"Aral the jack, formerly the noble Aral Kingsla... ...e best kind of hero: damaged, cynical, and ... ...t needing only the right cause to ri..."
—Alex Bledsoe, author of ...

"Once again Aral and his Shade, ...ss, find themselves in the middle of a royal mess—literally. Yet this time it is assassin versus assassin versus assassin. That alone promises readers some high-quality entertainment. But Kelly McCullough adds several twists, back-bends, and handsprings that only a mind as devious (or demented) as his could possibly conceive." —*Huntress Book Reviews*

CROSSED BLADES

"Kelly McCullough has once again written a magnificent story which deals with love, betrayal, and redemption." —*Fresh Fiction*

"The Blade novels are absolutely fabulous. The author, Kelly McCullough, takes you into a fascinating world of characters that have many skins." —*Night Owl Reviews*

"If you are seeking a fantasy unlike most others, you will not go wrong by choosing any title by this author. Kelly McCullough's writing style is indefinable, his imagination is creative and unique, and his [plot] execution is simply exquisite!"
—*Huntress Book Reviews*

BARED BLADE

"The second Fallen Blade fantasy stars an interesting hero with an irreverent, self-deprecating attitude . . . Fans will appreciate the magnificent McCullough mythos." —*Genre Go Round Reviews*

"Full of action, fun characters, and an interesting plot."
—*Whatchamacallit Reviews*

continued . . .

BROKEN BLADE

"Creative world-building really helps the reader to immerse themselves . . . A strong beginning to a new fantasy-mystery hybrid series."
—*Fantasy Book Critic*

"*Broken Blade* explores a different side of dark fantasy than the typical European/medieval fare . . . I could definitely spend hundreds of pages wandering around in the wilds of McCullough's newest creation."
—*Flames Rising*

"*Broken Blade* is a compelling read that was hard to put down . . . Mr. McCullough has the ability to make even his dastardly characters sympathetic."
—*Fresh Fiction*

"Filled with multifaceted characters, layered plots, and the type of quixotic scenarios that only the imagination of Kelly McCullough could possibly create. The author, once again, crosses genres . . . Stories by Kelly McCullough are one of a kind—just like him. I found Aral's world to be compelling and highly addictive. Brilliant!"
—*Huntress Book Reviews*

"McCullough's atmospheric little tale of betrayal and skullduggery is brisk, confident, intelligently conceived, and suspenseful . . . With as promising a start as this, McCullough's new series is looking like one sharp blade indeed."
—*SF Reviews.net*

"*Broken Blade* is perfect for a fan of political/hierarchal conspiracy in a fantasy series . . . It's also filled with some heart-pounding action . . . The story is positively bursting with excitement."
—*Whatchamacallit Reviews*

"The world McCullough sets up was certainly the highlight of the book for me. I enjoy fantasy-world politics and dark humor, both of which are in abundance here."
—*Night Owl Reviews*

More praise for the novels of Kelly McCullough

"Entertaining and rapid-fire."
—*San Francisco Book Review*

"One long adrenaline rush."
—*SFRevu*

Ace Books by Kelly McCullough

The WebMage Series

WEBMAGE
CYBERMANCY
CODESPELL
MYTHOS
SPELLCRASH

The Fallen Blade Series

BROKEN BLADE
BARED BLADE
CROSSED BLADES
BLADE REFORGED
DRAWN BLADES

DRAWN BLADES

Kelly McCullough

ACE BOOKS, NEW YORK

THE BERKLEY PUBLISHING GROUP
Published by the Penguin Group
Penguin Group (USA) LLC
375 Hudson Street, New York, New York 10014

USA • Canada • UK • Ireland • Australia • New Zealand • India • South Africa • China

penguin.com

A Penguin Random House Company

DRAWN BLADES

An Ace Book / published by arrangement with the author

Ace Books are published by The Berkley Publishing Group.
ACE and the "A" design are trademarks of Penguin Group (USA) LLC.

For information, address: The Berkley Publishing Group,
a division of Penguin Group (USA) LLC,
375 Hudson Street, New York, New York 10014.

ISBN: 978-0-425-27000-4

PUBLISHING HISTORY
Ace mass-market edition / November 2014

PRINTED IN THE UNITED STATES OF AMERICA

10 9 8 7 6 5 4 3 2 1

Cover illustration by John Jude Palencar; dragon © iStockphoto/Thinkstock.
Cover design by Judith Lagerman.
Interior text design by Laura K. Corless.
Maps by Matthew A. Kuchta.

For Laura. With love in our twentieth
wedding anniversary year, which happily coincides
with the writing of my twentieth novel.

Acknowledgments

Extra-special thanks are owed to Laura McCullough; Jack Byrne; Anne Sowards; Neil Gaiman; my mapmaker, Matt Kuchta; and cover artist John Jude Palencar and cover designer Judith Lagerman, who have produced wonders for me.

Many thanks also to the Wyrdsmiths: Lyda, Doug, Naomi, Bill, Eleanor, Sean, and Adam. My Web guru, Ben. Beta readers: Steph, Dave, Sari, Karl, Angie, Sean, Matt, Mandy, April, Becky, Mike, Jason, Jonna, and Benjamin. My family: Carol, Paul and Jane, Lockwood and Darlene, Judy, Lee, Kat, Jean, and all the rest. My extended support structure: Michael, Lynne, Bill, Nancy, Sara, James, Tom, Ann, Mike, Sandy, and so many more.

Penguin folks: Rebecca Brewer, Anne Sowards's wonderful assistant; managing editor Michelle Kasper; assistant production editor Julia Quinlan; interior text designer Laura Corless; publicist Nita Basu; and my copy editor, Mary Pell.

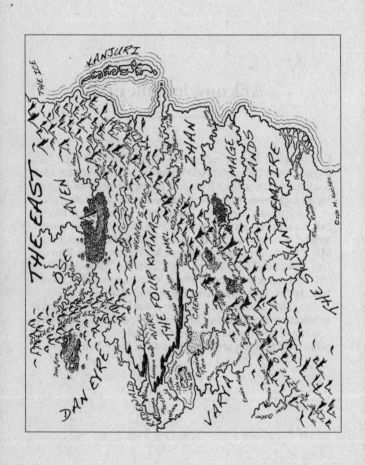

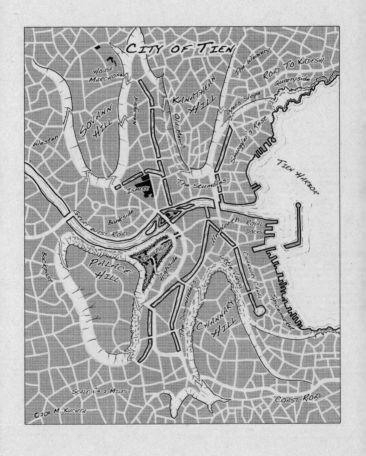

CITY OF TIEN

House Marchon
Sovann Hill
Western
Kanathean Hill
Newgard
Old Mews
The Weavery
Road to Kadesh
Quartyside
Dyer's Slope
Smuggler's Rest
Ismere
The Stumbles
Tien Harbor
Great West Road
Bankside
Backport
Royal Palace
Lilworth
Royal Docks
Palace Hill
Highside
Chancel Canal
Little Vona
The Daymarkers
Channary Hill
Spice Market
Scale 1" = 2 Miles
Coast Road
©2011 M. Kuchta

1

---◆---

Smoke without fire.

That's how it began. With swirling darkness on a cold stone hearth. Or, in a bar, with a beautiful woman, who had a problem. It all depends on how you look at it.

I had come back to Tien after months away. Not for me, but for Faran, my apprentice. She needed help I couldn't give her—delicate and difficult magical healing—so I had brought her to a friend. Treatment was slow and painful for Faran, but it seemed to be working. Her sight had fully returned and the headaches were much better. So I'd decided I could leave her alone for an evening and visit old haunts.

Mistake? It all depends on how you feel about powerful magical sendings and other people's problems.

The Gryphon's Head was a dive bar of the worst sort, full of criminals and other shady types. It was also coming home. I had spent six years living in a tiny room over the stables there. I'd made my money as a shadow jack in those days—the underworld's all-purpose freelancer. It was a very long fall from the days when they'd first called me Aral Kingslayer and the mighty had feared the coming of my shadow. Well, and lately, they had begun to call me that again, but that's another story entirely.

You see, I'm an assassin, or was once—one of the best in the world—and my shadow lives. His name is Triss. He is my familiar, a thing of elemental darkness and magic . . . which brings me back to the smoke.

Triss saw it first, and whispered into my mind, *Aral, ware the hearth!*

I turned in my chair, and saw the first twisting coils of smoke begin to rise from the bare stones. I wasn't the only one. A pair of Cobble-Runners—one of the local gangs—who were sitting closer, noticed it about then, too. They leaped out of their chairs and backed away from the hearth, shooting the occasional glance my way as the smoke built slowly.

They were only the first. Within a few moments the whole bar was shifting attention between whatever was building on the hearth and me. The bar's owner, Jerik, came over as the ball reached the size of a kneeling human.

"Aral?" he called. "What have you brought into my bar this time?"

I wanted to tell him I hadn't brought anything, but honesty forbade me. I didn't know what the thing on the hearth was, or where it had come from, but the chances were good that it was there for me. My life has taught me to doubt coincidence, and the odds that a piece of magic like nothing I'd ever seen before would appear in the Gryphon's hearth by chance on the same day that I finally returned after so long away . . . Well, let's just say that I wouldn't take that bet, and leave it there.

"I don't know," I said. "I : . ." I trailed off as the thing stood up.

I say "thing" where I should call it a woman, because that's what it had become. A woman of smoke. Tall and slender and very familiar. She wore the loose pants and shirt of the order I had once belonged to, and the swirling loops of smoke perfectly mirrored the dyed patterns of my own grays.

The hood of her cowl was drawn up to hide her face, and the smoke blurred what features I could see within, but the shape of her body and the way that she moved were instantly recognizable, even in smoky avatar—which form made her slow and deliberate as though she were underwater or might come apart at any moment.

Siri, the Mythkiller, First Blade of Namara. I recognized her at a level below thinking and beyond question. This was Siri, my sister in the service of Justice, my better in the arts of magic and the assassin, and perhaps the only person in the world who could ask for my life and expect me to give it into her care without thought or question. Both duty and honor demanded no less. I met her halfway to the hearth.

"Siri?"

The smoke swirled under her cowl, and a twist of white might have been a smile, but the figure spoke no words. After a long moment, she nodded. It was a slow movement—as they all had been—and it feathered the edges of her cowl.

"What do you need?" I asked.

Triss whispered into my mind. *Careful, Aral. You can't be sure it's really her.*

But I was. *No. This is her. I'm certain of it.*

The figure extended its left hand, palm up. With the other it gestured me to touch the extended hand with my own. When flesh met smoke I felt a faint electrical tingle, like distant mage-lightning, but no other sensation of contact.

Her right hand came forward and began a slow but intricate dance of gesture over our joined palms. I almost jerked away then, as I recognized the motions a priest would make at a handfasting, but forced myself to stillness. No matter how strange the manifestation, this was something of Siri. I could feel it in my soul, and I owed her whatever she asked of me.

When she was done, that white swirl of a smile flashed within her cowl once more. Then she fell apart, splitting into a hundred wisps on the breeze.

"What was that all about?" asked Jerik.

"I don't know," I answered. "But I think I'd better find out."

Aral, Triss spoke into my mind, *she left you a ring.*

Looking down, I saw that he was right. There, wrapped around my wedding finger, was a ring of smoke. It was only as I examined the ring that I realized none of what I had just seen bore any light of magic, and the only enchantments that I knew of that acted that way were god-magic. . . .

* * *

"It's marvelous. I've never encountered anything like it."
Harad moved careful fingers this way and that as though he
were trying to twist my new ring. "It doesn't *feel* like god-
magic, but it certainly wasn't made by any normal mortal sort
of spell. I have no idea what it is."

I gave the ancient librarian a hard look. "You don't have to
sound so happy about it."

"I'm six hundred years old, Aral, and a master sorcerer for
five hundred and fifty of those years. I have been the chancellor
of one of the great Magelands universities and studied more
varieties of magic than most spellwrights are even aware of.
Finding something wholly new is a treasure beyond price." He
paused and rubbed his chin. "Though, I will be very sorry if
it devours your soul before I have time to get it sorted out. . . ."

My shadow twisted itself into the silhouette of a small and
rather worried-looking dragon. Triss rose up off the floor so
that he could sniff at the smoke ring. "Don't worry," the Shade
told me. "If it tries anything like that I'll bite your finger off
before it gets the chance."

"Um . . . thanks, Triss." I turned back Harad. "Is that really
likely?"

"It was a small joke on my part, nothing more." Harad
frowned. "Though it seems to have gone wide of the mark. You
didn't look nearly as alarmed by that prospect as I had hoped
you might, but then, it's hard to read you. You do grim and blank
as well as any man I know."

I shrugged. "It's not something I'm going to dance about,
but my soul's pretty badly mortgaged already. Between my
failures since the death of my goddess and the need for efik
chewing a hole in the back of my mind, there's not much left
for anything else to carve off a piece."

Triss winced—because he worried—but he didn't say
anything.

"The cravings haven't eased in the months since the Kitsune
first forced you to eat those few beans, then?" It was the question of a healer who considered me one of his patients. "I had
hoped it would pass, but with the death of Namara you seem
to have lost your immunity to the darker side of the drug."

That immunity wasn't all I'd lost when the goddess of Justice was murdered. The list was long and brutal. Most of my magical protections. My home. My family. My friends. My reason for living. No, my efik problem didn't even make the top five, however much harder it might make my life.

Again, I shrugged. "I have good days and bad, just like with the booze, though efik hunger is sharper, and the hooks in my soul are deeper. But what can you expect? I tried it first shortly after I entered the temple, though I didn't really acquire the habit till my teens. But I never touched so much as a drop of alcohol until after my goddess was murdered."

"Horrible stuff, whiskey." A girl's voice—drifting down from the shadows atop a nearby set of bookshelves.

"Ah, Faran," I said to my apprentice. "I was wondering when you were going to let us know you were there."

She released the shadow that enshrouded her as she dropped silently to the floor. She landed a few yards beyond Harad, and I revised my earlier "girl" to "young woman" when I met her gaze. At eighteen or thereabouts, I had to admit that she'd grown up a lot in the last year. The cloud of living darkness that had concealed her from view on the shelves now flowed down to the floor, becoming the shadow of a phoenix.

My eyes immediately went to the scar that ran down from her forehead across her left eyelid and onto her cheek. It looked better than it had before her sessions with Harad, but I still winced whenever I saw it. She'd picked it up guarding my back, which made it my fault.

"You knew I was there?" She flicked her dark hair angrily back over her shoulder. "How? My form was perfect, and I know you didn't cross my shadow trail. What gave me away?"

"Your nature," I replied. "I know you, and I know you wouldn't have missed me coming in to consult with Harad. You didn't greet us when we entered. That means you decided to make a game of stalking us." I gestured around the large open reading area at the end of the narrow stacks. "There's only one place in this entire room where you could both listen *and* be sure Triss wouldn't sniff out Ssithra. That's atop the shelves. Therefore . . ."

"Fair point." Faran smiled and bowed to acknowledge the hit. "Now, let me see what the fuss is about." She reached out

to touch the smoke ring on my wedding finger, then abruptly
snatched her hand back. "Hey, it bit me!"

Ssithra flapped shadow wings and lifted off the floor, putting herself between Faran and my ring.

"It bit you?" Harad asked brightly. "Let me see."

Now it was Faran's turn to give the librarian a hard look as
he pulled her hand toward him. "The thing *bites* me, and
you act like someone gave you a damned Winter-Round
present?"

"Hush, child. I'm working. Hmm, no blood . . ." Harad
reached through a hole in the air with his free hand and pulled
an emerald quizzing glass from the pocket dimension where
he kept most of his more delicate tools. He held the lens above
Faran's injured finger. "*Very* interesting."

I looked over his shoulder. The crystalline lens showed four
tiny black marks on Faran's fingertip—marks invisible both to
magesight and my mortal eyes. But only for a few heartbeats.
Then the spots wisped up like smoke and blew away.

"What was that?" asked Triss.

"It really did bite her." Harad dropped the emerald back
through the hole in the air and it vanished. "Though, what it
drew wasn't blood."

"I told you so," said Faran.

"Why would it do that?" I asked. "And, how?"

A huge grin spread across Harad's face. "I have *no* idea."
Then he paused and looked thoughtful. "I take that back. I have
no idea about the how, but I think I can make an educated guess
about the why."

"Which is?" Faran demanded.

"Smoke or no, it's a wedding ring. That's a very specific
and ancient sort of magic. My assumption would be that it saw
you as a potential rival for Aral's affections."

"I . . . Wait, it what?" Faran blinked several times, blushed,
then shook her head. "That's idiotic!"

Harad grinned. "It quite likely is, but I don't think the ring
thinks so."

"Stupid ring," grumbled Faran. Then her expression shifted
suddenly from annoyance to something like shock. "Hold it.
If it's a wedding ring, does that mean that Aral and Siri are
married now, for real and legally?"

"I don't know about legally," said Harad. "But magically and symbolically, yes. That's a sort of marriage that's deeper and more profound than mere laws, and *far* less disseverable."

Faran rounded on *me* now. "Aral, did you know that was going to happen when the smoke figure offered you that ring?"

I shrugged. "Siri didn't offer me the ring precisely, but she did make it pretty clear she wanted my participation in something like a formal handfasting, and marriage is where these things typically lead, ring and all. Given that we had consummated our relationship in the traditional way long ago, I probably should have realized the implications."

"And you're all right with that?" she demanded.

"Of course. If Siri asked me for my life, I would give it to her. Why would I refuse to marry her if that's what she needs of me?"

"You haven't seen or heard from Siri in eight years!" Faran's voice started angry and got angrier. "Then a smoke figure that may or may not even be her shows up, asks you to get hitched, and you just say 'yes' like it's nothing? You don't even know what sort of person she is now, Aral. That's insane!" She glanced at Harad as though seeking his support, but the old librarian had an even better blank expression than I do.

"Perhaps it is," I replied. "Perhaps Siri *has* become a monster in the years since I last saw her. I can't imagine it, but I couldn't imagine Master Kelos betraying the order and our goddess either. None of that changes what Siri once was and the duty I owe her."

"How can it not?" demanded Faran.

"Because what I owe Siri isn't about her. It's about me, and my duty here is perfectly clear." I paused for a long moment, trying to think of how best to explain the thing properly. Faran was my apprentice and if that was going to mean anything I had to let her see my thinking. "I don't have much of my old soul left, but what there is, is bound to the service of Namara, whether that takes the shape of the goddess herself, her ideal of justice, or simply the word of her First Blade. I *can't* turn Siri down if I want to remain true to what little remains of Aral the Blade."

Faran glared at my shadow now. "Triss, don't you have anything to say about this?"

The little dragon flipped his wings back and forth

noncommittally. "I am concerned about the manner of the thing. But what we have heard from those who *did* betray the goddess suggests that even Kelos believed Siri was incorruptible. It's one of the chief reasons why he sent both Aral and Siri away when the temple was about to fall."

Ah Kelos, my mentor and master—two-hundred-year-old lord of assassins, and the father I never had. The Deathwalker. He was perhaps the greatest Blade who ever lived, and, without any doubt, the greatest traitor to our order. His actions had materially contributed to the death of our goddess. I knew that he deeply regretted her murder, but I also knew that he would do the same again in the same circumstances if he believed it would achieve his goals. He was brutal and ruthless, and yet he had spared both Siri and me as much because he loved us as because he wanted to preserve our talents. I could not hate him as I did, did I not love him, too.

Ssithra spoke for the first time, breaking my reverie. "Siri is the Mythkiller, and one of the greats of our order. I would marry her if she asked me. Or Kyrissa, her Shade, for that matter. I think that if you had completed your training you would do the same."

Faran scowled. "I . . . You . . . I can't even . . . Aral, this is one of the stupider things I've seen you do. And I've seen you pull some really dumb moves. You *married* someone you haven't seen in years simply because she asked you to. No. Because a . . . a fucking smoke *effigy* of her asked you to. Do you have any idea of the magical implications of this?"

I shook my head. "No."

Faran threw her hands into the air and snarled.

"Faran," I said, trying one last time, "Siri is my sister in the order, my master in the arts of the Blade, my friend, and my lover. My honor is her honor, and what she asks it is my duty to give."

"Augh!" Ssithra suddenly puffed into a black cloud, rolling forward to envelop Faran in impenetrable darkness.

It was always a startling transformation, even for one who had performed it as often as eating. One moment, Faran was there with Ssithra at her side, the next she became a sort of hole in the center of my vision. A simple blot of shadow would have been easy to pick out against the lights and sights of the library, but some magic of the Shades made the task infinitely harder, more a place you couldn't see than a patch of darkness.

Even trained eyes had trouble focusing on an enshrouded Blade. You had to learn to look for what you couldn't see, and it was surprisingly difficult. That shroud of shadow was the most powerful tool possessed by those of us who had once been Justice's hidden weapons—Namara's Blades. I lost track of Faran and Ssithra within moments as they moved rapidly away, slipping into one of the aisles between shelves.

"She seems angrier than she ought," I said. "Any idea why?"

Triss looked over his shoulder at me and contracted briefly in the loose Shade equivalent of an embarrassed shrug. "No idea. Harad?"

"I wouldn't care to venture a guess," he replied.

That wasn't a "no," but years of association had taught me better than to call him on it. Harad would share what he wanted when he wanted, and nothing anyone could do would change that. Instead, I raised my beringed hand between us. "Any further thoughts on what to do about this thing?"

He nodded. "Shang informs me that he would like to have a look at it through his own eyes since it's new to him as well."

I blinked at that. Triss assumes the form of a dragon. Shanglun *is* a dragon, and not a petty dragon either. Shang is a river dragon, one of the greatest of the noble breeds, a power of the world, and Harad's familiar—though I didn't learn that last until after I'd known the librarian for more than a decade.

While such bondings aren't completely unheard of, they're so rare that you had a better chance of winning ten straight rounds of lin-hua against Ping Slickfingers than of actually meeting such a pair. He was also the reason for Harad's great age, as the lifespan of any familiar-bonded pair will always conform to the longer of the two partners, and dragons live as long as they wish.

Normally, Shang prefers to slumber in his tank below the library and, dreaming, look out through Harad's eyes. That he was interested in seeing Siri's smoke ring through his own was both an honor and more than a little alarming. It drove home the unique nature of my new trinket in a way that Harad's childlike delight simply couldn't. This was a *dragon* and he wanted to see my ring because he'd never seen anything like it before.

Oh. My.

I gestured toward Harad's apartments and the secret stair that led down to the library's equally secret underwater entrance. "By all means, let's go show it to him."

The reservoirlike tank that Shang used as a bed lay in a deep, barrel-vaulted chamber under the river side of the building. The Ismere Library held the city of Tien's largest private collection of books, including many volumes that had been officially banned by the government at one time or another. Protecting that collection from forces both official and un- was one of the chief reasons the library had such a powerful sorcerer as its chief. It had been founded four hundred years earlier by a Kadeshi merchant-adventurer—see also smuggler and pirate—and the underwater tunnel that connected the tank to the river was probably a legacy of the founder's original line of work.

When we entered the vault, Harad waved his hands. In response, the blue and green magelights that picked out Zhani glyphs on various surfaces slowly brightened. In combination with the flickering reflections from the pool and the deep green moss that covered many of the stones, the magelight produced an illusion that the whole room lay deep under tropical waters.

As we crossed to the reservoir, a column of water lifted up out of the tank. It rose and twisted, extruding bumps and whiskers that slowly formed themselves into the features of a large dragon. As the face took on shape and character it darkened in whorls and swirls, like a fine tea when you first stir it. Its scales shaded in from the lightest hint of jade at the center to an oversteeped seaweed green along the edges.

The change rolled back from a head longer than my own five feet and eleven, coloring in his thick, ropy neck and the many looping coils of his snakelike body. Shang was big, perhaps a hundred feet from nose to tail, though he was dwarfed by Tien Lun, the guardian of the city's bay. He smiled at Harad when he bent down to touch his nose to the old man's forehead—a disconcerting expression that exposed teeth longer than my forearm.

Once he had greeted his partner, he turned my way. Dark green eyes the size of an extended hand fixed on me and he spoke in a deep, watery mindvoice. *Hello, Aral, what trouble have you found for yourself this time?*

I responded in kind, sending my thoughts along the same channel I used to communicate with Triss. *I don't find trouble. It finds me.* I held up my beringed hand. *This came to me. I didn't seek it out. Besides, who's to say that it's trouble.*

Shang laughed into my mind. *It's a wedding ring. They exist for trouble. I have watched your people for two thousand years, and yet this magic is a new thing for me. When such takes up residence on your hand, you can bet that trouble will follow. Beyond that, I would have thought your experiences with the Kothmerk and the Signet of Heaven would have taught you to avoid such pretty baubles.*

He's got a point, Triss noted, his mindvoice wry. *Rings have not been good luck for us.*

I couldn't argue that, but there was something about Shang's tone that made me think he was teasing me as much as advising me. It's hard to tell the difference with dragons.

I bow to your wisdom, venerable one. Which I did, giving him the full formal court version. *But I'm afraid that the lady made me an offer I simply couldn't refuse.*

Such is the way of women, said the dragon. *Now, let me examine this fancy of yours.* He bent lower still and twisted his head to the side so that he could bring one great eye within inches of the smoke ring.

Hmm. He pivoted and looked at it with his other eye. Then he touched it with one of his long whiskers.

Very interesting. Hold it out and let me smell it. My entire hand slid into a nostril big enough to engulf my head, though I could still see it through his translucent flesh. *One last test.*

He opened his mouth and a tongue that was bigger around than my waist and long enough for two of me to lie end to end on shot forward. Before I could think to protest, Shang licked me from toes to top—the two forks of his tongue wrapping around me like a lover's arms. It was a profoundly weird sensation, as the dragon's substance split the difference between animate-water and mortal flesh.

I would like to see this Siri of yours now, said the dragon.

That's a lovely idea, I agreed, somewhat sarcastically. *Any thoughts on how to manage it?*

He nodded. *First, you will need to make a fire. . . .*

"Faran," I said aloud. "Would you be so kind as to fetch some wood from Harad's apartments? I believe there's a basket of it beside the fireplace."

A snort issued from an unusually dark shadow at the base of the vault by the door. "Why me?"

"Because fetching and carrying is the reason they invented apprentices." I smiled. "Aren't you going to ask how I knew you were there this time?"

"No. You know the same way you did earlier, by knowing me. I may not always like the lessons you give me, but I do learn. And, yes, I'm off to fetch that wood now."

Twenty minutes later we had a nice little fire going beside the pool. "Now what?" I asked.

We wait for it to burn away to nothing. Fire devours its prey entire. Smoke is the ghost of the consumed—shadow and flame. The sacrifice must wholly burn away before the true element can arise.

"That's going to take hours," grumbled Faran, who had dropped her shroud once again—though her mood seemed only marginally improved.

"It needn't." Harad stepped forward, put his hands out over the fire as though he were warming them, and spoke a single word in the language of ancient Kadesh.

A thread of spell-light—invisible to the normal eye—jumped from Harad's hands to a point between Shang's eyes. The dragon opened his mouth, and a great flood of spell-light burst forth, engulfing Harad in an aura of green and blue. As the light flowed down Harad's body to his hands it changed color, becoming a scarlet torrent that shot from his fingers to the flames below.

It all happened in the pause between two heartbeats, and the very next instant the fire roared and flared like a burning building collapsing. There was a brief burst of heat almost too intense to bear. Then the fire was gone, leaving behind ashes and a thick curl of smoke.

Shang leaned forward, touching the smoke with the tip of

his long tongue. "Come!" he said, speaking aloud in a voice like the Grand Rapids below Kao-li.

The smoke curl twisted back on itself, forming the rough outline of a human figure. It looped back and back again, until the whirls and swirls of smoke took on the character of the woman I had so recently married.

"Siri?" I said.

The figure nodded, but made no further answer.

Shang touched the figure with his tongue again. "I lend you my voice, that you might speak."

The smoke woman bowed to the dragon and spoke in the rippling tones of a lively brook, "Thank you, great heart, you have saved me hours of pantomime." Then she turned to me. "Hello, Aral. I need you to come to the Sylvani Empire. It's a matter of souls and buried gods and unfinished business."

2

―――・◆・―――

When the gods make mistakes the world suffers.

That's the story of the Sylvani Empire. Not to mention the Temple of Namara, but that's another tale entirely. For the moment, let me stick with the Sylvain. We of the eleven kingdoms aren't the first children of the gods. That "honor" belongs to the four kindreds of the Others: the Durkoth, the Vesh'An, the Asavi, and the Sylvani—who were all once one people but are no more.

I will relate a part of that tale now, because it is important to all that comes after, and I will tell it in the manner it was told to me by Master Kelos:

"It is said the gods created the Others because they wanted a people to share the wonders of the world they had newly formed. That the first Others looked and acted much as the Sylvani do now. That they were arrogant, and sometimes cruel, and that this drove a wedge between them and the gods, and that the gods were forced to bind their magics and confine them to the lands of the Sylvain. That the Vesh'An and the Durkoth refused the bargain of the gods and lost their magic because of it. Many things are said by the priests who serve

the Son of Heaven first, themselves second, and their gods next before all others.

"But here in the Temple of Namara, Goddess of Justice and champion of those who cannot champion themselves, a different tale is told. The gods created the Others without limits on their magics because they wanted powerful servants and they were arrogant enough to believe that none could ever challenge them. But all too soon some among the Others began to rival their masters, and this the gods could not abide. So there was a war between the gods and their first children, and much that was wonderful in the world was unmade.

"The old gods were the more powerful and they defeated the Others, but only at great cost. Many gods died in the war, including the first Sovereign Emperor of Heaven. All of the great ones among the Others were thrown down, too, but some had grown too powerful for even the gods to destroy without dying themselves. These mightiest of the Others were bound into the earth of the Sylvain in a state halfway between life and death. The rest of the Others were bound as well, tying their magics to their buried mighty.

"The Sylvani and the Asavi accepted this confinement and limited themselves to lesser magics and the lands of the old empire. The Durkoth and the Vesh'An refused, forsaking magic for the deep places of earth and ocean that they loved more than power. The bound ones . . . they do not sleep easy or accept their fate. They fight against the injustice of the gods and ever they strive to rise from their graves to challenge Heaven once again.

"Namara never forgave the other gods for what they did to the Others, but neither did she make an effort to free the fallen. For they had become horrors in their own right, terrible and mighty, desiring only to renew their war with Heaven. And they would tear the world apart to wreak vengeance. In these days they are known as the buried gods, and now and again one will rip free of the earth and seek to regain the power they once held."

It was in confronting one such risen god that Siri came to be called the Mythkiller. That was the mission that made her a legend and me second among the Blades of the day. The fight more than half killed her and it left her with many scars and a lifetime of nightmares.

That's why I had been so surprised when I first learned she had forsworn the lands of man and gone south to the Sylvani Empire after Namara was slain. It seemed a . . . strange choice. One that seemed stranger still if she had become involved with the buried gods once again. There was nothing in the world I wanted to do more than stay out of the affairs of the gods, dead or otherwise. But if Siri told me that she needed me to do so, I would make war on Heaven itself.

"How soon do you need me?" I asked the figure of smoke.

"As soon as you can get here by land." This time she spoke with the deeper tones of a river running slow and wide.

"A ship would be faster," I said.

Harad leaned forward. "And there are spells that could send you as far as the Wall of the Sylvain faster still."

"No, it must be by land or the connection will fail." The figure shook her head—a quicker movement than any she had made yet. It blurred her features as the air currents pulled at the smoke. "The logic of smoke requires it."

"The logic of smoke?" Faran lifted an eyebrow. "How so?"

"I don't have time to explain," said Siri. "Already I can feel the ghost of the fire failing. The magic involved is . . . complex. Suffice to say that the ring requires certain conditions to be met if it's to work properly."

Harad cleared his throat. "What, exactly, will it do if it works properly?"

"More importantly," said Faran, "what happens if it doesn't?" She gave me a hard look. "I *really* don't like this."

Ssithra flipped her wings and rose into the air, agitation showing in the ruffling of shadow feathers and the tension in her neck. "Child, for once in your life, respect your elders. This is the Mythkiller you're talking to and she has a need for haste."

"Phoenix," said Siri. "That means Ssithra, and you must be Faran." She turned eyes of smoke on the younger woman. "You were a clever girl, and very promising. I'm glad you escaped the fall. Please, trust me that this is necessary."

Faran nodded reluctantly and bowed her head, stepping back.

"Where are you?" I asked.

"South of Tavan, near . . ." Her voice fell away to nothing. And then, with a faint puff, the smoke form collapsed in on itself and Siri was gone.

"Next time," I said to Faran as gently as frustration would allow, "please save the arguments until *after* the important questions are all asked and answered."

She looked down at her feet, but nodded anyway.

"When do we leave?" asked Triss.

I thought about it for a moment. "We'll have to stop at the house and the fallback at the abandoned warehouse both to collect all the supplies we'll need for traveling before we hit the western road. That'll take some time. We really ought to leave here within a quarter of an hour if we want to get clear of the city yet tonight."

"I'm coming with you," said Faran.

I was not feeling in charity with her, and I immediately shook my head. "No, you're not. You have to complete your healing here, with Harad."

"Look," said Faran, "we can have this argument, and you might even win. But if you do, I'll only sneak out and follow you like I did the last time, and the result will be the same as if you'd just agreed in the first place. Besides, Harad says that I'm at a stopping point in his treatment anyway, so the timing is perfect."

I looked at Harad.

He spread his hands noncommittally. "What I said was that we needed to take a break from your sessions so that you could rest and see how the healing was working. A two-thousand-mile speed run across the eastern edge of the eleven kingdoms isn't exactly what I had in mind. . . ."

Faran looked stubborn. "It'll be *much* more restful for me than staying here would be. I'd fret myself into a mess worrying about all the trouble Aral will get himself into if he doesn't have anyone to watch his back."

"Hey!" Triss flicked his wings grumpily.

"You know what I mean, Triss," said Faran. "Given the sort of trouble a buried god is likely to pose, can you honestly say that you won't need all the help you can get?"

"There is that," Triss agreed reluctantly. "But I'm not taking you anywhere unless Ssithra and Shang both agree."

Ssithra contracted briefly in a shrug. "I gave up arguing with her when she gets this tone in her voice years ago. But you're right. If Shang doesn't think it's a good idea, we're not going."

At that point, all eyes turned to the river dragon. While Harad might be the one formally in charge of Faran's treatment, it was Shang who was ultimately responsible for her progress. The curative powers of the great water dragons were without peer—most of the healing springs of legend had drawn their magic from a resident dragon.

Shang slid his huge head down and forward till he was inches from Faran. Then, much more gently than he had done with me, he extended the tips of his tongue to touch either side of Faran's forehead. He stayed like that, perfectly still for several minutes before finally drawing back and canting his head to one side so that he could look deep into her eyes with one of his own.

"I know your vision is much improved, though it will never be perfect again. But tell me true, child, how are your headaches?"

"Bad," Faran said in a small voice. "But not nearly so frequent as they were, and never so awful that I think about killing myself anymore."

The dragon sighed, then nodded. "If you do this thing, I do not believe that you will backslide. But neither will you get better. It is true that you need a time away from my active care to set what we have done so far. But if you spend the time moving about rather than resting, what might have taken a few weeks will take some months at the least, and I won't be there to soothe the pain for you."

Faran winced. "I know, but I won't be resting if I don't go with Aral either. I'll be stuck here alone with Ssithra and going mad with worry, just like I did when he went to face the Son of Heaven alone. He's too gentle, and that's going to get him killed one of these days."

Shang turned his other eye on me now. "The gentle assassin—now, there's an interesting turn of thought. What do you think of that, Aral?"

There was something about the dragon's tone that didn't brook dissembling. "Faran's right that I prefer not to kill anyone I don't have to," I replied. "But I am not so gentle as I was when last Faran and I went a-hunting together. My definition of who needs killing has . . . widened a bit since our visit to the Magelands last year."

"Really?" Faran looked doubtful—she'd been all of nine when the fall of the temple had cast her out into the world alone. It had hardened her in ways I didn't think were entirely healthy. She killed with a cheerful remorselessness that didn't suit one who should have grown up to become a champion of Justice.

But Triss nodded. "He's coming around nicely, actually." Like most Shades, Triss had never shied from killing anyone that he thought needed killing, and he had often chided me for letting loose ends keep breathing.

"What changed?" asked Faran.

"I remembered what I am," I said. "When I was younger, I gave my conscience into the hands of Namara, and I killed who she told me to kill, knowing that I served justice as well as Justice. I was content with that. Then Namara died. And, for a very long time, I was lost. But I finally realized that the death of Justice the goddess didn't free me from my obligation to do justice. There are many monsters in this world, and for some the only justice is death. It's what I was born for and trained for, and ultimately death is what I am."

"Death," said Faran, and I nodded. "That's a little dark for you, but I think I like it." She smiled. "If I take the house and you hit the fallback we can save an hour. Meet at the bridge where the Great West Road crosses the Zien?"

"Done."

Pick up my gear and head out. A simple task, but important. Many of the tools of my trade are things that you have to make for yourself. Cornerbrights, drum-ringers, opium-and-efik-packed eggs for knocking out watchdogs, the blanks for making wardblacks . . . The list is endless. Others are hard to come by or expensive, like eyespys, good silk rope, spare Blade grays, etc. And, while things like bedrolls and silk tents can be picked up at most of the larger markets, it's infinitely quicker and easier if you already own such things to collect them from storage.

Which is why I had come back to the long-forgotten warehouse that was my main fallback at the moment. At one point, the stone and timber building had probably fronted one of the many narrow lanes that spurred off the nearby canal road. But somewhere along the line someone had simply walled off the ends of the alley to make a new building, orphaning the small warehouse and cutting it off from the commercial lifeblood provided by the canal. That was likely when the main entrance got bricked over, though it could have been ten years before, or half a hundred.

When and who had cut the door-sized hole into a sidewall that accessed a dead-end alley not much broader than my shoulders was an open question. Though it had to be noted that whoever had done it had almost certainly been planning on using the rotting old building as a tuckaside for smuggled or stolen goods. At least, that was the conclusion I'd reached given how carefully they'd concealed the door's construction.

Later still, the dead-end alley had been closed off, too—possibly by repairs made after one of the many fires that had burned through the area over the years. At that point, the only way in or out of the old warehouse involved either climbing down into the alley through a gap in the rooftops above, or heavy work with a saw and maul. Great for concealment, less so for quick entry and exit, and a major problem now that something had followed me to my hidey-hole.

I first heard it come into the alley behind me when I slipped through the warehouse's hidden entrance. I'd dropped the heavy bar in response, but it forced the door within a matter of moments. By then, I'd gotten up onto the balcony above, though I hadn't had the time to make it all the way up to the concealed loft where my gear was stored.

The creature was patterned and colored like a tiger, but it moved more like a hound. Big, bear-sized, maybe six hundred pounds. It came through the broken door slowly, head low—sniffing along my back trail. I could see it tracing the route I had followed after I entered. I didn't know how good its eyes were, or anything else about it, really. I'd never seen its like before and it practically reeked of magic. For that matter, nothing that big and obviously dangerous should have gotten anywhere near this deep into a city the size of Tien. Which made it a sending of some sort—quite possibly conjured directly into the alley.

Shrouding myself in Triss's substance, I drew my right-hand sword and leaped lightly onto the railing that separated the balcony from the lower level, slipping back toward where I had come in. When the thing passed below me, I dropped. Landing to one side of the creature's head, I swung my sword in a beheading arc. The short, curved blade hardly slowed as it passed through the thick neck—such were its goddess-forged enchantments.

A moment later, I skewered the head on the tip of my sword and lifted it for a better look. It was heavy, even for a head, and ugly—a nightmare of extra teeth and tusks—and it nearly cost me a broken leg. I was so busy examining it that I almost missed seeing the swing of the body's right forepaw—almost.

The long claws shattered a crate as I crow-hopped back out of the way—the best I could manage with that head weighing down my sword. I cleared my blade and turned to face the still-standing body, drawing my second sword. It was looking right at me—if anything without a head can be said to look. The gaping wound of its neck pointed straight at my heart as it continued to slowly drool blood. The headless body took a ponderous step toward me. I backed up again and it followed.

Now what? Normally when I beheaded something, it stopped coming after me. Especially when I used my goddess-forged swords. I wasn't at all sure how you killed a thing that could shrug that off.

Triss? I mindspoke.

No idea.

I had a problem. A big, ugly, magical problem. The blood stopped dripping off the end of its neck about then, and . . . I realized that I had a big, ugly, *regenerating* magical problem. Even as I watched, the thing had begun to grow a fresh head. I glanced down at my sword then, checking to see if someone had somehow managed to substitute an ordinary steel blade for my own.

But no, the light-absorbing black steel of the goddess was as familiar as the hand that held it. More so, since flesh could be bent to new shapes by the right spell, while Namara's steel was immutable and all but unbreakable. But that same divinely forged blade should have acted to magically cauterize the wound and prevent any regeneration. For that matter, it should have broken whatever spell bound the thing to life and killed it even if beheading didn't.

The whatsis swiped at me with a paw again. I was tempted to slice it off, but a nasty thought occurred to me then and I simply slipped aside. I looked around for the fallen head and discovered that I'd made the right decision. It had begun to grow itself a new neck—and presumably, given time, a whole new body. I mentally pointed that out to Triss as I put one of the pillars that held up the balcony between me and the thing.

We need a plan, I sent. *Ideally yesterday. I don't suppose you could send it into the everdark?*

Not in any reasonable amount of time. It's too big and too magical. Maybe if you could get it to hold still for an hour or two . . .

Somehow I don't think it's going to cooperate.

It struck again, shattering the thick wooden pillar and sending splinters flying every which way. One thick sliver embedded itself painfully in the back of my hand, and I snarled an angry curse. When I yanked it out with my teeth, the taste of tarred oak gave me the first ghost of an idea, but I needed a bit more time to let it grow into something solid.

I slipped sideways, keeping one sword between me and it to fend off any more sudden attacks. When I got to the next pillar, I used a long vertical cut to shear off a corner, effectively making myself a short wooden spear.

I quickly returned my left sword to the sheath on my back and slid a foot under the jagged piece of wood, flipping it up into my hand. I was only just in time, as the beast charged me then and I had to cartwheel out of its way to avoid a vicious swipe from freshly regrown tusks. Moving in behind the whatsis, I jabbed the rough spear through one of its hind feet and down into a crack between two flagstones. It wouldn't stop it for long, but it ought to—

"Oh, fuck." I swore aloud as the damned thing kept moving forward without slowing. Sure, its hind leg stretched out briefly like some boneless bit of tentacle, but then the flesh simply parted around the wooden spike and grew back together afterward, like water cut by a knife.

That's not good, sent Triss.

No. I think we're going to have to do something pretty drastic.

Any idea what?

Maybe, yeah, but it's ugly dangerous. I need you to go to sleep for a bit while I see about making a fire. I hate using fire as a weapon, but I didn't see a lot of choice given the thing's regeneration.

A low growl from behind warned me that the original head would soon be providing me with a second whatsis to deal with. I needed to end this fast, and I could only see one way to do that. I silently kissed off the supplies that I'd not yet had the time to retrieve and set about implementing my plan.

For starters, I took over from Triss, who had slipped into the dream state that allowed me to use his powers and senses as my own. The whatsis seemed to favor scent over sight, which meant there was little point in shrouding myself, but any sort of complex magic required that there be only one of us pulling on the reins. Honestly, I suspect he would be better at the spell-work than I was if we could arrange things that way. But, with the notably bizarre exception of the Dyads, that's simply not how the mage-familiar relationship goes.

Magic works much like swordplay, with the mage in the role of the hand on the hilt and the familiar playing the part of the blade. I drew my shadow up from the floor and across my skin, forming it into a coating thinner than the finest hair as I bent Triss's substance to my will.

When it covered my face and head, my senses expanded into the realm of shadow in ways that are hard to describe in any human language. Darkness took on tastes and textures that no mortal tongue or eyes ever experienced—light howled, color vanished, and textures whispered. The first time I'd clothed

myself in Triss's substance, the utterly disorienting mishmash
of sensation had driven me to my knees. It had taken years of
training to allow me to interpret the flood of new information
in any useful way.

I got out ahead of the whatsis again now. Easy enough, since
it didn't seem to be in all that big a hurry to kill me. That was
convenient, but also worrying. When someone is trying to murder you in a leisurely sort of way, it's usually because they're
not at all concerned that you're going to get away. Hopefully,
that was out of ignorance of who I was and what I could accomplish, but somehow, I doubted it.

I took down the pillars holding up the part of the balcony
overhanging the secret door—shutting it forever. That nar-
rowed my exit options considerably, since the main entrance
had been bricked over years before. It was one of the things
that had attracted me to the potential fallback in the first place.
That and its location deep in the Downunders where structures
didn't so much get built as they accreted, which was all the
more reason to feel a pang of regret for what I was about to do
to the place.

I began to work my way around the periphery of the building. I moved as quickly as I could. But the necessity of dragging
one sword tip to score a continuous line along the stone flags
behind me made for slower going than I'd have liked. That gave
the whatsis and its slightly smaller twin time to catch up to me
before I'd quite finished inscribing my circle of protection. I
was just speaking the word of closing and binding as I brought
my scored line back to bite its own tail when they came at me
from both sides.

Even the fanciest of footwork only barely sufficed to get me
clear as I took two running steps up the wall and then back-
flipped into a swords-tip cartwheel. The maneuver would likely
have resulted in my breaking my idiot neck only a year or two
before, and it certainly would have shattered the lesser swords
I'd been wielding at the time. As it was, I barely held on through
the shock of first one blade and then the other striking the hard
flags tip first as I vaulted through the narrow gap between
monsters. My hands and wrists felt like someone had struck
them with hammers.

As I raced out into the center of the warehouse, I sheathed

my swords and extended my arms toward the ceiling. Triss whimpered in his sleep as I shot magefire from my palms—Shades and the element of fire make for a painful mix, but it was the only plan I had, and I was all out of time. In a matter of instants, the main trusses sprouted blossoms of red and gold and I closed my fists—quenching the fires of magic. The building was aflame, and soon it would be falling in on itself.

Now I just had to get out. . . .

3

---◆◆◆---

The flame that burns the bones. Call it bonfire if you like, or the older and more honest bonefire. Whatever name you give it, a burning skeleton holds a terrible beauty.

Whether it belongs to a man or a building older than any mortal span, the result is much the same. All-devouring chaos claims another victim. From the outside it can be gorgeous, even cleansing. From the inside, all that matters is getting out.

I had deliberately left the central pillar of the warehouse untouched when I called the magefires to my service. But, before I could even begin to mount that rough-cut length of timber, the whatsis and its likewise-evil twin were upon me again. There was no subtlety to their approach—a small mercy that brought them straight in from the front. I hadn't the time to draw my swords again, nor, frankly, the inclination—they'd done me little enough good so far.

Magic might have done me better service, but I am no Siri, nor even Faran. The finer points of spellwork have always eluded me. Beyond that, the same flames that I hoped would save me now circumscribed my shadow-centered magic as thoroughly as any chains or bars of irons would have prevented more ordinary means.

So, I put my trust in luck and a good grip where another of my order might have chosen fancy bladework or a well-tempered spell, and simply leaped as high as I could up the pillar, wrapping arms and legs tight around its rough girth and hoping that it would be enough.

The shock of impact as the paired monstrosities struck and shattered the bottom six feet of the pillar very nearly finished me. Aged oak a foot thick and iron hard though it was, the wood burst to flinders when the great beasts struck it. Slivers drove deep into ankles suddenly clutching air. The ceiling dropped a good yard, and me with it, leaving the remains of the pillar hanging from the cross braces above instead of supporting them.

I had just enough time and presence of mind to shimmy up out of reach of my ungentle friends before they could strike again. This time, with no support left, the pillar merely lost a bit more of its end. Then I was up and away, climbing into the fiery rafters above and hoping to find some hole where I might squirm out before fire devoured us all.

I could feel Triss tossing and turning deep down in the sleep of magic. As too-real nightmares of fire and sun chewed at the Shade's substance, I pushed him farther and farther into my own weak and mortal shadow, shielding him from the flames as best I could with the stuff of my own flesh. It wasn't enough, and the fires I had started tore angrily at my familiar, racking me with guilt.

I lost track of the creatures below as the fire and smoke that ruled the upper reaches of the warehouse became the whole of my world. By the time I reached the rafters, there was no path left to me that didn't pass through flame. Leaping from my pillar to one of the rafters, I sprinted along its fiery length, grateful for the low boots that kept my burns to something time might treat even without the aid of magic.

Soon, I reached a point where the cracked and aging terra-cotta tiles of the roof hung inches above my head, with only the threadbare bamboo matting between them and me. By then, smoke owned my sight and had taken a good bite from my lungs as well. It was break through or die.

Five feet more, and I paused to flip the rough silk of my hood and muffler into place, costing me precious but necessary seconds. Then I unsheathed my swords and crossed my arms. Bracing the blunt back sides across my shoulders and the back of my neck, I formed them into a rough triangle pointed toward the sky.

Picking a spot more or less at random, I put the paired tips of my swords against the bamboo and drove upward, punching through matting and shoving tiles aside to create an opening into the world above. For one brief, beautiful moment, cool air and bright light surrounded me—heaven. But I hadn't the time to enjoy it because I knew what must come next.

I took a quick, shallow breath, then closed my mouth tight and forced the desperately needed clean air back out through my nostrils, as I leaped upward. Fire followed me, erupting up and out in a huge column as the air-starved flames below suddenly found a fresh route to the sky and the fuel it brought with it. My forelock burned away, but my silks protected me from the worst of the blast, and exhaling through it all kept me from scorching my lungs.

I hit the roof on fire and rolling. Again, the thick raw silk of my assassin's grays meant that my burns, while painful, weren't crippling. I stopped rolling when a low and broken chimney caught me in the ribs. The roof tile was hot enough to cook fish, and my elbows burned through my sleeves as I levered myself back to my feet. Smoke was everywhere, blinding and confusing, and I might have died then if a thick twist of it hadn't suddenly shaped itself into something like Siri's slender form and led me through the chaos.

At least, that's what I think happened, though the pain of my burns and a head made too light by shallow breathing and caustic fumes might have sent my mind astray. Whatever the cause—madness, or method, or merest luck, I had almost reached the edge of my strength when I passed from a smoky maze into clear air and bright sun. It happened all in an instant as I stumbled over the low coping between one roof and the next, and, with that, passed the line of protection I'd drawn to circumscribe my fire.

I fell to hands and knees, and then onto my side, gasping and coughing as I tried to breathe enough to catch up for what felt like a life's worth of inhaled smoke. A towering cloud of gray and black rose behind me, threaded here and there with the brighter colors of active fire where it angrily clawed the sky. A few feet away, just on the other side of the magical line I'd drawn with steel and magic, stood the shape that might or might not have been Siri. It seemed to blow me a kiss in the instant before it blew away itself. And that made me doubt its existence more than anything—Siri never mixed her pleasure with her work, though she did both with rare verve and focus.

I was still trying to sort out what I ought to believe about those mad air-starved moments in the fire, when a new shape appeared where Siri's might once have been. This one was big and broad, moving like a crippled bear, and all too familiar— my whatsis come calling again. Fire rode its back and shoulders, a burning cloak that haloed the beast and consumed it, though not quick enough by half.

It staggered as it reached the line that divided fire from freedom and went to its knees. I struck then—though I hadn't known I had it in me till I moved—rolling up onto my own knees and driving both swords deep into the monster's chest. It reared back, teetering on the edge of balance. I followed, using its motion to lever myself to my feet. Letting go my hilts, I took a long step back. Then I pivoted and kicked with all the strength I had left, striking the paired pommels of my blades and driving them hilt deep into charring flesh.

Before I could move to recover my swords, the whatsis staggered back out of easy reach, though whether it was dead at that point or simply overbalanced I couldn't say. It flailed its great paws for one brief instant, then went over backward, smashing into and through the burning and weakened roof with a tremendous crash and another eruption of flame. I had one moment of clarity to curse myself for letting it take my swords with it and to wonder how long I would have to wait for the fires to cool so that I could retrieve them. Then the sky tilted up and away from me, taking the world with it.

"**Old** fool." It was Faran's voice sounding angry and worried and oh-so-very-far away as she spoke quietly. "What were you thinking?"

My laugh turned into a hacking cough as I opened one eye. My apprentice was hovering just above me, her face dark and hidden by her cowl, with the stars behind her. "Not much, actually, my young monster," I replied, or husked, really—speaking hurt. "I was too busy simply surviving."

I took a mental inventory of my condition and, despite a host of places both hot and tender, I found that I felt better than I had any right to. I could sense Triss hunkered somewhere down deep in my shadow, though I couldn't tell whether he was sleeping still or unconscious. I decided not to try to wake him. Given the element of fire, he would need more recovery time than I did.

"What time is it?" I asked. "And where am I?"

"A bit after midnight," answered Faran. "The quarter hour just chimed. And you're atop a water tank about a hundred feet from where I found you. I didn't want to move you so far given the condition you were in, but I had to get you away from the Crown Elite and their damned stone dogs before one of them decided you were close enough to dead that they could safely get away with pushing you the rest of the way over the line."

"Elite?" I blinked my other eye open to try to get a better view of Faran's face, but shadow and more than shadow continued to hide her expression. "I think the dance moved on without me there. What do the Elite have to do with anything?"

"Did you hit your head along with all the burns?" Faran asked, her voice going sharp and acerbic. "Who did you think was going to show up to investigate when a damned great magical fire consumed a building no one knew was there? Especially when the famous Aral Kingslayer—assassin and former lover of the new queen—was found unconscious on the roof right at the edge of the circle that bound the flames to that one building? The royal hunt?"

"Point, though I'd have expected Captain Fei's people to get here first."

"The guards' Silent Branch? They did, which is the main reason you're alive. Fei herself sent me a whisper as to where to find you, and to come double quick, too. Royal pardon or no, the Elite still hate you far more for the two bad kings you killed than they could ever love you for putting a good queen on the throne. You're the living symbol of their worst failures, and not a one of them would have thought twice about tipping you back into the fire and watching you roast, if there weren't any official witnesses about to whisper in the queen's ear."

"True enough."

The Elite were tasked with making sure that whoever happened to wear Zhan's crown at a given moment stayed alive, well, and firmly in power. Utterly loyal to the throne and ruthless in pursuit of their duties, they were among the best mages and warriors in the eleven kingdoms—right up there with my own order or the Dyads of Kodamia.

Their familiars—earth elementals who took the shape of lion-like dogs the size of small horses—were just this side of unkillable. Tougher and much smarter than the whatsis, the stone dogs have come close to killing me on several occasions. The Elite made brutal and bitter enemies, and they hated me. Both for the pair of kings I'd ghosted out from under them, and for the rather large number of their fellows I'd sent to guard those fallen masters on the far side of the grave.

All of which made a bad idea of lingering in the vicinity any longer than need forced us to. I started to push myself into a sitting position, but Faran put a hand gently on my chest and spoke quietly. "Stay low. The tank's a small one with a low rake."

I nodded and rolled over rather than sitting up. In a city like Tien, water tanks were among the assassin's best friends. They tended to sit up high, and most of them had dished tops to collect the frequent rains and reduce the amount of lifting and pumping involved in keeping them full. Perfect for hiding. But the smaller the tank and the lower the rake on the roof, the smaller the cover it provided. That made me plenty cautious as I crawled up to the low edge and looked for what was left of the fire I'd started.

The answer was a few errant wisps of smoke rising from a black and gaping hole in the rooftops, and not much more. . . . A gaping hole in the rooftops absolutely surrounded by Tienese officialdom. I counted three Elite, a dozen or so Crown Guards, and perhaps fifty Stingers—as we called the yellow-and-black-clad city watch. It was past time to wake Triss and get moving again, and I said as much to Faran.

She gave a relieved nod. "Wonderful, let's be gone."

"There's only one little problem we have to settle before our departure."

Faran sighed. "Of course there is. Let me guess. Your swords are in yonder big smoking hole in the ground, right?"

I smiled. I didn't think she'd have missed them going missing. "They are indeed. On our way out, we need to amble over there, slip through the crowd, climb down the still-hot walls, and root through the ashes, all without drawing any unwanted attention."

"Would a really big distraction help?" she asked.

"Did you have something in mind?"

"In fact, I did. I was thinking that a tiny little rooftop water tank coming apart when the enormous dragon that has wedged itself inside makes its exit is probably high up on any list of things that would draw the eye."

I blinked at her. "Wait. What, now?"

She smiled sweetly. "Do I need to repeat myself using words smaller than 'dragon' and 'water tank'?"

I touched the top of the tank with my palm. "Shang . . . is in here?"

She nodded. "You were pretty badly cooked when I carried you up here. You didn't actually think you'd recover as much as you have just from a couple hours of lying unconscious on a rooftop, did you?"

"Shang wedged himself into this tank for me?" A dragon five times the size of the container?

"Of course not. He did it for me." Faran rolled her eyes. "Silly old man." Then she grinned. "Have I ever mentioned how much fun it is to make the legendary Aral Kingslayer gape like an idiot?"

Was that a joke? Triss said into my mind. *I think it was actually a joke. She's come such a very long way from the place where we found her.*

She has indeed, I silently replied.

When I'd first encountered Faran she was not yet sixteen

and making her living as an eavesman—or private spy—listening at windows for the highest bidder along with lifting state secrets and the occasional precious bauble. It was a job that suited her talents and the training she'd received at Namara's temple before the fall, and she had grown quite wealthy doing it. But it hadn't leant itself to trust or humor, or any of the softer emotions.

In the first days after the fall she'd spent so much of herself on simply surviving when every hand had turned against all of our kind, that most of the light had been squeezed out of her soul. Seeing it come back, and—more—helping with that process, made it much easier to deal with the aggravations inherent in dealing with a girl who'd had to mostly raise herself as she tried to figure out how to become a woman. Not easy by any measure, but easier.

"No, my young monster," I said to Faran, "you hadn't mentioned that. But I figured it must give you some pleasure considering how very often you do it."

Faran laughed quietly. "And that's a point to you. Now, shall we retrieve your swords and get on our way?"

I nodded. Slipping past the Elite and a contingent of Crown Guard is no easy thing, even for a pair of fully shrouded Blades. Not under normal circumstances, at any rate. But Shang would make for a most excellent distraction.

"Why don't you circle around to the northeast corner, while I go down the southeast," I said.

"Or you could stay right where you are for five minutes and I'll bring the swords to you." The voice that spoke on the breeze was female, gruff, and brim full of vinegar.

It belonged to Kaelin Fei, Tien's chief of police corruption, and the city's main interface between shadowside and sunside. As head of the watch's silent branch, it was her job to make sure that crime happened quietly and with a minimum of unnecessary bloodshed.

Back in my shadow jack days I'd worked for her from time to time. In the years since, we had become friends, which is why I barely blinked at her voice speaking out of thin air. Well, thick air, really. The message came via her familiar, Scheroc, an air-spirit. Faran and I were among the tiny number of people who knew Fei was an unfaced mage—the only kind Tien had in its city watch.

Historically, the Zhani aristocracy were very suspicious of mages holding any kind of authority, a fact that had greatly complicated my efforts to help Maylien to her rightful place on the throne. To say nothing of how much it was going to complicate her tenure now that she'd taken possession of that royal chair. Fei's familiar spirit brushed invisibly across my cheek by way of greeting, then flitted off to tell her that it had achieved its mission. The creature was sweet, if nowhere near as smart as one of the higher elementals like Triss or Shang.

A few minutes later Fei's scarred face popped up over the edge of the tank. "You really don't need to go all dramatic and skulky for this one, Aral."

Faran laughed aloud. "But it's so funny when he does. You should have seen the look on his face when Scheroc gave us the whisper. His whole plan to outsmart and outsneak that crowd over there went up in smoke." She poked me in the ribs. "I half think you were disappointed at losing a chance to add another caper to the Kingslayer legend."

"That does sound like our Aral," Fei said as she finished her climb. "All dark and drama all the time."

"If there was no need for drama," I grumbled, "why did you send for Faran to come rescue me earlier?"

Fei snorted. "Because this is Tien and nothing is simple. There's no question that the Elite would cheerfully kick you off a ledge into a fire if they thought word of it wouldn't get back to Her Royal Majesty. 'And died of his wounds while being treated' describes the end of any number of Elite enemies. I figured that until you were able to fend for yourself it was best to remove the temptation. But now that you're self-mobile . . . you could have just walked over and demanded they let you retrieve these." She tossed me a long slender bag—it clanked as I caught it out of the air.

"Somehow, I don't think it would have been quite that easy," I said.

Fei shrugged. "I suppose it depends on how you feel about answering four or five hours' worth of pointed questions about that fire. Speaking of which: care to share anything on the subject? I *am* going to have to file a report . . . and it would be nice to know what I ought to leave out."

I grinned. "When you put it like that, how can I resist? There's not much to tell, really. I was using the place as a fallback. I stopped in to pick up some supplies on my way out of town. A horrendous and, to me, wholly new sort of carnivorous beasty showed up and tried to use me for a chew toy. I objected. Strenuously. The rest is collateral damage."

"Tell me about the monster."

"Triss?"

At my prompting, he shifted out of my shadow, taking on the shape of the monster.

"It looked like that, and it acted, well, stupid for starters, but it made up for dumb with all kinds of tough."

I gave Fei a thorough rundown of my encounter, at the end of which she shook her head. "That's a new one on me, too. I don't like that one little bit. But you said something about leaving town. . . ."

I nodded. "We have business in the south."

"'We' meaning just you and Triss? Or, are you taking little miss floods and fires with you?" She nodded at Faran, who grinned back—their first meeting had been . . . fraught, and very nearly involved Faran starting a three-sided war between Zhan, Kodamia, and the Durkoth.

"I'm going, too," said Faran.

"Oh good." Fei nodded. "I'm always a bit less on edge when I don't have to worry about what new hell you might visit on my city." She pointed at the bag. "So, I'm going to step aside and you can take those and her and get out of my jurisdiction soonest."

"No curiosity about where we're going or what we're up to?" I asked.

Fei shook her head. "Not in the least. You are an absolute lodestone for trouble. And, from what I've seen, she makes the effect about ten times worse. The idea of you taking whatever horror you're up to this time on the road fills me with nothing but a sense of peace and joy. I just hope it's *far* south."

I laughed. "It is that. Thanks for retrieving these for me." I pulled the first of my swords from the bag and froze as the rich blue of the lapis-inlaid guard seemed to stare at me with the eye of a goddess long dead.

It was only a momentary thing, and I quickly moved on to sheathing it and its mate, but I knew that Fei had caught my hesitation, that Triss couldn't have missed it, and that Faran had probably noticed as well.

Only Triss was willing to broach the subject, and that silently: *Aral?*

Not right now, please. Aloud, I said, "If you'll excuse us, Fei, it's time we were gone. Faran?"

"I was ready hours ago." She vaulted over the side of the water tank and vanished.

I started to follow, but Fei held up a hand and I saw real concern in her eyes. "I don't know what that little start was about, but the last time I saw that look on your face you'd just kicked back a glass of efik liquor complete with a couple of beans as garnish."

"And it very nearly destroyed me, yes." Though I would never have told her anything, Fei knew about my efik problem by simple dint of having been there when I'd gotten my first dose since the fall of the temple. Cold fire ran through my veins at the mere memory of it, like a jolt of triple-distilled need. I could feel sweat start at my temples, but I didn't let it touch my expression or take the flatness out of my voice "Your point?"

"I care about what happens to you, Aral. You saved my life and more. If you need anything . . ."

"There's nothing you can do about this, Fei, but I do appreciate the concern." Again I started to turn away, but this time I stopped myself. "I notice that you haven't let your hair grow back beyond the barest minimum needed to pad out a helmet."

When I'd first met Fei, and for most of the years since, she'd worn a long thick braid. It had always been her one concession to vanity. She'd cut it all off during the same mess that had resulted in my getting a damned big hit of a drug that was about a hundred times worse for me than the alcohol I'd nearly destroyed myself with.

Now she ran a hand through the inch-long stubble on her head and smiled a sad little smile. "No, I haven't."

"Why not?"

"It hurt too much to slice it off. I'm not willing to risk the pain again."

"Then we have something in common."

And with that, I followed Faran.

4

———❖———

The eyes of the dead do not judge. That's what I kept telling myself, but somehow, as I stared into the deep lapis blue eyes made by the paired guards of my swords, I couldn't believe it.

I had surrendered those very same blades back to the goddess once upon a time, leaving them in the hand of her idol on the floor of the sacred lake. I was away on a mission at the time of the fall, and I had survived when so many others had not. By failing to die in defense of my goddess, I believed that I had failed her, that I had rendered myself unfit to wield her weapons or to serve the cause of justice any longer.

Later events had forced me to rethink my responsibilities, if not my failures, and so, I had returned to the lake and recovered my swords. I would do what I could for justice once again even if Justice herself had gone beyond service. But I had wanted . . . no, *needed* some way to acknowledge that while I might still try to follow the path of my goddess, I would never own her clarity of sight. So, I had painted over the oval guards of my swords, and with that painted over the Unblinking Eye of Justice that they had been made to represent.

Now . . . I turned the swords again, using the light of our

small campfire to look for . . . something, though I didn't know what.

I don't see the problem, Triss sent. *The swords are inde-structible. The paint was not. Why does it worry you so?*

I thought about that. *It's the soot.*

What soot?

Exactly! The fire didn't leave any behind.

All you have ever needed to do to clean anything from the swords is to flick them. It's part of their magic. Nothing clings to them.

Not even black paint?

I don't . . . Oh. Yes, the paint ought to have come off sooner, oughtn't it? Why didn't that occur to either of us before now?

I don't know. I badly wanted to acknowledge the closing of the eyes of Justice, and the paint seemed the best way to do that. Maybe, in wanting that as much as I did, I didn't think it through. But somehow I don't believe that's all of it.

The swords have always been amenable to the will of the wielder. Perhaps the paint stayed because *you wanted it to stay.*

Then why did it come off now?

"What are you two discussing so earnestly?" Faran asked from across the fire.

"Is it that obvious?" I asked.

She shook her head. "No, not to anyone who didn't know about your trick, or to anyone who didn't know *you* quite well for that matter."

"Good." Triss and I were unique among Blade/Shade pairings in our ability to speak mind-to-mind—a side effect of a bit of magic that had almost gone horribly wrong. "I'd hate to be so transparent."

Now she laughed. "I don't think transparent is a word that's likely to come up much if anyone ever writes the biography of the Kingslayer. Harad has it right when he calls out the blank stare as your most effective expression. It's certainly the one you get the most practice with. If I didn't know you it'd be scary as hell. But you still haven't answered my question."

"He does that," Triss said from his place on the ground beside me—I'd moved a log to provide him a screen from the fire. "Constantly. It's very aggravating."

I gave my shadowy partner the hairy eyeball. "I'm getting there." I shifted my gaze to Faran. "It's my swords."

"Really? I'd never have guessed that from the way you keep playing with them."

The shadow phoenix perched on a branch in the small tree behind her made a disapproving noise. "Aral is still a master and your teacher. You should show him more respect."

"I *should* do all sorts of things that are never going to happen, Ssithra. I'm sure that Aral will get over it."

I sighed and nodded. "Aral got over worrying about respect about the same time he crawled into a whiskey bottle to die. Crawling back out again hasn't changed that." I flipped one of my swords end for end, catching the flat of the blade between fingers and thumb so that the back faced my palm. "Here." I extended the sword to Faran.

She took it gently, almost reverently. "These are so beautiful. I wish . . ." After a couple of silent beats, Faran shook her head. "I wish a lot of things."

Triss slid over to Faran and touched her knee with: "I'm sorry that you were thrust out into the world so young and unprepared. You ought to have had the opportunity to finish your training and take up the swords of the goddess instead of those cane knives you use. You would have made a marvelous Blade."

"Thanks, Triss." She reached down and scratched the ridge behind his ear—a favorite spot. "That's only one wish among many, though it is a big one. Besides, the cane knives aren't so bad." She tapped one of the crossed hilts that stuck up over her shoulders—she preferred the older style of back sheath, where I had shifted to hip-draw. "They're better than most swords for close quarters."

She was right there; short and forward curved, the cane knives were brutal weapons that shared as much lineage with hatchets as they did with knives. Now she looked at me down the length of the sword I'd handed her. "I don't see a thing wrong with this darling. What am I missing?"

"Nothing," I said. "Which is exactly what worries me."

"Care to elaborate?"

"I painted over my guards."

"I'd noticed that, though I didn't want to ask. Neither about that nor about taking them up again. It seemed too personal a thing for me to pry."

"Thank you." I didn't think the Faran of even a year before would have had that delicacy, but I did her the courtesy of not praising her for the change. "I didn't come to either decision easily."

A long but not uncomfortable silence grew between us as she twisted my sword this way and that in what looked like a vain attempt to catch the fire's reflection. They were assassin's blades, and the goddess had shaped them to drink light as surely as any Shade could. Finally, she turned the sword around—far more carefully than I had—and handed it back to me.

"So, what's the problem?" she asked.

I quickly explained to her my thinking about the fire and the paint and the distinct lack of soot. When I'd finished she looked very thoughtful. "I suppose you could try painting them over again to see what happens."

"I've considered it, but I don't know. Maybe it's a message of some kind. If so, wouldn't it be disrespectful of me to erase it like that?"

"The dead are gone forever." Her voice came out flat and hard—the return of the merciless killer who shared a body with the ill-used teenager that was Faran's other face. "Namara passed through the final gate and went to the lords of judgment, as we all must someday. Don't fool yourself into thinking otherwise."

"I know that. None better."

But, even as I said it, I couldn't help thinking about the handful of times I had experienced something . . . numinous over the last few years. Not the return of Namara, certainly, but maybe something like the echo of her ghost—a sort of sense of beneficence that . . . Well, whatever it had been, I wasn't going to share it with anyone. I hadn't even really talked about it with Triss.

I frowned, reaching for the right words. "I wasn't thinking of a message from Namara, Faran, so much as . . ."

"As what? Some other deity trying belatedly to apologize for their role in murdering ours?" Her words came out angry but cold. Calculated and deadly. "I spit on every last one of them."

I paused then, trying to figure out what I wanted to say to that. "Justice the goddess is dead, but justice the ideal . . . Now, there I'm not so sure."

Faran snorted. "Somewhere down deep, you're still an idealist, aren't you? Even now, after the death of Namara and five years of selling bits of your soul to make the price of a bottle of whiskey and a spot to sleep in the hayloft. You still believe, somehow, that there's justice in the world, don't you?"

I held up a hand and said, "No, not—"

But Triss flared his wings angrily at Faran, interrupting me. "What's wrong with that? The world *needs* justice."

"I wasn't finished," I said quietly before she could respond. "Faran, I agree with Triss that the world needs justice, but no, I don't believe that it's just out there waiting to happen or anything like that. What I believe is that someone has to make justice happen—that *I* have to make justice happen when and where I can. I don't have Namara's pure vision, which is why I painted over her eyes, but I'll be damned if I'm ever again going to close mine to what needs doing."

I jumped to my feet. "When I talk about the ideal of justice living on, I'm not talking about an abstract. I'm talking about these swords and making it happen myself."

"And your idea of a message?" asked Faran, her voice quieter and more thoughtful, but still cold, a killer's voice. "Where might that come from?"

"I don't know. Maybe it comes from here." I touched a fingertip to the spot over my heart. "The swords have always listened to their wielder. Maybe the eyes of Namara opening once again is me trying to tell myself something. Or maybe it comes from out there." I spread my swords wide, opening my arms to the world. "Maybe the world needs something from me and used the fire to deliver the message."

"Or maybe," said Faran, "whatever nasty thing is going on with Siri is trying to get an entirely different sort of message across. That's certainly how I read the arrival of the thing you killed in the fire. Who's to say that peeling the paint off your swords wasn't simply the dying act of a monster that wanted you dead."

"Could be," I agreed with her. "I don't know the *why* or the *what*, much less if there's a *who* involved. Which is why I keep staring at my swords and making up theories without any further evidence. Honestly, yours sounds like as good an explanation as any."

Faran looked baffled. "Well, if you didn't believe all that stuff about some cosmic message, why did you sound so convincing?"

"Maybe because I wanted to be convinced. Wouldn't it be marvelous if the world *were* crying out for the return of justice?"

"You're impossible," she said, but it was the voice of the confused teenager this time, and not the killer. "And a crazy old man."

"And you, my dear, are a cynical young monster. Yet here we sit, master and apprentice, or something very like."

"You want to teach me something? Paint the guards over again and see what happens. Call it a test of faith."

"Fair enough."

I reached for my trick bag—which held most of a Blade's standard tool set. For reasons I hadn't been able to fully articulate even to myself I'd tucked the little paint pot I'd used for the task into my permanent kit. Maybe it was because I *did* want to be convinced. Though, I had to admit I wasn't sure of what exactly it was that I wanted to believe. Whatever the reason, I had Namara's eyes closed again in a relative wink. Then it was time to eat, and to desperately try not to think about how nice a glass of whiskey or a cup of brewed efik would chase it down.

Aral, wake up.

I did, instantly and fully, but without moving—a faculty I'd recovered since letting go of the booze. *What is it, Triss?*

Nothing dangerous, or at least not immediately so. Open your eyes.

All right . . . I did, and saw Namara's staring back into my own from the paired hilts of my swords—I always slept with them in easy reach. *Oh.*

"Faran," I said quietly.

"Yes." She had received the same training I had, and there was no muzziness in her voice as she woke and answered me.

"The swords are clean again."

"Interesting." I didn't hear her move, but she was squatting beside my head a moment later. She reached out a finger and touched the ground. "There's paint dust under them. It looks like it just fell away by itself. Huh, score one for the something-unusual-is-going-on-here theory, I guess." Then she shrugged. "Are you cooking breakfast, or am I?"

"I am," I said quickly—the quality of Faran's cooking was . . . erratic. "But I want you to help. Poisons are one of your weakest subjects, and the foundation of a good poisoning is a good meal."

"Hey, I've gotten much better. I barely burned the fish yesterday morning."

"And today you'll do even better."

An hour or so later we'd cleaned up the remnants of a very nice meal and repacked all of our gear onto the horses. I'd initially planned to walk, since feet could cover more ground and faster than hooves over the kinds of distances we had to travel. But Faran had talked me around by the simple expedient of buying horses and overpacking before she came to collect me at the burned-out warehouse. I could have insisted, but the thought of sleeping on a thick pad instead of wrapped in my poncho and being able to eat real meals made an excellent argument.

It was late spring in Tien, which meant the day started warm and headed quickly for hot. It also meant Faran and I both wore the lightest of our grays.

Given that the order of the day was dusty plodding on dirt roads under a brutal sun, I ditched my shirt and my cowl with its wraparound muffler in favor of a loose vest and a broad conical hat in the peasant style. For lack of concealing sleeves I also took off my wrist sheaths, though Faran kept hers. If we'd been walking rather than riding, I'd probably have swapped boots for peasant sandals as well. Faran's vest was tighter, but other than that, and the differences in our weapons, there was little to distinguish our outfits one from the other.

Our road ran a touch south of west, loosely following the line of the Zien River as it flowed down from its confluence with the Vang. We had very nearly four hundred miles left to cross before we hit the Great Mountain Way that trailed along the eastern edge of the Hurnic Mountains. Faran had chosen our horses for endurance over speed, and we were lightly packed by horse standards, but even so, we'd be close to a fortnight just getting to the mountains, and then it would take us a month or more from there to the edge of the Sylvain. It wasn't going to be a fast trip, nor an easy one.

Zhan is a rich country with a dense population and a recent history of war with its neighbors, all of which would help us on our way. Thauvik might have been a miserable bastard of a king where it came to shedding his people's blood, but he'd valued keeping the roads in good repair to make it easier to move his armies. And lots of people meant frequent inns and lighter loads because of that—we'd only camped the first couple of nights because I'd wanted time alone to think about the meaning of the change in my swords.

That night we stopped at our first inn, a long low building with a raked gravel garden in the middle of the central court-yard. It was typical of the Zhani style, with wide windows and open-walled galleries to catch the summer breezes, while broad overhangs provided cover from the rains of winter.

A young woman in pants and a vest met us at the guesting gate that arched over the turnoff into the grounds of the inn. Her loose brown clothing was cut much the same as the outfits we wore, though they were of a significantly cheaper grade of silk and she had on sandals rather than boots.

"Welcome to the Five Dancing Turtles, noble oyani. I am Yian, eldest daughter of the house."

Yian called us by the honorific that denoted outland nobility as she bowed low in the center of the gate. While I might have been able to pass for a local lord with a bit of scandalous blood in the ancestral closet, no one would ever mistake Faran for Zhani. Where I was a touch on the dark side, she was simply too pale. But that was no problem given that we were riding the main travel route between the lands that lay west of the mountains and those on the east. Even so deep into the countryside, foreigners were common, and our weapons and the richness of our clothes gave us a courtesy promotion to the nobility.

"Do you wish accommodation, or are you merely seeking refreshment?" Yian asked as she stepped to the right side of the gate, formally inviting us onto the grounds.

"We need two rooms and stabling for our horses." I slid out of the saddle—it was far from a graceful dismount, as I was some days yet from recovering my seat for riding.

Faran, younger and spryer, hopped down without so much as a wince. By then, a boy had arrived to take care of the horses. Faran and I claimed the smaller saddle bags from the riding horses, then fell in behind Yian.

She led us to a table in the eastern gallery, only a little way from the fountain. "Please wait here. Will you take tea or wine before you bathe? It will be a few minutes before we have your rooms prepared."

"Cold tea," I said. I still didn't much enjoy the stuff, hot or cold, but I no longer hated it.

"I will see to it." She bowed and headed for the arch that led to the back courtyard and the inevitable summer kitchen.

A few moments later a girl appeared with a tray holding small handleless cups, and a porcelain tea bottle still damp from the cold well. By her looks she was probably Yian's little sister. She poured our tea without speaking, then returned to the summer kitchen.

It was half an hour shy of sunset and a few of the locals began to roll in while we were drinking our tea. Mostly, they ignored us as they filled in the tables around the central garden. One fellow among a particularly rough-looking set of laborers gave us the once-over of a man thinking about starting a fight. He even started toward our table, but when he got close enough to really see us he suddenly took a deep interest in a previously tight sandal strap. Sensible. By the time we finished our drinks, the place was about two-thirds full, though there was a wide circle of empty tables around ours.

Yian came to lead us to the baths then, showing us which rooms were ours on the way. Like most public baths, the one at the Five Dancing Turtles had lockers where we could tuck our gear before scrubbing down and plunging into the big hot pool on the highest terrace. I laid a light spell of alarm on the lock, more out of habit than concern. With so many of the locals just finishing work, the baths were crowded, but a large space opened up around us as soon as we entered the soaking pool.

No one was rude, of course, but it was obvious that we made many of them uncomfortable, as what had been a lively group conversation faded into several smaller and much quieter groups. After a few minutes of everyone politely ignoring us, one ancient woman with a pile of gray hair pinned up on top of her head half walked, half swam over to us and bobbed her head in the bathhouse equivalent of a bow. I nodded back.

"Soldiers?" she asked in politely curious voice.

I shook my head. "No. Just simple travelers."

She laughed. "Pull the other one, young man. Simple travelers do not have such scars." She pointed to the sharp white line that ran across my chest at collarbone height where the Kitsune had very nearly managed to kill me, and then the scar that nearly took Faran's left eye.

"True enough," I said in the same moment that Triss sent, *She's got you there.* "Though, we're still not soldiers. . . ." I trailed off, letting silence ask the question for me.

"Call me Auntie Hua. My family owns this inn." She cocked her head to the side. "I won't ask, so don't bother making up false names. Warriors, but not soldiers, and not bandits, not with the clothes you wore in. Foreign. Hmm . . . Oyani for real, perhaps, or mages. That or couriers or some other type of royal agent. Safe enough. I hope your stay with us is one you remember fondly."

She bobbed her head again, then turned and glided back to the place where she'd been talking with a few other old woman. The atmosphere grew much more friendly after that, and the invisible wall that seemed to travel with us got a bit smaller.

Dinner was fried pork with mushrooms and broccoli—one of the last of the winter vegetables—on a bed of thick brown noodles. There was also a carp soup, and sweet rice balls.

The Five Dancing Turtles was typical of the bigger inns along the western road. From here on out we could rely on cash to feed and house us and other hands to deal with grooming the horses and getting them saddled in the morning. Which is exactly what we did, with one day blurring into another all the way to the mountains.

There, we turned south onto the much less traveled Great Mountain Way—north-south trade mostly traveled by ship along the coast. Add in the history of raids back and forth across the border with Kodamia and the villages became smaller and more scarce. With them went most of the inns and taverns. Though we would be able to put up at farms some nights, we provisioned up before leaving the western road.

Once again I was glad Faran had talked me into horses. It meant we would eat better. I'd walked thousands of miles on tight rations in service of my goddess back in the days when she had sent me all over the eleven kingdoms bringing death's justice to those the law couldn't touch. They were some of the best years of my life, but there were parts I didn't miss at all. Bad food and cold nights on hard ground without enough blankets were high on that list.

The landscape changed now, with large patches of dense woodlands starting to appear on both sides of the road. Here, closer to the mountains, the weather was consistently cooler, and that was reflected in the trees, which looked more like those in the forests of my homeland than the remaining patches of coastal jungle around Tien.

Three days after we turned south, we were laying our bedrolls out under the stars again. We camped near a small brook where Ssithra and Triss amused themselves by fishing up some fresh stirby for our dinner. I set our fire against a rocky ridge that hid the light from the road, and cooked the fish with a bit of pepper sauce and noodles, while Faran added in some berries she'd picked for dessert.

We'd had a long hot day on the road, and not long after sunset both Faran and I quickly fell asleep. Triss and Ssithra had mostly slept the day away to avoid the sun. Now, with night rolling in and darkness bringing them into their greatest strength, they took over watch duty. Very little could get past a single Shade in its element, much less two.

Which is why I was very surprised to wake suddenly in the cold hours before dawn with the distinct feeling of being watched.

Triss? I sent.

You sound worried. What is it?

I don't know. I just have a feeling we're no longer alone. Have you sensed anything moving in the night?

A fox, two skunks, more bugs than you'd care to count.

But nothing big?

No. Let me consult with Ssithra. A brief mental silence followed. Then, *No, nothing.*

That was when I saw the face in the stone. The little cliff we'd built our fire against was a mottled gray green, taller than a man on horseback, and roughly flat on the side facing us. I hadn't paid much attention to it beyond that, but I was quite sure it hadn't possessed a face when I had gone to sleep. I'd have noticed. Especially this face.

The features were human in number and order, but genderless, and utterly inhuman in their perfection. Even the most beautiful of mortals has flaws, one ear a fraction higher than the other, a faint scar under the eye, eyebrows that come too close to meeting. Something. This face looked like something out of a dream . . . or a nightmare. The eyes were blank spheres the exact same color as the rest of the face and the stone around them, and the expression was equally blank. Again, inhuman.

"Durkoth." I flipped my blankets back and sat up, crossing my legs as I faced the Other in the stone. "What do you want?"

The face's expression retained the same blank stare but it moved now, sliding slowly upward until the eyes were on a level with my own. It also pushed forward a few inches, so that most of the ears were exposed. As the face moved, the rock flowed around it like water passing smoothly around a stone. It was a profoundly unnatural effect, and I knew that I would never find it anything but discomforting.

"Your kind usually prefers to start a conversation with inanities," said the face, in a voice as genderless as its features. "Yet you have chosen to speak directly to the point. May I ask why this is?" Though the Durkoth was asking a question, neither tone nor expression betrayed any sense of curiosity.

I glanced over at Faran's bedroll and saw that she was no longer in it. "Certainly," I said to the face. "Though, I'm surprised you care. I didn't think the Durkoth found us ephemerals all that interesting."

"Most of us do not. As for me? Of yourselves, no. But I am a speaker. It is my role to hold converse with the lesser races. I have performed this task for some thousands of years, and it is my experience that behavior that does not fit the normal pattern sometimes points to a shift in societal patterns, and sometimes is merely an individual peculiarity. In the former case it is important for me to take it into account in future

conversations. In the latter, I needn't concern myself with
it. So?"

"Individual peculiarity."

"Noted. Thank you."

"You're welcome. I note that your features remain the color
of the surrounding stone. The Durkoth I have met before have
generally reverted to a pure marble white at some point. I had
taken that to be your natural color, but you have not shifted.
Am I incorrect?" I tried to keep my voice as neutral as the
Other's.

The Durkoth actually smiled then, a small enigmatic gesture, quite possibly assumed solely for my benefit. "That is
something of a philosophical question among our kind, at least
when phrased as you have put it. Generally, we live in stone
and reflect the color of the stone around us. It is only when we
venture into the outer air that the colors of the earth leach out
of us. Since spending time above the earth is unnatural for us,
can the color we assume in that circumstance be said to be
anything other than unnatural itself?"

"Interesting. And now, for indulging my curiosity, it is my
turn to thank you."

"You are welcome."

"Which puts us back where we started. What do you want?"

"To continue the conversation we have begun."

I found myself blinking at that. "I am . . . surprised. Is the
conversation a goal in itself? Or, did you have a specific thing
you wished to discuss with me? In either case, if we're going
to continue to talk, it would be nice to have a name for you.
Can I offer you tea or . . . anything? You're welcome to join
me by the fire."

The face smiled again, and this time I thought it might be
genuine. "Let us begin with names. You may call me Thuroq,
which is as close a rendition of mine as your speech apparatus
will allow. I *do* have a specific thing I have been directed to
speak with you about. And, thank you, but no. I will remain
within stone while I converse with you. Your companion killed
many of my people during the unpleasantness that first brought
you into our awareness. I would prefer not to give her the opportunity to add my name to her ledger."

Faran's voice spoke out of the darkness. "You think that

rock wall would protect you? I'm holding a blade of the goddess in my hand. I could drive it through your forehead before you so much as blinked."

I glanced over at my sheaths and saw that Faran had indeed managed to lift one of my blades practically out of my lap without my noticing. "That's not going to be necessary, Faran. Please put the sword back." I turned my eyes back to Thuroq, desperately glad that Faran hadn't decided to try anything hasty. "Pardon my apprentice. She's had bad experiences with the Durkoth in the past."

That was putting it mildly. In her former role as a spy Faran had stolen the Kothmerk, a signet that held enormous cultural value for the Durkoth and Kodamians both. The incident had nearly started a three-way war and a lot of people had died, both human and Durkoth. Many of the latter had fallen at Faran's hand.

"It is of no matter," replied Thuroq. "I am not in any danger, nor have I been while we talked." The forehead of the stone face parted, exposing only more stone. "I am deep within the rock, too deep even for your divine blade to touch. A good decision, I think."

"And the face?" I asked.

"Mine, but not. Sister stone acts as both my mirror and my voice."

Faran stepped out of shadow and returned my sword to me before crossing to look at the stone face from much closer. "That's an interesting piece of magic."

Thuroq's lips thinned ever so slightly. "It is *not* magic. The stone and I are children of the same mother. She shapes herself to my will out of love, nothing more."

"Of course," said Faran, her tone broadly sarcastic. "Nothing magic or coercive about it."

"Faran." I shot her a quelling look when what I really wanted was to shake her. "Don't." She knew as well as I did that the Durkoth absolutely hated having their command over stone compared to human magic—it was tied up with their religion and the Others' ancient war with the gods.

She winked at me, then slipped back into shadow before I could say anything more, effectively removing herself both from sight and the conversation. I turned back to Thuroq.

"I do apologize again. You were about to tell me why you're here, I believe. Something about having been directed to speak with me . . ."

"By the King of the North, yes. I am here because of the ring."

I had a brief nightmarish flashback to the mess with the Kothmerk, but then realized I might have leaped to the wrong conclusion.

"Wait, do you mean this one?" I raised the hand bearing the smoke ring.

Thuroq nodded ever so slightly, his expression going grim.

"What about it?" I asked.

"It is a wedding ring."

"Yes, I was aware of that. Why does that matter to you?"

"We have felt it calling through the earth each time you sit beside a fire, smoke singing underground, a link to the south and our buried past."

Triss gave a little shiver in my shadow at that. Though he remained silent, I could sense his concern and shared it. There was something here I was missing. Something important.

"Is there a problem?" I asked.

"Yes. When a mortal such as yourself weds one of the buried gods of our ancestors, there is most definitely a problem."

5

————◆————

The Others called him the Fire That Burns Underground, or Smoke in the Ashes. Humans knew him as the Smoldering Flame.

Whatever you chose to name him, he was one of the buried gods—a thing out of evil legend and twice dead. He'd been put into the ground once at the end of the godwar by the Emperor of Heaven, and then again by Siri Athalos in the year 3209—a feat that earned her the use-name Mythkiller and made her the pride of Namara's temple.

But while we may *call* a buried god *dead*, they are ultimately beyond the true death, and some part of the fallen god had begun to stir in his slumber once again. According to Thuroq, the Durkoth had felt the first rumbles of his unquiet sleep echoing through the bones of the great mountains some years past, but had paid little enough attention at the time. The buried gods are ever restless in the grave, and their struggles against the bonds of divine magic and enchanted earth surge and fade as endlessly and inevitably as the waves in Tien's harbor.

"But then something changed," I said, as Thuroq wound his story toward its end.

"It did," agreed Thuroq. "The Fire That Burns Underground

was one of ours at the beginning, a child of earth and stone. Because of that, he may yet persuade his element to aid him from time to time, despite the deathlike sleep that holds his soul, and the anchors the gods set into the Wall of the Sylvain, which bind the greatest part of his magic."

"Excuse me," Faran cut in sharply though she maintained her shroud, "but I'm getting kind of tired of all the blah-blah-blahs. Could you maybe get around to the point of this little lesson in the history of boring? You implied that Smoking Mayhem, or whatever you want to call him, had married himself to a mortal—presumably Aral here. Or, possibly, Siri. You weren't very clear on the whole thing. . . ."

"It's not a simple matter," said the Durkoth. "The ring around Aral's finger is born of the Fire That Burns Underground. We can hear it singing to its mate through the deep ways. But, as far as we can tell, it is not the god's waking will that it obeys. He remains entombed, and though he stirs, he is not yet risen. That much is easy to read even over so great a distance as lies between us and the buried lands. To learn more, we must examine one ring or the other. Since we will not pass the Wall willingly, that means this one." He nodded toward my hand.

"You're going to have to come out of that rock if you want a really good look at it," said Faran, and I caught a smug and dangerous note in her tone.

"Not I," replied Thuroq. "I have not the necessary skill. I merely speak."

At last, Triss said into my mind. *I think we finally approach the true point of this whole endeavor.*

I flipped my hand palm up. "And . . ."

"And my master, the King of the North, has bid me here to ask you if you would consent to a brief detour on your path south. I can promise you that it will cost you but a little time and not an hour of it drawn from your road."

"That's an interesting offer," I said, and I might be inclined to consider it given a bit more information. I might be willing to offer up my life if Siri needed it, but I would prefer not having to do it blind. "Though I wonder how the one can be managed without the other."

"Both concerns are addressed easily enough. The king wishes that you see one of his Uthudor and allow her to look at your ring."

Uthudor? Triss sent. *I don't know that word.*

Before I could echo his question aloud, Thuroq continued. "Dame Krithak is a . . . scholar? . . . Yes, I think that is the closest word in your tongue, though student or surgeon might also strike near the mark. The Uthudor are scholars of the earth. Though she long ago left court, Dame Krithak remains among the most revered of Uthudor, and she resides not far from here as the tunnelworm bores. If you will agree to go to her, I will open the way for you."

"And we won't lose any time out of our travels?" I asked.

"Quite the contrary. Once you are done with the Uthudor and have returned to your companion here, I will speed you along on wings of earth for three nights running."

I don't like the sound of that, Aral. We shouldn't allow them to separate us from Faran.

I'm not thrilled about it either, but taking Faran to visit a Durkoth elder is a bit like taking a mongoose along on a visit with a cobra. Besides, this is the one opportunity we've had to get any information independent of Siri about what's going on.

So, you don't *completely trust Siri.*

Of course, I don't. The only person in the whole world that I trust entirely is you. I may owe Siri anything she asks of me, but that doesn't mean I'm going to give it to her blind if I can avoid it. This is the first real chance we've had to get any real information about the ring and what the hell is going on. I think we have to take it.

Aloud, I asked Thuroq, "*Returned* to my companion? I take it that means you want me to leave Faran here?"

"Yes. I'm sorry, but the one we call the *Stonecutter* must remain at your camp. Dame Krithak has only consented to see one."

I opened my mouth to argue, but Faran touched me on the shoulder before I could speak. Stepping out of shadow, she knelt to put her face on a level with Thuroq's stone mask, fixing him with the coldest of stares.

"I can't speak for Aral, but I don't trust you, nor any of your kind. I have minimum conditions that must be met. If Aral agrees to go to this Uthudor, that's on him, but you will remain here with me, aboveground where I can reach you. If any harm comes to him while he is with your Uthudor, there will be a reckoning that will *begin* with my killing you on the spot."

The rock wall parted like a curtain, creating or exposing an arch and stairs that spiraled down into the earth. Faran rolled backward in response, drawing her cane knives and slipping into shadow once again. At the same time, Thuroq rose into view, coming around the curve of the stairs some half dozen steps down. I still couldn't say whether the Durkoth was male or female, though if pressed I'd have bet on the former.

As I had come to expect with Durkoth, he didn't actually climb the stairs, but simply stood statue still as they bore him silently up from the depths. Both his flesh and hair seemed to have been carved from a single block of white marble. He was barefoot and wore nothing but a simple black knee-length tunic of onyx.

I didn't make the mistake of thinking that was some sort of illusion, as I might have before my extended dealings with the Durkoth during the Kothmerk mess. No, despite the fact that the hem fluttered around Thuroq's knees like fine silk, the tunic was undoubtedly exactly what it looked like—a piece of living rock that weighed several hundred pounds and moved only as its wearer willed it. Past experience suggested that it would also double as excellent armor.

"If you will agree to see the Uthudor," said Thuroq, "I will abide here as hostage for your safe return. My king anticipated such a request and commanded that I honor it if so asked." The Durkoth gestured to the stairs. "This will lead you to the way which has been prepared."

Triss?

I say yes, though it's reluctantly, and with deep reservations. You're right that we don't really know anything about the ring, or what's happening with Siri yet, or about this Fire That Burns Underground. The Others normally refuse to speak about the buried gods with our kind. We can't pass this up.

I nodded. I didn't like it either, but that didn't change the facts. "One more question, Thuroq. You say that you will speed us along on wings of earth. I have to travel the distance from Tien to the Sylvani Empire in a way that maintains the contact between my ring and Siri's. . . ."

"The rings sing one to the other through the deep ways. What I propose will not interfere with their song. If anything, it may amplify it."

"Then I will go."

I rose and quickly donned the harness that held my swords and other working gear, then headed for the arch in the stone. As I put my foot on the first step, I called over my shoulder, "I won't be gone long, Faran. I expect to find Thuroq alive and in one leak-free piece when I return."

Faran didn't answer me, but Thuroq added, "That would be ideal, yes."

The stairway spiraled down through earth and rock for about fifty feet, ending abruptly at a rough wall of granite. As I put a hand on the stone, Triss reshaped my shadow into dragon form and slid upward to meet my fingers.

Somehow this isn't what I expected, he said into my mind.

Yeah, it makes for a mighty short trip unless we're supposed to swim through stone the rest of the way, and I wouldn't do that again, even if I could.

I'd taken such a trip with the Durkoth outcast Qethar once upon a time, and I couldn't even *imagine* a circumstance where I would agree to do it again. I was about to turn around and head back up the stairs when I felt the bottom step shift beneath me, angling itself downward. That was all the warning I got before the base of the wall opened up in front of me, forming itself into the top of a chute with walls as slick as volcanic glass. Before I could do much more than take a deep breath I slid downward into darkness.

I dropped another fifty or so feet in a matter of instants, then abruptly the chute or tube, or whatever you wanted to call it, angled back upward. I'm not sure how far up I moved before sliding over the top and moving down again at a much shallower angle. Reason dictated it couldn't be any farther than I'd come downward, but reason didn't get much say in what the Durkoth could do with stone. A fact that I found further reinforced as the trip lengthened and I had time to think instead of simply reacting.

A dim red magelight pulled from my trick bag allowed me to examine the space around me. Where I had expected to see darkness fading away into the distance both above and below me, I instead found paired stone concavities no more than a yard away in each direction. I wasn't sliding through an open-ended tube so much as I was riding a tapered cylinder of stone through the depths of the earth. The effect made me think of a particularly fat rabbit passing down the gullet of a snake barely big enough to swallow it.

That's disconcerting, I sent to Triss. *What happens if the will that's moving us decides to stop suddenly? Do I run into the bottom hard? Or does the whole thing collapse?*

I'm not sure that's quite how it works, Triss replied after a couple of long heartbeats. *You probably can't see it, but the tips of the cones above and below us are open about a finger's width. I can extend myself through the hole and a considerable distance into the tiny tube beyond, and there doesn't seem to be any end in sight in either direction. I suspect the one above reaches all the way back to the stairs we came down, like an impossibly long strand of hollow reed.*

And ahead?

There, too, I expect. Thuroq spoke of a way that had been prepared, like it was a thing already done. Perhaps this is sort of a self-operating transport spell, only without the magic.

You realize that doesn't make a lick of sense, don't you?

Hmph. We're dealing with Other ways of doing things here. You need to step outside of the human frame of reference. In the everdark there are currents of shadow, much like ocean currents. If you know how, you can ride these from place to place, traveling great distances without having to exert your-self to do so. Maybe the Durkoth have ways of tapping similar currents in the earth.

I suppose that's possible . . . though I couldn't begin to imagine how. I mean, I know the earth can move on its own—we got caught in that quake in Anyang, after all—but that's a very different sort of motion.

Yes, but . . . wait, I see light ahead. Be ready.

I stowed my little magelight and checked the hilts of my swords—I wanted to make sure that sliding so far on my back hadn't done anything untoward to the catches that held them in their sheaths. Then I braced myself for a sudden stop. I needn't have bothered with that last, as I slowed almost to nothing a moment before I broke through into open air. There, I was deposited neatly and gently on a sort of stone chaise. It was surprisingly yielding and comfortable, reminding me of the clothes the Durkoth wore—simultaneously fabric soft and rock hard.

As I got up from the low couch, it pivoted, while the opening above slid down the wall, transforming the chaise visually from the bottom end of a chute into the top of a scoop. Watching it made me feel a bit queasy—stone oughtn't to flow and shift like that. It especially shouldn't do it in such a manner that every single step from start to finish looked as permanent and solid as if it had always been that way and always would.

The chaise centered one end of an egg-shaped room perhaps twenty feet across the long way. There were no doors or windows and, with the narrowing of the tube by which I had entered, no apparent way out. But the shape of the room and the pale sourceless light that illuminated it focused my attention on the end opposite the one by which I had entered, so I headed in that direction.

Before I had half crossed the distance, an archway opened itself in front of me. Beyond lay an enormous natural cavern, or such a good counterfeit of one that the distinction seemed hardly worth considering. It was filled with that same sourceless light that obscured as much as it exposed.

One of the first things I noticed as I crossed the threshold was the gentle music of falling water. It rolled slowly down countless spears of rock that hung from the ceiling and dripped from their tips. Sometimes it landed on upthrust points that mirrored those above. Sometimes it splashed into one of the irregular pools that serpentined their way among the rough spires and pillars.

The predominant color was a milky white, though pale blues and pinks could be seen veining the stone like the lines in a fine Varyan cheese. Here and there, translucent curtains of marble and travertine created smaller galleries or chambers that prevented me from seeing any great distance in one direction. Add in the rippling reflections from the pools, and the whole area took on a dreamy mazelike quality.

"It's beautiful," I whispered as I looked around. "And . . . somehow, holy."

"To human eyes perhaps," said Triss. "I find it more disturbing than anything. There are too many reflecting surfaces, and this light that comes from nowhere makes my soul ache. There are no true shadows here, and I do not belong. I would very much like to keep our time here brief."

It was not the first time that Triss and I had a divergence of aesthetics—no surprise given our differing senses—but it was certainly one of the strongest. Well, no matter how lovely I might find the vista, if it made Triss that uncomfortable I would do what I could to hurry our departure. That meant I needed to get my meeting with Dame Krithak over in short order. A matter that would have been much simpler if I'd had any idea where to find her.

I took a dozen or so steps out into the cave, then stopped, looking for any signs that might point the way. At least, that was my intention. But, while I stopped walking, I didn't stop moving. It was a most disconcerting feeling, made infinitely more so by the ease with which I remained upright. I'd had a certain amount of practice at trying to keep my footing on a floor half-covered in marbles, emphasis on *trying*. It's a nearly, but not quite, impossible task, and this felt quite like that, only . . . not.

Maybe I'd better back up. In a perfect Namaran execution of justice, the goddess's Blade moves in without being seen, kills the target silently, and is gone before anyone knows they were even there. In the real world, that rarely happens. So, our training had focused as much on the techniques of escape as it did on the methods of infiltration and the delivery of death. Basically, we spent a lot of time learning how to run away.

Speed, silence, and agility are at the top of any list of skills involved in the getaway. Since the emphasis of the Blade is on personal action, acrobatic ability, climbing, and slipping through narrow gaps come in next. But not far behind is the deployment of various sorts of deterrents to pursuit. Caltrops, trip wires, oil slicks, and scattered marbles can all do wonders, and I had practiced planting each and every one of them for hours at a time. But such things can trip you up as easily as your enemies, and Master Kelos had insisted we learn as much about dealing with them as we did about delivering them.

The ground under my boots now had some of that same stomach-twisting unsteadiness that you felt when you hit a carpet of marbles on a stone floor. I could feel it rolling me along at a speed not much below walking. Deep in my gut I *knew* that my feet ought to be shooting out from under me at any second. At the same time, the floor had a sort of . . . grippy, tacky feel to it, like when you stand where some sweet juice has been spilled.

The weird combination of slick and stick made my brain twist in uncomfortable ways and I was very happy when the ride came to an end. The floor took me around a thick fall of stone, rotated me a half turn, and deposited me neatly in front of what at a quick glance seemed a half-finished sculpture of a gorgeous woman on a pink marble throne. That first impression was, of course, wrong.

Dame Krithak sat . . . on? in? had merged with? a massive, low-backed chair of pink marble. There were no seams where the pale sleeveless dress that covered her met the stuff of the chair, no tiniest gap between the flesh of her forearms and the arms of the throne. For that matter, it wasn't entirely clear where dress ended and Durkoth began. She was all of a piece, and that piece flowed continuously down from the top of her head through the throne and into the floor. She looked as though some sculptor had started to carve her free of one of the stalagmites that rose from the floor only to stop with the job three-quarters finished.

For all that, she looked far more human than either Thuroq or Qethar, simply because of the place she had chosen to set her throne. Though few people in the eleven kingdoms were half as pale as the finely whorled pink stone whose color Krithak had assumed, it was at least a shade that one could imagine seeing in skin. That appearance of life was somewhat muted by the fact that her hair and downcast eyes were the exact same mottled shade, but I still found it vaguely comforting.

"Dame Krithak, I presume?" I asked after long silence let me know that she would not be initiating our conversation.

She blinked several times, moving with that classic Durkothian stop-start-stop motion that always seemed to happen in the interstices of awareness so that you never actually *saw* them change position. Then her chin slowly lifted and blind-seeming eyes met my own.

"I am."

I let another long silence fall between us before I continued, "I'm Aral. The King of the North asked me to come here and show you this." I held up the smoke ring.

She reached out then and caught my hand, pulling it closer to her eyes. I wasn't expecting her action or I would have moved the ring closer myself. That, or leaped back out of reach. I had been touched by the Durkoth before . . . and much to the same effect. Durkoth look as cold and hard as the stone where they dwell, but they are not. Oh, no, far from it.

They are warmer than we are, with skin like hot silk, smooth and supple and . . . I shook my head, trying to shake off the sexual glamour with it. But the tight pressure of my erection practically screamed my failure. There would be no easy escape from the sudden and intense desire I felt for the woman in front of me.

It didn't matter that she was far more alien than she looked. It didn't matter that she probably had as much interest in taking me to her bed as I might have had in screwing the sculpture she had appeared to be only a moment before. It didn't matter that she was old by the standards of a people that lived until something external killed them. She looked young and beautiful and I wanted her. I wanted her right now.

But impulse is not action, and while I might not be able to rule my body's response to the glamour of the Durkoth, I would sure as hell rule my own actions. Though I was practically trembling with lust, I forced myself to hold perfectly still and to breathe slowly and evenly while she turned my hand this way and that in her own.

Time moved with an impossible, almost syrupy, slowness that made the process an exquisite sort of torture that went on and on and on. When she lifted the ring up and touched it to her lips and the tip of her tongue, I had to bite the inside of my mouth to keep from responding.

Finally, finally, she released my hand, and the pure unreasoning wanting of her began to fade. I remained hard, and I don't think I could have resisted for even a fraction of a heartbeat if she had invited me to take her there on the cold stone of the cave floor. But she evinced no more interest in me than I might have shown a piss-pot. In fact, she ignored me completely, and, ever so slowly, the physical aftereffects of my glamour-driven lust began to fade.

Once I reached a point where I could imagine speaking without begging her to bed me, I spoke into the silence, my voice harsh and husky. "Did you learn much?"

"Many things," she said. "Most of them are beyond one who has no fathudor, no . . . sense-of-stone, but a few I think might be of use to you, Kingslayer."

It was the first indication I had that she knew anything at all about me beyond the fact of the ring and the single name I had given her earlier. "Things such as . . ."

"The ring you wear is indeed a thing of the Fire That Burns Underground." She touched the arm of her throne. "This dorak-ki, this throne of earth, sits atop one of the threads that binds the bones of the mountain. It is connected stone to stone in an unbroken inkathiq to the tomb of the one your people call the Smoldering Flame in the Brimstone Vale. Through it I can feel the essence of his shekat, his soul. That essence is reflected in your ring, though darkly, as through a warped and smoky mirror."

"So, I *am* married to the Fire That Burns Underground?"

"No. Or, not directly. You are married to the echo of the Smoldering Flame as it burns in the heart of she who returned him to the tomb. I do not understand all of the implications, but you . . ." She held up a hand. "Wait! I sense something—"

Her words cut off abruptly as a cruel iron point suddenly appeared between her breasts. At first I didn't understand what had happened, but then a torrent of the rich purple blood of the Durkoth began to flow out around the point of the spear that had been driven through the back of Krithak's throne and out through her chest.

It was only in that instant that I realized that the gallery behind the Uthudor now held a pair of Durkoth. One still had his hands clasped around the base of the spear. The other was sliding around the throne, a soot-blackened iron axe held low in front of her.

6

———◆———

Life is simplest at the edge of the knife. When someone is trying to kill you, there is no time for second guesses or melancholy regrets. There is only the anticipation of blood and the question of who will spill it.

The axe came in fast and low. The woman wielding it brought the spike-tipped shaft upward from knee height in a jabbing cut that would have emasculated me if I hadn't thrown myself backward into a reverse handspring. I landed with a splash as my left foot came down in the nearest pool, and I more than half expected it to slide out from under me. But the wet and angled stone seemed to grab onto my foot with some of that same sticky grip I'd felt earlier.

As I brought my arms down from their extension, I popped the catch on the knife in my left wrist sheath, flicking the hilt into my hand with the same gesture. A moment later, I flipped it at the axe-wielder's face while I reached for a sword with my other hand.

The best thrown knife is unlikely to do much more than slow an opponent down, and this was little more than a snap toss. But even the toughest and most calculating of warriors will have a hard time ignoring a piece of pointed steel flying toward their eyes. The woman twisted aside in a move that was simultaneously inhumanly quick and impossibly statue slow. It looked like a series of painted pictures rifled quickly—each motion a moment of stillness that simply jumped to the next rather than flowing smoothly as a human's would have.

Watching her sent a spiral of nausea eeling through my belly. I had to fight the impulse to look away as she turned the twist into a stomach-churning spin that brought her axe around at the side of my head with tremendous speed and force. But forcing her to dodge had given me time to free my second blade, and I caught the head of the axe on the back of my sword, lifting it up and over my head as I drove my other sword straight into her left thigh.

Goddess-forged steel hit the thin stone of her bloused pants with a harsh *chunk* that stung my hand and jarred all the way up to my shoulder. A normal sword might well have snapped. It certainly would have slid off her stone armor. But Namara's swords are made of tougher stuff, and it went as deep as any hammer-driven chisel.

The Durkoth woman's leg gave and she fell. She was still turning from the impulse of her failed swing and she landed hard on her back, sliding into the pool to my right and sinking instantly. The stone of her trousers clung to my sword and very nearly wrenched it free of my hand in the process, but I managed to hold on, turning the blade as I did so. The edge levered its way out through the big muscles in the front of her thigh and the stone layer above them as she went down.

Ware! Triss shouted into my mind.

The effort of hanging on to my sword had spun me half around, putting me badly off balance as the woman's companion came rushing in. He'd left the spear in Krithak and had drawn a short mace, which he swung at me now. There was simply no way to parry the blow, so I threw myself into an awkward sideways dive instead and the flanged mace passed through the space I'd occupied an instant before.

I expected to hit the bottom of the pool and slide a few yards through shallow water, but plunged deep instead, fooled by its crystalline clarity. I hadn't had the time to take a deep breath and I caught a mouthful of water now. Touching bottom fifteen feet down, I kicked off immediately, aiming up and toward the far shore. Again, the clarity of the water deceived me, and I drove face-first into the steeply shallowing floor of the pool.

Stunned, I slithered forward through the knee-deep water, pushing my head up into the air and gasping for breath. I'd barely had time to register the bright blossom of red my broken nose left in the water below me when Triss yelped again and a hot silky hand caught my ankle from behind, yanking me back under. The mace clipped the side of my knee with a blow that might have shattered it if not for the dual protections of water slowing the Durkoth's arm and Triss's aid. My familiar pulled magic from my soul and used it to give himself greater physical presence as he wrapped my knee in the stuff of his own substance, briefly armoring me.

I pivoted in the water and stabbed downward along the line of my leg, but the Durkoth had already loosed his grip. I looked to see where he had gone, but couldn't find him through the cloud of blood coming from my nose. I tried to kick myself back to the surface, but full boots and the weight of my gear only dragged me deeper.

Triss, where is he!?

Below you, I—

The mace struck again, skidding across my thigh. Again, the water and Triss saved me from serious injury. If the Durkoth had had a blade of some sort or kept his spear I'd have been finished.

Triss, give me some fins!

I won't be able to armor you, he sent, but I could feel that he had complied as my madly kicking legs suddenly met sharp resistance and I shot upward through the water.

I felt a tearing pain as the mace smashed into my left calf, and roughly dragged down across my heel, but it didn't break the bone, and a moment later I was in the shallows again. This time I made it out of the water. I immediately dragged myself upright despite the injuries to my leg, staggering back from the pool's edge as I did so.

The water of the pool, so clear mere minutes before, was a muddy soup now, full of blood and silt kicked up from the bottom. I couldn't see what had become of my erstwhile attackers and I kept the points of my swords moving back and forth to cover the whole of the pool. Even so, I barely made my parry when the male Durkoth erupted out of the water like some lesser cousin of the dragons.

We went back and forth for a few passes after that, but I had both the better weapon and greater speed. With the element of surprise gone, the conclusion was all but inevitable, and he soon lost his head. I kicked it into the nearer pool and was about to do the same with his body when I noticed something odd on the breast of his shirt—a flat circle about the size of a silver riel. It looked to be made of a different stone from the rough granite of his shirt.

I waited another minute to make sure his companion wasn't going to resurface. She didn't, and I had to conclude that either the leg wound or the water had done for her—wrapping yourself in stone is not the best strategy for a swimmer.

Then I knelt and examined the circle. It was a delicate red marble and half-covered by a thick fold of his shirt. There was no way I was going to be able to get it off him without shattering it utterly. The little badge bore a simple intaglio design—a rough lump of something with a wisp of smoke rising off of it.

Once I'd fixed the image in my mind I kicked the body into the water and limped my way around to Krithak's throne. I expected to find her dead, but the blood staining the corner of her mouth continued to bubble faintly and I could hear labored breathing. When I got closer, she turned a hand on her throne, beckoning me close with one crooked finger.

". . . come," she husked, her voice softer than a whisper. "Listen. I have things still to tell."

Looking at the angle of the spear in her chest, I didn't think she could possibly have much time left. But I knew removing it would only cut what little she had even shorter. Knowing I could do nothing more for her than obey her final request, I knelt and put my ear close to her lips.

"Fire Underground cultists . . . can tell by the smoke-darkened iron they carry . . . true Durkoth wield stone."

"He wore a badge, a coal maybe, with smoke rising off of it. . . ."

"His emblem . . . yes." She paused for several heartbeats. "Buried gods all have . . . followings among the First. To our . . . shame. They want to . . . refight the godwar. You must be wary. . . ."

Again she came to a halt. This time the silence lasted so long I thought she must have passed the final veil. But a sharply indrawn breath told me otherwise and after another few heart-beats she continued.

"With this burnt iron in my chest I . . . could . . . not stop them completely. But I locked the shekatudor, the . . . the stone's soul, against them . . . prevented them from per-suasion."

"Thank you," I said. "You probably saved my life." I had wondered why the cultists hadn't used the stone against me as Qethar had in our battle. Now I knew.

"My cave, my dorak-ki, my rule." Despite her lack of air, these words came out hard and cold—absolute, a queen speak-ing from the heart of her power.

She coughed then, a deep tearing sound, and more blood leaked out around the head of the spear.

"You must . . . remove this." She pointed her finger at her chest.

"It will kill you."

"Almost certainly"—another cough—"but I will not die with this . . . accursed spike pinning me like . . . some . . . filthy slink. Do it."

"Now?"

"Now."

I stood and walked around behind the throne. The spear had a heavy barbed head like the harpoons monster hunters used when going after gryphon or other ferocious prey. Pulling it backward would tear Krithak's heart out, if I could even get it to come out that way. The back of the throne seemed to have closed around the shaft—probably to keep Krithak from bleed-ing out. I'd seen Durkoth fashion bandages from stone before.

"I can't make it gentle," I said. "But I can make it fast."

"Do it."

The spear was short—probably for weight reasons, as it was solid iron from haft to tip—with no more than four feet sticking out of her back. I positioned myself carefully, took a deep breath, and then spun to the side, kicking the end of the shaft with the heel of my foot. It drove the spear forward the better part of three feet, and my second kick finished the job on that side. Four quick steps took me around to the front, where I grabbed the blood-slick shaft just below the head.

Triss, give me a hand here.

Of course. He slid down and interposed himself between my hand and the barb of the spear. With one fast move I wrenched the spear the rest of the way out of Krithak's chest. A flood of rich purple blood followed it, and Krithak's head slumped.

I was sure she was gone then, but again I'd underestimated her toughness, and she somehow lifted her chin once more, holding her head high as the stuff of her seat flowed up and over her, encasing her in a second skin of pink stone. Pores in the surface opened up and somehow pulled all the blood inside, leaving the marble pure and unstained.

I left her then, looking much as she had when I arrived—an unfinished statue of a beautiful queen. Tomb, monument, and death mask all in one package. The spear I threw into the pool with the corpses.

Then, painfully, and with a lot of help from Triss, I forced my nose back into its proper shape. As I waited out the worst aftereffects, I had time to think about how things had gone since Siri came back into my life, from the whatsis to the Durkoth, and how much harder the latter had hit me.

When I mentioned that to Triss, he sent, *It's always easier to fight a stupid foe than a smart one, no matter how powerful the former. Now, we should get moving. We don't want to leave Faran alone with Thuroq for too long.*

I nodded and forced myself back to my feet. *True.*

As we made our way back to the entrance of the cavern, he sent, *There's much to think about in what the Uthudor had to say.*

And even more that I wish she'd been able to share. Perhaps we can learn more from Thuroq.

Why do I not believe it will be so simple?

Because nothing ever is, I replied.

Not since the temple fell, no.

Which was not something I wanted to talk about. Fortunately, a perfect change of subject presented itself at that moment as the light in the cave began to dim.

Triss, is it me or are the lights going out?

It's not you. The process started when Krithak died, but it was very slow at first—so slow I didn't think I need mention it. Things just speeded up.

Oh good. I hope you're right about how that thing works. I indicated the stone chaise with a jerk of my chin. *If not, we're going to have a hell of a time digging our way out.*

For all that I kept my tone light, the idea of being trapped so deep in the earth left me cold and sweaty. Doubly so with the lights going out. I have no fear of the dark, but who knew what else might fail now that Krithak's will no longer mastered the cavern.

When have I ever steered you wrong? Triss asked rather smugly, but I could feel the hidden worry under the surface of his words, too.

Never yet, but there's always a first time. I eyed the lounge dubiously, half-afraid to try it in case it didn't work.

Just sit on the damned thing and get it over with.

So, I did, and the reverse trip went much the same as the first one had. The stairs at the far end were tough going, and I paused before limping around the last turning.

Triss, shroud me up.

What? Why?

Because I don't want Faran to do anything hasty if we come staggering around the corner soaking wet and covered in blood and bruises.

Good point. Thuroq won't do us much good with a second smile three inches below the first. Do you want to hold the reins?

No need. Just keep me covered and we should be fine.

Done. Triss and I spent a lot less of our time arguing since I'd quit drinking, and I found it incredibly soothing to be so much in accord with my companion once again.

My view of the world went away as Triss expanded into a cloud of shadow. His substance thinned as his volume increased, like cream whipped into a froth. Soon, I could no longer feel him as a physical presence at all. My knee ached and my heel jarred painfully with every step and the muscles in thigh and calf had very colorful things to say on the subject

of stairs, but I forced myself to the discipline of silent movement as I climbed up and out into the night.

Triss's senses differ from mine in many ways. When I am
enclosed within the lacuna created by his shroud, I am forced
to borrow his *eyes* and see the world in the manner of the
Shades. Color loses most of its meaning, as does what we think
of as shape. Textures and the interplay of light and shadow
dominate the picture.

When I *saw* Thuroq upon a stone chair in front of the fire,
sitting as statue still as the Uthudor I had left in the deeps
below, it was a very different picture than my eyes would have
painted for me. The places where firelight reflected off his
polished skin flared bright and prominent, and the fire itself
hurt to look at. The deep folds of his onyx tunic held gradations
of shadow that no human tongue could adequately describe.
Where I would normally have seen nothing but black, Triss's
view of things supplied a darkened rainbow of meaning.

Faran was nowhere to be seen—no surprise there; she
loathed and distrusted the Durkoth. I flicked my focus around
the full circle of possible perception supplied by Triss's sense
of light and shadow. That omnidirectional field of view was
probably the hardest thing for a human mind to cope with.
We're very linear creatures at root, and it's almost impossible
for us to make full use of that aspect of Shade senses. Even so,
Faran is particularly good at the arts of hiding and shadow-
slipping and I couldn't spot any sign of her, leaving me to guess
at her whereabouts.

After a few seconds, I decided that she was probably in the
tree directly above Thuroq, where his sense of the earth around
him wouldn't be able to detect her. She could as easily have
taken up position farther away—she had several weapons that
could kill over a distance—but Faran preferred to slit throats
where she could. She had a tendency to over-personalize the
business of death.

"Faran," I called. "I'm back. Don't kill anybody."

Thuroq looked up and in my direction when I spoke. He
would have felt my arrival through the bones of the earth, but
chose—rather wisely in this case—to wait for me to announce
myself.

"Why are you shrouded?" Faran's voice came from directly behind me, and I had to suppress the urge to jump aside.

"I had some . . . difficulties below," I said, then quickly added, "None of them Thuroq's fault."

"But you took injury?" This time her voice came from the far side of the campfire.

"Don't. Kill. The. Hostage."

"If you insist." Her voice moved again.

"I insist. Also, how are you doing that with your voice?"

"Neat trick, isn't it? I've been trying to figure it out ever since you told me that the Kitsune had used it on you. I'll show you how it's done later, once we've gotten rid of the body."

"We're not going to kill Thuroq. That's final. Now, I'm going to step out of shadow. Don't overreact. Most of the blood's not mine." *Triss?*

My shroud fell away as my shadow reshaped itself into the silhouette of a small dragon.

I heard a sharp hiss from the tree directly above Thuroq, followed by the tiniest of thumps as Faran landed behind the Durkoth. Her shroud dropped away, revealing Faran with her index finger held a fingernail's width above the artery in his neck.

"You live for Aral's sake," she said quietly before coming to check me over. "What the hell happened to you?"

"Long story." I told her and Thuroq what had happened below while I cleaned up in the stream and dealt with my injuries. With the exception of my nose, most of what I had were bruises. I was going to be one stiff old bastard in the morning, but otherwise all right.

At the end of my story, Thuroq shook his head angrily. "My master will be most unhappy about the death of Dame Krithak."

"Will he search out these cultists, then?" asked Faran. "I'd like to see a lot more purple blood spilled over what they did to Aral."

The shadow phoenix that had taken up a perch on her shoulder bobbed her head in agreement.

Thuroq's blank expression reappeared. "I'm sure that my king will take action to see that anyone responsible for the incident suffers appropriately."

"That's a weasel's answer," she snapped.

"Faran." I gave her a sharp look.

She shrugged. "It is." Then she got up and walked away from the fire.

Thuroq neither moved nor spoke during the exchange. Nor did he betray any sign that he wanted to do either after her departure.

After a little while, I asked him, "What can you tell me about the cultists?"

"Nothing."

More silence.

Nice, sent Triss. *I told you it wasn't going to be simple.*

"You mean you don't know anything more about them?" I asked Thuroq.

"I mean I can tell you nothing."

"Why not?"

"Because there is nothing to tell. Krithak had many enemies and many eccentricities. That she ascribed the one to the other is no surprise."

"Wait a tick," Triss said. "Are you saying that you don't believe it was cultists who killed her?"

"I know nothing about any 'cultists' real or imagined. What happened in the days of the war between the First and those who name themselves gods is a matter of no interest to the Durkoth of today. Anyone who says otherwise can have no other motivation than trying to stir up ancient troubles. Now, will you retrieve your apprentice so that I can dispense my obligation to you, allowing me return to my king and my *real* duties? Or must I continue to wait here on a child's whim?"

I felt the ridge of scales along the back of Triss's neck rise angrily beneath the palm I'd been resting on his back, and he sent, *I'm starting to see the merits of Faran's attitude toward the Durkoth.*

"I'll call Faran back, and then we can go." I looked the Durkoth square in the eye. "But don't think it's for your sake, or that I can't see that you're trying to make me angry enough to do something that will allow you to break our bargain and avoid questions you'd rather not answer. I'll do it because I need to pass the Wall of the Sylvain as quickly as I can manage for the sake of someone I love dearly. You are a means toward that end, nothing more."

The Durkoth's face remained unreadable. "Your reasons are your own. They are of no matter to me."

At that point, there was nothing more for either of us to say. I could have gone for something scathing, or threatened Thuroq, but I didn't see any reason to bother. It was quite obvious that neither would have moved him. For that matter, I've never been much for bluster, and issuing threats is of very limited utility.

I *have* made the occasional conditional promise of later violence when circumstances called for it. But generally it's simpler and wiser to kill someone quickly when they need it rather than give them any warning that it's coming. That's certainly how I would deal with Thuroq if it became necessary. The Durkoth are too dangerous to play with.

When Faran returned, Thuroq had us move our horses and our gear a few hundred yards down the creek to a place where a long slab of tilted shale stuck up a few inches above the surrounding earth. The rock, which lay at the base of a low ridge of the same stuff, was perhaps fifteen feet by thirty at the widest, loosely diamond shaped, and not much thicker than my thigh.

"This should suit," said Thuroq. "Make sure to tie the horses." He gestured, and a thick stone arch rose up in the center of the slab.

"Now what?" I asked as Faran and I looped our reins around the impromptu hitching post.

"Do whatever your kind do when they settle into a new camp." Another gesture raised a low thronelike chair facing outward from the narrow point of the slab. He settled into it with his back to us. "Though I would advise against a fire. The smoke, you know."

I was just about to ask what he meant, when I noticed that the ridge was moving. Or rather, that we were, sliding silently along the ground beside the creek like some great stone barge with the Durkoth as its figurehead. At first, we moved very cautiously, slower than a slow walk, but after a few minutes we reached the road. There we turned south and began to pick up speed.

I walked a slow circuit around the slab, eyeing the line where the stone met the ground around it. At the front we had a curling bow wave not unlike what you might see on a swift sailing ship of the sea, but it quickly settled back down as it rolled along the sides.

Behind, the only evidence of our passage was the much-improved condition of the road. In front there were numerous ruts and potholes, as well as occasional washed-out patches along the shoulders. In back the royal road looked as smooth and flat as if the crews had only just finished grading and packing the dirt surface with their mattocks and spades and what have you.

The horses didn't much like the experience, especially at the beginning—they'd have bolted if we hadn't tied them up. I couldn't really blame them; it was a most disconcerting way to travel. But they settled down after a while and I expected that I would, too.

Eventually.

Maybe.

I laid my bedroll out a few feet from where Faran had already curled up and gone to sleep. Putting my saddle at one end as a pillow, I stretched out and tried to convince myself I was on a river barge. It didn't work. No barge in the world had ever moved as smoothly and silently as that slab of rock did. There were always little splashes or the occasional rocking motion on a barge to remind you that you were on the water and moving.

Our stone raft had none of that. The only way I could tell we were going anywhere was by watching the treetops go by against the backdrop of stars overhead. The speed of our passing created a breeze as well, but without the visual cue of the trees there'd have been no way to distinguish it from the night wind. The whole experience made me vaguely queasy, and sleep remained far away all through the night. Not being able to breathe through my nose didn't help.

Right before dawn Thuroq slid the great slab off the road and into a small clearing. As he rose, his seat sank back into the rock and the hitching post did likewise. I was exhausted by then and barely listened to his promise to find us again at day's end, wherever our travels took us. A few heartbeats after he'd disappeared into the earth, Faran vaulted to her feet and did a quick circle around the clearing before coming back to hobble the horses.

She gave me a pitying look when she returned. "You should at least try to get a quick nap in while I get breakfast together and pack us up."

I nodded thankfully and was asleep before she'd turned away. Now that the rock had stopped moving, my normal ability to sleep anywhere had returned.

. . . Aral.

What is it? I sent.

Faran asked me to wake you. She thought it would be gentler if I did it.

That was kind of her. Do you think she's feeling all right?

Aral! I felt sharp disapproval roll down the link that bound us together. *She kills easily, but she's far from heartless. She's very devoted to those she cares about, you especially. You know that.*

I winced at the acid in his tone and acknowledged that I'd earned it. *You're right, that was unfair of me. This waking up on little to no sleep shit does not make for a happy Aral. I could really use about four more hours.*

And I could use a month of lounging in the everdark. Your point?

I'm moving, I'm moving.

In deference to the beating I'd taken the night before, I sat up slowly. Despite the spell doctoring I'd had the night before, it didn't help all that much. I found myself groaning and gingerly prodding my aching knee.

Faran laughed. "Your age is showing, Grandpa. Do you need me to cut you a cane?"

"Only so I can shake it at you, monster child. It's just the damned bruises slowing me down. I've got a good couple of hundred years left in me."

Which was true, for certain values of truth. Shades live a very long time, and my span would measure itself to Triss's. But that assumed I died of old age, a dicey sort of assumption at best. Even in the days when my goddess yet lived and the temple provided a refuge for those Blades who had passed into age or infirmity, it was a rare thing for one of us to die by any cause other than violence. Without that shelter . . . well, if I were a betting man, I wouldn't lay down money on my chances of dying a gentle death. Not at any odds.

While I ruminated over my mortality and my bruises, Faran brought me a thin piece of flat bread wrapped around some cold sausage and yesterday's noodles. The tea was hot, though, and almost palatable—I was slowly beginning to acquire a taste for the stuff. Mostly by default, since I could no longer have even small beer without waking cravings for something stronger. Drinking unadulterated city water was a recipe for spending the night in the privy if you were lucky. If you weren't, they'd be fitting you for a winding cloth.

Faran collected my saddle and bedroll while I ate. By the time I finished, she had everything stowed but my tin cup, and a space waiting for that. Within minutes, we were ready to mount up. Getting onto my horse hurt, and riding even more so, but I just clenched my teeth and tried not to think about how much mellower I'd feel with a tucker bottle of whiskey to help me relax my aching knee and thigh. Or, better yet, a few efik beans.

After a while, both the sun and my mood rose. Which was when the bandits arrived. Naturally.

7

———✦———

Sometimes, the only answer to the absurdity of life is laughter. Which was not, I think, the reaction the bandit chief was expecting.

The first sign that we were in for a bit of a diversion from the day's original plan was the tree downed across the road. It was well placed, coming at a curve in the road with steep slopes on both sides. A major foothill forced the road up into a long bend that rode high along its shoulder, so the fallen tree wasn't visible from either direction until you were practically on top of it. Add in thick forest on the slopes to make leaving the road doubly difficult, and the fact that the trunk was neatly parallel to the ground at waist height, making it impossible to take a horse either under or over, and you had to admire the thought that had gone into engineering the thing.

The handsome bandit chieftain sauntering out of the greenery on the far side of the fallen tree with a cocked crossbow in one hand and a short sword in the other really was the crowning touch. It was such a classic moment that I simply couldn't help pointing and laughing.

I'll say this for the fellow: he was smarter than the average city thug. He demonstrated that fact by waiting politely for me to stop laughing rather than doing anything I would have been forced to make him regret. He didn't even raise the crossbow.

"Would you mind letting me in on the joke?" he asked once I'd finally lapsed into a smiling silence. "Because, from where I'm standing, you don't have much to laugh about."

That very nearly set me off again, but I managed to keep it to a grin this time. "I'm laughing at you, sir."

He glowered a little bit at that, but again he didn't do anything rash. "That doesn't seem terribly wise."

"I'm sorry," I said. "I will admit to impolite, but as to unwise, well, you'll have to judge that for yourself. I presume that at some point here in the near future you are going to tell us that you have dozens of followers in the trees around us, and that they all have crossbows pointed our way."

He nodded, and the glower faded a bit. "It had crossed my mind, yes. Mostly because it's true."

"And then you were going to tell us to get off our horses and hand over all of our valuables?"

"Yes, that was the plan. I take it you're going to suggest it's a bad one?"

"Terrible."

Faran rolled her eyes at me. "You're far too sentimental, Aral. We ought to just kill them all and get this over with."

The bandit chief glanced from Faran to me and back to Faran again. He had begun to sweat. "Mages?"

"That, too," I replied.

"Too?" He looked me over more carefully now. "The girl called you Aral."

"She did."

"That's a foreign name."

I nodded. "Varyan."

"Would you happen to have a family name to go with it?"

"Not that anyone remembers."

The bandit bent and carefully set his crossbow on the ground. "Two swords, all in gray silk, accompanied by a girl wearing two hilts and gray as well. I think I might be able to put a second name to you if I tried."

"Now would be an excellent time for trying," I said.

He swallowed visibly. "Would you be the Kingslayer?"

I smiled.

"I was afraid that might be the way of it," he said. "I'm going to propose a bargain, and I'd really appreciate it if you said yes."

I opened my hands. "Propose away."

"It goes like this. My mob comes down here and gets this tree out of the way. Then we all march down the road a mile or so to the bridge over the Loudwater River." He gestured back over his shoulder. "Then we all toss our weapons in the water and head for someplace far away."

"What do I have to do?" I asked.

"Nothing at all. Not a single thing. In fact, not doing anything would be the whole of your end of the deal, especially not doing anything involving blood and killing. How does that sound?"

"I think you might need to find a new sort of employment as well."

"We'd be happy to swear an oath on it."

I nodded and Triss spoke into my mind. *You're not really contemplating letting them go, are you?*

Actually, I am.

They've certainly killed travelers here in the past. He sounded more curious than indignant. *Lately you've been talking a lot about walking the path of justice again. How does this fit into that?*

I've no doubt they have a good bit of blood on their hands. But back in Tien when I was playing the shadow jack we dealt with people who'd done murder and worse all the time. But we never killed anyone who wasn't actively trying to harm us. Namara didn't make us what we are so that we could do the watch's job for it, Triss. She wanted us to handle the big injustices, the things the law couldn't touch. Kings, generals, high priests. This man . . . Well, as long as he follows through on his part of the bargain, I don't see that he's really our problem.

Fair enough.

I raised my eyes to meet the bandit chief's again. He'd done a lot more sweating in the silence while Triss and I conferred, and his skin looked about ten shades lighter than it had when he first asked his question.

I nodded at him. "That sounds fair to me. Do it."

"Thank you, kindly, Kingslayer." He bent down then and cut the string of his crossbow with his sword before putting the blade away.

There were a score of bandits that came down onto the road, about half of them women.

Faran leaned over as they started to march down the road ahead of us. "You know there are at least a half dozen still in the trees back there, right?"

"I do, but it's not worth the effort to go after them. Most of this bunch would feel obliged to fall in with their friends, and then we'd have to kill the lot of them."

"And?" Faran looked baffled.

"I can't speak for the goddess, but somehow I don't think she'd want us to choose that much blood over giving them a chance."

I waved a hand to indicate the group in front of us. "Some of these are certainly rotten to the core, but most of them probably fell into banditry when the farm failed, or the landlord foreclosed on the shop, or their parents died. It seems to me that it wasn't all that long ago that a certain young woman of my acquaintance had to make her own way in the world after her side lost a religious war."

Faran's eyes went very thoughtful at that, and she lapsed into a long silence.

That was well done, sent Triss. *And so is this*. I felt a shadowy pressure across my chest as he indicated the group of bandits walking in front of us. *You're right, by the way. I think this is what the goddess would want us to do.*

Thank you, Triss. That means a lot.

I felt a wave of love flow along the link that bound us and then a silent chuckle. *I was going to say that you are becoming more and more the man that you once were, but then I realized that I was wrong. You are better than that.*

How so?

The Aral who killed Ashvik would probably have let these bandits live, but he would have done it for the wrong reason.

Oh?

He would have done it out of sentimentality. Faran is right about you there—you're prone to a softness that is unusual for

a Blade. Or, you were before the fight at the abbey two sum-
mers ago, at any rate. But that's not what's happening here.

No? I was fascinated. Like Faran, and Jax for that matter,
Triss had always been somewhat confused by my choices where
it came to sparing my enemies.

*No. You have changed. You killed your first king for Justice
the goddess. You killed your second for justice the ideal. You
are letting these men and women live for the same reason, and
not merely because you prefer not to kill when you don't have
to. You have grown. But the sun is high and I must retreat into
the deeps of your shadow now. Wake me if you need me.*

A little while later as we sat watching the bandits throw
their weapons into the river, Faran leaned over to me again.
"What will they do now?"

"I don't know," I replied. "Why?"

"Look at them. Their clothes are ragged and worn. Thieving
hasn't provided them with a very good living. Without their
weapons, they're going to have a hard time of it."

Faran sounded genuinely concerned and I turned to give
her my full attention. "That's true."

"I think we should give them some money."

I raised an eyebrow. Compassion, from Faran? Very
interesting.

She clenched her jaw and gave me a hard look. "What you
said about the fall of the temple and how I had to make my own
way afterward? It made me think. *We're* robbing *them* now."

"You were ready to kill the lot of them not an hour ago."

She shrugged. "That's different," she said, her tone blithe. "If
we'd killed them they wouldn't have any need of anything. Now
they will."

"You sound like you'd still be willing to kill them."

"Of course." I blinked, but before I could say anything she
continued. "It would no longer be my first choice—I think
you're right in your reasons for not killing them—but willing?
Certainly, why wouldn't I be? And what's that got to do with
giving them money now? We're the ones who have turned them
out of their current life. Don't you think we ought to give them
a decent chance of starting a fresh one? I've plenty of coin, and
I can always get more."

I was still trying to think of some reasonable answer to that when the bandit chief came toward us slowly. When I looked up at him he went to his knees and put his forehead on the ground in the formal bow of a peasant greeting his lord.

"I'm no noble," I growled—the very thought made my bones itch. "You don't need to kowtow to me." Then, when he stayed down, "Oh, stand up already. What do you want?"

"To thank you for letting us live," he said. "And to ask if you would share our noon meal before we all move on. It would honor us."

"You're welcome," I replied. "Though I'm a bit surprised about the offer of lunch."

"You are the Kingslayer. If I have children someday, I would like to tell them that I once ate a meal with you."

"Why?"

He began to unbutton his tunic. "Let me show you something."

"All right."

When the last button opened, he stripped the garment off and turned around. "Ashvik gave me these in his final year on the throne." His back was a lattice of deep whip scars. "Not personally, of course, but it was his orders that put me in the hands of the office of agony. I was a soldier once, a sergeant, but I got on the wrong side of my lieutenant during Ashvik's last war. He gave a stupid command, one that would have gotten a lot of my men killed."

He slipped his tunic back on. "I didn't contradict him, but I took a different path than he'd ordered. In a better army, I'd have gotten a medal. In Ashvik's, I got sent to the torturers. And not just me. They took my wife, too, as a *lesson* to my men. She died. I would have, too, but Ashvik beat me to it. When you killed him, Thauvik took over. He was a soldier once himself, a ranker. He pardoned all the soldiers in Ashvik's prisons and offered us our places back."

"I killed Thauvik, too."

The bandit shrugged. "Eh, he might have let me off my chains, but it was you who gave him the chance, and he was near as bad as his brother by the end. Never been gladder than the last couple of years that I turned his offer down and came out here instead. I've had enough of kings, and I'd very much like the chance to break bread with the last of the Blades."

"What's for lunch?"

He smiled. "Rice, fish, fruit. It's humble fare."

"It sounds fine to me. What's your name?"

"They call me Chiu. Thank you. What you did for Tien . . . well, a lot of my mob could tell you similar stories. Maybe not so dramatic, and maybe not as can be linked so directly to this king or that one, but it all flows from the top. When the top is rotten . . ."

Which is how we ended up lunching beside a fire with a bandit chief and drinking tea—they'd put away the wine when I told them I didn't drink. The food was good, and the company rough but friendly. Despite what we'd done to them, they really did seem honored by the chance to share a meal with Faran and me. Triss woke up briefly when we dismounted, but with the sun still high and a fire so close by he soon went back to sleep. When we finished, the bandits started gathering up their things and smothered the fire, sending up a slender ribbon of pale smoke. It was time to get back onto the road.

Chiu bowed deeply as I stood up. "Again, I thank you. This day could have gone a lot worse for my mob if you were a less forgiving man."

I bowed back. "Just see that you find a new line of work, and I'll count our bargain fulfilled, Chiu, though, I think my apprentice had a thought about altering the deal."

Chiu had a better measure of us now, and he didn't actually blanch, but I could see him tense as his eyes flicked to Faran. "Oh. What did you have in mind, Madame Blade?"

She smiled. "Something I think you'll need if you're really going to keep up your end of things." She crossed to our pack horse and reached deep into one of the bags hanging across his shoulders. "Here." She pulled out a fat purse and tossed it across to him. "It's hard to walk a straight path when you can't afford to eat. I've been there. I know."

He bowed again, this time to Faran, and even more deeply. "Thank you, Madame Blade. I . . . just thank you." Chiu's voice was husky, and his eyes were very bright.

Faran looked embarrassed. "You're welcome, Chiu. I . . ."

Her eyes shifted past the bandit chief and she trailed off. "Uh, Aral, I think what's left of the fire wants to have a word with you."

Sure enough, the ribbon of smoke had thickened and darkened, twisting itself into Siri's familiar shape. Those bandits who were still close to the fire pit made various sorts of alarmed noises and moved quickly away. A couple of them even bolted, though Chiu held his ground.

As soon as my eyes met the darkness in her smoky cowl, Siri beckoned me closer, her finger twisting and blurring with the motion. Three long steps put me close enough to touch and she lifted her left hand, palm out, slowly spreading her fingers to emphasize the one whose ring matched my own. The message was obvious, and I raised my own hand to mirror hers. She nodded then, and bent forward, kissing my palm with lips of smoke.

The touch was softer than the brush of a butterfly's wing, but I felt a jolt like trapped magelightning. It ran from my palm to my heart and back again to my ring finger. The smoke of my own ring swirled wildly and darkened in response.

Fire and sun! Triss surged awake. *What's going on?*

Siri, I replied. *Bide a bit.*

I glanced at her finger and saw that the ring there looked lighter and thinner than the hand wearing it. Bending from the waist, I kissed her palm in turn. More lightning touched my heart, this time sparking along my lips and down my throat to my core. Siri's ring darkened now, becoming almost black—a sharp contrast to the grays that made up the rest of her.

I . . . That's very . . . interesting, sent Triss. *I wonder what it means.*

I have no idea. I wish I'd thought to really look at my ring beforehand. I think it might have been fraying a bit around the edges.

Siri had begun to lose her form in the very instant that her ring finished its transition. A coil of white curled her mouth into a brief one-sided smile, then a breeze caught her and she puffed out of existence entirely.

"Renewing your vows?" asked Faran, and I couldn't mistake the angry undercurrent I heard there.

I nodded. "Apparently."

She threw her hands in the air. "You know this whole thing is crazy, right? You married smoke. That's not normal. And, what if it's not really Siri?"

"That demon of smoke was the Mythkiller?" Chiu's voice came out in a sort of half squeak.

"Yes," I replied, in the same instant that Faran said, "Maybe."

"And she's not a demon," I continued.

Again, Faran said, "Maybe."

"You didn't have to come with me," I growled at her.

"This is beyond me," said Chiu. Most of his people had slipped entirely away by then. Now the bandit leader bowed quickly. "I think, Kingslayer, that it is time for me to leave you. Your life leads you to places that I would not go for any reason. I wish you success." Then he was gone.

I looked at Faran. "Are you coming with me, or do you want to walk away, too?"

She clenched her fists angrily, but then took a deep breath. "I may think this is a terrible idea, but I am *not* going to let you follow that thing into the Sylvain without someone to watch your back. You bailed me out when I got in over my head with the Durkoth. I'll be there when you need me to do the same."

I wanted to argue, but all I said was "Thank you," as I mounted my horse.

We were back out on the road and heading south shortly thereafter. Hours passed in a sort of truce of silence while we rode toward the Sylvain and nightfall. When the mountains started to claw the sun down out of the sky, we turned off into a small bamboo grove and built a fire to make dinner. Faran cooked again while I napped. Thuroq hadn't shown up by the time I finished eating. After renewing the healing spells on my bruises, I curled up by the fire and closed my eyes, assuming that Triss or Faran would wake me when Thuroq arrived.

I found out I was wrong about that when I half woke in the middle of the night and rolled over, bumping into a low rock wall that hadn't been there when I went to sleep. Instant disorientation, followed by sheer cold panic as I came fully awake. Reflex put my swords in my hands as I vaulted onto my feet and wrenched Triss into a shroud around me.

Aral, it's all right. You're all right. Everything is fine.

I didn't put my swords down or relax physically, but Triss's mental voice soothed the worst edges off my panic. *Where are we? What happened?* I was reaching outward through Triss's senses as I spoke—trying to reorient myself.

We're on the road with Thuroq, he answered. *When he arrived you were so deep asleep that Faran and I decided not to wake you.*

By then, I'd had a chance to really "look" around. Our campsite seemed unchanged except for the wall and a stone chair where Thuroq sat facing away south. The horses were still tethered to the same broken stump, and Faran had gone to sleep on the far side of our nearly burned-out fire.

I was confused. *But, but the wall . . . and I could have sworn I haven't moved. This feels like the same place I went to sleep.*

There weren't any good rock outcroppings nearby, so Thuroq pulled one up from below and just took our whole campsite along for the ride. Faran insisted that he raise the wall to protect you and the fire from the wind.

Oh. I let my hold on Triss go, releasing the shroud. Then I sat down with my back against the little wall. As I did so, Triss twisted into dragon shape and put his head in my lap.

I know we should have woken you, but I could feel how exhausted you were. I didn't want you to spend another night staring into the sky and not sleeping. I'm sorry.

I scratched the scales behind his ears, paying special attention to the spot that always itched. *It's fine. You were right, I needed the sleep, and I wasn't going to get it any other way. I overreacted when I woke up. It's just that . . . I haven't had a moment like that in a long time. . . . Where I woke up and things were different than the way I had left them—not since I quit drinking. I'm used to knowing what's going on around me again, even when I'm sleeping. It made me feel like I'd slipped back into the old nightmare.*

Triss stood up, putting his front feet on my leg. Then he brought his head up so that his face was on a level with mine and very gently butted his forehead against my jaw. I felt a wordless sorrow resonating along our link, along with guilt and an aching desire to both comfort and be forgiven.

I put my hand on the back of his neck and pressed my forehead against his. *It's all right, really. You had the best of intentions. You surprised me is all.*

I didn't know, he whispered into my mind. *I didn't think. I'm sorry.*

I'll be fine, truly. I gave him a squeeze and leaned back against the wall.

Triss settled beside me, his head in my lap once again. After staring at the embers for a while, I picked up a log and gently set it in the pit, and then another. They didn't burn at first, so I pulled a small folding fan from my pack and gently fanned the coals till the bark caught. I checked the fan's condition carefully before putting it away. Magesight showed a dusting of faintly glowing glyphs on the thick paper, all of them in good order, so I folded it neatly and tucked it back into the pack.

"Did you really just use a scent-breaker to get the fire going?" Faran asked, jerking her chin to indicate the bag where I'd put the little fan. Other than that, she didn't move.

I nodded. "Kelos taught me to do it. He said it works much better than blowing on the thing, and you aren't sticking your face down in the smoke and the heat, which means you can keep a better eye on your surroundings."

"I suppose . . . but the fan's supposed to make it hard for scent hunters to follow or find you, and they're not easy to make. Doesn't the smell of the smoke affect the charms?"

"Not at all, or at least not that I've ever noticed. It *will* catch fire if you're not careful and get it too close to the flames, but that's really the only risk. I—"

Faran cut me off with a waved hand and a touch of her finger to her ear. As soon as she did so, I realized she was right. The night sounds had changed, something subtle, like a new susurration or— The ground lurched sharply, pressing my back against the little wall, as our briskly moving campsite shocked to a halt in the middle of the road.

Faran rolled backward across her shoulders and vanished into shadow as she landed on her feet. I did the same, momentarily taking control of Triss and drawing my swords, as I spun myself upright and into darkness.

Triss?

Nothing's changed that I can see.

But even as he spoke, Thuroq was standing up. "Attackers below!" He launched himself forward into the earth—very much in the manner of a man diving off a dock into shallow water. He vanished beneath the dirt without a splash or ripple.

8

———◆———

When you cannot trust the ground beneath your feet, you cannot trust anything.

Fire. Water. Air. These are the elements of change. We expect them to turn on us. We have seen the burning house, the drowning man, the wind that rips away the roof. But earth is supposed to be reliable, solid, the ground in which we root ourselves. The betrayals of earth cut the deepest, for they are the least expected.

I felt a cold shudder building from the base of my spine as I looked through Triss's "eyes" at the place where Thuroq had gone into the ground. *Attackers below!*

"Trees," called Faran. "Quickly, but as smooth as you can. Durkoth can feel the impacts of your feet on the ground when you walk or run, and to a lesser extent the vibration as you move among the branches."

"Thanks." I knew that, but only because Faran had told me about it before, and I appreciated her reminder—she had far more experience with the Durkoth than I did, whatever the difference in our ages and training.

Fading now, Triss sent as he fully submerged himself in the dreamlike state that gave me control over our joined consciousness.

I dashed for the nearest tree, running low and as near to silently as long years of training could teach. I'd almost reached the edge of the road when an iron point came surging up out of the ground in front of me aimed at groin height. I didn't have time to swerve or dodge, and only barely enough to push off extra hard on my next step, throwing myself into a forward flip. The spear rose farther as I went over it, burning a line of pain from a few inches below my belt line down to midthigh as it ripped through my silks and tore a strip out of the flesh beneath.

The cut threw my jump off and I landed hard on my left side and hip, grunting at the impact. But I didn't dare stop, so I jackknifed into a half roll that brought me back to my feet at the base of a big cypress. I leaped upward and caught a low-hanging branch a bare few inches ahead of the next upthrust of the iron spear. This time, the Durkoth wielding it came partially out of the ground, as he shot upward trying to skewer me.

Mistake. His hips were just broaching the surface when a flicker of shadow reached out from behind and his head flew off his neck—Faran striking from behind.

I hand-over-handed my way higher into the tree, letting my legs hang free for now. I could feel blood streaming down the front of my right leg from the long wound the spear had given me, and I didn't want to strain anything in case it was worse than it felt. But I had no sooner stopped climbing than the whole tree begin to tilt back toward the road, forcing me to move again. The Durkoth were taking it down.

With a whispered prayer to a goddess long since dead, I let go my hold and dropped onto a large branch that was now pointing about thirty degrees up from the horizontal. My leg twinged but held, and I ran up along the moving branch until it started to bend alarmingly under my weight. Bouncing once to get what benefit I could from the natural spring of the wood, I launched myself toward the next tree.

I caught a branch and immediately swung onto the next, and the next after that, monkeying my way deeper into the forest as quickly as I could. Several more trees went down behind me, but only one of them that I had passed through directly so I dropped my shroud and my hold on Triss, asking him to see what he could do about sealing the wound. The next few minutes blurred past in a light-headed haze—I had already lost a lot more blood than I liked to think about.

Once I was fairly certain I had shaken my immediate pursuit, I gently pulled myself into a sitting position on a high branch so that I could check over the gash in my leg. Triss had formed himself into a thick pad of shadow-stuff that wrapped me from knee to hip bone, the cool touch of the everdark easing the pain considerably.

How bad is it? I asked.

I've got it under control, and I can keep it that way, but if you want to wear a shadow, or me to do anything else at all, you'll need stitches. You're also going to need to stay off of it for at least a couple of days. I'll do what I can to speed the healing and keep it clear of infection, but it's more of a rip than a slice, and those are always nasty.

I didn't like the sound of that. *I don't know what's going on with Faran and Thuroq. I have to double back soon to see if they need help.*

No. Triss sent the word flat and hard, with no room for argument. *You need to stay put, unless the Durkoth find us. Faran can take care of herself—better than you can, I sometimes think. And Thuroq isn't your problem.*

I—

Not going to happen, Aral. If you try to move one inch from this spot I will tie your legs together.

All right. I'll sit, but only for a little while. If I don't get a signal from Faran in the next half hour or so . . .

She'll be fine. That, or dead, and there's nothing you can do for her in either case, not unless you want to bleed yourself unconscious.

I decided not to argue the point any further. Not until I had to. Given the nature of the familiar bond and our relative strength of will, I could probably force the matter, take control of Triss against his will and *make* him let me do what I wanted. Some schools of magery did that sort of thing all the time, but I had never in all our years together exercised control over him when he had set himself against my will, and I would rather die than use him like that. He was my partner, not my servant, and always would be.

And so, because my partner demanded it, I settled in to wait in silence. Back toward the road I could hear the occasional crash of a tree going down, and once, a gurgling shriek of the sort that signaled a poorly cut throat. But mostly, whatever was happening happened very quietly—either deep underground or with a Blade's practiced stealth.

Aral, wake up.

Wha . . . I blinked my eyes open and only then realized I had fallen asleep in the tree. Well, more passed out, really. Apparently, I had lost more blood than I thought. *Have we heard from Faran?*

She's at the base of the tree with Thuroq. You need to climb down to them. Can you can manage it? From the worry in his tone, I could tell Triss had his doubts. *Or should I get Faran up here with a rope?*

I think I can make it. I would have liked to be more firm, but clearly I was not in the best shape. *I'd really rather avoid the rope if possible. She worries too much about me as it is.*

I thought you'd see it that way, which is why I woke you up before answering. She just called up a moment ago to ask how you were.

Got it, thanks. Then, aloud, "I'm all right. Sorry to cut out on you like that, but I caught a spear tip. I'll be fine with a few stitches and some time off my feet, but it put me out of the fight." I eased myself off the branch and began a careful climb down using only my hands. "I take it we won?"

Faran laughed. "We did. It was more of your cultists, judging by the iron weapons. I killed four, and Thuroq here says that he took care of three more . . . though I have my doubts."

I was close enough to the ground to see the Durkoth turn and look down his nose at Faran. "Doubts, why?"

"Because yesterday you told us that the cultists didn't exist, and it's awfully hard to kill a figment."

I was about ten feet up then, but I had run out of branches.

Triss, I'm going to have to drop the rest of the way, see if you can't brace that thigh a bit. I'll try to take the brunt of it on my left leg but . . .

But try doesn't always translate so well into do, got it.

Exactly. I let go.

And went away for a while. When I came back, I found that I had one arm across Faran's shoulders and she was helping me make my limping way through the woods back to our run-aground campsite.

What happened?

We lost you for a couple of seconds there, but you stayed upright.

Lost me?

Yeah, you wouldn't respond to either Faran or me, and I couldn't sense you at the other end of our link. It was scary, but you caught hold of the tree and stayed on your feet. Apparently your ability to grip is independent of your ability to think. We practically had to pry your hands loose.

I didn't think the cut was that bad, and you stopped the bleeding. . . . "Why is this wound hitting me so hard? The spear wasn't enchanted. I'd have seen that." I hardly realized I'd said that last bit aloud until Thuroq answered me—I was still really hazy.

"Hasheth, cursed iron." Thuroq was sliding along beside us, statue still, borne along by the ground itself.

"What?" I turned my head to look across Faran's shoulders at the Durkoth.

For the first time his face took on something like a real human expression, a sort of rueful embarrassment. "There are no cultists of the various buried gods. That is the official position of my lord and liege, and I will not in any way countermand that position."

Faran coughed. "But . . ."

"But, if there *were* such cultists, well, then it might be the case that there were stories about them. All lies, of course."

"Of course," I agreed. "Since they don't exist. What might such lies say about the wholly fictional cultists of the buried gods?"

"They might say that those wholly fictional cultists send weapons across the Wall of the Sylvain to be consecrated in the unquiet tombs of their buried patrons. They might also say that sometimes the buried ones bestow a special favor on such items, granting them hasheth—a curse, in your tongue—so that they bite deeper, or cause infection, or even wound the soul."

Faran let out a low whistle. "Nasty, but shouldn't we be able to see that sort of enchantment?"

Triss spoke aloud for the first time in Thuroq's presence, "Not if it's god-magic. The enchantments Namara put on her champions' swords are invisible to magesight."

"I thought the buried ones weren't considered true gods," said Faran.

"Perhaps not among your people," said Thuroq. "But what makes a god? Is it a matter of worshippers? Inherent nature? Or is it simply power? The buried ones had plenty of that last, and even now they have no small number of the first. It is only on the question of inherent nature that they fail the test as your 'gods' would have it."

"Not *my* gods," I said, and was surprised at how angry those words made me. "Namara died at the hands of her so-called fellows. I want no part of such *gods*."

Faran nodded. "I'm with Aral. Fuck the gods. They've caused me nothing but pain."

"Those are dangerous words to speak in the lands of man," said Thuroq. "But I do not think you will find many among the Durkoth who would disagree. Those who call themselves the *true gods* have no friends among the First. Though we may have lost our war to be free of them, we do not wear their shackles gladly."

I took an off step then, and my whole world went wobbly for a while. It returned to normal about the time we reached the road. We came out of the woods fifty feet from where we'd left our campsite. The rough oval of grassy ground looked utterly bizarre in the middle of the long pale stripe of the dirt road, like someone had simply dropped it in from another place entirely with its fire pit and low wall and the little stand of bamboo at the front end. Which, I suppose, they had.

Faran helped me down onto my blankets beside the fire while Thuroq steered our little slice of elsewhere off the road and into a clearing in the woods. Once he had us solidly out of sight of any travelers he came back to speak with us.

"I need to leave you for a time while I report this attack to my king. I don't think that I will be back before dawn, so I will have to find you on the road again to complete my bargain."

"I don't think that's going to work out so well." Faran had started the messy job of stitching up the long gash in the front of my thigh—working by magelight—and she shook her head now. "Aral isn't going anywhere for at least a couple of days, though I'd rather he stayed off this leg for a week. If this wound really is cursed . . . well, I don't have any idea what that'll mean in terms of healing time."

"That is . . . unfortunate, given tonight's . . . events," said Thuroq. "I'm certain that my king would prefer to see you moving farther from his borders faster."

"I'd prefer that as well," I said. "I have places I need to be. But it doesn't look like it's going to happen anywhere near as quickly as either of us might like."

"We'll see," said Thuroq. Then he was gone, sinking into the ground like a stone let go in deep water.

"That's the creepiest damn thing," said Faran. Then she sighed and went back to stitching my leg. "I *really* don't like the color of this wound. Triss cleaned it out just fine, and it doesn't look infected, but the edges have a very nasty orange tint to them."

"**Aral,** wake up. Thuroq is back."

I opened my eyes to find Faran kneeling beside me. Above and behind her was what looked like the inner surface of one of the domed felt tents the traders of Radewald favored, and I could no longer see the fire. What light there was came from the magelight Faran had used earlier to work on my leg.

"Where are we?" I asked. "I don't remember moving." The pain in my leg had kept me from doing much more than dozing. Unless I'd flat passed out again in there somewhere, I couldn't figure out how she'd managed it.

"We haven't moved an inch." Triss said, lifting his head from my chest to meet my eyes.

Faran added, "Thuroq raised an earthen dome around us so that the Durkoth healer could look at you without having to enter the surface world."

"Another Uthudor," said Thuroq. "Not a healer, a scholar of stone. As part of his discipline he prefers not to leave the embrace of sister earth."

I turned my head and saw the Durkoth standing alone on the far side of the low chamber.

"This guy is here to look at Aral's wounds, right?" Faran asked. "To see if he can make them better? By my lights that makes him a healer."

The Durkoth's face took on a pinched expression. "No. He's not interested in Aral at all. It's the effects of the hasheth that he cares about, the god-touched iron."

"So this *won't* help Aral?" said Triss. "That's not what you said when you arrived."

"It will almost certainly help him," said Thuroq. "That's why I asked for the Uthudor to come—because my king ordered me to see you taken care of and to speed you on your way as quick as I may. Healing Aral serves that goal. But *my* wishes in that regard have nothing to do with why the Uthudor chose to come here. He is not a healer. He cares nothing for Aral as Aral. He wants only to undo that which the hasheth has done, *because* it was done by the hasheth. He would do the same if the hasheth had marked a stone wall or a tree trunk instead of Aral's leg."

"That doesn't sound very reassuring," grumbled Triss.

"It is not meant to," said Thuroq. "Now, since this Uthudor is not a patient soul, can we dispense with further *discussing* and move on to dealing with the hasheth?"

I could feel Triss's frustration, but instead of arguing, he simply nodded and shifted off my chest.

"Fine by me," said Faran. "What does this Uthudor need from us?"

"Put out the light, and *try* to remain quiet."

Faran picked up the enchanted stone of the magelight and dropped it into her trick bag, sinking us in darkness. It felt like coming home. Much of my life has been spent in darkness, and I am always more comfortable at night than under the light of the sun.

As usual when darkness took me, I shifted more of my attention to my other senses, allowing sight to fade into the background of my mind. With greater focus, the scent of the earthen walls seemed suddenly sharper and stronger. The sound of Faran's breath and the nearly silent shifts of her gray silks loomed larger. Even the pressure of the blanket against my skin took on greater depth and meaning. Once I had grounded myself in my own senses, I was ready to reach outward.

Triss? I sent.

On it. My familiar flowed over me, enclosing me in a second skin—a necessary prerequisite to lending me the use of his darksight and other shadow senses.

A heartbeat later, I used Triss's "eyes" to watch a second Durkoth rise out of the ground between Thuroq and me. He was clothed in a floor-length robe of some porous stone that drank light so deeply that even Triss "saw" him mostly as a sort of deeper void in the darkness around him. He wore a cowl of the same stone, and something like a veil, completely concealing his features. As he slid toward me, his bare hands and feet suddenly flared in Triss's unvision, shifting to some highly reflective color—though whether that was the usual white, or silver, or even yellow was something I couldn't read through Triss's senses.

The ground beneath me rose into a high couch as he approached, lifting my wounded hip to the height of the Uthudor's ribs. Faran had cut away my pants earlier, and now the earth of the couch tugged aside my blanket, exposing the dressing over my wound.

The Uthudor glanced over his shoulder at Thuroq. "Yathraq, patis!"

"He wants you to remove the bandages," said Thuroq. "And please don't speak to him as you do it."

Faran stepped forward—no doubt borrowing Ssithra's "eyes" to guide her—and sliced my bandages away with a few deft flicks of her wrist dagger. She didn't resheathe it when she finished, spinning it into an underhanded grip instead, so that the blade lay concealed along her forearm. It was a shift as quick as any street conjurer's sleight of hand, and I doubted whether the two Durkoth would have followed it.

The Uthudor leaned forward and held his palm a few inches above the wound in my leg for several minutes. Beyond the gesture itself I had no indication of anything happening. Neither through magesight, nor Triss's senses, nor any sensation at all. Finally, he lifted his hand away and reached into the sleeve of his stone robe. I saw Faran tense at that, ready to protect me, but she relaxed again when the Uthudor's gesture produced nothing more threatening than a smooth stone of the sort you might find on any riverbank.

He rubbed the stone between his hands, shaping it into a perfect sphere. Then he set it at the top of the gash—just above and inside the point of my hip bone—and gently rolled it up and down the length of the wound several times. It should have hurt, simply from pressing against my wound, but it didn't. Instead, it relieved a pressure I hadn't known was there until it eased. It felt a bit like having an infected wound lanced, but much smoother and without the sharp jab of the lancet.

When he finished, the Uthudor lifted the rock away and turned it inside out by pressing on one side with his thumbs until the stone pushed through and out the other side, folding back on itself. The end result was an egg-shaped rock about half again larger than the original. He set it beside my leg on the earthen couch, barked a quick phrase at Thuroq in Durkothi, then slid down into the earth again.

"Don't touch that. I'll be right back," Thuroq said before following the other Durkoth into the ground.

"Did it work?" Faran asked me.

"It certainly did *something*." I reached down and touched the wound lightly. It hurt, but not, I thought, as much as it would have earlier. "I don't know what, though."

"To me it feels better." Triss collapsed back into a dragon-shaped shadow as Faran fished out the magelight to look at the wound.

Faran nodded. "That orange tint around the edges is all gone. Now it just looks like your basic mess of ripped-up flesh." She pointed at the rock. "I wonder what the story on that is."

"Me, too."

Ssithra leaned down from her perch on Faran's shoulder, stretching her long bird's neck so that she was scant inches away from the thing as she turned her shadow of a head this way and that above it. "I see nothing but a stone," she finally grumped.

That was all that I saw as well, but when Thuroq returned he lifted the thing in the air, and said, "This is a hasheth-ctark now." He pronounced the second word with a harsh coughing sound. "The Uthudor has encysted the hasheth of the Fire That Burns Underground in the stone. If you were to crack it open, you would find it hollow and the inside lined with tiny orange and red crystals. It is like a . . . What's the human word? Ah, yes, a geode."

"So, the curse has become a part of the rock?" I asked.

"Not quite, but your language doesn't have the words, and that is quite close to the truth. The curse is contained within, so that it can be dealt with properly."

"What do we do with it?" asked Faran.

"Take it beyond the Wall of the Sylvain. The hasheth is a thing of the buried gods. It should never have left the lands beyond the wall. Nothing of the buried ones should. You can do whatever you wish with it once you are there, though I would recommend that it be destroyed. That's the only way you can be completely certain it won't remain tied to the wound, even long after it has healed."

"I could send it into the everdark right now," said Triss. "Put it out of this world entirely . . ."

"No! The buried ones are of a place. I do not think that they could use such a small thing to access another plane, but they should not be afforded the opportunity. Take it beyond the wall and smash or bury it there. Or, if the chance arises, return it to the tomb of the Fire That Burns Underground—that would be the best solution of all."

"Is there any harm in touching it now?" I asked.

"No. As long as the rock remains unbroken, it is merely a rock."

Faran took the rock. "And what happens if we break it?"

"I honestly don't know, but it's a minor sort of curse. It might do nothing at all. It might return to your leg. It might simply root itself in the nearest available vessel. The Uthudor didn't say and he has gone."

I wanted to pursue the subject further, but could see it wouldn't get me anywhere.

"Now," continued Thuroq, "we need to see you on your way. My king wants you gone, and he has given me the tools to make that happen." He raised his hands above his head and made a gesture of parting.

In response, the low earthen dome sank back into the ground around us, revealing a bright dawn that made the Durkoth squint and pull a stone cowl over his head to protect his skin. Another gesture reduced my couch to nothing. A third brought our long-dead fire up from a sort of bubble in the earth, exposing a thick stone floor beneath it that hadn't been there before. A fourth carved a stairhead into the earth and stone at the front of our slice of misplaced land, and a fifth put a sunshade over the top of the opening.

"That all looks pretty elaborate," I said.

"As I said, my king wants you gone. Since you can't travel on your own, that means that we must transport you."

"We?" Faran eyed the stairs suspiciously. "There are more of you below?"

"Yes. Now. The king's orders called for haste. By myself I can only move you along the road, and that runs the risk of unwanted attention if we travel under the sun's gaze. With others to clear the way and close it behind, and to take my place when I tire, we can avoid the eyes of your people and travel both day and night. Add in the escort the king has sent to prevent any further incidents, and you will travel in state the like of which few mortals have ever known."

Faran made a bitter face. "Delightful. Will we be seeing much of this escort of yours?"

"Only me. None of the others speak your language or wish to spend time here above the true world."

"How far are you taking us?" I asked. "We must be close to the border of your king's lands already."

"We are very nearly there. If we had not been attacked by the . . . Durkoth bandits disguising themselves as wholly mythical cultists, we would have reached the place where I would have had to leave you tonight."

That sounded interesting. I raised an eyebrow. "And now?"

"My king feels that we cannot simply leave you at the border anymore. If the . . . bandits followed you over into the lands of the Queen of the South after his interactions with you through me, the queen might choose to see that as an act of religious aggression on the part of the North Kingdom and act accordingly."

I thought I was beginning to see where this was going. "I take it that would embarrass your king diplomatically?"

"I have no official opinion on the matter," Thuroq said with the blankest expression I'd yet seen on his face. "But it is possible the queen might choose to see it that way. Rather than allow her to make that misapprehension, my king has chosen to have us take you all the way to the Wall of the Sylvain."

That made me sit up despite the pain it woke in my thigh. "That'll take us down the whole length of the South Kingdom, won't it? I thought you were trying to *avoid* a diplomatic incident."

Thuroq didn't so much as blink at my question. "It would, *if* we remained in the foothills, but neither kingdom claims the lands that lie beyond the edge of the mountains. We will go south and east and travel above the empty country rather than following the line of the mountains to the southwest."

"That'll take us through some pretty heavily populated parts of southern Zhan and the Magelands beyond. Isn't that going to pose a problem in the not being seen department?"

"No. Your people have no sense of fathudor. Avoiding them with the resources I now have available will be easy enough." He smiled. "But even if we were seen, there would be no *diplomatic* problem, merely embarrassment. My people do not recognize the boundaries yours have drawn above the earth, so there is no question of violating them. Now, I must leave you before this light does me any more harm than it already has. I am weary as I have not been in a thousand years or more. If you need anything, come down and ask after it."

He turned and descended the stairs. A few minutes later, our campsite began to move again, sliding south and east through a forest that parted ahead of us and closed in behind. Despite my discomfort with our mode of travel, my injuries weighed heavily against my consciousness, and I soon fell asleep. My dreams were filled with the sound of cypress boughs brushing gently one against the other as they slipped out of our way.

After a few days of travel I grew more comfortable with the

stone raft. Some of that was familiarity. More was exhaustion. Healing, even magically aided healing, takes a lot out of you, and I spent much of my time sleeping.

The horses did not join me in my slow accommodation with our unnatural transportation. They didn't like standing on ground that moved, not one little bit. I'm not much of a horseman, and I prefer my own feet to riding, but I hated to see the beasts so unhappy—eyes wide and white, ears constantly flickering. Blinders helped, but only so much. I don't know what we'd have done with them if the trip had lasted much longer than it did.

The Durkoth steered that slice of earth as quick as any sailing ship with fair seas and a following wind, and they never stopped moving. In one eight-day week they covered a distance I had expected to take us at least a month without my wounds slowing us down.

Rather appropriately it was late afternoon on the day named for the Sylvani when the Wall of the Sylvain finally hove into sight on the southern horizon—the first Sylvasday in the month of Opening. We were still a half mile short of the wall when our earthen barge slid to a halt in a small wood. The wall was barely visible through the trees.

There is nothing in the eleven kingdoms of the East quite like the wall. It is simultaneously a magical ward that defines the line between the human lands and the ancient empire of the First and one of the most densely populated cities in the world—a city a thousand miles long and forty feet wide.

9

---·◆·---

"A stone snake five thousand miles long coils its way around the empire, a city riding on its back. Within is the oldest and mightiest civilization in the world, a dreaming land of decadence and corruption ruled over by ancient immortals fallen from grace. Beautiful and terrible they were in the power of their youth, and beautiful and terrible they remain, though they are ruined now and their strength broken—a decayed remnant of the world that was, bound forever within a wall built by the gods."

That is how I first heard the Wall of the Sylvain described in my childhood by my mentor, Kelos Deathwalker. I remember the words exactly, both for the grandeur they evoked in my young mind and for the sadness with which he spoke them. I remember, too, the sigh and what followed after.

"That's how the poet put it, lad, but it's not quite true. The part about a city five thousand miles long, at least. It's actually several cities and only one of 'em even a thousand miles. Great sections of the wall run through wastelands where no human can live, and the bulk of the wall's inhabitants are human, just as the bulk of the empire's are these days. The Sylvani simply don't breed fast enough to keep up with us. It's a poor life for a man—grubbing after the crumbs of the inhuman empire."

"Still," I said, "a thousand-mile city, that's . . . I don't even know. Please, tell me more."

Kelos let out a gruff laugh. "A thousand miles long but only forty feet wide. The wall encloses the entire Sylvani Empire in a near-perfect half circle. It runs from the great eastern ocean around the Sylvain and back to the ocean, and it is made of two parts. The first is the wall proper. That's the bit the gods made—the second part, the city, came later. I don't know what the wall is made of or how they built it, but it's exactly eight feet tall and eight feet wide. Hard as diamond, it is, and it looks more than a bit like some exotic gemstone."

"How so?" I remember being utterly fascinated.

"It's translucent. That means you can see a few inches into it, though if you lay a finger along the top corner and try to see it through the edge, you'll be disappointed. It's mostly green as fine jade, but calling it a stone snake is fair enough. It's got other colors running through the stone in regular patterns like a snake's skin—reds and golds mostly."

"Do you think it might be a dragon? Frozen into stone by the Emperor of Heaven to keep the buried gods inside?" Even so young I had heard stories about the buried gods.

Kelos shook his head. "No, I don't think so. The godwar was more . . . complex than the way your local priest probably told it. You'll get more of the story here in the temple as you get older. For now, let's just say the Emperor of Heaven's powers don't stretch as far as you might think they do, and that no dragon who ever lived was big enough for the task. Mostly, I think, it's just one giant monster of a ward."

"A ward against what?"

Kelos shrugged. "What remains of the power of the buried gods perhaps. Or maybe the magic of their children. It's certainly true that no Sylvani lord can cast a spell this side of the wall. It contains and limits the power of the Others and prevents the buried gods from crossing into the lands of man, whatever its master purpose might be."

I wasn't sure if I liked his answers. My parents and the people around them had been pretty convinced about the power of the Emperor of Heaven. But I knew that I belonged to

Namara now, and she had her own ways of doing things, so I nodded politely now and moved on to a different sort of question.

"Tell me about the city. Why is it only forty feet wide?"

"It's something about the way the gods built the wall. For exactly sixteen feet on either side of the wall the ground is almost as hard as granite and flat—perfect for building. Beyond that, the ground looks normal but isn't really for a good hundred yards. If you try to dig, the hole fills in behind your shovel. If you hammer a post in, the ground spits it back out. If you put a tent up, it falls over. They call it the Fallows."

"That's amazing!" I remember clapping my hands together with delight at a world so strange.

"The wall is a strange place. I've heard that back when it was new, people tried to dig under the Fallows, to run tunnels into the Sylvani Empire, but those filled in, too. The only thing that freely crosses under the line of the wall is water. A half dozen major rivers and any number of streams flow beneath the wall, and there are places where it provides the only bridge."

"So, you can pass the wall in a boat?"

Kelos shook his head. "No. The wall-stone extends right down to skim the surface no matter the level of the water, and a boat simply won't fit. For that matter, I once saw a man try to swim underneath it on a dare. He went down, and never came up again, though fish pass through easily enough.

"You can't build atop the wall either, though it's easy enough to walk across it. That eight-foot stretch of stone stays perfectly clean and clear all year round. Neither snow, nor dirt, nor any of the works of man will stay atop it for any length of time. You can walk or run on it, but if you stand still for any length of time you'll find yourself slowly sliding toward the nearest edge. The people who live in the city of Wall use it as their only street, and every building has two main doors, one on each floor. The lower opens into the Fallows. The upper onto the wall."

Memory is a funny thing. I hadn't thought of that moment in years, but seeing the city there along the wall, it suddenly pressed in on me in a way that felt more real than the present did. It hurt me to remember those days, when I was young and free of all the cares and betrayals the years would later pile on my shoulders. It hurt to remember how much I had loved the man who had acted as my father in the service of Namara, Kelos Deathwalker.

He was my mentor, my friend, and my goddess's greatest traitor. For years I had thought him dead, fallen with so many others in the destruction of the temple. Now that I knew better, I wished that I did not, that I had never learned of his betrayals. And yet, I couldn't help but wonder where he was now, and whether he was well or ill. He was as responsible as anyone alive for the destruction of my way of life, but somewhere down deep in my soul where the child Aral yet lived, I loved him still.

"Aral?" Faran touched my shoulder. "Are you in there?"

I shook myself free of memory and realized that our Durkoth guide had not come to the surface when we stopped moving. "I am now. Where's Thuroq?"

Faran pointed at the place the stairs used to be. "Gone. At least, as far as I can tell. After we stopped, I went forward to speak with him. The stairs closed in my face." She jerked her chin over her shoulder. "The little wall's gone, too, and the stand of bamboo. Even the dirt's changed. It matches the local stuff now. The only thing they left us is the stump where the horses are tied."

"Huh. I would have liked to have a final word with him, but I guess that's moot." I sighed. "Come on, we should get the packs on the horses. We have a wall to cross."

The Durkoth had chosen their stopping place well in terms of staying out of sight, leaving us in a scrubby patch of woodland far from any Magelander roads or farms. We had passed some fifty miles east of Gat—one of the five great university cities that governed the Magelands—and traveled more or less due south from that point on.

The major wall crossing points were almost all to our east, nearer the coast and the Ruvan Delta. The one exception was a couple of hundred miles north and west at the point where the river Uln went under the wall below Tavan, providing a natural transshipment point.

People crossed everywhere, of course, and the city along the wall extended all the way from the mountains to the sea here in the north, but the population thinned out a bit in places like this. Here you might go fifty feet between buildings, and they rarely stood taller than the two stories needed to provide easy access to the top of the wall. A thicker cluster of buildings stood a bit to the west of us, which likely meant a crossing house, so we pointed our horses that way and started moving.

The trees ended at the edge of the Fallows in a line as sharp as a sword's cut. There were a few scrubby bushes here and there in the open strip before the wall, but mostly the plants hugged the ground. And nothing in the Fallows grew higher than the eight-foot line of the wall's top. A sort of low grass was the dominant growth, striped yellow and brown like a Kvanas' slink. The one horse who tried a bite didn't take a second, though the sheep grazing in small flocks seemed to like it well enough.

I had only passed the wall twice before, neither time for a mission—the goddess had rarely interfered in Other matters— but I knew to look for a crossing house, and we soon found one. It was the widest building in the little neighborhood, easily identified by the ramp that started on ground level on our left, wrapping up and around the back of the building as it climbed to the level of the wall. At one of the busier crossing points it might have had an iron gate across the base, but here there was only a wooden bar that could be easily lifted out of the way.

As we approached the base of the ramp, I called out, "Hello, the house!"

There was a bell as well, but I didn't need it, as a plump matron stuck her head out of a second-story window before we'd quite brought the horses to a stop.

"What's your rate for three horses and two riders, no trade goods?" I asked.

She looked us up and down, quite obviously gauging how much the market would bear by the cut of our clothes and the quality of our horses. "Five silver kalends."

"That's extortionist," Faran growled in a low voice.

I agreed with her, though I didn't much care. We had the funds, and I'd have cheerfully tossed her the coins without any argument if that wouldn't have burned us deep into the woman's memory. Everyone haggles.

"You're right," I said loudly to Faran. "Let's move on to a house that's in the business of border crossings instead of highway robbery." I tugged on the reins, turning my horse's head away from the gate.

"Three kalends," the woman called, "and you won't find cheaper in a hundred miles."

"Two." I didn't turn back, but I didn't ride away either.

"Three, and I'll throw in a dinner you can eat in the saddle. . . ."

We eventually settled on two kalends and three fivers—the kalend is shaped like a five-spoked wheel and can be broken along the lines of the spokes—and no dinner. I wanted to find us an inn a bit farther west along the wall since we'd crossed well to the east of where Siri was expecting us. We'd get our dinner there. I tossed the woman the coins once we had our bargain and she reached out and pulled a rope that lifted the bar aside. We rode up the ramp, around the corner, and out onto the wall.

As I crossed the line, I felt a sort of tugging on my harness as though phantom hands had briefly grasped at the sheaths on my back, and I thought I heard the faintest echo of a metallic chime. But both things passed in an instant, and, when I asked Faran if she'd caught the noise or felt anything, she just shook her head.

We paused atop the wall for a several long beats to look at the endless line of the thing stretching away both east and west. There was something utterly inhuman about the perfection of that view. It rolled up and down with the terrain, but without any of the lumps or bumps such a wall would have had if it were made by the hands of man. The surface was as smooth as a pool of clear water in the heart of a windless day, unmarked by any line or blemish. Sure, it varied in color and pattern like a snake's skin, but it did so with a geometric exactitude that you could have used to place the knots on the world's most accurate measuring cord.

Within a few minutes, the horses started to stamp. Nothing that touches the top of the wall stays there. Though the magic sliding the horses along toward the edge was slow and subtle, they could clearly sense the movement. At some level, the wall didn't want them there, and they were in ferocious agreement. So, long before I was tired of the view, we finished crossing the wall and rode down the other side of the ramp into the Sylvain.

Eight feet. It was a distance I could have easily traveled in a single jump, and yet it took us into an entirely different world. To start with, the Fallows grass on the Sylvani side was of a lusher variety, deep green shading into blue, and the horses liked that just fine. But that was the least of the changes. We let the horses graze for a little while as we tried to adjust to the shift.

Shifts, really, since *everything* was different to some degree or another, including the weather. It was noticeably cooler despite how far south we'd come, which should have made the reverse true. Clearer and sunnier, too. Most of all, things felt . . . richer. Everything was more itself, or maybe more like you imagined it ought to be. The trees in the distance were greener and stronger and more treelike. The sky was bluer, the clouds puffier; even the wind tasted more like wind should. The earth itself felt more solid and real.

You could feel the change in the ground coming up through the horses, like water rising in a fountain. It was there in the way they planted their hooves and moved their bodies, in the set of the saddle and the hang of the stirrups. The whole thing ought to have felt marvelous.

It didn't. It felt old and alien and inimical to mortal life. This world didn't want us in it. Or, at least, that was how it felt to me.

"It's beautiful!" Faran slid off her horse and knelt to touch the ground. "And so alive. Can you feel it, Aral?"

"Vividly."

Faran turned and gave me a concerned look. "Are you all right? Because you sounded a little funny there."

She's right, agreed Triss. *Your voice had a sort of vibration to it, something that I don't recall hearing before.*

I don't know, I replied. *There's something not right. . . .*

As I tried to articulate my feelings, I looked down and saw that I was twisting at the smoke ring with the thumb and forefinger of my other hand. That was when I realized I could feel something else as well—a sort of pulsing or throbbing in the ring, like something alive and suddenly awake. I held my hand up where I could see it better. The smoke band had grown thicker and wider. It was more active as well, rolling and coiling wildly where before it had slowly swirled in a way that ebbed and flowed.

"Aral?" Faran had one of her cane knives out and a calculating look on her face. "I'm pretty sure I can take that finger off without touching the others if you spread them just a little bit farther."

I closed my hand into a fist and shook my head. "I'm going to hold off on that option for a little while, if you don't mind. The ring isn't doing anything really drastic, and we probably should have expected some changes when we crossed into the Sylvain, given its suspected origins."

"Suspected?" Triss asked aloud—a sure sign he wanted Faran's support . . . or Ssithra's. "Don't you think that's understating the case a bit, given the Durkoth cultist attacks, and the way the King of the North reacted to them and to your new-found bauble?"

"Possibly, but I trust the Durkoth slightly less than I would your average gutterside runner. While it's unlikely they staged the whole thing for reasons presently unknown, I'm not going to completely rule it out. Also, I'd like to give Siri a chance to tell me her side of the story before I make any irrevocable choices."

Faran lifted both her eyebrows. "That sounds like you're finally feeling a bit more skeptical about this whole wedding thing and Siri's part in it. I approve."

I sighed. "The buried gods aspect of the matter definitely makes it harder to believe Siri was acting in good faith." I held up a hand before Faran could respond. "But, and this is a big *but*, I owe Siri both duty and honor. She is, or was, the First Blade of Namara. I can *feel* her soul speaking to me through these sendings of smoke, and I know that she never betrayed the goddess or justice. As long as all of that holds true and *anything* remains of her, she can ask me for my life and I will give it to her. Can we drop this now?"

Faran took a deep breath and let it go before speaking. "I don't understand why you feel that way, and I don't like it, but I can see it's true. Maybe I *would* understand if I had completed my training, but I doubt it. I think this is more about the kind of person that you are than any lessons I missed out on. Now, let me just ask you one question before we get back on our way. It's a question about the kind of person Siri is. Would Siri, if it truly is her, *ever* ask you for your life?" She turned away before I could even start to respond, and vaulted back into her saddle.

It's a good question, Triss sent as Faran kicked her horse into a fast walk.

And one I can't answer without talking to Siri. Not now. In the old days, when Namara yet lived and Siri was her First Blade, I would have said yes. Namara did not spend her Blades lightly, but in her name Siri might well have asked me to take on a task knowing that my death would be one result. Now . . . I just don't know. Let's hope we don't have to find out.

The Fallows made for excellent riding—with little chance of gopher holes or other hazards—and the horses were fresh. So, we trotted the sun down before looking for a place to spend the night. We found it in a large inn centering a miles-long stretch of buildings. The bottom floor of the inn was mostly stables.

When we handed our horses off to the grooms—young, female, and human—they gave us chits with our stall numbers and pointed us toward a small booth at the base of the central stairs that led to the upper level. There was an older woman there, human as well.

"Welcome to Wall," she said as soon as we were close enough to speak without shouting. "At this hour, I'm guessing you'll be wanting beds as well as dinner. We're mostly full, but we've a few of the rooms as are cheapest and a few of the most expensive left open. By the cut of your cloth and the fact of your horses, I'm thinking it's the latter you'll be enquiring after."

"It is," I said.

She gave us a more thorough looking over. "Swords, and good ones, plus knives enough to outfit a spare kitchen or I'm no judge of subtle bulges. I can offer you the last of our tower suites for six silver kalends. No way in but the common room at the base of the stair, and bars on the windows. Very secure."

"And not yet booked an hour before midnight," I said. "Which means it's likely to go begging if we don't take it, especially here so far from a major crossing. Let's say three silver kalends, and you throw in whatever's left in the pot at this hour."

She snorted. "What's left in the pot is a sweet lamb curry with dates and almonds, flat bread buttered with garlic and ginger, and a cream custard with caramelized sugar and blueberries on top. Throw in the house red wine, and call it four kalends. Have we a deal?"

"Done," said Faran, before I could think to argue. "It's my money, and that sounds delightful."

"'Tis," said the old woman as Faran handed across the coins.

"Fine," I said. "But we'll take tea instead of the wine." Faran didn't like booze, and I couldn't have it, though the thought of a Sylvani red made my mouth water.

"Suit yourself. Here's the key." The woman handed across an elaborate bronze artwork designed to open a Durkoth-made lock with at least nine pins. "There's a spiral stair back of the hearth farthest west. That unlocks the gate at the base. Tell the first serving maid or boy you see where you want your dinner—sitting room or common room—and I'll have the grooms haul your luggage up."

We took the steps to the level above, where a long and narrow common room spread out like wings on either side of an open kitchen and central bar. There were eight hearths not counting the huge iron grill centering the kitchen and the various stoves and cooking fires that surrounded it.

We told a boy at the kitchen to have our meals brought to a table somewhere near the stair to our rooms. It was getting late enough that the bulk of the local crowd had gone home. That left a few workmen, a couple of near-unconscious drunks, a minstrel counting his hat, and one Sylvani lord eating alone—the first nonhuman we'd seen since crossing the wall. Even here on the edge of their ancient empire, the Others were few and far between, outbred by the peoples who had succeeded them in thralldom to the gods.

About forty feet along we came to the third hearth on the wall side of the inn. It was a warm night with open windows, and the fire was obviously laid on more for atmosphere than warmth. No one was paying much attention to this particular hearth and it had nearly burned itself out. As I glanced at the smoldering coals, the fire finished dying all in an instant, making a subtle whumph noise as it did so, rather like someone had smothered it with a lead blanket. An instant later, a thick rope of dark smoke billowed out of the fireplace, twining itself around me briefly, before moving on to form a churning column in the air a few feet away.

I drew my swords by reflex and saw Faran match my gesture with her cane knives as she sidestepped right to box the smoke between us. Startled cries broke out from here and there in the long room as other patrons noticed something strange was going on. Most folks started moving away from the smoke, but the Sylvani lord drew a serpentine sword and matching dagger as he rose from his chair and headed our way. He was tall and armored in indigo crystal and he quickly stepped in to form the third point of a triangle around the pillar of smoke, with Faran and me at the other corners.

Before I could get a close look at him or decide how I felt about that, the smoke bent and twisted, collapsing in on itself to become a tall slender woman with a burn-scarred throat and her eyes fixed on mine.

Siri.

Unmistakably so and in the flesh this time. Yet also transformed in ways both subtle and stark.

Things that had not changed: The deep icy black of her skin. The hard lean muscle of her arms and shoulders. The swords of our goddess riding high on her shoulders.

Things that had: Thick curly hair worn short and dense against her scalp had given way to scores of long braids that seemed two parts smoke for one part Siri. Eyes with irises every bit as smoky as her hair. A bittersweet half smile like no expression I had ever seen her wear before. The ring of smoke on her wedding finger. And, most of all, her shadow.

I would normally have expected Kyrissa to hide herself within Siri's shadow, but the Shade had made a different choice. The shadow curled up from Siri's feet to hang in the air behind her in the form of a winged snake. The same smoke that had transformed Siri's braid into something more than half of another world had touched the Shade even more deeply. Where once Kyrissa had worn bat's wings and a serpent's scales, she now had feathers of smoke. Only her face remained smooth and wholly a thing of a shadow.

Siri waited a beat to let me take in all the changes, then she nodded at me, and for an instant her smile lost its bitter undertone. "Hello, Aral, you made good time. Now, bide a moment."

10

If the Durkoth are marble idols, their Sylvani cousins are crystalline figures filled with the fading sorrow of twilight.

There are eight major elements: light, shadow, earth, air, water, fire, death, and life, though we only know of corresponding elementals for the first seven. Just as the Durkoth aligned themselves with earth, the Sylvani gave themselves to the light. In the beginning, they shone with the bright star of morning, but that was long ago, before the godwar broke their power. These days, their light is all but extinguished, but still it shines through, illuminating them from within, however dimly.

The tall Sylvani lord who had risen to face the smoke with us was a perfect example of the type. Like the Durkoth, he was beautiful in a way no human could ever hope to match. But there the resemblance ended, for his face was full of expression and life. This was no carved effigy, but a centuries-old man with all of a man's passions and needs and twice his sorrows. There were lines on his face, fine as the purest calligrapher's stroke. Lines of pain, and lines of grief, lines that told the story of fighting the long defeat. I found him far more attractive than any Durkoth.

When the pillar of smoke transformed itself into Siri, those lines twisted themselves tighter still, and I had little doubt that he saw in her the echo of the buried gods who had fought a war with Heaven and lost. But his hands remained firm and steady, his blades ready to attack or defend. If he suspected that he couldn't win the fight he had chosen, he accepted the chance and would not back away. It was a sentiment I could salute in another, even as I recognized its echo in my own losing battle for the ideals of justice after the fall of Justice herself.

So, when Siri pivoted to face the Other, I stepped forward without thinking to put myself at his side. She quirked an eyebrow at me, but kept her hands open, palms outward, showing the Sylvani no slightest hint of hostility. He held his blades ready, but made no further gesture of aggression.

She gave him the same nod she'd given me a moment before, only without the smile. Siri is taller than I am, but she had to look up to meet his eyes. She spoke a long fluid string of what sounded to me like a high-court version of the dialect the Sylvani used among themselves, then—I didn't speak even the common version well enough to make sense of it.

Her voice was gentle, but cold, and, knowing Siri as I did, I suspected there was more than one hidden message buried beneath the musical words of high Sylvani. When she was done, she quirked a faint smile at the lord and crossed her arms.

The Sylvani turned his head to look at me. There was a question in his eyes, but not one I understood, so all I could do in answer was shrug and put up my swords. His glance flicked from them to the pair on Siri's back, and his eyebrows climbed toward his silvered widow's peak. Finally, he nodded and sheathed his own blades. It was a liquid movement and very fast.

He touched the first two fingers of his right hand to forehead, lips, and the breastplate of his crystal armor just above the heart, ending the gesture with a flourish the elegance of which would have raised envy in the heart of the most polished human courtier. Then, without ever having spoken a word, he turned away and returned to his table and his dessert, settling in with his back to us as though nothing had ever happened.

As soon as he was gone, Siri smiled that bittersweet smile

again. "Will you put away your swords now, Aral? Or, were you planning on testing your edge on me?"

I bowed from the waist, inclining an apology as I returned them to their place on my back. "Honestly, I'd more than half forgotten I still had them unsheathed."

She arched a brow at me. "I will believe that Aral King-slayer has forgotten the placement of his blades by the tiniest fraction of an inch roughly one hour after the sun rises in the west." Then she laughed—a deep, rich, booming sound. I hadn't known how much I missed that laugh until the tears started in my eyes as she stepped forward to draw me into her arms. "Ah, my friend, it half unbreaks my heart to see you still alive."

It is Siri! Triss said into my mind, but I was too busy holding her as we both cried to answer. *And Kyrissa—though her soul tastes more than passing strange.*

For a little while I let go of everything but the joyous pain of a reunion I'd never expected to see. But every moment must end, and, after some unmeasured strand of time had passed away, I felt Siri's hands press less tightly on my back and I let go my embrace as well. Stepping back, I took her hands in my own and turned her to face Faran with me.

The younger woman had as sour an expression as I'd ever seen on her face, though she *had* put her weapons away as well.

"Siri, I don't know how well you remember my apprentice, Faran."

"*Your* apprentice?" Siri's question came out with a distinct note of curiosity as well as the faintest dash of disapproval. "That's the language of a mage school, not the temple."

I nodded. "Namara is dead and her temple is in ruins, but her onetime novices still need instruction. I have undertaken Faran's, and she is under my protection."

Faran snorted at that. "That's one way of looking at it, though I've spent nearly as much time watching Aral's back as he has mine."

Siri pulled away from me and spoke to Faran. "I'm glad you found each other, little sister. From what I've been able to discover from here at the far end of beyond, he was badly in need of someone to live up to." She extended her right forearm to the younger woman, hand open.

Faran eyed the hand for a long suspicious moment, rather as though she wanted to refuse the formal greeting and with it the implied kinship Siri had offered. But then she stepped forward and clasped forearms with Siri. "Maybe you are who you seem to be, after all . . . sister."

Siri released her and stepped back. "I am, and I am not. I have become as you see me." She touched a finger to the smoke in her hair. "I am . . . infected with a god."

Through all of this Kyrissa had hung silently in the air behind Siri, though I knew that she and Triss had exchanged the greetings of their kind while we embraced. Now the smoke-feathered serpent leaned toward me, bringing her nose within a few inches of my own.

"We are both become infected, Aral. Which is why I asked Siri to marry you."

Interesting . . .

Very, I agreed with Triss. *I wonder*— I began, but was interrupted by the advent of an extremely worried-looking boy carrying a tray full of food and drink.

"Excuse me, milord mage, but did you still want to eat this down here? Or would you prefer to take refreshment in your rooms?" His tone made it obvious that he was hoping we'd take our little freak show upstairs. "Also, the grooms have your baggage, but they need your key to let them in." He jerked his head back toward the kitchen where a pair of young women were pretending to be part of the counter.

"I think we'd better have you take this upstairs. Oh, and we'll want a third meal, I think." I looked at Siri, who nodded. "Come on."

Half an hour later we were all ensconced in large chairs around a fresh fire—Siri had insisted. The way that smoke kept wisping off the logs to slither around her legs like a cat in search of attention before returning to roll up the chimney was deeply disconcerting. Even stranger, Kyrissa had curled up on the floor less than a foot away from the flames.

I don't like it, Triss said into my mind. *It's not natural. I can't share darkness with her without getting painfully close to the fire. For that matter, I'm not entirely comfortable doing so. The smoke has changed her ssassisshatha . . . her soul's*

signature, if you will. She still tastes of Kyrissa, but . . . not.
His mental voice sounded very frustrated.

He and Ssithra had settled in between us and Kyrissa and were whispering away with her in the way of their kind, though neither of them was actually overlapping her shadow as would have been more normal at such a gathering. The familiar combination of the susurration of Shade speech and being able to actually reach over and touch Siri if I wanted to gave me a weird, out-of-time feeling, like we'd never been apart. I felt simultaneously more comforted and more homesick for the temple and my old life than I had in years.

I kept having to refocus on the present moment to keep myself from sinking too deeply into the want of a world gone forever. Fortunately, the food provided an excellent anchor to the here and now since it was nothing like the fare we had eaten at the temple. Not even while practicing poisons for court use. The inn had adopted many of the spices and staples of Sylvani cuisine, which we simply hadn't covered in our poison lessons.

The bread was bread, if particularly well made—there are variations, but the basics are much the same across the whole of the East. The curry, on the other hand, was subtle and sweet and full of alien flavors that delighted the tongue. The tea . . . well, the tea was like nothing I'd ever had before, rich and dark with a blend of sweet and sharp spices added. I actually *liked* it, and even found myself wishing for more when I'd finished the pot.

We ate mostly in silence because none of us wanted to start the more serious conversation that was all too likely to shatter the comity of our reunion. Though I doubted she would ever admit it, I think that Faran was also rather enjoying the idea of sitting down to a friendly meal with *Siri the Mythkiller*.

Eventually, though, Siri looked me square in the eyes. "Aren't you going to ask me why I suddenly showed up and insisted that you marry me before dragging you down the whole length of the East?"

"No."

"No?" She blinked, several times, and the smoke in her eyes swirled a little more wildly. "What about the ring itself? Aren't you going to demand answers about that?"

"Nope."

"Why not?"

"Yeah," said Faran. "I'd like to hear the answer to that one, too."

Triss had lifted his head at "no" and I could feel his full attention weighing on me.

I shrugged my shoulders. "We both know that if you want me to know the answers to those questions, you'll tell me. If you don't, nothing I can possibly say or do will pry it out of you. What point could demanding an answer possibly serve?"

Siri's face went very thoughtful. "You've changed, Aral, a very great deal."

I laughed. "Said the woman with smoke braided into her hair."

"Point. Though, that's not what I meant. I'm talking about inside. Whatever he looked like on the surface, the old Aral would never have sat there quietly eating dinner and waiting patiently for me to crack and spill my secrets. You were not a patient man in our temple days, not when you had anything like a choice in the matter. A patient man would not have gone to the goddess and asked her to make him a Blade before his time so that he could go after the King of Tien."

"I was a boy when I killed Ashvik, with a boy's patience. The world has taught me many lessons since then, none of them gentle."

Siri looked into her tea and slowly swirled the cup. "When you speak like that, with such a weight of weariness in your voice, you almost remind me of the way Kelos spoke in the old days."

"The Deathwalker is not dead," I said flatly. "He betrayed us all in pursuit of an impossible idea of what the world ought to be."

Siri nodded, her expression blank and closed. "I know. He's here in the Sylvain now. I've spoken with him. A bit less than a month ago, actually."

I saw Faran tense at that and look around as though she were expecting the Deathwalker to appear from behind an arras like something out of a Zhani melodrama.

"What happened?" I asked.

"He came to me, and asked if I would help him track down an item."

"Did he tell you that he arranged for both of us to be away on missions when the temple fell . . . so that we would live?" I could feel every muscle in my body tightening like a garrote.

Siri nodded again.

"What did you do?"

"I let him walk away alive." Her face remained blank, but her hands were fisted and I could see the cords on her forearms standing up from the strength of her grip.

It was a remarkable statement. The last time I'd crossed swords with Kelos, I'd lost badly. But I had no doubt that she could have killed him if she'd wanted to. Siri was that good.

"Letting him go was one of the hardest things I've ever done," she continued. "Afterward, once I was sure he was gone, I asked you to marry me."

"I take it the two are related?"

"The item he wanted me to help him find . . . it might help me with this." She touched a finger to the smoke in one of her braids. "It's . . . complicated. I'm going to tell you a story about how I got like this." She touched the braid again. "The question is where to begin. Give me a moment. . . ." She trailed off, staring into the fire like someone thinking deep thoughts about another time and place.

As the silence stretched out, I noticed something strange. When Siri let go of the braid, her hand dropped into her lap, landing palm up, fingers half-curled. A natural enough gesture. Except for the fact that her fingers were moving in a slow but distinct pattern, like someone playing an instrument, or trying to convey a silent message.

If your work happens in the dark and in silence you must have some means other than speech for communicating. While it was rare for Blades to work together, it wasn't wholly unheard of, and we'd had to learn a very rudimentary sort of squeeze code for such occasions. The vocabulary was tiny, fifty words or so. Come, go, right, left, guard, etc. Siri's hand was making the code for "watch" and "trap" and "false" in a loop, though she didn't seem to be paying any attention to it.

"Take all the time you need." I reached over and put a hand on her forearm. "This can't be easy." I gave her a comforting squeeze that said, "Yes, watch."

"I'd be lying if I said it was," said Siri. Her hand signaled "yes" twice, when she said "I" and "lying." She continued, "Not all of it, of course. Nor even most, but some . . ." Siri's hand made no further motions, and I took that to mean she'd told me what she needed to—that I couldn't trust all of what she had to say.

"I understand," I said. "The biggest lesson I've learned since the fall of the temple is that there is no black and white in the world. *Everything* comes in mixed grays."

"Like smoke," said Siri.

What did I just miss? Triss asked. *I could tell the two of you were having more than one conversation, but couldn't follow the details.*

I'll tell you later. The important thing is that Siri has warned me that we can't fully trust her. Can you let Ssithra know what's up without giving anything away to Kyrissa?

No. It'll have to wait for later.

All right. It's not like Faran's going to trust a word she says anyway.

Siri sighed. "I guess that's as good a place as any to begin. It started with smoke."

"The Fire That Burns Underground," I said.

She nodded. "Exactly, though Namara called him the Smoldering Flame. It was a bit over a year after you killed Ashvik that the goddess summoned me to her island. I was surprised, of course. Personal summons were always rare, and virtually unheard of for someone as young as I was at the time."

The goddess usually preferred to give assignments through her shadow council, or occasionally by way of the First Blade or the high priest. Summoning a Blade bare months after her investiture such as Siri was at that time was almost as unheard of as my own decision to go out to the sacred island and beg the goddess to assign Ashvik's death to me.

"When she rose from the waters and spoke to me . . ." Siri trailed off and I could see a mix of awe and sorrow and longing in her eyes.

I looked down because I couldn't bear the pain her

expression woke in my heart. "I've been there. I know what it means to have the goddess hold your soul in her hand."

Check in with Ssithra, I sent. *This is a topic that has to hurt her and Faran.*

Triss came back after a moment. *She says that they will be fine, but some of that feels like bravado.*

A long painful silence had opened up so I prompted Siri with, "Smoke?"

Siri started. "Yes, sorry. Namara told me that she had been watching my training and how I had done with my first few assignments, that she needed someone with my magical skills and *flexibility* of mind to assay a mission. I went to place my forehead on the ground at her feet as I promised that, whatever she wanted of me, it would be done. But she caught my chin with a fingertip and stopped me. She said that she didn't know if what she was asking *could* be done—that she needed me to slay smoke, but that smoke could not die. Her words troubled me."

Siri stood and walked to the fireplace, putting her hands on the mantel and leaning down to stare into the flames. Kyrissa looked worriedly up at her partner. After a few moments, Siri turned around and leaned back against the mantel. The smoke from the fire wisped back and forth across her calves, blending with the twisting patterns of her grays.

"I have never possessed the certainty that you do, Aral. I believed in Namara with every fiber of my being. But, justice . . . I cannot always see the true path. I can kill with the very best of them, but sometimes I waver in my understanding of what's right. To know that Namara could be uncertain about something, too—that shook me in a way that I don't think would have touched you, or Kelos, or Alinthide. The goddess saw that, and I knew that she had. It made me ashamed."

"It shouldn't." I got out of my chair and crossed to put a hand on her shoulder. "One of the most important things I've learned since the fall of the temple is that certainty is a trap. Believing you're right is one thing." I started to pace. "The very idea of belief carries within it the seeds of doubt. But *knowing* you're right . . ."

I shook my head. "When you *know* you're right you develop a special sort of blindness. That can be okay if you *are* right, but if you aren't . . ."

"It's funny that you should put it that way. The goddess said something similar. She told me that it was my very uncertainty that fitted me for the mission ahead, that you couldn't fight smoke if you didn't see all the shades of gray."

"You're making it sound like the goddess actually approved of . . . of . . . moral ambiguity," interjected Faran. "That can't be right! The priests always told us that Namara could see the way of justice in any situation, that her sight was always clear."

Faran sounded genuinely shocked and more than a little outraged. And, I felt . . . I felt like someone had taken my past and scrambled all the pieces when I wasn't looking. My whole life had been built atop the belief that the goddess never wavered and always knew what was right. That was my bedrock.

Siri nodded at Faran. "It bothered me, too. I would never have dreamed of questioning the goddess out loud. I tried to not even *think* what you just said, but I couldn't help myself for the same reason I couldn't help having doubts. Of course, the goddess heard my thoughts."

"And?" I asked. My voice sounded far away to my ears and I could taste brass.

My pacing had taken me around behind the chair I'd vacated a few moments earlier—putting it between Siri and me. Now I caught hold of the back, squeezing hard enough to make the joints creak. I didn't know what I wanted Namara's response to have been, but I knew that I had to hear it.

"And the goddess chuckled," said Siri. "Then she spoke into my mind, *'Priests say many things about the gods. Some they say because they are true. Some they say because we tell them to say them. Some they say because they tell themselves they must be true.'*

"I told her that I didn't understand, and she chuckled again. *'Daughter, we are not so different, you and I. Sometimes you worry that you will make the wrong choices. So do I. Sometimes there is no clear way. But you believe in me and trust me to guide you to the right path. And I believe in justice and trust that belief to guide me to the right path.'*"

Triss hopped up into my chair so that his head was level

with Siri's. "You're truly claiming that the goddess didn't always know the right?" To me he sent, *Maybe this is the lie she warned you about?* His projected words sounded even more confused than his spoken voice had.

I don't think so, Triss. Siri isn't giving me any signals, and this feels *like the truth, Namara help me. . . .*

Siri nodded again. "That's what she told me."

"Why?" I whispered, though I wasn't at all certain what I was asking for, or even who I was asking it of.

"I think it's because she knew that I needed to hear it. I had seen how certain you were, and Kelos, and . . . well, so many of the others. But I didn't have that certainty, and I was having a major crisis of the heart because of it. The goddess wanted me to understand that it was all right to doubt yourself, that doing so didn't make you somehow less than those who never wavered. I believe that she wanted me to understand that doubt itself could be a tool for seeking the truth.

" '*Doubt,*' she told me, '*is exactly why I have chosen you, my daughter. I am sending you to face one of the most powerful of the buried gods. He is the lord of smoke, a master of deception and misdirection. From the moment you cross the wall of the Sylvain you won't be able to trust anything you see or hear or smell. The habits of a doubting mind will be your greatest ally, certainty a trap that will get you killed.*'

" 'Then what do I hold on to?' I asked.

" '*Justice,*' replied the goddess. '*True justice. I am the least certain of goddesses. Much that my kind has done is . . . open to question. It is quite possible that you would all be better off if we had simply abandoned this world after your creation. I am absolutely certain of one thing only, and that is that might does not make right. The strong must not be allowed to prey on the weak with impunity. Someone must be prepared to call the mighty to account. In this case, that someone is you.*'

" 'But I don't know if I can do this!' I wailed. 'Why not send Kelos, or Illiana, or even Aral?'

" '*I don't know if you can do it either, but I know that Aral could not. Nor Illiana. Nor even Kelos. None of them have the doubt for it. Aral is like the arrow shot straight at the heart; you are the night falcon sent to bring down game in the dark.*

You *are my choice for this job, Siri. If any of my Blades can do this thing, you are the one.'* "

Siri threw up hands. "What could I say to that? So, I took the sacred dagger Namara offered me and went out to put a god who cannot die back into the grave."

11

"A sword may cut smoke, but it can never slay it. Steel cannot kill that which is already dead, and smoke is nothing more than the ghost of fire's victims," Siri said. "I could see no way to kill a buried god.

"But I had been assigned to do just that . . . and damn me if I didn't succeed. But that's a story you've heard more times than I'm sure you'd care to count. So, let me skip ahead to the aftermath."

She turned to look at Faran. "You were prevented from completing your training, so you haven't had the experience of the goddess giving you the dagger we call Namara's eye."

Faran shrugged. "No, but I've seen them and I never figured there was all that much to it. Take the eye, kill the target, use it to pin a list of the target's crimes to their chest. Seems simple enough."

"Yes and no. The goddess sealed each eye to the soul of the Blade she assigned the task, and consecrated it to the death of the target. It was nothing like the kind of power she invested in our swords, but there *was* god-magic involved and it did tie each dagger irrevocably to the wielder. Which is where things started to go wrong. When I pinned Namara's list of the fallen god's crimes to his chest, I set steel to the heart of smoke, steel tied to my very soul.

"At first, there were no ill effects. I put the god back in his tomb with my knife in his heart. Then I returned to the temple where Namara made me First Blade, replacing Aral."

Siri looked at me with a question in her eyes, but I just shrugged. "It never bothered me, Siri. I might have slain a king, but you killed a legend. Besides, Namara wished it. Despite anything the goddess might have told you at the time about her own lack of clarity, I had never had the slightest doubt that every choice she made was the right one."

"And now?" Siri asked me.

"I don't know. If you had told me this story before the fall of the temple, and I had believed you . . . it probably would have broken me. Since then, I've had to make a lot of difficult choices. I held the life of the Son of Heaven in my hands, and I walked away without taking it. I set out to kill Thauvik, knowing it might start a war that would kill more people than his death might save. I believe that I did the right thing both times, but I don't *know* it. The idea that Namara didn't *know* either . . . I'm not sure whether I find that terrifying or reassuring at this point."

Siri smiled. "You *have* changed, Aral. More than I would have believed possible."

I smiled a sad sort of smile. "My entire world was founded in the rock of Namara's temple. When she died, my world shattered and I shattered with it. The Aral you knew died that day. The new Aral . . . Hell, I don't even wear the same face as the old version."

"I wondered about that. I heard that you had changed your face, but I didn't fully believe it until I saw you through my smoke avatar. It's a stunning bit of magic, and I wouldn't have believed it was possible if I hadn't seen the results. I'd love to learn it sometime, if it can be taught."

"It's called the bonewright and I wouldn't recommend the process. It involves reshaping the bones of your face while you're wide-awake, and doing so without any sort of numbing. I wouldn't have attempted it if my need had been one shred less dire. It very nearly killed me."

"But it worked," said Siri.

"Yes, and I think I could manage it again now, having done so once. But I would have to be *very* desperate to try it."

You would also have to convince me, sent Triss. *That would be . . . difficult, if not impossible.*

"If we live through this, I would like you to teach it to me," said Siri.

I nodded. "As you wish." Namara might be gone, but Siri would ever and always be First Blade. I owed her whatever she asked of me.

Faran leaned forward. "Speaking of living through this, could we get back to the part where you were explaining exactly what 'this' is?"

Siri laughed. "The surest sign you're getting older is that the young grow impatient with your digressions and remembrances. A few weeks after Namara made me First Blade, I woke in the middle of the night with a coughing fit. I figured it was some aftereffect of all the smoke I'd breathed in during my fight with the buried god, but within the hour Namara summoned me to her island.

" 'I think that I have made a grave mistake, daughter.'

" 'What do you mean?' I asked.

" 'I heard you coughing in the night.'

" 'It's nothing.'

" 'It *is the buried god. I should never have given you an eye for him. That tool was grossly insufficient to the task, and the nature of it is already causing its slow but inevitable failure to rebound on you. I will have to take steps to freeze the effects it is having on you.'*

" 'I don't understand.'

" 'Let me show you.'

"She touched a finger to my chest, and I found myself coughing again—coughing up pale smoke. Before—in the darkness of my room—I hadn't been able to see that. Its wispy nature had prevented Kyrissa from noticing it either. 'What's going on?' I asked.

" 'The Durkoth call the one that you have returned to the tomb the Fire That Burns Underground. Though his greatest power lies in smoke, it rises from the flames within. The smoldering fire of his body is consuming the blade that pins him in his tomb. The steel burns. Imbued as it is with my power, it* *burns slowly, but it* does *burn. Because it is sealed to your soul, that burning echoes back through you.'*

" 'Will it kill me? Or . . . worse? How quickly will it work its magic?' I was worried, of course. But losing my life in the service of the goddess was how I had always expected to die, and I was nowhere near as frightened as I should have been.

" *'Nothing so horrible, daughter. Now that I know what is happening, I will protect you from the effects. I do not think it would kill you, even if I did nothing. But it might . . . infect you with something of the god. Whether you would simply take on some of his nature and powers, or become a sort of avatar of the Smoldering Flame, I cannot say.*

" *'I should have crafted a better remedy for him than I did. What a Blade's sword can slay, it may also lay to rest. Your efforts demonstrated the first, but I did not think ahead to the second. I would have to forge a sword just for him, unbound to any wielder to properly blunt the effects of his power on the one who put him back in his tomb, but that is what I ought to have done.'*

"The goddess touched me on the forehead and told me that she had taken care of the problem. Then she sent me back to my rooms to sleep. As the years went by, I mostly forgot about it. . . ." Siri trailed off.

"But then Namara died," I said.

She nodded. "Then Namara died. I knew the temple had fallen before I ever heard the story or saw the ruins. I knew it in the instant that Namara's fellows murdered her, because I felt it here." Siri touched her chest. "I coughed up smoke for three days after the death of the goddess. When it finally ended I had the first wisps braiding themselves through my hair and Kyrissa's wings had fledged. Not long after that I came south looking for answers and hoping for help."

"How'd that work out for you?" Faran asked, her tone a shadow's breadth shy of insolent.

I gave her a quelling look, but let it pass otherwise.

"You'll have the chance to judge for yourselves," replied Siri. "Tomorrow morning we ride for the castle of Ashkent Kelreven and his lady, Kayla Nel Kaledren—called Kayla Darkvelyn by the Sylvani. He is a high lord of the empire, and the only other living soul who has laid one of the buried gods unwilling in the tomb. She's a duchess of the Kreyn and fifth in line for the Oaken Throne."

"Kreyn?" I asked.

Siri nodded. "From within, the Sylvani Empire looks much less the monolith it does from without. In addition to the obvious exception of the Asavi, the First here are divided into many peoples. After the Sylvani, the greatest of those are the Tolar nomads, and the Kreyn who claim the mantle First of the First and that all the rest spring from their line."

I gave Siri a sharp look. "I'm a bit surprised at how much respect you're giving those titles, Siri. I didn't think you held the nobility in any higher esteem than I do."

Siri snorted and then grinned. "Ahh, now, there's the old Aral. I'd begun to think you'd left him behind completely. But there he is, as angry at all the lords and ladies as if he was fresh minted in the service of justice. It's not the *titles* that makes me respect Ash and Kayla—though those can come in mighty handy on this side of the wall—it's what they've done that makes them exceptional. Or, did you miss the part where I said that Ash was a Mythkiller, too?"

"And this Kayla?"

"She's the best mage I've ever met, bar none. Her absolute power is limited by the conditions the gods imposed on all of the First when they bound them to the earth of the empire. But she has more skill at spellcraft than I could hope to achieve if I lived ten thousand years."

"One more question," I said. "What did Kelos want your help for?"

"I was wondering when you were going to get to that," replied Siri. "How much do you know about the godwar?"

"Which version? Kelos made sure that I didn't take Heaven's story at face value, but I didn't care enough about the subject to learn more than the most basic take on Namara's side of things. The First and their lore never interested me."

"Does the name Sylvaras ring any bells?"

"First emperor of the Sylvain?" I hazarded.

"That, too. He was probably the most powerful sorcerer who ever lived. And, depending on who's telling the story, either the greatest traitor in the history of the First or the savior of the world. Sometimes both."

I held up a hand as a vague memory tickled the back of my brain. "Wait, something-something, died alongside the first Sovereign Emperor of Heaven in the final battle of the godwar-something?"

Faran interjected, "The Goodvelyn?"

"That's it," said Siri. "On our side of the wall, the story always has the buried gods threatening the very existence of the world if they don't get their way and the Emperor of Heaven sacrificing his life to save the world and bind the Others. Sometimes it's mentioned that a few of the Others helped out the true gods and died in the final battle. When they tell it that way among the First, Sylvaras is the leader of the traitors who bargained away the future of the First to end the war with Heaven. That one's popular among the Durkoth, the Asavi, and Vesh'An, though the Sylvani don't much like it."

"I take it the Sylvani write the story another way?" I asked.

"They do. In their version it's the Emperor of Heaven who threatened to end the world if he lost. And Sylvaras who sacrificed himself in order to break the power of the buried ones and save the world."

"How did the Emperor of Heaven die, in that version?"

"His fellow gods offered him the choice of an honorable suicide or a dishonorable abdication and interment with the buried gods."

"And this all has *what* to do with Kelos?" I prompted.

"In the version where Sylvaras is the hero, the true gods tried to bring him back from death so that he could join the ranks of Heaven and heal the rift with the First."

"The lords of judgment never give up the dead," I said flatly. "Once you've passed through the final gate you *must* go on to the wheel of rebirth. Everyone knows that."

"I agree with you," said Siri. "And the simple fact that Sylvaras never returned would seem proof absolute. But there's a thread of the legend that says the gods made a key for the final gate in honor of Sylvaras's sacrifice, a key that could only be used once, and only to resurrect a god."

I could suddenly see where this was going and it left me with a horrible cold feeling in my gut. "And, Kelos believes in this key. He thinks that he can use it to bring Namara back and reset the clock on his treason."

"That's not exactly how he put it, but yes, that's what it sounds like he wants to attempt." She frowned. "There was a lot about the history of the key in what he told me that I'd never heard before. He knew things that the rest of the world has long since forgotten. Do you think he could actually do it?"

Aral, are you all right? Triss asked me.

No.

"It can't work," I said aloud. I felt such a horror at the very idea of trying it that I couldn't even begin to express it. "Not even if the key is real. Turning back the wheel of rebirth would upset the foundational order of the world. I feel it in my soul. I don't know what we'd get if we tried it, but I don't think it would be Namara."

"That's what I've always thought, but . . ." Siri trailed off and shook her head. "I could have killed Kelos, but I knew there were things he wasn't telling me, critically important things. Where he believes the key is, for starters. Far more worrisome is the source of his information. Aral, I don't know where all the things he talked about ultimately originated, but they came *through* the Son of Heaven. That bastard knows everything Kelos does. Maybe more."

Another punch in the gut. "I wish I could say that surprised me. I don't want to interrupt the flow of this but, remind me to tell you about the Kitsune and what I learned from her about Kelos and the Son of Heaven."

"So, you really did meet the Kitsune?" asked Siri.

"I did, and she's dead now, but we can talk about that later."

"Right. Kelos told me the Son was putting together an expedition to recover the key for him, though he wouldn't tell me how he knew that or what the Son thought he could use it for. Kelos said that he was doing what he could to slow the Son down, but that he couldn't delay things more than a couple of months at the most."

"It sounds like he still has connections within Heaven's Shadow," said Triss. He turned to Siri. "That's what the Son calls Blades that went over to him after the fall."

She nodded. "It was obvious there was a lot more going on under the surface than some mad scheme to get Namara back. That more than anything is why I let Kelos walk away. Whatever he's plotting I was afraid it wouldn't die with him. That's part of the reason I reached out to you. He told me something about your last meeting in Heaven's Reach. He loves you like a son, Aral. If there's anyone who can get him to open up, it's you."

I rubbed my forehead. "Things would be simpler if you'd killed him. You know that, right?"

"Could *you* have killed him?" asked Siri. When I didn't answer she added, "He was *my* master, too—the father I found when the temple took me away from my parents."

"I know." I found myself with a sudden and terrible desire to ask Siri if she had any efik, or, failing that, to simply call down the stairs for that bottle of house red I'd turned down earlier. It had been a while since the cravings hit me so hard, and I bit my cheek by way of distraction.

"Aral." Faran touched me on the shoulder—I hadn't even noticed her moving. "You're shaking. Are you all right?"

"It's nothing."

There was no disguising how I felt from Triss, though, and he suddenly blurted out, "Faran, you mentioned the Goodvelyn. And, Siri, you called this Kayla, Darkvelyn. Is there some relationship?"

It was a clumsy attempt at changing the subject, but I appreciated it and sent a silent wave of love and gratitude flowing down the link between us once the first shock of need faded.

Siri looked at me worriedly, but nodded to Triss. "Yes, there is. 'Velyn' is a Sylvani word that describes the First. We don't have anything quite like it for ourselves, though 'human' probably comes closest."

"I see where you'd get Goodvelyn," said Faran. "But Darkvelyn sounds kind of negative."

"It is," replied Siri. "The Kreyn still live in the ancient forests like the ancestors of the First, making their homes in giant trees or natural caverns. The Kreyn *hate* Sylvani-style cities, and most of them won't use steel or farm with plows that break the earth. In turn, the Sylvani think of the Kreyn as primitive and uncivilized, barbaric even—hence darkvelyn. They used to want to force them into the empire proper."

"Used to?" As the craving eased a bit, I forced myself to look for more distraction. "What happened?"

"The Sylvani lost three or four wars in a row and gave it up as a bad job. The Kreyn are deadly fighters and some of the best mages among the First."

"So, how did this Kayla end up with Ashkent, then?" Faran asked. "I thought you said he was a High Lord of the Sylvani. . . ."

Siri grinned. "I asked her that myself once."

"And?" demanded Faran.

"She smiled, and said, 'Love is passing strange.' Then she went back to working on a tricky little death spell she'd been composing. I've never gotten another word out of her on the subject. But, I've talked enough for a while. It's your turn."

Siri looked at me. "Aral, I want to hear about the Kitsune at some point. And, Faran, I definitely want to learn about what you've done since the fall of the temple. Especially, how you came into Aral's care. But first, Jax, Devin, Malora, Kaman, Loris . . . what can you tell me about the order?"

"What do you know already?" I asked. "You've clearly got some good sources."

"Pretend I don't know anything. News of the human lands is hard to come by here, and I know that a good deal of what I hear is lies. Until very recently I thought Devin and Kelos had died with the goddess. Oh, and I heard that you'd killed Kaman, but that can't be right."

I looked away from Siri. "It is. He was close to dying already and more than half-mad from torture—they'd crucified him and staked Ussiriss out in the sun. I offered to try to free them, but he begged for death instead. If it happened now, I don't know what my answer would be, but at the time I more than half wanted to die myself. I gave him what he asked for."

"Oh, Aral, I'm sorry." Siri put her hand on my cheek, but I didn't look at her.

"Jax and Loris started a school for the novices and journeymen among the survivors," said Triss. "Those they could find, anyway. Loris has since gone to the lords of judgment—he died in a battle we fought with the Son of Heaven's forces—but Jax continues the work. Faran can tell you more about that. She studied at the school for a while."

"Only because I was too badly injured to do anything about

it when you ditched me there," she grumbled. "Well, really it wasn't so bad. But after years of taking care of myself it felt like getting sent back to train with the children."

"And Devin . . ." Siri trailed off.

"Is working for the Son of Heaven," I said. "But you must know that if you know he's alive. His name was put up among the fallen, as were all who went over to the Shadow."

"Tell me about that."

So I did, and many more things as well. Faran left us by the fire after an hour. I could tell by the way she rubbed at her scars as she walked away that she had one of her headaches coming on, though she didn't speak of it.

Later, after we had talked ourselves out, Siri followed me up the second set of stairs to my room. She went through the door first, slipping her shirt off as she did so. As usual when the possibility of human sexual activity came up, Triss slid deep down into my shadow and pretended to ignore me. Whether that was for my privacy's sake or simply because the act bored him, I couldn't say.

Siri wasn't wearing anything under her shirt, and she was as lovely as ever, but I found myself hesitating on the threshold. Unless I'd lost all facility at reading her, she'd given no signals nor slightest intimation that she wanted to bed me.

"It's been a long time," I said. "And, you haven't exactly been flirty tonight. Are you sure you want to do this?"

She smiled and stepped in close, putting her hands on my hips. "Very."

"But . . ."

"Ah, and there's the new Aral again. I don't think you ever hesitated for so much as an instant when I offered to take you to my bed back in our temple days. Well, except for that year when you and Jax were engaged. You went all boring and monogamous there for a while."

I couldn't help but grin at her tone and the memories of times we'd shared a bed in the past. But I still didn't cross the threshold. "True enough, but you always seemed more interested then."

"That's a lie, and we both know it. Yes, I've been focused tonight, but I've *always* focused when there was work to be done. Think back to the training grounds. When we were fencing did I ever once let it slip that I was going to tumble you after a match?"

"Well, no, but that's different. You were always serious when you had to be, but tonight we were just talking, and . . ." She raised a sardonic eyebrow at me and I ground to a halt. "Oh. Right. Tonight we were sharing information on the eve of a war, weren't we?"

"Exactly," said Siri. "From now until this thing with the Key of Sylvaras is resolved, we are on a mission. Of course that's going to be my focus."

"So, why this?" I ran my hands up her ribs to cup her breasts. "Normally you've no interest in mixing pleasure with business."

"Aral, I love you. Not in a husband and wife sort of way. That's never going to be my thing, despite our present circumstance. But you are one of my oldest and dearest friends in all the world, and I enjoy bedding you. Isn't that enough?"

I shook my head. "That's not all there is to this. If it was, you wouldn't be mucking around with sex at the opening of a mission."

"I think I liked the old Aral better, at least where it came to getting you into bed. It was sooo much simpler." She sighed. "All right. No, it's *not* all there is to it." She reached out and touched the smoke ring on my finger. "That's a wedding ring."

"Yeah, I got that part."

"You're not going to make this easy for me, are you?"

"Which part? Getting me into bed? Or explaining why?" I winked at her and she growled low in her throat, but then she laughed.

"Fine. Marriage is one of the deep magics." She touched the ring again and then raised her hand to show me the matching one there. "These bind us together in a way that simultaneously allows me special access to you while giving you certain protections from the buried god that has become a part of me. For the moment, with the god still in his tomb, those protections don't matter all that much, while the access does. But, if things change suddenly, your ring may be the only thing that can save you from him . . . or . . . me."

"Are you saying you're not fully in control of yourself?"

"I honestly don't know. I think it's all me in here." She

touched the side of her head. "But with the smoke braided through my very soul, I can't *know* that. That ring on your finger is one of my insurance policies."

"And taking me to bed?"

"The deep magics don't just happen. If a ring is going to mean anything, should the time come, we actually have to *be* married."

"So, tonight is by way of completing the ritual." *That* definitely took some of the shine off the idea.

Siri rolled her eyes. "No."

"No?" I was confused.

"There is no *completing* the ritual. It's not one and done. It's a marriage. Both symbolically." She touched her ring to mine. "And, more . . . practically." Her voice dropped huskily as she reached down and slid her pants over her hips. Stepping out of them, she stood completely naked before me.

I couldn't help but notice a change. "Uh . . ."

"I shaved. Wherever I have hair, the smoke is. I didn't want that coming between us. Now, are you going to come in here and take me to bed like a gentleman? Or am I going to have to resort to wicked enticements?" She gave a whole-body shimmy that made my heart jump into my throat.

I swallowed hard. "Now, that sounded a lot more like the Siri who used to take me to bed. Less ritual magic, more lust."

"All right, enticements it is." She pressed herself tight to my chest and then slowly slid down my body. "Oh, there's a magic to this, all right, but never doubt the lust. I didn't have to choose *this* way to tie us together. But it's a lot more fun than any of the alternatives." She did something creative then, and I felt my knees go spongy. "Don't you think?"

"I do."

"It's about damn time you said that."

12

————◆————

There is no word for returning from that place that lies beyond longing, the place your heart goes when it finally understands that you can never go home again.

I have spent my entire adult life a hunted man. The very first thing I did on becoming a Blade in full was to kill a king. Since that moment there has never not been a price on my head. The only place in the whole world that didn't hold true was the Temple of Namara. It was the only place I could feel entirely safe and at home. When the temple fell, I entered a land beyond homesick, a place where the very idea of home could never be anything more than a dream. At least, that's what I had believed for eight long years.

But then I woke up in Siri's arms, and for the first time since the fall of the temple, I knew I was home.

It hurt.

It hurt like having an arrow pulled out of your heart might hurt if it were possible to live through such a thing.

It hurt like only healing can.

I wanted to cry. I wanted to sing. I wanted the pain to last a thousand years. But even as I clutched at the joyous ache of homecoming and tried to draw it tighter to me, it started to slip away. I might be at home in my heart, but I was still a-sea in my head.

Let me take a step back. I woke in a feather bed, with Siri's head pillowed on my chest. I had been here before. Not in this bed perhaps, but in this position with this woman whom I loved as a friend and honored as my sword-sworn sister in the service of Namara. That was familiar, and I treasured it, but that wasn't where the feeling of homecoming originated. This wasn't a thing of memory. It lay deeper than that, in the blood, and the bone, and the soul.

The moment didn't create the feeling. The feeling informed the moment. I could sense the awareness of home somewhere deep inside me, like a spring of clear water bubbling invisibly away at the bottom of the lake it feeds. It was wonderful, and I wanted nothing more than to let it fill me with peace and contentment, but I *couldn't*. Not without questioning the source.

When you spend your whole life training to kill by stealth, you spend your whole life learning all the ways that stealth can kill you. The blade in the back, the poison in the chalice, the spell striking from shadows. You learn that the easiest time to kill someone is when they are happiest. Happy people inhabit the moment. They don't want to question what lies beneath or beyond, and that makes them vulnerable. I had been taught to *always* question those things. Instead of simply lying back and savoring my happiness I started digging away at the place inside me where I felt the happiest. I couldn't not.

I didn't have much luck at first. How do you search inside your own heart? But then I started thinking about where I was and what had happened in the last few hours. I ran through each and every moment in my head. That's where I found it. In a single, simple word. *Married*. Thinking it made my heart thrum like the strings of a harp.

That's when I knew what the feeling meant and where it originated. It was that deep magic Siri had talked about the night before. I *wanted* it to be a thing of hearth and home and heart. I wanted it desperately. How could I not? But I recognized that wanting didn't make it true. I loved Siri. Always had, always would, but never in that truly-madly-deeply way of the joyously wedded. I might not have recognized the strangeness

of this sudden absolute sense that Siri represented home if I hadn't almost married Jax.

You see, I had tried truly-madly-deeply with Jax. It was wonderful and wild and it had shattered into a thousand tiny pieces somewhere along the line. I knew how it felt when a deep love built from within. This was something different.

God-magic, Triss said into my mind.

What? I was startled to have him answer a question I hadn't asked.

It's been there since you accepted the ring, though I couldn't feel it as much more than an itching of the soul at the time. It was too tenuous then. When the Durkoth talked about your ring speaking to Siri's through the deep ways, I knew the connection had to be there, though I couldn't find anything when I went sniffing after it. But when you and Siri consummated your marriage, it began to build into something I could sense. It's grown steadily all night. I felt it peak in the moments right after you woke this morning. Then it dropped off a bit. It's holding more or less steady now.

You've been listening to my thoughts? That was new.

No. I can hear them sometimes when you dream, or occasionally when you're really focused on figuring something out. But I think that's mostly because you're sort of talking to yourself as you do it—thinking in words that spill over into our link.

So how did you know what I was thinking about just now?

I didn't. Still don't, for that matter. But I could feel you focusing your attention on the channel of energy that runs between you and Siri now. I've been watching it closely ever since I finally identified it last night. When you started to poke at it, too, I figured I'd let you know what I had learned. Which is that it's god-magic. Well, no. The connection isn't only god-magic, but there's god-magic all through it. It tastes of smoke and charcoal.

The Fire That Burns Underground, I sent.

That part of him that is expressed through Siri at any rate. I think that the connection between the two of you would exist even without the god's presence within her reinforcing it, but the thing would be different. Gentler, quieter, more natural.

"Aral?" Siri raised her head from my chest. "What's that buzzing sound in my mind?"

"Buzzing sound?" I was confused.

"Yeah, like hearing a faint conversation in another room. Only, when I try to listen in, it sounds like some language I can recognize but don't actually speak. But the whole thing is happening inside my head. It's *very* strange."

Do you think she can she hear us now? asked Triss.

Kyrissa suddenly lifted up out of Siri's shadow—a sort of hybrid pool of smoke and darkness that I hadn't really thought about until it took on the familiar shape of the winged serpent. "It's Triss." She twisted her head this way and that, like she was trying to catch a distant sound. "They speak mind-to-mind."

"They what?!" Siri sat up, spilling the silken sheet that had half covered her into my lap. "Aral, is that true?"

"Uh . . . yeah, it is. I guess I neglected to mention it. Huh." Our ability was unique among Blade/Shade pairings—a result of actions Triss had taken to save my life when the bonewright spell went horribly wrong.

Siri gave me a very hard look. "Yes. You did. Why is that?"

It was a thing that Triss and I hadn't shared with anyone, though Faran had guessed it. "I . . . I don't really know." Though, a moment's thought told me it was mostly a matter of a lifetime's habit of always keeping a knife or two hidden up my sleeves.

"You don't fully trust me." Siri's words came out flat and even—a statement, not a question.

I couldn't really argue with her. Many familiars could speak mind-to-mind with their mages. Because of that, most people wouldn't rule out such a thing happening between Triss and me. But Siri was a Blade. Every Blade *knew* that Shades and their Blade partners couldn't do what we did. If it was a hidden knife, it was one that could best be used against another Blade.

I opened my mouth to try to explain, but Siri cut in before I could start. "Don't. It's fine. You *shouldn't* fully trust me." She touched a finger to the smoke in her hair. "This means that *I* don't fully trust me. I'm not mad at you."

Through the link that we now shared I could feel that she was telling the truth. A painful silence opened up between us even so.

I'm sorry, sent Triss. *If I'd known they would hear us, I'd have kept quiet.*

It's all right, Triss. I'm not upset.

"Aha," said Kyrissa. "*There* it is."

A moment later, I felt an odd sort of buzzing sensation in my head, like someone speaking in another room of my mind. Siri nodded then, and I realized Triss and I were no longer unique in our ability to speak silently.

"Deep magic indeed," I said.

The buzzing continued as Siri nodded at me. "That is . . . unexpected. And . . . lovely." A tear suddenly appeared at the corner of her eye. "Thank you, Aral."

She leaned in to give me a kiss. We might well have proceeded to other things from there had we not been interrupted by a harsh metallic pounding somewhere below.

"What's that?" I asked.

"The gate to the tower, I think." Siri rolled out of bed and reached for her swords.

A clear inhuman voice yelled, "Open in the name of the empire!" The shout was followed by a tremendous crash, like someone trying to smash the gate open.

I had a moment to worry about Faran, but there wasn't a hell of a lot I could do about it, so I pushed it aside.

"Oh, hell." Siri vanished into shadow . . . and smoke.

The strangeness of what happened then caused me to freeze for an instant as I tried to sort out exactly what I was seeing. The smoke of the god had touched Siri's shroud as deeply as it had the rest of her. Normally, the effect produces a hole in your vision, a place where you simply can't see *anything*. If you don't know to look for the place you can't see, your brain sort of refuses to believe it's there and jumps over it without registering its existence.

But with Siri, the blind spot had become something fuzzier. If I looked directly at where I knew she had to be, I could dimly see through the hole in my vision to the table on the other side of her, as if she weren't entirely in our world. I suspected that it would make her much harder to spot than a normal shroud would, especially at night.

Aral! Triss yelled into my mind.

Right. Worry about it later. Shroud me up.

Darkness enveloped me as I rolled out of bed. I scooped up my sword rig as I went, and I already had my arms through the shoulder loops by the time my feet touched the floor. I landed in a crouch, fastening the harness's chest strap with one hand while I used the other to check the position of my hilts. It was just like a thousand practice sessions.

I could practically hear Master Kelos running through the drill in the back of my mind. *Shroud first. Then sword rig. Shroud, swords, sheaths! Pants if you have time. Boots even if you don't. That'll give you two more knives, and you don't want to run the rooftops barefoot if you can avoid it. Nor the jungle either, for that matter. Wrist sheaths if you were dumb enough to sleep bare. That's all your steel. Trick bag should be attached to your sword rig before you go to sleep. If not, grab the bag, idiot! Still have time? Cowl, pack, poncho, and move! Move! MOVE!*

Another metallic clang came from the gate below as I pulled on my pants, but it didn't give. That meant I had time, so I grabbed the lot. I even snagged my shirt off the back of the chair and tucked it into my straps as I heard the gate finally crash open. It *should* have been tucked through the straps holding my trick bag to my rig, but I'd been sloppy last night.

Siri was as well, leaving her clothes where they'd fallen just inside the doorway, and I spared a brief thought to wonder whether she'd had the time to grab everything. It wouldn't slow her up if she didn't—like most female Blades she was small breasted. Even if she weren't, the women's version of the sword rig supplied a bit of support for those who needed it.

The blind spot that was Siri slid into position on the hinge side of the door. Ours was a small half circle of a room with the morning sun peering in through a high barred window on the northeastern wall. Intense golden light spilled across the lower half of the bed and a big patch of floor. That left me the top of the wardrobe as the only halfway decently shaded spot where someone charging into the room wouldn't immediately bump into me.

"Fight?" I asked quietly as armored boots came pounding up the stairs from the suite's sitting room below.

"Not if we don't have to. They're the buried god's enemies, not mine. Will Faran be—"

Before she could finish her question and a bare heartbeat

after I'd pulled myself up out of the way, the door burst asunder with a flash that blasted a loose cloud of shattered wood into the room. I tensed, ready to pounce on intruders or to vault over them as circumstance demanded. But whoever was out there, they decided not to rush in blind.

Instead, a cautious voice called, "We've got a god-sniffer. We know you're in there . . . whatever you are. If you surrender gracefully, we won't have to take drastic acti—urghk!" The words ended in a sudden moist gurgle that told me Faran had run out of patience.

A second voice cried out a split second later, "Mother of—aghhs!"

Then a third. "Fuck, fuck, fuck! I can't see what—gack!" The distinct sounds of a body falling down a flight of stairs followed. Then silence.

Shadow blotted out the doorway, visible through Triss's senses in a way my eyes never could have perceived it. Faran.

"Come on through to my room," she said quietly. "I forced a window. Hurry! I've cleared the stairs, but there might be more below." The shadow vanished.

Siri's blurrier presence occluded the door a moment later as I dropped to the floor. "Dead. All of them. Is she always like that?"

I crossed to the door as Siri moved into the hall. "Efficiently ruthless and cheerful about it?"

"That."

"Yes." I stepped over the first of the bodies, a tall Sylvani woman with her throat slit. Beyond her another Sylvani slumped against the wall—male this time, but likewise with a slit throat. The—presumably dead—owner of the third voice was somewhere out of sight around the curve of the spiral stair.

"Huh," said Siri. "I think I'm going to like this girl."

"I rather thought you might." I bent and tore the small crest free of the first corpse's short cape for later examination—Triss's senses didn't lend themselves to the finer points of reading heraldry. Then I stepped over the body and moved on.

Faran's door was open, the room beyond it empty. The bars of the southwestern window lay on the floor, and the glass was broken out. The window briefly wavered and fuzzed out as Siri went through. I followed her a moment later, dropping ten feet to land on the roof of the common room. My thigh twinged a bit, but the older injuries in calf and knee seemed to have pretty well healed.

"Now what?" Faran asked. "Do we collect the horses?"

"No, let's head westward along the rooftops for now," I said, suiting action to words. "Even if there aren't more soldiers below, we might have to kill some of the stable hands. I think we've already made enough unnecessary corpses for one day, don't you?"

"Aral." Siri's voice came out soft but cold as she followed me along the roof. "Don't second-guess the girl. This wasn't the way I intended to play that scene, but you weren't in her position, so you can't know if she had any choice in the matter."

I nodded, though no one could see me. "Point. Faran?"

"I don't know. That first woman had a big rod thing she was aiming into your room—looked like some kind of heavy-duty magical siege equipment maybe."

"See?" Siri said rather smugly. Then, "Sounds like you made the right call, Faran. Well done."

"Thanks . . . but, don't get me wrong. I was planning on killing them all before I ever saw the rod."

I repressed a petty urge to tell Siri "See?" in the same smug tone she had used on me.

"You were?" Siri asked Faran.

"Anyone blasting in the doors of the place I'm sleeping is an enemy. Especially when I'm having one of my headaches and they make so much noise about it—I thought the top of my skull was going to come off when they smashed your door. I popped mine open as soon as I heard them pounding up the first set of stairs. One of them stuck a nose in my room, but I was shrouded up and they moved straight on to yours. I was less than five feet away when they hit it with a burst from that rod. Damn, but that was loud. *And*, the flash hurt Ssithra."

"How bad is your head?" I asked.

There was a long pause. "Bad. Ever since they blew out your door I've had a fucking bolt of rainbow lightning running right across the center of my vision. It feels like someone's trying to shove a hot iron ball through the side of my skull. It wasn't great before that, but after . . . Damn!"

"Can you run?" If the Sylvani who'd broken in the door

really were imperial officials of some sort, we probably needed to pick up the pace.

"Won't be much fun, but yeah. Just try to keep up, old man." Then she blurred past me.

The morning sun made it easier to keep track of my companions' shrouds but harder to maintain my own. Triss remained mostly dormant in the face of the intense light. I had to constantly feed nima into it to fight against the abrading power of the sun and I could feel it drawing down the well of my soul all too quickly. Two miles and a quarter of an hour later, I knew that if I didn't release my shroud soon I was going to keel over. I hated sunrunning.

"Can't keep this up much longer," I panted as we dropped into the shade of a broad chimney to take a brief rest. "Sun's way too fierce, even if it is cooler on this side of the wall than in the human lands."

Faran dropped her shroud then and pressed her forehead to her knees. "Feels like my head's gonna come apart."

I released my own shroud as I reached over to lay a hand on her shoulder. "There hasn't been any obvious sign of pursuit. We can stop here for a bit and let you recover."

Siri stepped out of shadow and knelt in front of us. She looked as fresh as if she'd just climbed out of bed after a long night's sleep—though whether that was due to her own reserves or additional protection provided by the god I couldn't say.

"Aral's right. You need a break." Siri caught my eyes. "I think it might be best if we split up for a while. The Sylvani mentioned a god-sniffer, which means it's me they're really looking for. If they've another, there's no good way for me to shake them off afoot, and I'll be a risk to you as long we're together."

"You know more about the way things work on this side of the wall than I do." I wasn't entirely convinced about splitting up, but it was Siri's call, and I wouldn't argue. "Which reminds me, what's a *god-sniffer*?"

"It's a who, not a what. After the godwar the Sylvani didn't want to have anything more to do with any kind of gods ever, so they created a sort of imperial anti-religion, the nuliphate. Initially there wasn't much to it, but the buried gods do not rest easy in their prison-graves. They have enormous power still and most of them have cult followings of one degree or another. When they started to reach beyond the bounds of their tombs and draw cultic followings, the emperor created the office of the disquisition to investigate and deal with the problem of the cultists and merged it with the nuliphate."

"And the god-sniffers?" I prompted.

"I was getting there. They're a suborder within the disquisition—Sylvani mages who've attuned themselves to the magical signature of the buried gods. They can suss out the presence of even very minor manifestations of the buried ones. They can also track them over short to medium distances when the trail is fresh enough."

"That doesn't sound good." I suddenly remembered the badge I'd taken from the corpse and pulled it out. "I picked this off one of our late visitors. Let's see if it has anything to tell us."

It was a disk of translucent crystal an inch and a half across. The outer edge was a sort of dusty rose that glowed faintly from within. The stark outline of a leafless tree was etched into the surface of the facing side. It stood on a low hill in front of a westering sun, likewise faintly glowing. I recognized the lowering sun as an emblem of the Syvani emperor, but the tree . . .

"What's this symbol?"

"That's the emblem of the disquisition. It's a dead grave tree. The Sylvani plant them over the burial places of their fallen in the way we might put up a stone. Normally, they're shown thick with leaves to symbolize the continuation of life in the face of death. They're incredibly hardy and long lived—ten thousand years or more. But every single one of them that stands on the grave of a buried god died within a century of being planted."

Siri took the badge from me. "There are three shield pips here on the lower left." She shook her head. "This belonged to a hierarch of the disquisition, one of their senior anti-priests. If there isn't another god-sniffer close at hand already, there will be soon. We definitely need to split up."

"Won't they scent this?" I held up my wedding ring.

"Surely, but it's a paltry thing compared to the god reek I trail around these days. They'll see me as the greater threat. Besides, you can cross over to the human side of the wall where they can't follow you."

"Why can't we all just do that?"

She touched her hair. "I can't cross the wall either. Not at the moment, at least. My divine infection has grown too intense to pass the ward."

"What will you do when they catch up to you?" I asked.

"They won't. Once I've drawn them out of the area, I'll light a fire and 'poof.' Being able to vanish in a puff of smoke comes in very handy."

"It would. All right. All right, I don't like it, but I see the need. Where should we meet you?"

"Head west for another fifty miles along the wall, then turn south. Give me five days, then light a fire and smother it. I'll find you."

Before I could argue or ask any more questions, she shrouded up and vanished.

"Faran, are you ready to move?"

She didn't lift her head. "No, not really, but I can if I must." She pushed herself to her feet, took a step, staggered, and barely stayed upright. "I don't think I have the will left to hold Ssithra in shroud form."

That was a problem. As long as we stayed in the sun, the Shades would have a terrible time of it no matter how much of our nima we fed them. Triss was older and more experienced than Ssithra and I doubted his ability to maintain himself in shroud form under the circumstances—a big part of why I was running things at the moment. If Faran couldn't hold the shroud herself . . . We had to get out of the sun, and we had to do it now.

"Can you clear the wall?" I pointed to the narrow street that ran down the center of the thousand-mile city.

"Eight feet?" Faran snorted. "With one broken leg, and a blindfold. If that ever changes, cut my throat and leave me for dog food."

"Then we're going to take Siri's suggestion and jump back to the human side of things. There are woodlands over there. We'll be visible on the way, but Triss and Ssithra should be able to keep us out of sight once we're mostly in shadow again. That should keep us out of the hands of any human allies the disquisition might send to our side of the wall."

Siri had said that no one would follow us there, but I'd spent too many years running from the authorities to take anyone's word on something like that.

"Anything this time?" Faran was flat on her back with a wet cloth draped across her eyes as she had been for most of the past three days. The Sylvani blasting rod had triggered the worst round of headaches she'd had since starting her treatments with Shang and Harad.

I stared at the spiral of smoke climbing up from my freshly extinguished fire. "Nothing." It was now ten days on from when we'd left Siri. "But the wedding ring's still happily smoking away. I expect something would have changed there if she'd been killed or the disquisition had taken her prisoner. They'd have to have ways of shutting down god-magic if that's their primary mission. She's probably fine." Yeah, right.

"Maybe. Or maybe you're married to the god directly now instead of at one remove. This side of the wall, he's bound to have a lot more power over you."

"Cheery thought, that. Thanks."

Faran didn't answer me.

I'm sure it'll be fine, sent Triss. *Siri can take care of herself.*

I hope you're right.

13

———◆———

The voice of a god speaking in your heart can never be forgotten. The silencing of your god can never be forgiven.

The latter truth came home to me with a brutal horror when the voice of the Smoldering Flame burned itself into my memory forever.

Awake, mortal. I have need of you.

There was no mistaking the voice for Triss. I heard the words in my mind, but it spoke in my heart, resonating through blood and bone and soul. It came up from the same place that that sense of home I'd felt with Siri came from. This was the Smoldering Flame speaking painfully through the channel that Siri had made between us.

The sheer force of the god's voice hammered at my mind like a giant shouting in my ear. But even worse was the way the unmistakable divinity of it woke echoes of Namara in my memory. That ripped at my soul. I tried to sit up and make it stop, but I found that I couldn't move. Not so much as the tip of my little finger.

What do you want? I sent along that same channel once I realized I couldn't break free.

I demand a service of you.

I felt an incredible compulsion to obey, but resisted. It burned my mind. *You have no right.*

WHAT?! The voice set my bones painfully ashiver, and my ring finger suddenly felt as though I was wearing a band of fire. *You dare question my orders? I am a god!*

Not mine, you aren't. My god was slain. Without that loss, I don't know that I could have fought the pressure I felt now. *If you want something from me, you will ask for it the same as anyone else.*

I will destroy you! The smoke ring burned even hotter on my finger, and I thought I smelled cooking meat. I wasn't sure whether or not the god could make true on his threat, but death scared me less than compromising who I was. I had only just gotten back to a place where I knew who that was.

Perhaps. But if you kill me that's going to make it very hard for me to perform whatever service you're trying to sweet-talk me into.

I do not sweet-talk. I command. I am obeyed.

The god's voice sounded just as loud and autocratic in my head as when it first began to speak to me, but the channel that tied me to Siri carried emotional freight as well as the words. And, there, I sensed something like confusion—the god didn't know how to deal with someone who would not be forced. That gave me more strength to fight against his will.

You may command all you want. I am no longer in the business of obeying anyone.

Shock, consternation, confusion . . . *But I need you to do something for me.*

Then it will be on my terms or it will not happen. I spared a moment to wonder what it would be like to contend with the god when he was unbound, and couldn't suppress a shiver at the thought. That would be a *very* different contest.

You are even more trouble than the Siri.

She obeys you when you attempt to force her? Somehow I have a hard time seeing that.

I could sense the god fuming away at the other end of the channel, but he didn't say anything immediately.

It's like this, I sent. *You can tell me what you want in a polite way, and I can decide whether or not I'm interested. You can try to kill me and end any hope of my cooperation ever. Or, you can hold me here on the edge of dreams for however long it takes Faran to wake up, walk over here, see the way my ring is burning my hand, and decide to cut my finger off. Those are your options.*

Would the child do that? The god's mental voice shifted, becoming more calculating.

She is no child, and she'd do it in a heartbeat. She's offered five times so far. If I am not free to stop her, she may well decide this is the perfect opportunity. For that matter, if she *doesn't do it, and you release me without us coming to some sort of arrangement, I'll cut the finger off myself.*

But what about the Siri? Is she not your bride?

She is. But I married her*, not you. Since Namara's death I have no use for gods. So, ask me your favor politely, attempt to kill me, or fuck off. Those are your choices.*

I felt frustration and a great weight of weariness followed finally by resignation. **The Siri is trapped and I am still too tightly bound by the dagger in my heart to free her. You are the only one I can communicate with whom I can trust to extract her from her present situation.**

Why not send a pack of cultists? The ones that attacked me on my way here seemed eager enough.

Anger! **Because *they attacked you on your way here.*** The Fire That Burns Underground sounded furious now. ***My truevelyn—those who walk in my shadow—hear me . . . imperfectly.***

They do not . . . approve of mortals usurping the power of the Smoldering Flame. If they could, they would see you slain and the Siri relegated to a . . . more symbolic state. That has led them to do something very foolish, and why I need . . . why I must ask you to perform this service for me.

If I do this thing for you, you'll get out of my head and stay out?

It hurts me to manifest my attention through so narrow a channel as the one that binds me to you through your bride. I do not use it willingly.

Not quite a yes, but I guess it'll have to do for now. Siri is important to me. I would do what I could for her with or without you. Tell me what needs doing. I felt cold and wet, as wrung out as the rags we used to soothe Faran's headaches—but I had won. For now, at least.

"**That's** crazy." Faran spoke very quietly. She was sitting up with her back against a boulder in an effort that obviously pained her. Ssithra was perched behind with her wings draped across the sides of Faran's head, using her connection to the everdark to cool and soothe her partner's hurts.

"Which part?" I asked. "The god speaking into my mind? Or the part about the cultists trapping Siri to use as an icon?"

Faran rolled her eyes. "Neither. I was thinking about the bit at the end, where you said 'yes.'"

"Siri's in trouble."

"And you'd jump into a fire for her. Yeah, I got that. That doesn't make it not insane. Quite the contrary, if you want my opinion."

Ssithra spoke, "Siri is First Blade."

"To a goddess who died eight years ago! Doesn't that change things?"

I said, "Not for me," in the same breath that Triss said, "Of course not," and Ssithra asked, "Why would it?"

Faran looked like she wanted to scream, but didn't dare for fear of blowing the top of her own skull off. After several deep breaths, she said, "Right, right, what *was* I thinking?" She sighed. "So, when do we begin our assault on this heavily forti- fied temple full of crazed fanatics armed with cursed weapons and dark magic?"

"*We* don't," I said flatly. "You're sitting this one out."

Faran shouted, "No, I fucking well am no—" But then she visibly paled and her hands went to the sides of her head. "Shit, shit, shit. This isn't fair," she whispered. "I was getting better."

"And you will again," I said, quietly. "But you need to give your body some time to heal right now. That means that Triss and I have to do this alone."

Faran glowered at the dragon shadow on the ground beside me. "Don't you dare let him get killed, Triss. He gets these stupid ideas about mercy and goes wobbly at the worst times."

"I'll see what I can do," replied Triss.

I started sorting through our gear. "If the Smoldering Flame is right, the underground temple is only about forty miles from here. That means I can leave everything but my weapons, a few magical tools, and a couple days' worth of dried meats and fruits here with you. Considering the state you're in, I don't think we could find a better place for you to hole up until I get back."

The main chamber of the cave was nearly thirty feet deep and half that across, though the roof was too low for standing. It had a nice little natural chimney at the back—a key point in the selection process, given our need for a fire to connect with Siri.

The only reason it didn't have any residents other than us and a few enormous fruit bats was the position of the only reasonably sized entrance. It was big enough to fit a person— barely—and it opened under a brittle shale overhang forty feet up a mostly sheer cliff that was over a hundred feet tall with whitewater running along the ravine at its base.

That same little river had almost certainly carved the cave at some time in the past. We'd never have found it from above without the Shades' ability to crawl down the narrowest cracks, and Blade training that included a good bit of instruction in how to locate defensible fallbacks in environments both urban and wild. Faran would be as safe here as anyplace.

My big worry was how well she'd be able to get out if I *didn't* make it back. I'd needed rope to get down to the cave. Faran needed that plus an awful lot of help from both Ssithra and me, mostly due to the giant rainbow-colored holes in her vision. The headaches had eased up a bit after we settled in and the auras went away completely. I didn't like the idea of leaving my apprentice in this kind of shape at all, much less in such a tight place a hundred miles from the southernmost edge of the eleven kingdoms of man, but I didn't have much choice.

Once I had my trick bag packed, I slung it to my rig. "I'll be back as soon as I can."

"You'd better." Faran waved me toward the door, then closed her eyes and laid her head back against the rock wall.

Even with the rope it was a tough climb—wet and slippery from the spray coming off the wild rapids below.

* * *

The entrance to the cultic temple lay in another water-carved ravine. This one was much broader—more a canyon, really—and it lay just on the edge of an incredibly ancient and dense forest. There were only two truly virgin forests remaining in the eleven kingdoms—places where the hand of man had never felled a tree. The heart of the gigantic wood around White Fang Mountain, and Twilight in Dan Eyre. This felt infinitely older and more dangerous than either of them. No surprise really since it belonged to the Kreyn.

According to Smoldering Flame, his cultists had built their temple where they did because the canyon lay in one of the undisputed territories that surrounded the Kreyn's ancient enclaves. Established by a treaty between the Oaken Throne and the Emerald, the territories provided an uninhabited buffer between the peoples. They were among the most lightly trafficked lands anywhere inside the wall—perfect for the cultists.

I arrived at the lip of the canyon shortly after dawn and about a mile below the temple's entrance. Yellow clay turned the river into a thick golden snake slithering ever eastward to the sea. As I worked my way carefully westward, the gentle rush of the water fifty yards below me slowly blurred into the deeper roar of the waterfall that lay just to the west of the hidden door to the temple.

The Smoldering Flame had written the plan of the temple into my mind in a series of intensely detailed pictures, very much in the way Namara used to brief us before a mission. It was a painful reminder of all that I had lost. I needed to slip past three guard posts on my way upriver, and it took me well over an hour to travel that one short mile.

The last of the three stood on a concealed platform high up in an enormous arimandro tree barely fifty feet from the hidden entrance. I crawled another ten yards before slipping in under some sort of low and thorny evergreen that reminded me of a juniper. It had a fair view of the falls—though I couldn't actually see the crack in the canyon wall where the door lay hidden—and provided a thick patch of shade.

Wake up, my friend. I reached into my trick bag and pulled out a handful of raisins and nuts.

Are we there yet? asked Triss.

As close as we're going to get this side of sunset. I filled him in on the details of our immediate situation while I ate a cold breakfast.

Can you see the smoke from the temple?

No, not even knowing exactly where to look. Another reason the cultists had chosen this particular site was the waterfall. By piping the smoke from the god's altar fires out behind the waterfall, they were able to hide what little came through the water in the mist. *Very neat work.*

Now we wait.

Now we wait. Are you up to holding the shroud? I'd love to catch a few hours' sleep. It was day, and a bright one, but the thick brush kept out the worst of it.

I think so. At least until the hour before the sun is highest. The days are longer and brighter here than anywhere on our side of the wall, but it's cooler, too. Strange magic, that. I wonder what drives it.

I shrugged. *Siri might know, but the deep theory stuff's beyond me.*

Get some sleep. I'll wake you if anything changes or if it gets too bright for me.

I closed my eyes and let Triss push me under. I surfaced for a few hours right around noon, but spent most of that time in a sort of half trance. Much of an assassin's job consists of long waits in uncomfortable circumstances. Efik's the perfect answer for easing you through those times without going mad, but that path was no longer open to me. That forced me to fall back on my meditation training, which was simultaneously less effective and harder to maintain. I was only too happy to sleep again when the sun sank low enough for Triss to take over again.

What do you think is our best approach? Triss sent.

We were hanging upside down in the top of the crevice that concealed the door. I quickly reviewed what the god had given me, then shook my head.

We don't have a lot of options. There are alcoves on both sides of the passage a couple yards in from the door. The guards are relieved every four hours. A human in that position would lose a good bit of their edge by the end of the third hour. Especially here in the wilderness where the chance of actually having to deal with intruders approaches zero. But that's hardly an eyeblink for one of the Others, so there's not much point in waiting. I say we pop the door and go in fast and lethal.

I don't like going straight in like that. Not if we can avoid it. What if we open the door and slip back up here—lure them out?

I don't think so. They've the means to sound an alarm. An open door with no one coming through it is as likely to make them call for help as anything. I wish I could do that shadow folding thing Siri invented for traveling short distances through the everdark, but the magic's way too complex for me.

Triss hissed. *And, I'm incredibly glad you can't. It's crazy dangerous even when you understand all the principles. That's why the council banned it. Faran was absolutely right to refuse to teach you.*

Faran was something of a magical prodigy. Back when she was playing the spy, she'd independently developed a variant on Siri's shadow origami trick that allowed her to tuck small items away in the everdark. Having a place to hide papers and the like where no one but she could get at them had come in very handy.

Later, when we were trapped in a collapsed tunnel, she'd been able to back-figure Siri's version of the thing with the help of Master Loris, who had been part of the council when it was originally banned. Since then, Faran had flatly refused to even try to teach me the trick. She said I didn't have the mathimagical underpinnings, and until I did it was nothing but an especially fancy way to commit suicide by stupid.

I sighed. *You're probably right, but it still rankles.*

I'm definitely right, and you'll get over it. Now, if there really isn't a subtle way to do this, I guess we're stuck with a frontal assault.

Only, sneaky like. I punctuated my sending with a mental wink.

Yeah, that, Triss replied wryly.

Might as well get it over with. I took a deep breath, and then another, focusing my attention entirely on this moment until nothing else existed. Then it was time to begin.

. . . I kick off with my feet, pivoting around the friction point of my braced hands. Rotating in the air, I land facing the concealed door. Slipping my fingers into the crack that hides the catch, I yank the right side of the door outward, using the same impulse to fling myself into the narrow passage beyond.

Short daggers drop into my hands when I flick my wrists. I hear clattering as the guards start to react to the door crashing open, hands slapping on sword hilts, the shush of steel sliding against leather.

Two lunging steps and I'm in the wide space between the guards in their alcoves. Though they can't see me, the one on the right has her sword more than half out of its sheath already. The other is slower, with barely three inches of steel showing. Bright reflections spike across my borrowed darksight—polished steel rather than cursed iron.

They are too far apart for me to take both simultaneously. I spin to the right, slicing my dagger across the throat of the faster guard. It cuts deep and catches. I let it go as blood fountains. At the same time, I collapse my shroud into a thick rope of darkness and solidify it with a burst of magic, snapping it across the eyes of the other guard like the tip of a whip. He yelps and turns toward the alarm bell—belatedly recognizing what he should have done from the first.

The first guard lets go of her sword as she tries to staunch the gush of blood from her throat. I catch the hilt out of the air and fling the sword at the other's shins. It doesn't really hurt him, but he stumbles as he reflexively tries to dodge the spinning blade. I put a foot on the wall at the back of the first guard's alcove and launch myself into a diving thrust that ends with my second dagger snapping as the point wedges under his kneecap.

He catches me across the shoulders with a downward swing of his sword. It's a brutal blow, but his blade breaks when it hits the goddess-forged swords in my back sheaths. I roll and come up behind him, flipping my rope of darkness around his neck like a garrote. He drags me forward as he staggers toward the alarm once more. I spin more magic into the rope, tighten my focus . . . The line across his throat contracts, becoming a black wire no thicker than one of the hairs on my head. The loop closes, and the guard loses his head.

Messy, Triss sent when I released him a moment later, dropping back into a more normal perception of time.

Tell me about it. I dashed back to close the hidden door. It had been open less than a minute. *See what you can do about that.*

Triss worked to clear the worst of the blood from my skin and clothes—sending some of it into the everdark and scraping away much of the rest.

I won't be able to do much about the stuff that's soaked in, not without investing time we don't have right now.

I know. Triss could probably clean the cloth out pore by pore, but washing it in cold water would be quicker and more efficient. *Just do what you can.*

Drawing one of my swords, I cut the alarm free of the wall and stomped on it. *That'll slow things down a bit if someone discovers the bodies, but from here on out, we're mostly going to have to rely on speed and luck.*

Pushing aside the past and thinking only far enough into the future to guide my immediate choices, I raced down the hall. Thanks to the Smoldering Flame I knew where I was going and what I would have to do to release Siri from the binding that has trapped her smoke form within the temple's ever-burning flames. The plan was a simple one, driven by the physical structure of the complex and the necessity of speed.

The passage angled slowly down into the depths of the earth, bending to the right as it went—toward the waterfall. An arch opened ahead of me and the passage widened beyond. There were more guards here in a room just beyond the arch. An iron gate stood ready to close the passage. But I was practically invisible and they were lax—relying on the first pair of sentries to give them the warning they would need to take action.

As I passed them, I spared a moment to be thankful that the Durkoth won't cross the wall back into the empire. The earth would reveal my footsteps to them, where the Sylvani noticed nothing. A few yards farther on, a small doorway opened onto a narrow spiral staircase on my right. I ducked through and catfooted my way down the short flight of steps.

The main passage—now behind me—went on, driving deeper into the stone as it wound through the living areas to reach the sanctum and the ever-burning cultic fires. These stairs led to a series of maintenance-ways running close to the surface of the rock face behind the waterfall to allow easy access to the chimneys and sluices.

As I left the bottom of the steps, I encountered a cultist returning from some cleaning task. He had an empty bucket and a large sponge. There was no way to slip past him in the narrow passage. I drew a short knife from my boot.

He paused a few feet short of me and rubbed his eyes—it's hard *not* to notice the blind spot when it completely obscures the path in front of you. Stepping forward, I hammered my knife between two ribs and into his heart. As he slumped, I grabbed the bucket, using it to catch the blood that spilled when I withdrew my knife.

A few seconds later I left body and bucket both hanging in an airshaft. Somewhere below, a room or complex of rooms would eventually start to catch the worst of a bad smell. But not soon enough to affect my plans. I was alone again, and unlikely to encounter more cultists, at least for a while.

I passed a whole series of such shafts and sluiceways as I worked my way along the back side of the cliff face. They were all large enough for a good-sized man to crawl through, allowing for proper maintenance. Farther along, a second spiral staircase plunged deep below the main levels, giving access to the waste outflows that flushed sewage into the cauldron at the base of the waterfall. But I moved quickly past it since my business was with that which went up.

Finally, at the very end of the tunnel, I came to the chimneys that vented the smoke from the temple fires into the void behind the waterfall. There were three, and they were the biggest shafts yet. The fires were never allowed to die, so any work on the chimneys had to happen with the smoke flowing through them. Make them too tight, and your chimney sweeps were likely to suffocate. I wanted the central shaft, which opened out of a hood directly above the fire pit that centered the temple.

Pulling my hood and cowl tight to block as much smoke as possible, I opened the iron hatch on the angled wall above me. The shaft climbed past at a steep but not impossible pitch. It was smooth and polished under the layers of soot, but there were no handholds. Once inside I closed the door and released my shroud.

Triss, can you drop the bar?

Reassuming his dragon shape, Triss nosed his way along the seal at the edge of the hatch. It was tight, but after a moment he stopped, sniffed carefully at one spot, and nodded. With obvious effort, he pushed his head and one foreleg through the paper-thin gap. A moment later, I heard a muffled clang. I kicked the door to check the seal, and it didn't even rattle. That was good. I needed it to stay tight.

Thanks, Triss, you know what to do next.

On it. Triss shrank and tightened, squeezing himself down into a shape he'd never assumed before.

This was where my plan diverged from what I had told the Smoldering Flame. He expected me to climb down through the smoke and drop into the temple below where he would protect me from the heat of the flames while I recovered a stone glyph buried amidst the coals. Removing the glyph from the fire and putting it in an airtight bag would break the first half of the summoning that held Siri trapped in smoke form *without* extinguishing the symbol of the Smoldering Flame's sacred presence. That part was very important to him.

Which was too bad. I braced my hands and feet on opposite sides of the shaft and started to climb up instead of down. Within seconds I noticed the smoke ring on my finger beginning to swirl and twist angrily.

What are you doing? the god roared into my mind.

Freeing Siri.

This is not how you told me you would do it.

And you *agreed to stay out of my head. In my book that makes us even.* I paused in my climb. *Oh, and before you try anything fancy like trying to possess me, let me direct your attention to the second ring on that finger, the one that lies below yours, the one made of shadow.*

Your familiar.

Yes. If I do anything but what I have told Triss to expect me to do, he's going to snip that finger right off my hand and you with it. We worked out the details on our way to the temple.

It had been a nerve-wracking conversation to begin, relying as it did on the god's seeming inattention and my untested ability to detect him if he intruded on my mind again. Because of the potential presence in my head, we'd carried the conversation out in whispers rather than mind-to-mind, hoping that would help keep from tipping him off. I honestly hadn't been entirely certain we'd pulled it off until Triss finally settled in place beneath the smoke ring right before I started my climb.

I began to move upward once again. *After Triss removes my finger I will continue on to free Siri in the manner I choose without you. Do you understand?*

I felt the god probing at my mind and chose not to resist this time. I had some thoughts about how I might fight such a battle should I need to, but I wasn't sure any of it would work twice. Since I didn't want to give any of that away prematurely, I pushed my current intent right to the top where he couldn't miss it. Hopefully, that would make him so mad that he wouldn't think to dig deeper.

A moment later, the god snarled into my mind, **What you are planning is basest sacrilege!**

I can't transgress against a creed I don't believe. Now, get out of my head and let me work.

I will make you pay for this, he growled—and I had no doubts that he would if he ever got the chance. But then he retreated and I was alone once again.

Soon I reached the top of the shaft. It opened less than ten feet below the lip of the falls, taking advantage of a deep overhang that kept water from rolling down into the shaft. Balancing on the lip, I leaned as far out as I could and sent a chain of jagged lightning out from my palm to strike the rock wall above me. Shards of stone exploded outward from the point of contact as the water permeating the top layers flashed into steam.

A shallow irregular channel formed, and I walked it up to the overhang, then started working the lightning back and forth laterally. After two or three passes a portion of the waterfall's lip gave way and I ducked back into the chimney shaft as water started sheeting down the cliff face. Most of it continued on toward the basin below, but the channel I'd carved directed enough into my shaft to more than half fill it. I held on to the lip for twenty long heartbeats as it hammered away at me. When I was done, I took a deep breath and let go, letting the raging flow carry me down into darkness.

14

───◆───

Wheeeeeeeeeeeee!

    As a general rule, the job of the assassin doesn't involve a lot of laughs. I am very good at killing people, and I feel more alive when I am working than I do at any other time. But it's not really what you would call "fun."

Normally.

Riding a watery torrent down a hundred-foot stone shaft in utter darkness, on the other hand? Pure delight.

As soon as I let go of the ledge, Triss moved back to cover me in darkness, surrendering his will to me as he did so. Down and down I went, sliding faster and faster until I suddenly tilted into a straight fall and dropped from darkness into ruddy light. Though the god's tribute fire had been extinguished by the rushing water, the dome of the sanctum was studded with magelights in all the colors of flame.

It was thirty feet from the bottom of the shaft to the floor of the temple, more than enough to break bones at the speed I was traveling. Without the water I would have had to use Triss as a sail to slow my fall. Instead, I balled up tight and took the impact on my ass and the soles of my feet, landing with a huge splash.

The god's fire was kept in a sort of stone well at the center of the sanctum. A low stone wall surrounded a shallow circular pit floored with coals and constantly fed fresh green wood that smoked heavily as it burned. With the water pouring into it from above, it quickly became a pool twelve feet across and half that deep.

I hit hard enough to drive me into the iron grating on the bottom, but not so hard that I took any injury from it. I did pick up a few nasty scrapes off the floating debris, but most of the bigger chunks of wood had been pushed out to the edges by the pressure of the falling water. Fortunately, the narrow chutes that led into the ashpits below made for a much narrower outflow than the chimney above or I'd have had a much rougher landing.

When my head broke the surface a few seconds later, I heard all manner of screams and shouts in the Sylvani dialect. But nobody actively tried to spear me—an excellent sign. I had to find the glyph stone before anything else, so I dove again as soon as I caught a lungful of air.

I started to quest outward from the well's center using fingers as well as my borrowed darksight and other senses to look for the stone on the grates. But I had barely begun my search when I found something else entirely—something that very nearly startled the breath out of me and sent me straight back to the surface.

Kelos had been there before me.

Every shadow has its own distinct *flavor* or *scent* for a Shade. The stronger the shadow, the more powerful the taste/smell. The strongest are associated with the shadow-elementals themselves. They are as individually identifiable as any signature, and Triss had taught me how to read them, though I only knew a few well enough to recognize them myself. When I started feeling around the bottom of the well, I tasted one such trail. But fire or direct sunlight will burn them away in a heartbeat and the only way such a trail could survive here was if it were laid down *after* the flame was extinguished. That meant the stone was already gone.

I angled toward the wall around the edge of the pit. When my head broke the surface this time, I heard more shouting and a brief clangor of steel on steel, followed by an agonized shriek.

I rolled over the lip of the wall, landing on fingers and toes and staying low. I wanted a moment to survey the room before deciding what to do next, but Triss's senses made an utter hash of the scene. The light-scattering smoke in the air combined with the wild reflections off the rippling water on the floor to baffle and shatter my borrowed darksight into a senseless noise of brightness.

I had no choice but to flick aside the shadow covering my eyes. Even then, I couldn't entirely make sense of the scene. The area behind me seemed relatively calm—I had come up on the side opposite the entrance to the sanctum, but the other half of the room . . . utter madness!

The great stone portal that opened out of the sanctum was closed up tight and sealed with a powerful spell that made it glow a deep angry purple, and the area between the door and the well was a churning chaos of spell-light. There were cultists everywhere, and all of them casting wildly, throwing spells and charms at every half-seen shadow.

Kelos had that effect on people. I forced myself to ignore the spell-lights and look for the most vulnerable target on the periphery of the scene because I *knew* Kelos. He wouldn't be anywhere near the heart of the storm. He would kill and then slide around the edge of things to kill again, and he would keep doing it until not one of his targets was left standing. He wasn't invulnerable, and with so many trying to fry him a lucky shot might well take him down, but he wouldn't waste a step or a draw of the knife along the way.

I hadn't yet decided on who his next victim was likely to be when I felt a shroud brush gently across my own and reflexively whipped my swords out of their sheaths.

"Easy, Aral, it's just me."

"Bastard!" The word snapped out of my mouth before I could even begin to think, but I put up my swords. More an acknowledgment of reality than anything—if I hadn't been able to bring myself to try to kill him the last time I saw him, I certainly wasn't going to change my mind when I could use his help as much as I could right then.

"Still angry," said Kelos. "That's good. It'll keep you sharp. I've got the glyph stone. Nipped in and picked it up as soon as you killed the fire. Now we just have to get out of here. My plan involved the gate, but that sealing spell's a thing of rare beauty." He chuckled happily at that—he seems to genuinely delight in having things go against him. A perverse reaction to two hundred years of successes, perhaps.

"It would take hours to crack the thing," he continued. "Even if we could manage it, the locks and bars are god-cursed cultic iron and I've no idea how to get around that. Magic seems to slide right off the stuff. Any clever ideas for our escape?"

"How are you even here?" I demanded. At the same time, I woke Triss up so he could listen in.

"Is that really important right now?" asked Kelos.

"No. Tell me anyway."

He snorted. "Short version. I've been following you ever since you crossed back over into the Sylvain a few days after parting ways with Siri."

"*And* listening to every word Faran and I have shared in that time."

"Pretty much. But we really need to get moving." His shroud brushed across mine again, directing my attention to the farther side of the room.

The spell-lights had shifted away from madness and into method, as the cultists organized themselves into mutually supporting ranks. There must have been a hundred of them, and every one of the Sylvani is a mage.

"Not good," I said. "And yes, I do have a clever idea, but it's going to need a hell of a distraction to give me the time I need to make it work."

"Right. I'll go play death-tag with the Sylvani while you get our exit sorted out. Make a flash when you're ready. Oh, and tell me where I need to be for the endgame."

"First, give me the glyph stone." I didn't trust Kelos even the tiniest bit.

"That's fair. Here." I felt his shroud impinge on mine in the instant before a cord looped itself over my head and a small but heavy leather bag fell across my collarbones. If Kelos had wanted to kill me then, I'd have died. Yeah, he was *still* that much better than I was.

I touched the bag, verifying that it held something of the right size and shape. "Keep an eye on the well. If the amount of water flowing over the edges drops, you'll know my play worked."

"The ashpits?" he asked.

"Exactly." They hadn't been an option with the plan I'd sold the Smoldering Flame, and they were never going to be my first choice given the inherent problems. But after I'd decided to cross the god and flood the well, they had become part of my thinking for possible backups.

"Tough to crack, but a good play. I'll get on the distraction." His shroud brushed mine once more and then he was gone.

I put my swords away and slipped back into the water. There, I started feeling along the edges of the iron grate. It was made up of two pieces, each of which must have weighed three hundred pounds.

It's nearly indestructible, Triss sent, after trying to send a piece of it off to the everdark. *I don't know if it's formally enchanted, or if it's just the effects of bathing in the sacred fire, but it feels a lot like those cursed weapons the Durkoth had. If we have to cut through it somehow, we're not going anywhere.*

Right. Well, I still have one thing to try, but it'll require a good deep breath first.

I surfaced long enough to fill my lungs and draw one of my swords before heading under again. There, I slid the blade between the two halves of the grate. Bracing my feet against the wall of the pit, I pushed on the hilt, using the nigh-unbreakable sword as a lever. Nothing happened for long seconds. Then, slowly, I felt it begin to shift—the grates moving ever so slightly apart. The effort had sent purple and gold fireflies sparkling across the edge of my vision, but I *had* moved it.

I surfaced and took another breath, then went down and shifted the placement of my sword, dropping my shroud as I did so—a risk I had to take. This time it was easier, even though I was trying to lift an edge. Opening the gap even the inch or so I already had was providing the water a better path into the lower levels and relieving some of the pressure holding it in place.

Your turn. I fed Triss extra magic from the well of my soul as he took my other sword and slid it into place. *Good, hold it!*

I grabbed another mouthful of air, then repositioned my first sword. That allowed me to brace myself against the bottom with one foot on either side of the sword. Of course, if I slipped, I was going to cut my own leg off. . . .

Two more rounds and I had the grate open wide enough for Triss to wedge it with a short log, and that opened up access to one of the pair of narrow shafts that led to the ashpits below. Siri probably could have figured a clever way to use magic to do the same work in half the time, despite the cursed iron's resistance, but that was well beyond my talents.

It was time to go, so I resheathed my swords, reshrouded, and pushed my way to the surface one last time. Taking a deep breath first, I aimed a palm at the ceiling and fired off a huge crackle of orange pink spell-light. It was a very distinctive color, and one every Blade was trained to look for from the first day they exhibited magesight. Then, without waiting to see if Kelos was even still alive, I dove for the bottom and squirmed into the gap between the gratings.

I didn't like the next bit at all, but if there was any good alternative, I wouldn't have been underwater in the first place. The rectangular shaft was short enough that it could easily be cleaned from below, and that meant it didn't need to be anywhere near as big as the chimneys. It didn't, in fact, need to be big enough to pass a man.

I *believed* that it would, but I wouldn't know for sure until I actually tried it, at which point the weight of the water above would make backing out all but impossible. With a small prayer to a dead goddess, I slithered my way into the mouth of the shaft. That was when the current caught hold of me and *yanked*!

My trick bag caught on the lip of the shaft when my hips slid over the edge, and suddenly I was pinned. Worse, I only had one arm free—the other was trapped against my chest. I'd have drowned then if not for the fact that I was playing the role of cork in this bottle's mouth and largely blocking the flow from above. That quickly emptied the short shaft of most of the water that had been flowing through it, allowing air to come up to me from below.

I couldn't reach anything with my free hand. When I scrabbled against the grate edge behind me with my feet I couldn't get any real purchase, and I didn't dare brace against the one above for fear of knocking the log free and trapping me even worse than I already was. I'd never felt more vulnerable, but I forced myself to breathe deeply and push aside the panic I felt rising in my chest. I *could* do this. I *would* do this. I had to think instead of simply reacting.

And, there was my answer—obvious once I got my emotions under control. I collapsed my shroud into a slender edge of shadow and cut the straps of my trick bag. The weight of the water did the rest—pressing me down and through the shaft in one sudden rush.

I landed hard and badly, with only one hand to catch myself, and a terrible angle for rolling out of the fall. It was a good thing the ashpit was partially flooded, or I might well have broken my wrist. As it was, I bounced my head off the stone floor, throwing sparks across my vision and sucking in a huge snootful of water as I lost my hold on Triss.

I came up coughing, spluttering, and tumbling in the current. Before I could so much as sort up from down, the water pouring out of the shafts in the ceiling washed me through the room's blown-out door and into the narrow hallway beyond. I'm not sure who was more surprised at that point, me or the Sylvani cultist trying to staunch the flood.

I plowed into him at knee height, knocking him over on top of me. He had a hefty pry bar, but my reflexes were better, and I gutted him with my boot dagger before he thought to use it on me. I was just dragging myself out of the worst of the flood and onto my feet when Kelos appeared in the doorway behind me. It was the first time I'd seen his face since the night I'd invaded the rooms of the Son of Heaven.

His shirt was gone, he had blood flowing down the side of his face from a long cut in the scalp, and a blistered burn on his shoulder and chest, but Kelos looked as calm and unruffled as always. He was a big man, taller and much more heavily muscled than I. There was a patch over the eye he'd lost to a basilisk, and his skin was basically nothing but scars, though the tattoos that wrapped his torso and arms in serpentine coils obscured many of them.

"Any trouble with the grate?" I asked. It had been tight for me. He shouldn't have fit at all.

"No."

"Of course not."

Aral, be cautious.

"You sound almost disappointed, Aral. Were you hoping I'd get stuck?"

I shook my head, though I wasn't entirely sure I hadn't been. Kelos simply wasn't fair. Two hundred years old with more kills notched on his hilts than any ten other Blades, and a casual confidence that always made me feel like a child all over again.

"Where to now?" he asked, his voice calm to the point of nonchalance—maddening.

Down! yelped Triss.

I threw myself at the floor, sending up a huge splash when I hit the calf-deep water. In that same instant I heard a tremendous crackling noise like someone dropping the world's biggest egg roll into the fryer, and the world lit up bright red above me. Triss screamed as a wave of heat rolled across my back—magefire— but some feet above me thanks to Triss's warning. Before I could react any further, something grabbed me by the cowl and dragged me forward through the water.

I tried to twist away, but Triss spoke into my mind, his words tight and hard with pain. *Don't fight. It's Kelos—pulling us in.*

My old mentor yanked me to my feet in the ashpit chamber a moment later. "Sylvani in the hallway," he said. "A bunch of them, including at least one really outstanding spell-thrower. He'd have cooked you good if you hadn't reacted so quickly. Being as soggy as a seal chasing after a fish didn't hurt either."

I tucked myself against the wall beside the door, drawing my swords in case they rushed us. "Any thoughts on how best to deal with them?" I hated ceding the initiative to Kelos, but the unexpected injury to Triss had thrown me off my game.

Triss retreated deep into my shadow and I could feel him drawing nima from the well of my soul as he worked to soothe his burns. *I'll be all right. I just need a few moments to recover.*

Kelos took the opposite side of the doorway. "We don't have a lot of options. That hallway's far too narrow for a shroud to do much good, and from what I could see when I poked my head around the doorframe, they've got a great defensive position at the base of some stairs. They can wait there indefinitely and nail us whenever we finally move. You're the one with the map of this place in your head. What was the plan from here?"

"If you turn right when you go through this door, there's a spiral staircase about forty feet up the hall. It leads to the upper maintenance-ways, and from there back to the tunnel to the main entrance. I'd hoped to get out that way, but that's no good with those cultists on the stairs."

He frowned. "And your backup plan?"

"If you go the other way down the hall, there's a trapdoor in the floor about thirty feet along. The waterfall has undercut the cliff pretty deeply over the years, and the door opens directly into the ceiling of the cauldron there. They use it to dump the ash from the fires above."

Kelos whistled. "That's a damn big falls, boy. The undertow has to be brutal. I'd hate to have to try to swim our way out through that."

I shrugged. "That's why it wasn't plan A."

"Point. Malthiss, go see what our friends in the hall are up to." The shadow of a basilisk rose out of the coiled tattoos on Kelos's back and shoulders, his cobralike head peering at me briefly before slipping under the surface of the water. "We might be able to slither down to your trapdoor without getting fried if we stay mostly submerged, but I have my doubts."

I had more than doubts given the depth of the water. I was about to say as much when a thunderous blast shook the entire complex. "What the hell was that?!"

Kelos cocked his head to one side. "Given the direction and the tone, I'd say someone just blew the front door in. Class three combat magelightning, if I had to make a guess."

I couldn't have gotten all that from one distant explosion—hadn't, in fact. But I didn't doubt Kelos's assessment. He really was that good.

"Who and why?" Triss inserted himself into the conversation for the first time as he climbed up out of my shadow.

Kelos shrugged. "No way to tell that from the sound of the blast. But given the politics of the thing, it almost has to be the office of the disquisition. That or a Kreyn special tasks unit—the Oaken Throne doesn't like the cultists any more than the Emerald one does."

He paused and looked thoughtful. "Well, or it could be one of the other buried gods trying to muscle in on the Smoldering Flame. Less likely, but still possible. In any case, our friends at the foot of the stairs are about to have worse things to worry about than our little blasphemy with the waterfall. Too bad whoever it is is likely to be just as happy to nail us up by our ankles as these guys are."

"There is that." I glanced down at the ring of smoke on my finger—I didn't think it would endear me much to any of the candidates he'd mentioned.

Malthiss's head slipped back into view above the waters. "They appear to have been demoralized by the blast, but they haven't abandoned their position yet. We will have to wait if we want to pass the door and live. I will keep watch, and call out when the way is open. Be ready to move quickly." Then he was gone again.

"While we're waiting—" began Kelos.

"I don't want to hear it," I snapped, and then immediately felt childish for doing so.

"I know," he answered. "That's what makes this the perfect opportunity. You're a captive audience."

"You betrayed the goddess. I will fucking kill you if you don't shut up."

Kelos chuckled low and deep but he kept his eye fixed on mine. "Never make a threat you can't back up, Aral. Especially when we both know you don't *want* to make good on it."

"I—"

He waved a hand, cutting me off. "Don't bother. You had the glyph stone and a way out. If you were serious about wanting me dead this go-round, you'd have skipped the flare and closed the grate behind you. Who knows, that might even have worked. But you didn't, which means you're not yet ready to go that far to get rid of me."

"Why are you here?" I shouted. Yeah, mature, I know, but there was something about Kelos that made me revert to the callow teen who'd practically worshipped this man.

"To make sure your rescue succeeded. I'd have thought that much was obvious."

"No, not here-here. Here!" I threw my arms wide.

"Listen to yourself, boy, you're babbling."

He's right, Aral. You need to calm down and think before you speak. He's deadly smart and the best manipulator in the order. You can't beat him by punching blind.

"Why. Are. You. Here," I growled, ignoring Triss.

"Seems clear enough to me. I care about your welfare. Yours and Siri's both. That's why I sent you away before the temple fell. I have an investment in your future."

"Fine," I said. "Don't tell me."

Malthiss popped up again. "We have a problem."

Before he could elaborate, a giant sheet of flame went roaring past the doorway, coming from the direction of the Sylvani cultists on the right. A split second later there was a deep ringing note, like a silver gong being struck, and the fire flowed back the other way even brighter and hotter. Screams followed.

"New players?" asked Kelos.

Malthiss nodded. "Sylvani lord, biggest bastard I've ever seen."

"Which makes him old," said Kelos. "This could get interesting."

The hallway lit up with a giant streamer of spell-light—magic so bright I had to blink back tears—again, coming from the left. It was followed by more screams. Briefly. Then silence.

"Triss," I said. "Take a look."

"On it." He stuck his head through the doorway, whipped it from side to side, and then jerked back. "The cultists are dust, but the Sylvani lord's just standing there. He's leaning on something that looks like a sword but isn't."

"What?" I asked. A sword that wasn't what?

Before Triss could answer, a high clear voice called out, "Aral Kingslayer, we need to have a long talk. But first, I need you to escape."

"Pardon?" I called back.

"My name is Ashkent Kelreven and we have . . . a mutual friend—resourceful young human woman with hair issues. You're holding the stone that binds her in a pouch around your neck right now. I came to collect it, but you're ahead of me, and that makes things much easier. Well, it does if you get out of here before the imperial disquisition sees you, anyway. At that point, things could get very sticky, so I'd really prefer we avoid it. . . . We haven't got much time."

"What do you think?" Kelos whispered, but I was already moving—if nothing else it would get me away from my former mentor.

"I'm coming out. Oh, and I've another . . ." I trailed off, Kelos didn't deserve the name of Blade anymore. "I've got an . . . ally with me—an ally of convenience."

Kelos lifted a mocking eyebrow, but I just shoved past him wordlessly. The Sylvani lord *was* huge. Well, tall anyway— seven feet if he was an inch. His shoulders were broader than Kelos's, but his height made him look slender. He was leaning casually on the crossbar of an absolutely ridiculous sword very nearly as tall as he was.

It was eight inches across at the base of the blade and it barely tapered from there to the sudden narrowing of the point a handspan from its tip. The blade was striped orange and black like a tiger's hide, and the pommel . . . the pommel was shaped into the head of a fantastical beast . . . A fantastical beast I had seen for the first time only a few weeks before, when one of them tried to kill me in a warehouse. The whatsis.

The Sylvani quirked a smile. "I take it from the way you've stopped moving and put your swords up that we have a problem."

I nodded. "You might say that."

"From the timing and the angle of your eyes, I'm guessing it's got something to do with my sword."

"The creature on the pommel," I said. "What is it?"

"Oh, is that it?" He lifted the sword off the ground and gave it a sharp shake like a terrier with a rat before turning the pommel so he could look it in the eyes. "What have you been up to, old devil?"

The sword gave off an angry tinging sound, and the Sylvani shook his head and glowered at it.

"Don't think I won't follow up on this," the Sylvani admonished the sword. Then he looked back at me. "I'm fairly certain that I will owe you an apology once I learn the story, but we don't really have time for it right now. The disquisition is starting down the stairs right now, and you have to be gone before they get here. The trapdoor's already open—that's how I came in. So, I'm going to step to the side of the hall here and let you go past. We can talk later."

"Put the sword down," said Kelos. "Then we'll go."

"It's not really a sword. And, again, I don't have time for details. Suffice to say that it will be *much* more dangerous to you if I don't keep a firm grip on its vicious little neck, and please, get moving." The Sylvani pressed himself against the wall, pinning the blade between himself and the stone. It let out a harsh and angry clangor, like metallic grumbling. "Now, go!"

Malthiss whipped up out of the water behind us. "There are footsteps on the stairs behind the fallen—many of them. We must choose quickly."

"You're Ashkent Kelreven?" I asked.

The Sylvani lord nodded. "I am. Though not always the happier for it."

"Fine." I sheathed my swords and started splashing my way quickly down the hall.

"Aral?" Kelos asked.

I didn't slow. "You can make your own choice, but he's a friend of Siri's." Then I was at the trapdoor.

White mist floated up through the opening, obscuring everything below, and I could hear the hammering of the falls. By reflex I reached for my trick bag and a magelight to help me navigate the night-darkened waters, then remembered I'd lost it. Still, light's one of the easiest enchantments, and I quickly set a temporary light on one of the rings of my harness.

I stepped into space.

15

―――◆◆◆―――

White and black. Water. Rocks. Froth and foam. Pummeling, tumbling, air-starved madness. I clip my head on something and the whirling and twirling of the world grows wilder still.

Something catches me under the ribs and I lose the last of the air in my lungs. I stroke for the surface, desperate to breathe again. Triss shouts into my mind, but the words make no sense.

My leading hand sinks deep into mud, and I realize I've gone the wrong way.

Black and red. My vision pulses with waves of fire and darkness. I know that I am drowning, but I can't seem to care.

A bar of iron closes across my throat. The spinning subsides, and the red fades away into nothing.

. . .

Gagging and retching, I return to the world of awareness. I am on my stomach, I hurt everywhere, and I appear to be vomiting up my lungs. Right, I was drowning. But, how did I stop?

There's a strange noise in my mind—hissing—but I can't make any sense of it. It sounds like: *Sshthisshesssthrssstra*, on and on and over again.

There is a heavy weight on my back. "Idiot!" It's Kelos, using that special tone he reserves for my more spectacular failures.

Am I fifteen? If so, my mentor rarely leaves the temple anymore, so that's where I must be. Perhaps I hit my head sail-jumping into the lake. . . .

I wrack my memory, looking for the beginning of the thread that led me here. For the longest time I can't make sense of anything. Kelos taught me to swim, but he would never have let me get that badly out of my depth, and the lake is placid, not at all like the madness of tumbling white and black that dominates the vision in my mind. I must have done something especially stupid.

ARAL—ARAL—ARAL! The voice hissing away in my mind suddenly resolves itself into my name repeated over and over again, and I recognize it as Triss's.

With that, I return to myself and the present day, and coughing up about a hundred gallons of yellow river water. I feel like a shucked clam. "Fuck. Me."

Kelos chuckled and got off my back. "You don't need any help there, boy. I thought you'd finally managed to kill yourself that time. I've rarely seen you do anything dumber than trying to swim that nightmare without the proper magical preparation."

For what it's worth, I've seen you do much dumber things, though rarely so thoughtlessly. I could feel Triss's exhaustion echoing through the link between us and hear it in the hollow depths of his words. *I'm going to take a little nap now.* And, he was gone.

Rolling onto my back, I looked up into the starry depths of the sky. "I take it you fished me out?" My throat felt like raw meat and it hurt to talk, but I was becoming more and more myself with each passing beat of my heart.

"Yeah. Sorry I didn't get to you sooner, but the turbulence in the main cauldron was awful. It took me a lot longer to get my charm of water-breathing going than I planned for. I wish we'd had time to deal with it before we went in the water, but Ashkent was right about the timing. I actually saw the first of the disquisitors enter the hall as I was dropping through the trapdoor, but I was half-shrouded and I don't think they saw me."

I nodded, but didn't say anything. Kelos had just saved my life. I didn't like the feeling of owing him something. Not at all. Triss continued quiet as well. I could feel him down deep in the shadow beneath me, a reassuring presence, though vague and distant at the moment.

"What happened to you?" asked Kelos.

"What do you mean?"

"Don't play stupid, boy. Why didn't you charm your lungs before trying to swim out of that mess?"

"I . . ." The answer was simple, but I hated to admit it to my first and most critical teacher. There *are* spells that will allow a man to breathe underwater and I have even learned one or two of them . . . sort of. But . . . "I'm still shit at the more complex magics. Give me an hour or two, and I *might* be able to manage something like that. But on the fly? In that madness of water and rocks? Never."

"Loris was right."

"That I'm no mage?" I couldn't keep the bitterness out of my voice. "Yeah, I could have told you that."

Kelos growled deep in his throat and spat into the water. "No. You're smart enough, and you've got the necessary power. What you lack, what you've *always* lacked, is the discipline of the magus. You could have been a good mage. Maybe not as good as Siri, but better than competent. Loris said you never got there because I spoiled you, and he was right."

That made me sit up. "Spoiled me?" Shouting made me cough—briefly and rackingly, and I had to spit out more water when I finished. "Funny, I remember a brutal taskmaster who demanded that I know every sword form perfectly backward and forward, a man who insisted that I know the ins and outs of shadow-slipping better than most of the instructors. I sure as hell don't remember being spoiled."

"That's because people who are, rarely do."

"Really?"

"Truly. You were good, boy, really good. Gifted even. Siri's the only student I trained in two hundred years that came close to you in blade work or shadow-slipping, and ultimately she bettered you in the latter. But she had to work five times as hard as you did to manage it."

Kelos started to pace. "You were such a natural with shadow and steel that I pushed you to be the very best on those fronts and let you slide on magic. I bailed you out of trouble with Loris more than once when I shouldn't have. I prized your heart and your stronger skills so highly that I didn't push you to be all that you could have been. If you'd put half as much work into spellcraft as you did the rest of your studies . . ." He sighed and shook his head.

"No," he continued, "*I* should have been harder on you, and I wasn't. Today that nearly got you killed. I'm sorry. It's too late for *me* to do anything about it now, and I know you've damn good reason not to trust a word I tell you anymore. But listen to me when I say that you could *still* be a decent mage if you would only give it the work it needs."

"Thank you for your advice." It wasn't worth the effort of arguing with him. I was a lousy mage and always would be, no matter what Kelos might think.

"There's no need to give me a pretty lie," said Kelos. "If you mean 'fuck you,' you might as well just say it."

"Fine. Fuck. You."

The shadow of the basilisk raised itself from his shoulders, hood spread wide. "If Aral can move now, we should defer this till later. We're less than a mile from the falls, and this beach is far too exposed for my liking."

"Fair point." Kelos extended a hand, offering to help me up.

I ignored it and got slowly and painfully to my feet unaided. The effort gave me another coughing fit, but I already felt considerably less shaky and more myself. After a quarter mile of hiking along the narrow beach—I was still in no shape to scale the cliff walls—we found a side canyon centered on a swift but shallow stream, and turned into it. Within half an hour we had climbed back up to the level of the bluff tops. By then, I'd blown through my initial recovery and out the other side, and I was pretty well spent. But Kelos insisted we travel on a little farther.

I made it fifty feet. That was when a sudden burning agony rolled up the front of my thigh and inside the point of my hip bone, like someone had dragged a branding iron along my skin. My leg gave and I collapsed, hitting the ground hard and starting into another coughing fit.

Aral! Triss's mindvoice sounded thick with worry. *What's happening?*

Between the pain and the coughing, I couldn't answer at first, not even mentally. The coughing eased first. *I don't know. It feels like that cursed wound has opened itself up again—that or started on fire.*

Where's the rock that Durkoth Uthudor used to contain the curse? asked Triss.

In my trick bag—I'd simply hung on to it for lack of a good plan about how to handle the thing—*which means it's back in that temple somewhere.*

Strong hands closed on my shoulders, pulling me up into a sitting position and sliding me back to lean against a boulder. "Easy there, boy, what's wrong?" Kelos asked.

"Not sure, leg hurts like a . . ." As suddenly as it had started, the pain stopped. I lifted my hand from where I'd pressed it to the old wound, more than half expecting it to come away covered in blood. "And . . . now it's gone."

I reached down and loosened the ties that held my pants up so that I could examine the injury. The scar looked rough and red, but no more so than I would normally expect from a wound as nasty and recent as this one.

"Tell me about it?" Kelos settled back on his haunches.

I *wanted* to spit in his face and stalk off into the night. I didn't trust the man, and I absolutely despised what he had done to my goddess and my people. But somewhere down deep in the bone, he was still my father in all but name, and I loved him where I couldn't hate him. Besides, I wasn't up to getting back on my feet, much less walking anywhere once I got there. For a little while at least, I was going to have to deal with him.

"Durkoth," I began. "Cultists of the Smoldering Flame . . ."

Kelos got up and worked at making us a camp as I told the story, but he stayed within easy listening distance. By the time I finished, he had built us a good-sized blind under a thick bush so that we could lie hidden during the day that was fast approaching. Given the nearness of the forces of the disquisition, we didn't dare risk a fire, which meant in turn that properly freeing Siri would have to wait at least another day.

After I wound my tale to its end, Kelos left me for a bit to go in search of food. He returned with some purplish berries, a couple of things he called muffin-fruits, and a score or so of freshwater clams. We ate it all raw—even the clams, which weren't bad after Kelos doused them with some insanely hot Sylvani pepper sauce he had in a small skin in his trick bag.

"Does amazing things for putting dogs off your scent," he said as he produced it.

"I bet it does. My nose is going to be running for a week."

Kelos chuckled. "Entertain a theory?"

"About what?" I tensed warily, and felt Triss do the same.

"The wound in your leg, of course."

"Oh, that. Sure."

"If the disquisitors found that cursed rock, they would likely have recognized it for what it is. At that point, they would have moved to destroy it. Given your doubled tie to the Smoldering Flame, the pain might well have been some sort of backlash from the rock's destruction."

"Seems reasonable to me," Triss agreed aloud, and I had to nod. Hopefully, I was well and truly done with the thing.

I yawned and stretched then. "I desperately need a little sleep. How do you want to set watches?"

"I've got it," said Kelos. "I can rouse you near sunset if you don't wake on your own, and we can move on then. We need to work quickly if we're going to get ahead of the Son of Heaven on this key thing. When you were seen in that tavern with Siri, the news spread quickly. He has ears in many places and the two of you together and active in the Sylvain will almost certainly cause him to advance his timetable."

There were at least three major assumptions involved in that statement, and I didn't like any of them. But I was too tired to have that argument, so I just grunted and rolled farther into the blind.

The shade is deep here, sent Triss. *I could keep an eye on Kelos. . . .*

Don't bother. If he wanted to betray or kill us, he's had plenty of opportunity. I think we can trust him at least until we find this key that brought him to Siri . . . or refuse to do it.

He seems to think he needs our help, or hers, at least. Of course, all bets are off if ever we actually get our hands on the thing.

You may be right. Triss didn't say anything for a long time after that and I was on the edge of sleep when he finally spoke again. *But somehow, I suspect it will be less simple than that.*

I didn't have a good answer for that, and his words followed me into troubled dreams.

I woke in midafternoon, alerted to some change in my surroundings by instinct perhaps. Triss was deep down in my shadow, oblivious to anything that happened up in the world of light. Without moving, I opened my eyes. Kelos's side of the blind was empty, and my thoughts instantly went to the glyph stone in the pouch around my neck. But the weight still pressed against my skin, and I didn't want to betray my wakefulness to any possible observers by checking it more carefully. Not before I had a better idea what had brought me out of the dreamlands, anyway.

"Your companion has gone down to the river to see about catching the two of you some lunch." The voice was clear and high, and though I had only heard it the once, I recognized it.

"Lord Kelreven," I said. And, *Wake up, Triss.*

"It's *Duke* Kelreven, actually, but I'd prefer that you simply called me Ash."

"Ash, then," I said as I rolled over. "And you may call me Aral."

I felt Triss come groggily awake. *What's going on . . . Oh.*

The tall Sylvani lord sat cross-legged on the ground a few yards away, his enormous not-quite-a-sword across his knees. It was unsheathed, but not exactly bare, as it had an intricate multicolored pattern of silk cords knotted around the blade. Spell-light ran through the network in weird pulsing lines. Daylight showed the fine lines in his face, and made his silver hair gleam. He was a beautiful man and one I would probably have found attractive in other circumstances.

I matched Ash's pose, crossing my legs and putting my empty hands on my knees. "Kelos?"

"He would not have left you if he hadn't felt certain of your safety. But he knew that you would be hungry when you woke, and he wanted to provide an answer to your need. He searched a wide circle before he went, making sure that you were alone and would remain so."

"But he didn't find you."

He shook his head. "I didn't want him to."

"Neat trick, that." I lifted an eyebrow. "I must admit that I'm surprised he left me at all, food or no."

"I wanted to speak with you by yourself before having dealings with the Deathwalker. I gave him a bit of a nudge in the direction of finding you a meal."

Spooky, sent Triss.

Tell me about it.

"He's not going to like that very much."

"That doesn't really concern me one way or the other, and I doubt that he'll ever find out if you don't choose to tell him. Now, as in our earlier meeting, we don't have much time before we are likely to be interrupted, and there are things we should speak of."

I had my doubts about his assessment of Kelos's ability to discover his machinations, but I let it go. "Interesting sword you've got there." I didn't know about the Sylvani, but the blade with its grinning pommel was close to the top of *my* list.

Ash smiled in the manner of a man inviting you into his joke. "We both know it's not a sword."

"More a suspicion on my part than real knowledge," I countered. "If you don't mind my asking, what *is* it if it's not a sword?"

"The trapped soul of a buried goddess, of course."

"Of course." I suppressed the urge to back away slowly.

That's got to be all kinds of volatile and unstable, Triss whispered into my mind, his tone rife with alarm.

"She was called Rakshifthra the Changer, and she wore two skins in life. One, a Kreyn priestess. The other, a filathalor . . ." His eyes went far away for a second. "I don't think there is a word for them in your language—they died out before your people first walked in this world—call it a tiger-boar and you will be close enough."

"Big bastard," I said. "Stripes? Tusks? Way too many teeth? Bad attitude? Regenerates? I had one try to eat me at the beginning of this trip."

Ash nodded. "So, I *do* owe you an apology."

"For . . ."

"This." He slapped the blade of his weapon, and it responded with an angry metallic growl. "The filathalor are extinct. If you've encountered one, it's entirely because my watch on the goddess slipped and she managed to summon one up from the grave to send after you."

"You seem pretty certain. How can you be sure it wasn't simply frozen in a spell somewhere? Or summoned by some other mage?"

"The filathalor are beyond dead. Their breed-soul is bound to the lifeline of the Changer." He touched his sword. "They *cannot* live in the world except through her will. The idea of one acting and existing independently of their goddess is as absurd as if I were to suggest that one of your hands might leave your body behind and go off on its own to strangle someone on the other side of the empire."

Breed-souls? sent Triss.

No idea.

I wanted to ask about that, and about how you bound a buried god into a sword, and all kinds of other things implied by his words, but it would have to wait. "Was there anything else you wanted to talk about before Kelos gets back?"

Ash inclined his head ever so slightly. "You cannot trust Siri."

"Uh . . ." Siri had told me much the same thing, but . . . "Given what she means to me, that's a pretty bold statement coming from someone I've only barely met."

"She is not alone in her head," replied Ash. "As the dagger that binds the Smoldering Flame in the grave burns away, the god will have greater and greater influence over her thoughts and actions. Just as the Changer may slip the leash and visit a sending on you away north in Tien, so, too, may the Smoldering Flame work his will in the world from the deeps of his tomb."

"I *owe* Siri—"

Ash cut me off. "I am not suggesting that you forsake her. Quite the contrary. I have great respect and affection for her. That one so young could bring low the Smoldering Flame—a mortal barely out of her second decade? That's remarkable. I *want* you to help her, but I also need you to recognize that you can't entirely trust her motives nor all of what she tells you."

"Are you suggesting I should trust *you*?"

Ash snorted and lifted the hilt of his sword. "Does this look like I am free of the influence of the buried ones? Of course you can't trust me. *I* don't fully trust me. To be bound to a god is to lose something of yourself. For three thousand years I have wrestled with the goddess in my head. I second-guess every choice that I make if it goes beyond what to wear or have for breakfast. Mostly, I think that I get it right. But the true horror of the thing is that the only way I will ever find out if I've gotten it badly wrong is if my bound goddess awakes."

Show him the ring?

"And this?" I held up my hand with its circle of smoke.

"Means that you can't entirely trust you either." He nodded. "I wish that Siri hadn't done that, and I told her as much, though I understand the reasons for her choice. If you are as . . . strong of will as she suggested, I do not think the god can bend you too much to his purpose. Not unless he completely suborns Siri first."

I felt the emotional equivalent of an amused grin echoing through my link with Triss. *Strong of will . . . Do you suppose that's Sylvani for* pigheaded?

Hush you.

"So, I can't trust Siri, or you, or me, and certainly not Kelos. Is there anyone you think I can trust?" I didn't mention Faran, and I wasn't planning on taking his advice on the matter in any case, but I wanted to see how he would respond.

Ash smiled sadly and shook his head. "Of course not. We are in the Sylvain." He said it like a man speaking a proverb. He opened his mouth as if to say more, then twisted suddenly and looked toward the river. "Kelos comes."

I figured it would be better to give my old mentor something real to chew on, and there were still things I wanted to know, so, "What keeps the goddess in the sword? And how can you risk carrying it around like that? Perhaps more important than all the rest, how did *you* end up with it?"

Ash smiled and nodded faintly, clearly acknowledging the purpose of my ploy. "The sword itself is a greater binding crafted over long years for the express purpose of trapping a god within the steel. When I was young, barely out of my first millennium, I craved power. There is no greater power in the empire than our fallen gods, so I forged this prison to catch myself a god. Later, my priorities . . . shifted, I gave up my quest for power, and I put the godsword aside."

Kelos appeared then, making rather more noise as he walked up than he needed to. He had a short string of fish slung over his shoulder. "If you gave up the quest, how did you come to be carrying around a bound goddess, Duke Kelreven?"

"Ash. The Changer came out of her grave on the edge of the lands ruled by my wife's line. The goddess killed hundreds of Kreyn and enslaved thousands more. We had not yet met then, but in her search to find a cure for this divine plague, Kayla augured out the existence of the godsword. She came to seek it as a way of freeing her people. She was brilliant and beautiful and her need was dire. I fell in love with her, but I didn't trust anyone with the kind of power this weapon might give them—not even her. Not then, at any rate. That left me only one option."

"Convenient for you," said Kelos.

"To be shackled to a devourer of souls? You don't know what you're talking about." Ash's tone was light, but layered with an ancient bitterness. "Pray that you never find out, child."

Kelos bristled. "I gave up praying long ago, velyn."

"Oh good, I didn't miss the dick-swinging contest."

I started at the familiar voice. "Faran?"

My apprentice stepped out of the shadows a few yards beyond where Ash sat. "You didn't really believe I was going to sit on my ass in that cave and wait for you to come back and rescue me like some frail princess from an old story, did you?"

I sighed. "No, more like an injured warrior smart enough to know when to rest and heal. Clearly, I gave you more credit for good sense than I ought."

Faran snorted. "Point, and I might even have done so if I hadn't caught this one's scent overlying your backtrail."

"Neat trick, that," I said. "Sniffing Kelos out while lying flat on your back in your sickbed in the cave, I mean."

She waved a hand around lightly. "I wanted to get some air. Which, I will admit, may not have been the smartest idea I've ever had. Getting up the cliff above the cave damn near knocked me flat. But, once I was up there, I didn't have to go ten feet to latch onto Kelos's scent. He was on you from the moment you cleared the top of the ravine."

Malthiss lifted out of the tattoos on Kelos's chest—the man still hadn't replaced his shirt. "Ssithra?" he said.

The shadow at Faran's feet twisted itself into the outline of a phoenix. "Yes, Malthiss?"

Triss gave a mental start. *Note that she doesn't offer him the title* resshath. *That's a very deliberate sort of disrespect.*

I responded with the mindspoken equivalent of a whistle and a nod. It took a *lot* to get a Shade to let go of their hierarchy.

Malthiss continued as though he hadn't noticed the slight, "You and your partner have grown much in skill. I did not sense the two of you until Faran spoke."

"No, you didn't," interjected Faran. "Not even when I stood behind you in the shallows of the river, knife in hand. You live because I didn't think that Aral would have approved of my killing you then. Well, more because of the fact that I didn't want to have a giant screaming argument about it—not when my head still feels so fragile—but why quibble?"

Malthiss jerked his head back at that and Ssithra vanished into Faran's shadow, but Kelos only laughed.

"Point," said Kelos. "Your tongue cuts deep, *Master* Faran, and I have no doubt your knife cuts deeper still. Thank you for staying your hand."

"It's not me you need to thank," replied Faran. "It's Aral's silly notions I'm indulging on this one."

The blade in Ash's lap rang sharply at that precise moment, sounding a note as clear as a struck bell, and continuing to jingle faintly afterward. The Sylvani lord stripped the cords off the blade and unfolded himself at that, rising to his feet in one smooth motion.

"If you don't want to have a rather lengthy discussion with the Imperial Office of the Disquisition, I suggest you all come with me." He crossed the small clearing to the base of an enormous and ancient tree—eucalyptus maybe. "A god-sniffer approaches, and I detect at least another couple of dozen breaks in my line of warding. I imagine it is the entire assault force that stormed the temple—or, all of it that survived."

"I thought they were with you," I said.

"Allies of convenience only. They would not slay me out of hand because of my rank and my marital alliance with the

Oaken Throne. But love me, they do not. Were they to find me with one who wears such a pretty bauble as that ring on your finger, they might take it as an opportunity long hoped for."

"All right, but how are we—"

But even as I began to speak, Ash spat out a liquid string of high Sylvani, and with it a cloud of spell-light—like some angry dragon's breath. Then he turned on his heel and swung the enormous blade in an underhanded cut at the tree, splitting its bark from ground height to perhaps ten feet up the trunk. A moment later, Ash spoke another mouthful of Sylvani, and the split opened like some enormous mouth, exposing a swirling blue void of magelight.

"It will not remain open long." Ash stepped into the whirl of color and was gone.

I crossed to the opening, but hadn't yet decided whether I really wanted to go through when Kelos spoke. "Let him go. We don't need him. We can shroud up and—"

I walked into the void.

16

Sometimes magic is as simple as walking through a door. One moment, I was stepping into a tumbling mass of blue magelight. The next, I was stepping out the other side into a large and rather elegant parlor, rich with dark woods and stunning tapestries. I moved to the side as soon as I was through, pivoting to see what this end of the gate looked like. It was another tapestry, floor to ceiling, showing a stylized portrait of the woods I had just left, with Faran in the foreground, and Kelos scowling over her shoulder.

Then Faran vanished from the tapestry, reappearing in the parlor a heartbeat later. Kelos came right behind her, though he left the fish. The scene in the tapestry blurred and faded, like the world through a scud of mist. The mist became a fog, the fog a cloud, the cloud a sheet of milkstone. That held for perhaps three heartbeats before the process reversed itself. At the end, I found myself facing a tapestry depicting a thick tropical jungle where an impossibly beautiful velyn woman sat astride an unsaddled tiger-boar. Her face was set in an arrogant sneer, her gaze directed straight out at the viewer.

"Welcome to Castelle Filathalor," said Ash. "Faran, Kelos,

you may wait for us here. I have something I wish to show Aral because of his ring. We won't be long."

I followed our host as he headed through the larger of the room's two doors. Faran looked rebellious and Kelos angry, but when I waved for them to stay there, they did. *And* visible. At least, they remained that way until I passed out of sight.

Do you think they'll stay? Triss asked.

I mentally shrugged. *Who can say?* The castle had *lots* of shadows.

Ash led me along a hall and down a long spiral of stairs that ended in an enormous room somewhere in the roots of the castle. The ceiling was cross vaulted and far above, the stone floor a single continuous piece as smooth as though someone had poured it in place and frozen it there. Lines had been etched into that surface and filled with some translucent gemlike substance. They formed a gigantic and intricate pattern centered around a half globe of black jade as big as a pony. Faint flickers of spell-light danced through the pattern in the floor and across the surface of the globe, like the pale echoes of some mighty spell long since broken.

"What is it?" I asked.

"Easier to show you."

As he started toward the central sphere, the blade in his hands began to bell and jangle like steel scraped across rough stone. It also started jerking this way and that as though it wanted to get loose. The Sylvani lord held on tight, his face as grim as the grave.

When we reached the stone, Ash took the sword in a double-handed grip, point down, and raised it high over his head. This time when he spoke a long piece in high Sylvani, he did so slowly and carefully, as though his soul depended on the proper pronunciation of each syllable. The words came out in a rhythmic cadence that reminded me of Aveni vadric poetry, though I thought I detected a rhyming structure, which no Aveni would ever use. As he spoke, sparks of spell-light like the ones in the floor and the globe flew from his lips to dance along the edges of the godsword.

The blade continued to shake and chime the whole time Ash spoke. As he neared what sounded like the peroration of his chant, its motions became weaker and weaker. Finally, Ash cried out a last word in a voice twice as loud as any he had used before and slammed the sword point-first into the apex of the globe. It hit like a knife going into flesh rather than a chisel into stone, and it sank a good three feet into the jade.

Streaks of orange burned their way through the midnight jade, forking outward from the point where steel met stone to split and roll down the sides until the entire globe took on the aspect of a tiger's hide. Once that process finished itself, the sphere began to bend and flow, taking on a new shape—the snarling head of a filathalor. The sword was buried deep in the center of its forehead. At the moment the transformation completed itself, and, all in an instant, the pattern on the floor crackled to life, filling with the most intense spell-light I'd ever seen.

That's a hell of a piece of magery, sent Triss.

Yeah, I think it might even impress Harad.

"The tomb of the goddess lies directly beneath the filathalor's head." Ash waved his arms to encompass the whole room. "It took me nearly a hundred years of work, every minute of it spent fighting the goddess, to inscribe the spell that encloses us now. *This* is what it takes to bind a buried god across the great deeps of time. Sheathing the sword puts her to sleep and holds her there, but even in her dreams she tests at the bonds, pushing and pulling and forever gnawing away at the edges."

I had a hard time encompassing the scale of the spellwork involved in the Sylvani's binding. "Why do you *ever* remove the sword from the stone?"

I was wondering about that, too, Triss sent.

"Because the binding is tied to my soul every bit as strongly as the goddess is. Were I to go beyond the grounds of Castelle Filathalor without bringing the sword with me, even for so long as a day, the spell would fail and rebound on me. I would become a hollow shell inhabited only by the will of the Changer."

"Is that what's going to happen to Siri?" I found it hard to even ask the question and I could feel that Triss shared my worries.

"I hope not. Initially, I made the sword to bind the power of an unburied god into a tool that a man might wield. Later, after I understood what that really meant and recognized my foolish vanity, I gave up the quest to command that power. But I could only make slight alterations to the sword. Your Namara meant to slay a god, inasmuch as such a thing is possible, to force the Smoldering Flame back into the grave and keep him there, and that was Siri's intent as well. That matters. Not enough perhaps, but it does matter."

"Why am I not reassured?"

"You should be. The danger is still terrible, but Siri used god-magic to bind a god. Lesser god-magic perhaps, and too weak by far for the task, but god-magic nonetheless. That gives her a chance that I would not have if my wardings failed. With luck and your help, perhaps it will be possible to free her from the influence of the god, or merely to hold it back for a few short hundreds of years. That is another place where her plight is less . . . fraught than mine. Time allows her the chance to escape into death without having to embrace it. That door is closed to me."

"Is that what this is really about? She told me that she called me here to help her with Kelos and the Key of Sylvaras."

"The key doesn't exist. I am seven thousand years old and I have never found any sign of it more substantial than the first whispers of the legend, though I looked for it long and hard in my youth. Others have devoted more years to that quest than I, some of them very great mages indeed, but no velyn has ever seen the thing. No, if it did exist, it would have come to light long years ago. And, if it had, every buried god within the compass of the wall would have torn themselves from the grave and made war on each other to possess it. There is no key."

Do you think that's true? I mentally asked Triss.

It makes a lot of sense, especially the part about the thing igniting another round of godwar if it did exist. On the other hand, Siri seemed to think that Kelos believed in it, and he's not easily gulled.

No, but he might be playing Siri to accomplish something else.

Or Siri might be playing us.

There's that, too.

"If the key doesn't exist," I asked Ash, "then what is Kelos really after? And Siri?"

The Sylvani shrugged. "That is something you will have to

sort out for yourself. But now, before we return to your companions above, I have one thing more to say to you, and this is the real reason I brought you here. I believe that here in this place, the godsword can free you of that ring you wear on your finger. Slide it along the exposed edge of the blade and the ring will break, trapping the smoke within the binding that surrounds us long enough for it to dissipate."

I felt Triss tense at the offer, but he didn't say anything one way or the other. Apparently, this one was up to me.

I looked at him. "I thought you wanted me to help Siri."

"I do." Ash nodded.

"But Siri said I would need the ring to do that."

"You might. It will protect you from some of the powers of the god while making you more susceptible to others. Certainly, Siri thinks it will help you, and no one knows more about the Smoldering Flame than she does."

"Then why are you offering to remove it?"

"Because I know what it means to bind yourself to a buried god for one you love. If I can help you to help Siri, I will. But if there is any shred of doubt in your heart about the rightness of what you're doing, or the binding you have taken on, I owe it to my soul to offer you the chance to escape it."

I looked at the smoke ring and thought about what I had learned over the last few weeks. "I'd walk into fire for her."

"You already have." His eyes were sad. "Is that your final word?"

I nodded.

"You're sure it's you speaking and not the god speaking *through* you?"

"I believe so."

It is, sent Triss. *I can feel it. I'm not sure that I agree with the decision, but it's definitely all you.*

Do you want me to cut the ring off?

I don't know. I look at what has happened to Kyrissa, and that frightens me even more than the changes in Siri. But, at the same time, I am not willing to abandon them. And, if we must go up against a god . . . even a dead god, we're going to need all the help we can get.

I think we have to keep it.

Triss sighed, but he didn't argue. Ash had waited while Triss and I went silently back and forth, though whether he knew what was going on was an open question. Now he nodded very faintly.

"I can see that your decision is made. It's the same one I would make"—Ash chuckled—"the same one that I *did* make." He put a hand on my shoulder. It was warmer than a human's, but the contact carried no hint of the sort of glamour the Durkoth wore. "I can't say whether the choice is the right one, but I hope that it turns out for you better than mine has for me."

Clear laughter sounded from the base of the stairs behind me. "Oh, Ash, my love, you make it sound like marrying me was the worst thing that could ever have happened to you." The voice was beautiful and throaty, and it made me think of green leaves under moonlight.

Ash's mood visibly lightened as he raised both his eyebrows and affected a stern demeanor. "You know very well that's not the decision I was speaking of, Kayla."

I turned then to see an achingly beautiful velyn woman approaching us. She was taller than I, though not so tall as her lord, with dark hair and darker eyes, and flawless skin the color of forest shadows.

She grinned and winked at me, dropping her voice into an excellent imitation of Ash. " 'I know what it means to bind yourself to a buried god for one you love.' " She swept her arms wide. "And so begins our play this evening: The Song of Kayla and Ashkent, a tragedy in three acts. Come, children, draw closer and listen to a tale of darkest woe and unplumbed pathos that would make the buried gods weep in their very graves. It begins in a glade where our intrepid hero broods over his terrible creation, the godsword."

By then she had crossed the distance between us, and—after bestowing a kiss on Ash—she offered me her hands. "I am Kayla Nel Kaledren, called the Darkvelyn by my shocked and horrified in-laws . . . when they will speak of me at all. And, you can only be Aral Kingslayer. Siri has had much to say of you, and not all of it I think untrue."

I was still trying to come up with anything that I could say that might stand up to such a tidal force of personality, when Triss formed himself out of my shadow and slipped between us.

"Cousin, well met." He lowered his head briefly, touching

his muzzle to her extended palms, then looked up into her eyes. "How did I not know that the Kreyn were shadow-kin?"

She smiled at him. "The alliance is a very old one, though not much remarked these days anyplace outside our ancient homes. I wonder, do they even speak of the Kreyn anymore in the lands beyond the wall? Or have we become simply another sort of Sylvani? More exotic perhaps, but still children of the light?"

Triss dropped down to stand by my side. Kayla's hands were still extended, so I cautiously took them in my own. They were cool to the touch and free of any glamour, though her beauty and vitality provided her with an appeal that struck even deeper than the Durkoth's—pulling at heartstrings rather than invoking sexual desire. I did not want to take Kayla Nel Kaledren to my bed, but I understood how very easy it would be to love her.

We only touched for a few brief heartbeats, but I could see that she read deeper into my heart than most ever would. She squeezed my hands once, then released them with a smile.

"Welcome to Castelle Filathalor, Aral, Slayer of Kings. Stay as long as you will. Depart in joy. Return often. While you are our guest, I am merely Kayla and bear no titles nor wait on any formality."

"And I am Aral. Thank you for your welcome . . . Kayla." Though I generally disliked titles and the nobles who wore them, I found it hard to treat this ancient woman as I might a mortal.

She laughed again. "Let it go, Aral. Dignity is a bauble for the young and the vain to wear, a costume they assume to hide their insecurities. The old and the powerful need it not, and I am both. I drowned my dignity in a river under mighty trees five thousand years before you were born. Do not try to wrap its corpse around my shoulders now. But come, we must collect your companions."

She turned and started back toward the stairs. It was only as I fell out of the center of her attention that I realized that I had been half holding my breath for some time.

I think I'm in love, sent Triss. Then, more soberly, *Trust not my judgment where it comes to Kayla Darkvelyn. She is flesh, but also a sister to shadows.*

She has power over you?

*Not directly, but she tastes of the everdark and has great
strength of will. My mind is my own, but my soul sees her as
a beloved sister long lost. I understand now how the Durkoth
can twist the wits of a stone dog. The effect of the First on their
allied elements is . . . intoxicating.*

A heavy arm landed across my shoulders and Ash leaned
down to speak softly in my ear. "Welcome to the eye of the
storm, Aral."

"I heard that," Kayla called over her shoulder.

"You were supposed to," he whispered back.

As we passed back through the castle on our way to the
parlor above, I realized that the building no longer felt like a
mere pile of stones elegantly arranged, but rather like something alive. A sleeping dragon perhaps, or an ancient power of
earth. The reason was obvious. The will of the buried goddess
below inhabited the place in much the way a soul inhabited a
body. She might sleep in stone, but the castle breathed with her
dreams. The art reflected her will as well, with the filathalor
represented heavily in the sculpture and paintings.

Faran and Kelos had taken seats in opposite corners of the
parlor, from which they glared at each other like two angry but
exhausted cats trapped in a sea trunk. Normally, I would have
expected to find their Shades somewhere in the middle, speaking civilly with each other regardless of the antipathy between
their human partners. That was certainly how Triss and Zass
behaved despite the fact that Devin and I hated each other's
guts. But, whatever Malthiss might wish on the topic, Ssithra
had signaled her own feelings toward him back in the glade.
They both rose as we entered.

"I'm surprised to find you both unmoved," I said. Triss had
swept for shadow signatures along the way, and there was no
evidence that either of them had trailed us down to the roots
of the castle.

"I *started* to follow you," Faran admitted. "But then Ssithra
said that the shadows were watching us and that there was zero
point in attempting to hide in shadows that refused to cooperate. It sounded fishy to me, but my head still isn't up to a real
argument, so I let her have her way."

"Malthiss agreed with Ssithra, though I didn't understand
the why until this very moment." Kelos met Kayla's eyes, and

then very formally bowed the bow of equals meeting on the practice field. "Sister to shadow."

"Call me Kayla, Master Kelos." When she spoke there was none of the warmth she had shown Triss and me. Next, she inclined her head ever so slightly to the shadow at his feet. "Resshath Malthiss."

"Just Kelos," he said.

Kayla shook her head. "I think not, Deathwalker. You are Aral's guest, not mine. I would no more think of addressing you so informally than I would one of Ash's noble relatives."

That's a deeper cut than many might have made with a sword and clear room to swing, sent Triss.

If he's bleeding, he doesn't show it.

He is still the Deathwalker. You could cut his head off and his expression wouldn't change.

True.

Kayla turned to Faran and Ssithra, holding out her hands. "Welcome to my house, children. How shall I call you?"

"Faran's all the name I own." She moved forward, and, together with her shadow, took Kayla's hands in her own.

Shadows shifted, and a dark phoenix rose to perch on Faran's shoulder, inclining her head to the velyn woman. "Ssithra."

Kayla smiled at them both. "So it shall be." Then she looked up, including Ash and me in her gaze when she asked, "Are any of you hungry?"

"Famished," I replied. "But I have things to do before I can eat." I touched my hand to the bag hanging around my neck. "I'll need a fire."

"We can certainly arrange that." Ash's eyes went thoughtful and far away. "But let's do it outside the bounds of the castle proper. I don't know what your method looks like, but anything that draws the attention of the buried ones ought not take place too close to the warding below."

"Ash, why don't you take Kelos along with you." Kayla drew Faran into place beside her. "If you're willing to skip the festivities, I may have something that will help with your headaches. It would not work for most humans, but your connection to the everdark makes you something of a Kreyn by proxy."

Before Faran could answer, Ssithra spoke. "Yes, please."

"But what about Aral?" demanded Faran.

Ssithra flicked her wings angrily. "I'm sure that he can spend an hour or two out from under your eye without getting into too much trouble. You may fool the others, but you cannot hide your pain from me. Do not let your bravery make you stupid."

Faran looked mulish for a beat or two, but then she nodded. "All right. I'm all yours, Kayla."

Ash led Kelos and me down to the castle's main stairs. These split at a massive landing ten feet above the floor of the entry hall, curving outward like wings. The twinned flights widened as they went down, defining a semi-enclosed crescent between them—a typical design, and one I had seen in several other castles.

What I had not seen previously was the row of brass sculptures that lined the curved wall from the base of one flight of stairs to the other. There must have been fifty of the things standing shoulder to shoulder. They belonged to an aesthetic that felt alien, even somewhat disturbing. Each of the figures was eight feet tall and humanoid but sexless.

Take a man, dip him in wax, and then pull him out to let it harden. Do that again and again until nothing is left of his features or individuality. Plane away every imperfection, and accent the edges so that the figure becomes as streamlined as a ship's beak. Cast what remains in brass, polish it until it glows, and you have the sculptures of Castelle Filathalor. Faceless. Sexless. Shorn of any hint of personality, yet projecting a sort of bright, emotionless vitality.

I found them repellent on some level below conscious thought. And that was *before* Ash sang one of them awake. As we reached the base of the steps, Ash pivoted into the open-fronted crescent. Pointing to the first of the sculptures on that end he sang a quick rhyme in high Sylvani, blowing spell-light into its face with the words. It breathed in the light of magic with a great sighing noise, then stepped down from the low pedestal that held it to kneel before him. He spoke to it again in his own language, his tone that of a man giving a servant instructions, and it rose to its feet, preceding us to the gate.

There, another pair of the brass figures stepped forward to lift the bar and swing open the thick ironbound doors. The first sculpture marched through ahead of us, its long legs driving it forward with the inhuman precision of shears clacking mechanically away at a fleece. A few yards after it crossed the drawbridge, it turned. It moved nearly as fast walking as a man running, and it vanished into the thick woods that surrounded the castle within a matter of seconds.

"I've sent it ahead to prepare a fire." Ash inclined his head in the direction the thing had gone as we followed it across the bridge.

"What is it?" asked Kelos—his first words since we'd departed the parlor above. "I've never seen the like."

"A living spell," replied Ash.

"I saw no light but your own," I said.

"God-magic animates the servants of the Changer. They are very reliable if you give them specific instructions. But without the will of their mistress to guide them, they become restless if you let them go too long without a suitable task. Kayla and I crafted a spell that settles around the gem they use as a heart and binds them in sleep until we have need of their services."

"Interesting," said Kelos. "Will you have to put the one you raised back to sleep when it's done with the fire?"

"No, without further reinforcement, my words of waking will last only until the next turn of the sun. When it grows sleepy, it will return automatically to its place in the great hall."

Kelos's one remaining eye took on a thoughtful cast. "I wonder if you could construct one using a more common sort of magery."

Why do I not trust him to use this information for anything good? asked Triss.

Because you don't trust him to use any *information for anything good?*

That could be it.

While I spoke with Triss, Ash was answering the question. "Of course you can, but it's hardly worth the effort. The spells have to be crafted and laid individually, so you can only build one at time. The things take three or four years to bring to full animation, and then they tend to run down after a bare handful of decades." Ash looked ahead, and pointed. "There's also that."

We had just entered a clearing split by a small stream. The

brass figure stood at the edge of the stream. As we watched, it pitched a chunk of log across the water. It landed in the midst of a loose pile of similar pieces. Before the log even finished bouncing, the thing pivoted, crossing to an old downed tree and ripping another hunk of wood free before returning to the stream to throw it amongst the others.

After three repetitions, Kelos whistled. "It's geographically bound, isn't it? It can't leave the castle grounds."

"Correct. This batch is tied to the tomb of the Changer. The ones that I made had a greater range, but even they could go no more than a mile or two from the place where they were first awakened. There is a very complex magical diagram involved in the final wakening and they are tied to that location even though the figure is actually destroyed in the process. I haven't been able to discover the cause."

"Too bad," said Kelos.

We waited a few more minutes while the thing finished tearing apart the old tree and tossing it onto the pile. Then Kelos and I waded the stream and kicked the logs into a tighter mass. Ashkent remained on the same shore as his brass minion, reminding me that he was almost as bound to the environs of Castelle Filathalor—or, really, the goddess—as it was. Next, Triss shifted around behind me for a few moments while I spilled magefire from my palms onto the logs.

Once the fire was going hot and bright, I tossed the bag with the glyph stone into the center. The leather tightened instantly, shaping itself into a second skin around the stone disk. Soon, cracks began to form in the leather, and then the whole thing burst into flame. A rope of dense black smoke rose out of the fire, centered above the burning bag.

The smoke twisted and turned, looping back on itself to shape a woman's figure—Siri's figure. But unlike my previous encounters with her smoky avatars, this one merely hung in the air, hands together, head down.

"Now what?" asked Kelos, his voice pitched to carry across the water and so include Ash in our conversation.

"We wait for it to heat up," I said. "The glyphs are made of iron. The Fire That Burns Underground said Siri could only be freed after they begin to glow orange."

"That's going to take a while." Kelos lowered himself into a cross-legged seat on the ground.

Across the water, Ash did the same. Kelos was right, but I resisted following his example simply because he was Kelos. Instead, I stood on his blind side, just far enough back so he had to twist his whole torso if he wanted to see me. I knew it was petty, but I couldn't help myself. Of course, if it bothered him, he didn't show it. He simply stared into the heart of the fire and never so much as turned his head my way.

It was late afternoon, and the sun was high, so Triss and Malthiss both stayed deep down in shadow. I could feel that Triss remained awake, but he didn't seem inclined to talk, perhaps for the same reasons that I found myself without any words.

This was the first time since the fall of the temple that I had spent more than five minutes with Kelos when we were neither in direct conflict nor threatened by nearby enemies. Without any such force to drive conversation, I found that I had no idea what to say to my old mentor. A quarter hour passed in silence, and not the companionable sort.

Then . . . "Why did you do it?" The words burst out of me without any preamble—I didn't even know I was going to say them before I spoke. Triss tensed within my shadow, coming fully awake and alert in an instant.

Kelos went perfectly still for several long beats, but then he took a deep breath and nodded without turning to look at me. "That's a fair question, and if I owe anyone an answer, it's you."

Good, he wasn't going to do me the discourtesy of pretending he didn't know *exactly* what I was asking.

"You fought the Kitsune?" he asked.

The Kitsune was a rogue Blade, a woman who had turned her back on Namara to kill for money, a legend who had battled the order to a standstill in a private war that lasted nearly a century. Her given name was Nuriko. She was brilliant and powerful and quite, quite mad. I had never faced a tougher enemy, and she had nearly destroyed me.

"She was your lover?" I countered.

"She was that, too, but first she was my enemy."

"I killed her," I replied. "You know that, right?" I kept my voice even, like it was no big deal. I wanted him to think it hadn't really mattered to me. "Drove one of Devin's swords into her heart." I wanted to *hurt* him.

Kelos didn't so much as flinch. In fact, he laughed. "You're not the first, you know. To kill her. That was me. I sliced Nuriko's throat from ear to ear, a sword cut two inches deep, blood everywhere. There was no surviving it. I've killed thousands, Aral. I know death when I see it. I saw the light go out of her eyes as Thiussus took her into himself. And then they both vanished into the everdark, from which there is no returning."

17

Sometimes, words strike like lightning. They come with no warning and no chance to get out of the way. A flash, a crash, and the thing they touch is destroyed.

That's how I felt now, blown apart. "I . . . I don't understand."

"Neither did I," said Kelos. "You know that Namara sent me to kill the Kitsune, right?"

"Of course."

He had brought her sword back to lay at the feet of the goddess—the Kitsune was the only Blade to carry a single goddess-made blade—a great-sword created especially for Nuriko in the mode of the Kanjurese Islands where she had been born. Kelos's execution of the Kitsune was the feat that had earned him the name of Deathwalker. But when I'd met Nuriko the previous summer, she was both very much alive *and* carrying the sword Kelos was supposed to have brought to the goddess.

Until this moment, I had assumed that the two of them had conspired to fake her death and then somehow return the sword to her. Now? I didn't know what to believe. You see, I, too, had seen the Kitsune die by my own hand. I, too, had watched as the spark of life drained out of her eyes, watched as Thiussus took his partner into the everdark, known it to be a trip from which there is no returning.

My first thought now was that Devin had told Kelos about that night—that Kelos was using Devin's descriptions of my actions to play mind games with me. But as much as I wanted that to be the story, I couldn't make myself believe it. There was a hard ring of truth in Kelos's words that I couldn't quite dismiss.

He continued. "We fought on the rooftops of Emain Fell. The Kitsune had killed thirty-one Blades over ninety-four years of war with the order at that point, and Namara wanted to end her once and for all. The goddess sent Master Pol to kill the Duke of Fell, knowing she was sending Pol into a trap. She did it without telling anyone but me. We knew the Kitsune had some way of getting information out of the temple and the only one Namara trusted absolutely was me."

"Ironic, that."

"Now, perhaps yes. Then, no. I was completely committed to Namara in those days. It wasn't until later that I realized her methods could never achieve her goals, and I had to make my choice between them."

How dare he! We don't have to listen to this self-serving ssissathshta! Triss trailed off into angry hisses in the back of my mind.

I think it's shit, too, Triss. But this may be our only chance to find out what he was thinking, and I need to know this.

Kelos continued, oblivious to our exchange. "The goddess sent me out after Pol. Not to save him, but to avenge him. I did both. Nuriko was a magnificent swordswoman, but you know that—you've killed her, too. Our fight was a close-run thing, the closest I've had short of when that basilisk took my eye. I have a dozen scars from that day with Nuriko, but her sword didn't cut half so deep as her words."

Kelos hunched his shoulders—the first movement he'd made since he sat down in the first place, and one that made him look beaten somehow. "It was a running fight and it lasted nearly four hours."

"Four *hours*?" That was an almost unimaginably long time

when you considered that a sword fight is usually decided in minutes, or even seconds.

"Much of that was spent chasing each other across the rooftops, or simply in gasping for breath between rounds. We were both utterly spent by the end. I think that the only reason I beat her was because I simply had more physical reserves to burn. I finally killed her atop the Temple of Shan, but I made a critical error first. Nuriko called hold and asked me for two minutes to speak. By then, I was sure I was going to win, and she was so damned good that I hated to have to kill her. So, I said yes. And that was my ruin. Did you speak with her?"

"I did, several times."

"Then you know what she's like. The intensity. The passion. The total commitment to the destruction of the system that creates the monsters Namara trained us to hunt . . ."

"The madness . . ." growled Triss.

Kelos laughed bitterly. "Perhaps, but if so, it's a divine madness. The first thing she said was that she knew that I was going to kill her, but that it was all right. She didn't blame me for not being able to see beyond my orders. I'd expected her to try to convince me to let her live—half wanted her to succeed, really—but she didn't. All that she did was ask me two questions. First, she wanted to know if I really believed that killing some corrupt king actually changed anything, or if it was a never-ending cycle, with new monsters popping up as quickly as we eliminated the old ones."

That fit with my experience. "She asked me the same thing."

"What did you tell her? Thirteen years ago you killed Ashvik, a monster of a king. You just killed Ashvik's successor a few months ago, another monster. Did killing Ashvik really change anything, or did it just push the problem down the road?"

It was a hard question to answer, but I thought back to Chiu the bandit chief and the scars on his back. "Sometimes, all you can do is hold back the darkness for a few seconds more. Executing Ashvik saved a lot of lives, even if Thauvik started the killing up again only a few years later. I don't believe the people whose lives I saved think I wasted my effort."

"We are neck deep in plague rats, Aral. Killing one king is like pointing out a particular rat and saying, 'That rat? I'm going to kill that rat, because it will make a difference.' That's all you're doing."

I wasn't going to have this argument. Not here. Not now. Not with this man. "What was her second question?"

"She asked me if I would open my eyes and look around and really think about the question over the years to come. And, if I was willing to do that much, would I promise to talk with her again later? We both knew by then that I was going to kill her, so it seemed like a ridiculous question. But she was brilliant and passionate and the greatest duelist I'd ever fought. I couldn't refuse her."

"And then you killed her."

"And then I killed her, and Thiussus took her into the everdark, leaving behind her sword and an empty suit of clothes. I brought the sword to Namara and I went back to my duties. But I couldn't forget Nuriko's questions, and the more corrupt priests and debauched earls I executed, the more I saw that nothing ever changed. Nothing. Ever. Changed. For seventeen years I killed and killed and killed again, and the world didn't get any better. And, somewhere in there, my heart broke. Nuriko was right, nothing we did mattered as long as the system itself was corrupt."

"Then she came back," I whispered.

"Then she came back." Kelos nodded.

"What did she say the second time you talked?"

"She took me to a distillery in Aven, and she showed me how they make whiskey."

That doesn't make any *sense,* Triss sent, and I echoed him aloud, "I don't understand."

"I didn't at first either, but she showed me a thing called a safety valve. It's a device that allows the still to let off pressure that might otherwise blow the whole thing up. She told me that Namara had become a safety valve for the evils of our system. That the goddess drained just enough evil out of the eleven kingdoms to keep the whole thing from exploding. She told me that without Namara to release that pressure we could bring the whole thing down and create a better world."

"How did you answer her?" Triss asked.

"I told her that she was crazy . . . the first time. But again, she went away and left me to think about things on my own. A year or two later, she came back and asked me what I thought now. Aral, she may be crazy, but that doesn't mean that she's wrong."

I looked away from Kelos, focusing my attention on the flames. I didn't want to hear any more. "The glyph is glowing orange."

Kelos turned around, staring up at me until I finally met his gaze. "Nuriko's coming back, Aral. You know that as well as I do. She is something more than human if less than a goddess. What will *you* say to her when she asks you her question a second time?"

I drew my right-hand sword. Kelos smiled sadly, nodded, and turned his back on me. I knew that he would let me kill him then if I chose to do so.

Aral! Triss spoke sharply into my mind.

I stepped forward and brought the blade down with all my might . . . shattering the glyph stone. As much as I despised what Kelos had done and become, I still loved more than I hated.

When the stone broke, the figure of smoke lifted her chin and looked me in the eyes. A second figure formed, splitting out of the first—a feathered serpent. It coiled itself around her shoulders, wings held high above her head. The smoke thickened and darkened. It took a step forward. Another.

One foot left the fire, becoming flesh as it touched the earth. Then the other. Siri stood before us, her face sweaty and strained, her eyes wide and staring. Shadow bloomed at her feet. Rushed upward. Infused the smoking serpent. Became Kyrissa. Siri stumbled forward, started to fall.

Kelos moved then, exhibiting that terrible speed that seemed impossible in such a big man. One moment, he was sitting on the ground a good two yards away from Siri. The next, he had caught her and lifted her back to her feet before her knees could touch the dirt.

"Are you all right?" he asked.

Siri's answer was deceptively calm. "Take your hands off of me, traitor, or I swear that I will turn you inside out and smoke your organs to feed to the dogs."

"I'll take that as a yes." He released Siri, and stepped away.

Siri swayed, but she stayed upright this time. She closed her eyes for a long beat, and the swaying subsided. When she opened them again, she turned my way. "Took your damned time getting me out of that thing, didn't you?"

I recognized her tone for what it was, and responded in kind. "I know how much you hate to have your elbow joggled when you're working and I didn't want to get my head bitten off for interrupting a daring escape." I shrugged and sheathed my sword. "Is it *my* fault that you somehow got miscast as the damsel in distress for real this time?"

"Fuck you, Aral." She looked around, spotted Ash and his brass man. "Castelle Filathalor?"

"I'm on the grounds," replied Ash. "The stream is the boundary."

"All right, then." She took a staggering step toward Ash, then paused. "Aral, get your ass over here. Help me up to the castle and I'll think about forgiving you your tardiness someday."

As I lifted her arm across my shoulder, I glanced over at Kelos. I thought I saw pain in his eye as he watched us, and love, but only for an instant. Before I could be sure of what I'd seen, his face reassumed its normal masklike expression.

"You wanted to know what I will tell the Kitsune when she comes back," I said over Siri's shoulder. "I will tell her what I learned at the bottom of a whiskey bottle. The world isn't a thing made up of black-and-white ideas. There is no *system*. There are only people. If you take a hammer to the *system*, that's really what you're destroying. People. When I kill a king, I kill a man. When you kill a system, you're killing a hell of a lot of innocents. If you're okay with that, then who is the monster? Really?"

"**You** want to go *where*?" For the first time since I'd met him, Ash looked genuinely disconcerted.

"The city understairs," Kelos repeated from the far end of the long kitchen table where we were all sitting. "That's where the Son of Heaven believes the Key of Sylvaras is hidden."

Kayla looked thoughtful. "If it actually existed, that'd be a damned fine place to hide it. You have to admit that, Ash."

The couple had put together a big meal for us all—food was one of the things that the enchanted servants of the Changer did an especially poor job at—and we'd eaten it in place rather than haul it all to the castle's great hall. Like the dinner we'd had back at the wall, the Sylvani-style meal was heavy on the curries and other complex dishes. We were drinking more of that lovely spiced tea, though they'd offered us a variety of stronger drinks that had brought the bitter longing sharply back to the surface for me.

"Back up," said Faran. "What's this city understairs?"

"Do you know much about the Asavi?" asked Kayla.

"Nope."

"Well, in the beginning, there were the Kreyn," Kayla began.

Siri held up a hand. "I hate to interrupt, but I know how the First tell stories, and none of us ephemeral types are long enough lived for you to do the whole thing properly." She turned to look at Faran. "There used to only be one type of Other. They split into a bunch of tribes and fought our gods. They lost. Two of the tribes chose to live on the human side of the wall, the Durkoth and the Vesh'An. Everybody else stayed here. You know that part?"

Faran nodded.

"Good. Most of the tribes that stayed are more like each other than they are like the Durkoth or the Vesh'An. The one exception is the Asavi. In making their alliance with air, the Asavi were transformed every bit as radically as their cousins on our side of the wall. For starters, they grew wings. But winged flight is hard when you're man-sized, so they shrank themselves as well." She held her thumb and forefinger about two inches apart.

"That's tiny," said Faran.

"It is," agreed Siri. "Life is different when you're that size. Very different. Their culture changed as radically as their bodies. They became insular and much more hostile to outsiders. They live in hivelike cities and their tempers are even shorter than they are. Think angry, immortal, intelligent, spell-casting bees, and you won't be too far from the truth. Their largest hive is built under the grand stairs of the Sylvani capitol. The stairs used to connect the palace with the port. They occupy some of the most expensive land in the city. But the big people no longer use them for fear of angry swarms of Asavi."

Kayla sighed. "You do realize how badly you've just butchered twenty-five thousand years of First history, don't you, dear?"

Siri assumed an air of startled innocence, and fluttered her eyelashes. "Is any of that wrong?"

"Well . . ."

"Then I just saved us all about six hundred hours of beautifully narrated blah-blah-blah blah-blah, didn't I?"

Ash laughed aloud. "The child's tongue strikes deeper than her swords."

Faran spread her hands. "Speaking of blah-blah-blah, what would it mean if the Key *was* there?"

Ash's grin faded. "It means that we won't be able to help you beyond delivering you to the city. The Asavi do not allow any of the other First within their hives."

As usual at any conference that involved their active participation, the Shades had assumed their preferred forms and taken positions along the walls beside or behind their respective partners. Triss flicked his wings now and leaned forward. "Wouldn't size preclude the entry of anyone but the Asavi in any case?"

Ash shook his head. "Once, maybe. But the migration of so many of your people into the empire has changed the way that most of the First live. In many of our cities, the human population outnumbers the First. Humans do much of the brute labor of the empire these days—even some of the lesser craft work. The Asavi are more insular than the Sylvani, but where their settlements overlap those of my people, they have also taken to employing human workers."

"How does that even work?" Faran asked, looking skeptical.

"The Mouse Gates," said Kayla. Then, when that drew blank looks all around: "The Asavi breed some of the best mages in the empire. They have crafted powerful spell gates. Enter from the city side, and you shrink to fit the Asavi mold. Reenter from the hive side and you return to your normal stature."

"That's one hell of a fancy piece of magic," I said.

Kayla nodded. "Yes, but it does have some rather sharp limitations. It only works to shrink and restore, never the other way round. You have to go out via the same gate through which you entered. It will not work on the First without special tuning, since the Asavi don't want the rest of us anywhere within their boundaries. Most importantly, the transformation is unstable. The gate stores an imprint of you when you pass through. If you don't pass back the other way within twelve hours, the gate sheds the imprint."

"That sounds mild enough," said Faran.

"It's not." Kayla pinched the flesh on the back of her hand. "We are made of more than this. Every fiber of our beings is infused with the essence of magic."

Faran nodded impatiently. "Yes, yes, nima, the stuff that fills the well of the soul. Varies wildly from person to person and defines the power of the individual's mage gift. Draw it down to cast big spells, etc. That's first week of mage school stuff."

Siri put a hand on Faran's forearm. "Be polite." Faran flared her nostrils, but nodded a moment later.

Kayla continued as though the exchange hadn't happened. "Mage gift defines the maximum density of magic that the vessel of flesh can hold. When you pass through the Mouse Gate, you don't become any more dense, so the extra nima has to be stored somewhere. A tiny part of it goes to feed the gate. The rest is held for your return. If you don't make it back in time and the gate sheds the imprint, it also flares off the excess magic . . . which is still tied to the person's soul.

"If you don't leave the city within twelve hours of entering, your flared nima will backlash through your body, burning you up from within. The more power you had going in, the bigger the effect. A normal human might merely die of fever. A hedge witch will broil from the inside out. A more powerful mage will literally burst into flame."

The smoke swirling in Siri's hair suddenly increased its gyrations as she turned to Kelos. "I know why Ash *doesn't* believe in the key, and I think he makes a damned good argument. Why are *you* certain the key exists?"

Kelos shrugged. "I'm not. But the Son of Heaven is. He wants it and he wants it very badly. That's reason enough for me to deny it to him even without any other potential uses we might find for it. The best way to do that is to grab it and put it out of his reach."

Faran boiled out of her chair and glared down the length of the table at Kelos. "A decade ago, you betrayed us all *to* the Son of Heaven. In the process, you killed almost everyone that I loved. Why the fuck should we trust you to be working against him now?"

If Kelos felt the least bit ashamed, he didn't show it in face or voice. "Beyond my efforts to manipulate Aral into killing the Son of Heaven two years ago?" he asked mildly.

"Yeah, beyond that. I don't believe that you actually wanted the Son dead. If you did, why is he still alive after Aral got close enough to leave those cuts on his face?" She turned and glanced at me. "No offense, Aral, but I think you got played there. You should have killed him, even if it would have made Kelos the next Son of Heaven."

Kelos smiled. "That's one place that we agree, Master Faran. Aral should have killed him, but not because it would have made me the Son of Heaven. I would have used the power to make the world a better place, but that was always a side effect of the plan, never its heart. No, Aral should have killed him for the very reason that those cuts have never healed." He took a deep breath. "Maybe it's finally time that I laid the whole story out."

Kelos looked down the table at me and raised an enquiring eyebrow. He was leaving it up to me, and I found that I both needed to know this and felt a sick fear at the idea. What if he somehow convinced me that he'd made the right decision? Wouldn't that make me in some way culpable in his betrayal? What if he didn't and it killed what love I still had for him? It felt like someone had just plunged an ice dagger into my guts, but I nodded. I had to know.

Kelos leaned back in his chair and put his booted feet up on another, looking as relaxed as a big cat after feasting on a fresh kill. "Aral knows some of this, but I will tell it all now. It started with the Kitsune. . . ."

He went on to relate the story he'd told me by the fire earlier. That part left Siri looking thoughtful, but it didn't touch the rage expressed in every line of Faran's body.

When he finished with that portion of the thing, he launched into territory I knew only slightly from my conversations with Devin and the Kitsune herself. "The third time Nuriko came back, she had a proposition for me. She told me that she had aligned herself with the Son of Heaven, and that he wanted to bring down the goddess and bring the order under the control of the 'Emperor of Heaven and the true rule of the gods.' Through himself, of course."

"And you found that convincing?" Kyrissa asked from her place on the wall behind Siri.

"Not in the slightest," answered Kelos. "Neither did Nuriko, for that matter. We knew he was lying to us, and we knew why. But we both saw our chance to bring down the whole damn system. You see, the Son of Heaven is a rapportomancer."

"A what?" asked Kayla.

"I don't think you have them on this side of the wall," said Siri. "It's a term for someone who has the familiar gift but no mage gift."

The First were their own focus—they didn't need a partner to cast spells. That need for an external focus was a limitation the gods had placed on human magic after the rebellion of the First. A way to keep us from following our forebears into war with the gods—one of many.

Siri continued, "Rapportomancy is incredibly rare even among humans, with two notable exceptions." She looked at Kelos now. "But I hadn't heard that the Son came either from the Kanjurese Islands or Kodamia."

The warrior caste who ruled the islands of Kanjuri were rapportomancers who bonded with the magically ensouled swords crafted by the mage smiths called Gojuru. The other exception, of course, were the Dyads of Kodamia—human-human mage-familiar pairings where the mage gift ran in one set of houses, and the familiar in another.

Kelos shook his head. "He's neither, though you never know

what you might find if you looked far enough back in his blood-
line. Where he got the gift doesn't matter. It's what it's done to
him that's important."

"Done *to* him?" I asked.

"Yes." He rose from his chair. "Once upon a time there was
a young priest from Dan Eyre. His name was Corik. In the
course of his duties ministering to the Kvanas, Corik had a
run-in with the wandering dead, one of the risen. It bit him.
Under normal circumstances the curse would have killed him
over a period of hours to weeks, depending on the strength of
his will. Then it would have resurrected his body as a new host
to pass the undead contagion on to a fresh victim. But Corik
was anything but normal. He was that one-in-a-million freak,
an undiscovered rapportomancer among a people with no history of the gift.

"That's where things get interesting, because the risen curse
isn't a spell. It's more like a magical disease. It possesses a sort
of life of its own, even a rudimentary will. As the curse
devoured Corik's life it also settled into his bones and soul.
Somewhere in there it met with his rapportomancy and bang!
Meld. Corik became the first human ever to bond with a living
curse of the undead. I don't know what kind of person Corik
was before he merged his soul with an all-devouring curse.
Pious? Ambitious? Cowardly?

"It doesn't really matter, though, because Corik was three-
quarters dead by the time he joined his soul to the disease—
well on his way into the all-devouring madness of the undead.
If it had happened a few days earlier he might have gained
complete control over the curse, maybe even changed the
course of risen history. A few days later, and he would have
been too far along. He would simply have become another of
the wandering dead with an especially close relationship to the
curse that controlled him.

"But as it was, Corik wasn't the only one who was transformed. In melding with the priest's soul, this particular strand
of the risen curse separated itself from the one that had birthed
it. That meant that Corik Half-Risen was the only victim carrying that particular strand of the disease. At least, at first. But
the curse had infused him with its need to pass itself along,
and the best way for him to do that was to amass worldly power

so that he could infect others. And, so, Corik arranged to 'trip' and slice the face of his superior with a jagged fingernail.

"Lacking Corik's inborn familiar gift, the older priest quickly succumbed to the risen curse. He became one of the undead, inhabited by a part of the disease that was Corik's familiar. In effect, he became Corik's slave, and anyone that he bit or clawed became infected with Corik's special strain of the curse in turn. Corik's rise to become Son of Heaven was swift, climbing, as he did, up a ramp made from the bodies of those above him."

"That explains so much," I whispered. I knew from Devin that the Son had some control over the risen, but Devin had thought it was something to do with the authority conferred upon him by the gods.

Kelos nodded. "But even that wasn't enough for the curse or for Corik. By the very nature of what they had become, it *couldn't* be enough. He wanted more. So, he began to arrange for the infection of nobles and officials at every level of government in the eleven kingdoms. The only ones that he couldn't touch were mages."

"Why is that?" asked Faran, her face and voice expressing a sort of creeping horror.

"Because when you kill a mage, you kill the familiar," I said—I had already figured some of this out in the course of helping Maylien, first to reclaim her barony, and, then, onto the throne of Zhan. What I hadn't known was how it applied to the Son of Heaven. "The curse can only resurrect the mage, never the familiar. Infecting any mage instantly reveals the curse. That's why the church has remained weak in Kodamia and Kanjuri, and the Magelands." Jax and I had briefly had a piece of that part of the puzzle, but I hadn't known what to do with it until now.

"Exactly." Kelos returned to his chair.

Siri rubbed her neck, putting her hands inches from the hilts of her swords. "And you *knew* this when you betrayed the goddess, Kelos?"

"Of course." Kelos crossed his arms. "Can't you see it?"

Hands drifted closer to hilts. "I see a monster who deliberately set out to help an even bigger monster take over the eleven kingdoms."

"Not at all," replied Kelos. "Nuriko and I set out to help him corrupt and control the rulers of the eleven kingdoms because we wanted to free the land from rulers altogether. You know how it works; kill the mage, kill the familiar. Right now, the Son of Heaven is pair-bonded to three-quarters of the most important governing officials in the eleven kingdoms. If he dies, they die, too. With one stroke of the sword, you can behead the whole damned lot."

18

————◆◆————

A good strategist can beat you. A great strategist can force you to beat yourself. A genius of strategy can make you believe that beating yourself is the only right thing to do.

Kelos was a genius. He wanted to tear the whole system down, and despite the fact that I disagreed with him in every possible way on the topic, I knew that at some point . . .

"I will have to kill the Son of Heaven," I whispered.

Kelos nodded. "Eventually, yes. But first you have to deny him the key. With it he can make himself into a god and put himself forever beyond the reach of justice."

"Justice!" I moved without thinking, snap drawing my swords in the same moment that I leaped onto the table. A half second later I stood with the edges of my blades touching the skin on either side of Kelos's neck—just above the arteries. "You dare to speak to me of justice after destroying Namara?"

Red ringed my vision, narrowing it to Kelos's face and the steel I held on either side of his jaw. Blood hammered in my ears and I wanted to kill him so very, very much. I pressed the swords into his flesh, dimpling the skin but not yet breaking it. It would take the tiniest of movements to end him. A short drawing cut with either hand. That was all.

"Go ahead. I deserve to die." Kelos's expression remained serene. "For what I did to the goddess. To you." His eyes flicked over my shoulder. "To Siri and Faran, and all the others, living and dead. I have earned the death you hold in your hands, Aral. I won't try to stop you or argue you out of it. Killing me *is* justice. Do it." He closed his eyes and smiled.

Aral.

Yes, Triss. Don't try to talk me out of this.

He deserves it, and the choice is yours, of course.

But? I had to ask. I didn't want to, but I had to.

He's still playing you.

And, because Triss was right, I let my swords fall away from Kelos's throat. "Clean up your own damned mess. You want the Son of Heaven dead so bad? You do it."

Tell him he's unworthy of those swords, said Triss.

All right . . . I didn't see where Triss was going, but I trusted him. "You're not worth bloodying the swords of the goddess." I turned my back on Kelos, resheathing my swords as I returned to the floor and then to my seat.

When I got there, Faran gave me a hard look. "What is it with you and not killing people who really, really need it?"

"He *wants* me to kill him, and I'm done being played."

"Can *I* kill him?" Faran asked, though she didn't sound very hopeful.

I just shrugged.

"I won't stop you," Kelos answered her.

Faran settled back into her seat. "I'll take that as a no." She sighed. "Right, since I'm the apprentice, I guess it's my job to ask the clueless questions. So, what does he think he's going to accomplish by having one of us kill him?"

"I don't know," I replied and Faran rolled her eyes. "Not all of it anyway." I turned to look at Kelos. "I do know that you believe that if I kill you it will somehow force me to go on to kill the Son of Heaven for you."

Kelos smiled but didn't say a word.

He's not wrong, sent Triss.

I am not *going to be responsible for the destruction of the governments of most of the eleven kingdoms, no matter how much he wants me to. It's madness.*

So, if Kelos were dead, you would simply walk away and let the Son of Heaven and his risen slaves rule the bulk of the eleven kingdoms? Knowing that they are willing to shed endless quantities of blood to feed the curse? Knowing that they will only continue to expand their grip on the lands of man until there is nothing left but a vast empire of the dead? You will let them win?

I growled mentally. *It's the Kitsune's plot. She can deal with it.*

We don't know how long it will be before she comes back. It took her nearly twenty years after Kelos killed her. We don't even know if she will *return this time. You're going to trust the fate of the human world to the possible resurrection of a madwoman. Really?*

Dammit, Triss, you sound like you want me to do Kelos's dirty work for him.

No, I am simply recognizing the fact that ultimately we may have no alternative. Kelos is very good at putting people in a position where they have to choose to do what he wants them to.

I'm confused. If you think that I'm just going to have to do what he wants in the end anyway, why did you keep me from killing him?

I stopped you because he wants it to be you. I suspect that has been his plan from before the temple fell. You heard what Nuriko had to say about Kelos. He believes in justice in his bones, and he believes that justice demands that the system die. But he also believes that betraying the goddess means that justice demands his death. He hates himself for what he's done even though he believes he had no choice. He sees in you his ultimate successor as the true champion of justice. Especially after you beat him in Heaven's Reach. If it's you that kills him, especially with the swords of the goddess, he will see it as Namara's will made manifest. It would offer him a sort of peace.

And that's why you told me to say that he was unworthy?

Yes. I want him to suffer. I want him alive and aware of his crimes and I want him to think that you don't believe he's earned the death of Justice. If he wants to expiate his sins by giving up his life and going on to face the lords of judgment, let him do it his own damned self.

Remind me never to piss you off.

Triss snorted mentally. *That ship sailed long ago, but this goes so far beyond merely being pissed off that it's another thing entirely.*

I looked at Kelos, who had continued to smile knowingly while Triss and I had our little talk. *He knows we can mind-speak, doesn't he?*

Probably.

And, he's still playing us. He thinks he's got things set up so he wins either way, whether we kill him or not.

He is Kelos, sent Triss, as if that was all the answer I needed.

And, in truth, it was. *Can we beat him?*

The only way to find out is to play the game out.

I sighed. "All right, Kelos. If any of us kills you, you win one way. I'm sure that you have a winning scenario plotted out if we don't kill you, too. What is it?"

His smile widened briefly. "Aral, you continue to make me proud for my part in your training." Then he shut the expression off in a way that made it perfectly clear that the smile was only one more tool in a very large set. "If you want to find that out, you'll have to go after the key."

I rubbed my temples. "I suppose you have some way to compel us to that course?"

"Do you want the Son of Heaven to get the key? Because his agents are already on their way. News of his plans in that direction is what moved me to go after it myself and to seek out Siri."

He turned to her now. "For that matter, now that the Smoldering Flame knows where to look, what do you think he will do about it? If you wish to remain Siri, you need to get there first *and* figure out how to keep the god in your head from using you to get what he needs to rise again. You *know* that I can help you there."

Siri ran her fingers through her braids, stirring the smoke into mad whorls. "For my part, he's right, Aral. I have no choice but to go after the key, and having Kelos at my side may make the difference between success and failure. But I won't ask you or Faran to come with us. Not after all he's done to you."

I held up my hand with its ring of smoke. "I didn't put this on idly, and I'm not going to abandon you now. Especially not to him." I nodded at Kelos. "That said, I would prefer that we left Faran here."

Faran crossed her arms and gave me a hard look. "And what if Faran doesn't agree to be left?" she asked.

"Then, given the success I've had in the past at enforcing my will on her, I imagine that she will be joining us."

Faran smiled. "So, he *does* learn. I had begun to have my doubts."

"You aren't the first to wonder about that," Triss said with a snort.

Kelos stood. "Shall we go? The longer we wait, the greater our chance of failure." He turned his gaze on Ash and Kayla. "I presume that if you wanted to, you could get us to Sylvas more quickly than we could make it by horse or the burning of boot leather."

Ash looked at Siri. "I see why you said this man was so dangerous, child. He manipulates like a Sylvani courtier." He canted his head to one side. "He lies like one, too, though the truths here serve his purpose as well as the falsehoods, making it very hard to sort one from the other. What would you have us do, Siri? Send you all along now, together? Or just the three of you." His gesture excluded Kelos. "We can do either."

"Much as I hate to say it, I'd rather have him inside the boat bailing water out than the other way round."

"It's your decision," said Ash, though he didn't sound the least bit happy about it.

"I'll take them," said Kayla. "The Changer is already riled from one outing. Let's not give her another chance at slipping the leash again when her anger at being returned to the great binding is still so fresh."

Ash sighed, but nodded. "That's probably best."

Sylvas was a city of jewels. The Sylvani had occupied the site for twice ten thousand years, and when they built to last, they built in gemstone. Towers of ruby and sapphire climbed into the sky, while jade fortresses squatted side by side with manors of white opal. All of it as smooth and pure as if it had been grown. The streets were sheets of diamond.

"How did they make this?" Faran ran her fingertips along a wall of yellow citrine at least a foot thick. She left a long trail in the grime that covered the stone.

"They begin with rough sandstone or tufa blocks—any stone that's easy to work with—laying them much as I am told things are done on your side of the wall," replied Kayla. "Where they need to, they will reinforce the construction with iron or timber. Once it's all in place, they fuse the stones together with magic, creating a single seamless skin of uniform material. The spells involved take years to lay and months to complete their work. But that is only the beginning.

"Transforming a tower of sandstone into one of ruby is the sort of magic that might take a score of your human generations to construct, and another dozen to play out, though stone to stone is an easier transmutation than wood to stone or any other cross-elemental spell. Five hundred years may pass between the laying of the first stone and the point when the building is ready for the arrival of its masters. But that's all the talk we have time for. The nearest of the Mouse Gates lies just ahead." Kayla's long belled sleeve billowed around her arm with the gesture.

Before leaving the castle she had changed into a loose flowing set of garments the color of sand. They covered her from head to toe, concealing both her face and her gender. When Kelos asked her about the choice, she'd laughed.

"The Tolar are not well liked in the capitol," she'd said. "But they are infinitely more welcome than Kayla Darkvelyn of the Kreyn. I find that it's a more effective disguise by far than glamouring myself into the shape of a Sylvani maid tall and fair, however well the illusion is cast."

"Why?" asked Ssithra.

"Fair seeming draws the eye. Seeing magic, the curious will then look deeper. Whereas the eye scorns the outcast, skipping on in search of visions more pleasant rather than seeking to pierce the veil of internal disdain. Your company will only enhance the effect. The Sylvani use humans; they do not love them. Hence this." Her gesture took in the filthy buildings, trash-strewn streets, and harsh looks from the few natives we had passed.

With Ash's help, Kayla had conjured us into an alley not far from a Mouse Gate that entered the Asavi city-within-a-city near the base of the grand stairs on the north side, near the center of the waterfront. Given its position, it ought to have been a wealthy neighborhood, and there were many once-grand houses to be seen on the street where we emerged from the alley. But the very presence of the Mouse Gate, and with it the heavy human traffic into the city understairs, had caused the Sylvani nobility who once lived there to seek fairer harbor.

The spells that kept sand and dust from accumulating on gemstone walls had long since fallen away, and a thin layer of grime covered everything. Here and there deep gouges showed in the stone where scavengers had tried their hands at chipping out a king's ransom in precious gems. A futile effort according to Kayla. The spells that had once transformed tufa to topaz were of a piece, and removing a bit of stone from the matrix caused it to revert to its original form.

In a few places, more enterprising souls had gone so far as to try to carve out massive chunks of stone in hopes of circumventing the failure of their less ambitious peers. They, too, had failed, and even more spectacularly, causing whole wall sections to degenerate back into the coarser stone from which they had once been formed. Given the surrounding architecture, the gate that led into the city understairs stood out like a crow among gaudy parrots.

"I see why they call them Mouse Gates," said Faran.

At our end, the gate was tall enough to accommodate a horse and rider, its opening shaped into the snarling mouth of a mouse backed into a corner by a rat. It was made of some coarse gray substance that looked more grown than built—the cocoon of some great moth perhaps, or the rough nest of ten thousand wasps. The surface felt warm and slightly yielding, almost alive, when I bent to touch the tip of the lower jaw.

"This is where I must leave you," said Kayla. "Good luck." With a swirl of sand-colored silk, she turned and was gone.

"Well, that's inviting. . . ." Siri pointed to the rapidly narrowing gullet that lay at the back of the open mouth.

Three young men wearing the clothes of common laborers slipped around us to enter the mouth. As soon as the first of the laborers crossed the threshold, lines of spell-light reached out from the tips of the mouse's teeth, fastening themselves at wrists and ankles, neck, heart, and forehead. With each step beyond, the spell threads pulsed and the man visibly shrank. By the time he reached the throat of the gate he had shed nearly two feet and both his fellows had fallen in behind. Watching them out of sight was most disconcerting.

Following them into the mouth of the gate a moment later and *feeling* it was ten times more so. Make a three-sided pyramid of oranges twenty tall. Take away the top orange, then the two below it on one side, and the three below that, and so on down to the bottom. You now have a pyramid that looks much the same, but it's only nineteen oranges tall. Do the same again, and now the pyramid is eighteen oranges tall. Now imagine how it might feel to *be* the pyramid. It was kind of like that.

"Slick." Siri was right behind me and we'd reached a point where we were perhaps ten inches tall. "Very slick. I'd love to take this thing apart and see how they do it."

A curtain of darkness hung across the path, blocking any view ahead, but I pushed on through what felt like a wall of cobwebs and staggered out the other end where we passed through a simple rounded arch. As I stumbled out into the Asavi city, I had a brief moment to compare the smaller end of the gate to the classic mouse hole as any sketch artist might have drawn it. Then I looked up and saw the stairs above. . . .

Each individual step that made up the grand stairs of Sylvas was a thirty-foot-long translucent bar of precious stone a foot wide and six inches high. Garnet, topaz, citrine, a graduated rainbow that ran for half a mile from harbor to palace. The Asavi had excavated a continuous gallery below that ran the entire length, like a hanging valley in the mountains where the sun shone down through a jeweled sky. It was breathtaking and I couldn't take my eyes off the view as I slowly walked out into an open plaza.

"I was expecting something a bit more . . . rat hole," said Faran. "This is . . . I don't even know what."

"Blood," said Kelos, and at first I thought he was talking about the light.

We had entered the city near the base of the stairs where ruby and garnet dominated and the light painted the plaza in shades of crimson.

But then he continued, "I smell it in the air. There's blood in the offing. We need to hurry, or we'll be too late." He started up the nearest street at a jog. As far as I could tell he hadn't even looked at that marvelous ceiling.

"He's right," said Siri. "The god just went quiet in my head."

The buildings were mostly made of some sort of dense stonelike material the color of honeycomb. Most of the people we passed on the street level were human, though the Asavi flitted this way and that in the air above. If they noticed those of us who needed to get about on foot they didn't show it. Though they remained some distance away and moved with frightening speed, I got enough of a look at them to decide that they reminded me more of the Durkoth than any of their other cousins. Impossibly beautiful and alien, with no slightest hint of humanity in the austerely arrogant cast of their expressions.

Both sexes went shirtless—presumably to allow their gossamer wings the maximum freedom. Most had needle-like swords at their sides, and many carried blowguns as well. The tiny sheathed darts reminded me of one of the few bits of Asavi lore I'd ever learned at the temple—poison.

Three of the deadliest that we had used in the service of Namara were imported from the Sylvain. Two of those were delivered orally and used heavily by the Sylvani court for eliminating rivals. The third was best administered via some sort of puncture and it came from the Asavi.

Since Faran had been too young at the fall of the temple to have done much more than begun her training with poisons, I touched her on the shoulder, and spoke quietly. "The Asavi invented ancubonite."

She whistled. "Good to know. That would explain why they're all carrying those itty-bitty little pin-pricker swords as if they were serious weapons."

Kelos suddenly stopped dead in the middle of the street. "Can you feel it?"

"What?" I had no idea what he was talking about.

"The blood tension is singing in the air," he whispered.

Do you think Kelos is cracking? I sent to Triss, but I couldn't help noticing the way the sun suddenly seemed to dim above the gemstone ceiling of the city.

How could he not? replied Triss. *But I don't think that's what this is about. I can feel it, too, a sort of pressure dancing along the edge of perception. It's more elemental than magical, but there's definitely something there.*

Before I had a chance to do or say anything more, a horrible squealing shriek came from somewhere down the street behind us. I drew my swords without thinking and spun into a defensive stance in the same instant that Triss rolled up my skin from below, bringing my shadow with him. Siri and Faran had whirled as well, slotting in on either side of me a few steps back. Without looking, I could feel that Kelos had remained facing up the hill, putting his back to mine and closing the fourth point of a defensive diamond.

The shriek repeated itself, followed this time by a sort of deep growling grunt. A few seconds later I could see something storming up the slope toward us. A trio of somethings. As they got closer details resolved themselves.

"Filathalor!" Siri snapped.

"Those tiger-boar things painted all over the Castelle?" Kelos asked from behind us.

"Yes," I replied as they roared closer. "Saddled. The riders are Sylvani warriors in crystalline armor and they have lances."

"I thought they only came out at the will of the Changer. Do you think that Ash and Kayla sold us out?" he asked, still without turning—that took a discipline that I'd have been hard-pressed to match.

"Impossible," said Siri. "Or, very nearly. But the key probably has the Changer stirring in her slumber, and she has her cultists just as all of the buried gods— Ware!"

They were almost upon us then, and I tensed my legs to leap aside. I'd faced these things before and I knew there was no way any of us could hope to take one head-on. An angry buzzing made me look up as they closed. A dozen of the Asavi were zipping back and forth in the wake of the charging filathalor, weapons drawn. Bright lines of spell-light zipped back and forth between the flyers and the riders, but none of it seemed to have much impact.

At the last possible instant the lead rider hauled on her reins and the tiger-boars swerved left, going around us without engaging. They passed close enough for me to see the hundreds of poisoned darts sticking in the necks and shoulders of the filathalor. I could also hear a high chiming, like crystal rain, as more darts struck the helms and cuirasses of the riders.

It was the first time I'd seen Sylvani armor in action, and I took a moment to fix it in my memory. Wherever a dart struck the armor it created a momentary splash of bright lines, like fractures radiating out from the point of impact. The magically charged crystal was refracting the force of the blow, dispersing it throughout the structure of the armor—transforming the physical attack into light and scattering it until it dimmed away into nothingness.

But even the fanciest of armor couldn't cover every gap perfectly, and one of the darts must have found a chink, because the trailing rider slumped in his seat and then tumbled to the ground a few lance lengths after they passed us. Neither of his companions so much as looked back, and his filathalor rode on without him.

"They must be here for the key," Siri cried even as the Sylvani cultist hit the ground.

"After them!" yelled Kelos, and he was away.

I slowed as I reached the fallen cultist and swung my right-hand sword in a full over-arm chop aimed at the crest of his helm. I had no doubt that the ancubonite would finish him if it hadn't already, but I was intensely aware of the Asavi flying above us and wanted to send them a signal about being the enemy of their enemies. I also wanted to see how the kinetic refraction of the armor would handle the god-magic of my swords.

Not very well, as it turned out. When the edge of my sword hit the top of the helm, it gave off a flash like brightest mage-lightning, and lines of light crazed their way through the translucent crystal. For one brief instant the helm was spiderwebbed with violet light. Then, with a crash and a tinkle, it shattered into a thousand pieces no bigger than the tip of my little finger. It did stop my blow, leaving the fallen Sylvani untouched, but only until my other sword parted his head from his shoulders.

Whether my demonstration worked or the Asavi just weren't that interested in armed humans when there were obvious cultists of the Changer to deal with, I couldn't say. But no darts fell upon us, and that was enough for me. I put on an extra burst of speed to catch up with the others. As I ran, I noticed a tugging at my ring finger and saw that the smoke there had grown thicker than ever as it whirled madly away.

Another of the riders fell off her filathalor before they turned into a filthy side street where we all ran headlong into a fight with at least four sides.

19

---◆—◆---

There is nothing poetic about a battle when the blood is still flowing fresh in the gutters and the stench and the screams are hammering at your soul. There is not much good to be said about the aftermath either, but that doesn't keep people from trying.

"Shroud!" Kelos yelled after we pelted around a corner and almost plowed into the back end of a filathalor.

It was an unnecessary warning. Blood and the opened sphincter smells of fresh death hung heavy in the air. By the time Kelos spoke, training as deep as instinct had already taken over. Siri and Faran and I each vanished into our own individual blind spots. Triss released control—and I lost track of the others within seconds as I dived into the narrow gap between two buildings—leaving me alone.

It was a small building and I quickly found the alley behind, moving along it until I reached a wide-open back door—presumably marking where the owners had very sensibly fled the battle out front. A ladder led upward from the back room to the rooftop, but I passed it by as I headed for the front windows. Normally, I would have made my way above to get an overview of things out front. But with so many heavily armed and potentially hostile flyers, I wanted a roof between me and the rain of poisonous darts.

Furnishings and the unmistakable stench of curing hides suggested that my temporary haven normally served as a leatherwork shop of some sort. One of the shuttered windows hung open and I pushed the shadow away from my eyes so that I could peer out into the small square fronting the shop. As I did so I felt Siri's shroud brush across the back of my own, gently letting me know she had followed me.

"Madness," I whispered as I looked out into the swirling chaos of a battle with no readily apparent objectives or obvious structure.

Blood and magic ruled the scene, with bodies and bits of bodies spread across the square every which way and spell-light flickering along every surface. I saw Asavi corpses and Sylvani, Tolar and Kreyn, the filathalor—apparently *something* could kill them—and a scattering of humans.

Most of the latter were obvious bystanders—likely caught in the initial explosion of violence. But I also saw one body in the loose silks of a Blade. One of those who had gone over to the Son and formed Heaven's Shadow, no doubt, given the reddish tint to his grays. Three more wore the ritually tied hair bindings that marked the Hand of Heaven—the Son's personal sorcerer-priests and shock troops.

That would explain the dimming of the sun earlier. The mages of the Hand were partnered by the Storms—powerful elementals that rode the thunder and lightning. They wore wings of deep black clouds and came in shapes that encompassed everything from lightning-tipped scepters, to spheres of ice or burning wheels spoked with slender whirlwinds. They *were* the weather, and the skies would mourn the violent passing of three of their number with a storm of massive proportions.

"Who's winning?" Siri asked me.

"I can't even tell who all the sides are. The Asavi, of course, and those who follow the Son of Heaven. The filathalor mark the presence of cultists of the Changer. Add all the fire magic out there to the way my ring's going crazy and I guess we have to count the Smoldering Flame among the cultic types. Beyond that? Who knows? It's a mess."

"Should we be worried about Faran?" asked Siri.

"No, or not much. With the exception of the trouble she gets into by trying to watch my back, she's significantly better at taking care of herself than I am. In that way, she's rather like you at the same age."

Siri snorted. "Fair enough. What do you think we ought to do now?"

"I honestly don't know." I slid down to sit against the base of the wall while I tried to sort it out. The thick stonelike material shook occasionally as spell blasts hit the other side, but it felt sturdy enough to protect us from all but the worst of direct attacks.

I felt Siri settle beside me. "Picking a side and wading in doesn't strike me as a good survival strategy given the amount of dying that's going on out there. This is no kind of fight for an assassin. Maybe we should just hole up here for a while and let the crowd thin itself out."

I nodded though she couldn't see me. "Hard to argue with that. I take it your divine affliction isn't telling you where to find the key."

Siri chuckled. "I'm afraid not. I *can* hear the god buzzing very faintly in the back of my mind when he talks to his cultists out there, but for the moment he's shut me out. Probably because he knows that I wouldn't surrender the key to him if I got ahold of it right now."

"Right now?" I emphasized her qualifier.

"Yes, right now." Siri's voice went grim as she answered me. "Later? I don't know. I can feel the dagger I left in his heart slowly burning away, Aral—feel it taking bits of me with it. In the early years it was a slow thing, more rot than fire, like a log crumbling in on itself in the woods. But since Kelos told me about the key, and, with me, the god . . . it's terrifying."

In all the years I had known her, Siri had never shown the slightest sign of fear. She had always been first in line to attempt the scariest jumps, or to try out a poison and its antidote. Hearing her say that she was terrified . . . that shook me. I tried to imagine what that might feel like, knowing that a will greater than your own was slowly devouring you from within, and that shook me even more.

"What can I do?" I asked.

"Nothing you haven't already offered." Siri reached through our overlapping shrouds to take my hand—the one with the ring. "I didn't know what you would do when I sent my smoke seeming to you, Aral. It had been so many years since I'd seen you, and in all that time I never even *tried* to find you. Not after the fall, and not later when I first heard that you had resurfaced in Tien. I abandoned you and all the others and ran to the Sylvain and Ash for help with the god. You would have had every right to turn me away."

"Siri—"

"Let me finish. You had no way of knowing who I was now, or that I wasn't about to betray you. When you didn't even hesitate over accepting my ring . . . I cried. It meant so much to me to be trusted when I felt like my soul was rotting away from within. I can never begin to thank you enough for that."

I squeezed her hand between my own. "You are *Siri*. We entered the temple barely a year apart. I have loved you in one way or another for almost as long as I can remember." I didn't know if this was the right time for this conversation, but then, I didn't know if we would live long enough for the chance to come again, so I plunged on. "I may not see us ever playing husband and wife in the traditional way, but I would happily give you my life. How could I deny you my hand?"

"How can you say that after all the betrayals you've suffered? Devin and Kelos and—"

I touched a fingertip to her lips to stop her words. "Devin is weak of heart. He always was. Though I thought of him as my brother once, I can't blame him for bending to Kelos's will. His spine is no stiffer now than it ever was. If he crosses me, I may have to kill him, but it's hard to fault a puppet for dancing when someone tugs on his strings."

"And Kelos? What about his betrayals?"

"You heard what he had to say. He fell to the weaknesses of his strengths. I might have done the same in the days before I learned to see the world in all its myriad shades."

"You can't mean that you would forgive him," whispered Siri.

"For my own part, I might someday. For what he did to the goddess, no. That I can never forget or forgive."

"Is that why you decided to give me your trust?" She

sounded genuinely baffled. "Because the goddess was gone, and the only one I could betray is you?"

"Siri, when you sent your seeming to propose to me, *giving* you my trust never entered into it. I didn't know what you wanted beyond my hand. I didn't know who you had become. For all I knew, you could have been contracted to kill me. None of that mattered. What mattered was the Siri I knew from the temple, the Siri that I loved personally and honored as First Blade. I trusted *that* Siri, and I owed her my life's blood if she asked for it."

"The more you speak, the less I understand you. You couldn't know that I was the same person."

"I'm sorry. To me it's very simple. In the old days, I wouldn't have hesitated to walk into a fire at your request. You've never given me any reason to believe that the woman who I would have done that for is gone. If I were to revoke my trust in you simply because of what the world has done to me or what you *might* do in your turn, then my trust is hardly worth giving."

"You're mad. You know that, right?"

"Triss tells me so often enough, but I'm not sure that I agree. What I do makes sense to me. And, really, is there any other measure that matters?"

Siri laughed, perhaps the first true laugh I'd heard from her since coming to the Sylvain. "I do love you, Aral, madman or no, and I'm sorry to have drawn you into this." Then she gave me a quick kiss on the cheek. "I'm still not all that enchanted with the idea of marriage, but if I had to marry someone, I can't think of anyone I'd rather it were."

"Thanks . . . I think." Then I poked her in the ribs in lieu of a wink, since I understood exactly where she was coming from. I had no interest in marrying either, but better to an old friend if it needed doing.

A lull in the sounds of the fighting outside caught my attention then. "Might be time to get back into the game." I turned and slid my eyes above the sill again, but the battle was still a confusing whirl with too many sides to keep track of, if somewhat slower. The biggest difference was that there were more bodies scattered about now. "I wish there was some way we could tell who has the key at the moment and slip up behind them. *That's* an assassin's fight."

"Truth. But I can't think of any way to pick out the key. Not without a lot more information about any magical signature it might have. Probably not even then. If it were visibly magical, or traceable by magic, someone would surely have found it before now."

"Maybe we can reason out its whereabouts." It was worth a shot, especially given the alternatives. I tried to shut out the sounds of death and mayhem so I could think it through.

Siri squeezed my hand. "I'm game, but how?"

"Start with the idea that the key's been hidden here for ten thousand plus years without anyone finding it. Yet somehow, the Son of Heaven winkled it out."

"It's more likely that someone tipped him off," replied Siri. "There are more humans in the empire than First these days. As much as you and I might have reasons to hate the Son of Heaven, he *is* the chief priest of the religions of man. Maybe someone here spotted the key and told their priest about it, and that's how it got back to him."

"Not a bad guess, that." My own personal hatred of the man tended to blind me to the place he held in the hearts of most of our kind. "But that doesn't really matter. What matters is that no one is likely to have happened along and turned up the key before the forces of Heaven's Reach got here specifically looking for it. They probably had the key in hand when this all started."

"Which means what?"

There was something important there, but I didn't quite have a handle on it. "Let me chew on it for a bit. At a guess, touching the key did something that alerted the buried gods to its existence, or at least to those of them who were close by or knew to listen for it."

"That would explain the way the Smoldering Flame suddenly went silent along about the time we arrived in the city understairs. Good. What else?"

"There's a single ex-Blade corpse out there—Mabung, I think; his Shade took the form of an alligator—but I see no other evidence of our former brethren." I could sense that part of it was important, but I didn't know why yet. "All the humans still fighting at this point are Hand. They're fanatics totally dedicated to the Son, and willing to die for him. . . ."

Then I had it. "The key's already gone! The Shadow took it and left the Hand behind to confuse the issue and slow down any pursuit."

"We have to find their trail!"

"And quickly." I started pulling Siri toward the back door. "I wish we had some way to tell Faran what we were doing." Kelos could rot for all I cared and I didn't mention him. Neither did Siri.

"**Now** I see why you say she can take care of herself," said Siri.

"Funny, I was just thinking the opposite," I grumbled.

We had found the shadow trail we were looking for. The initial track was made by a pair of shrouded Blades and very fresh—no more than half an hour old. It was hard to believe the fighting had started so recently, and that we had arrived more recently yet. A battle distorts time even if you're only sitting on the edge of it. There was also the fact that the storm raging in the world above had dimmed the late-afternoon sun into something that approached an artificial night.

I didn't recognize either of the original pair of shadow signatures—I'd only learned the art of detecting them at all in the last few years and I had yet to master it—but I had little doubt they belonged to a couple of our former brethren who had gone over to the Son. I did, however, recognize Kelos's signature following along atop the others perhaps fifteen minutes ago, and Faran's trailing his a few minutes behind.

"She should know better than to go after a pair of Heaven's Shadows without me," I said. "And that's without adding in Kelos and whatever game he might be playing."

"That's not entirely fair," said Siri. "Not when we didn't make any attempt to track her down before going after them ourselves."

"That's different. She's eighteen, incompletely trained, and you and I were both First Blades once upon a time."

"She snuck up on Kelos as recently as yesterday. Close enough to cut his throat as I recall the story. She survived completely on her own for years with a price on her head starting at the age of nine, and came out of it wealthy. If the temple hadn't fallen, what are the odds she'd have become First Blade herself somewhere along the line?"

"Point. But don't *ever* tell her I said so. She's hard enough to manage without anyone doing anything to add to her extraordinarily good opinion of herself."

"Said the man who went to the goddess to ask her to make him a Blade ahead of his year so that he could be given a mission that had already claimed the lives of three of his far more experienced elders. Is that not right, oh Kingslayer?"

"Again, that's *different*." But this time I said it with a laugh.

The trail led us through a series of narrow alleys and gaps between buildings back to the Mouse Gate.

"That doesn't look good," I said from our vantage across the plaza from the gate.

"Not one little bit, no."

Smoke was rising from the arch of the magical gate, and showers of sparks periodically shot out of the dark hole that centered it. Spell-light danced along the edges as well, and the whole plaza smelled like burning hair.

"What do you think happened?" I didn't know a tenth as much about spellwork as Siri and I had no idea what might have gone wrong.

"At a guess, servants of the buried gods happened."

"You lost me."

"Kayla told us that the gates wouldn't pass velyn unless the Asavi made special adjustments to them. I imagine the cultists used some sort of god-magic to force the passage, and that it wasn't a gentle process. It doesn't look like it did the gate any favors."

"Do we chance it?" Given that the shadow trail clearly headed that way I didn't see any alternatives, but Siri was the magic expert.

"I wish we had a choice," replied Siri. "But the gate is obviously close to failing, which means we'd better get through it as quickly as we can. Come on." She caught my hand and headed straight across the plaza at a dash, forsaking the trail and dramatically increasing our risk of being sighted.

I was more than a bit surprised that she had chosen to abandon the direct trail even if we were likely to pick it up again on the far side, but I picked up my pace to match hers anyway.

"What happens if the gate gives up while we're passing through?"

"No idea. At the moment I'm much more worried about what happens if it fails *before* we get through it."

I started to ask, "Why . . . Oh." Then trailed off as an ugly thought occurred. "It's going to flare off the excess nima, isn't it?"

"At the very least. Anyone who passed through this or any other forced gate who doesn't get back out before they fail is going to end up cooking in their own skins. We should be damned glad Faran has preceded us."

I felt sweat break out over my whole body at her words. We were almost to the gate by then, and it was *probably* just a nervous response to the idea of suddenly bursting into flame, but I put on more speed nonetheless. We hit the darkened opening of the gate together. This time, instead of cobwebs, the resistance to our passage was more like diving deep and hitting a muddy river bottom. It felt much thicker and harder to pass through, for one, and I got the distinct impression that things were only going to get worse and worse the farther we went.

I hadn't gone two steps before my shroud simply collapsed in on itself. I tried to wake Triss in response to see if he knew what had happened and why, but I couldn't pierce his dreams to bring him back to the surface. It didn't feel like he was in pain, but all that I could hear of his mindvoice was a distant sort of delirious babbling. The kind of thing you might expect from someone caught in a heavy fever. I wanted to do more for him, but I had to let it go as I devoted more and more of my attention and will to forcing myself through the gate.

Ice and fire thrilled along my skin in weird tiptoe spatters, and I lost all sense of which way was up and which down. The only reason I could tell forward from back was that forward was more difficult—a sort of cold resistance that felt like it *wanted* me to stop. Once or twice I stuttered to a near halt, but then Siri would tug on my hand, and I would push on again. I did the same for her, or thought that I did at least. It was hard to know anything for sure in that bizarre maelstrom of sensation.

Eventually, we did break through into the gullet of the gate, though the far end was obscured by a wall of hammering rain brought on by the death of the Storms. On the way in, spell threads had gently fastened themselves to hands and feet, neck, heart, and face.

Now firelike ropes burned down from the walls, reaching deep and painfully into my flesh, and I could feel a torrent of nima pouring into me. It came in faster and faster as I staggered along the gullet and back toward my normal size—filling the well of my soul to overflowing. It burned inside me, bright and hot and harsh, more by far than I had given up on the way in.

"What's happening?" My words sounded long and warped in my ears—like noises heard underwater or through a fresh concussion.

"'S beginning . . . to flare out," Siri answered, though I found her speech hard to parse through the garbling effect of the gate. "We're caught in . . . overflow."

Moved by an impulse I barely understood, I lifted my free hand and pointed my palm out toward the open mouth of the gate ahead of us. A burst of magelightning as thick around as my leg and far more powerful than anything I'd ever dreamed of attempting blasted out of my palm and the tips of my fingers. It felt raw and wild and somehow wicked, and it brought with it a sort of deep relief in my chest, like some impossible weight of pressure draining away. When the lightning hit the sheeting rain at the mouth of the gate, droplets flashed into steam with a hiss and a crackle, filling the air with a hot fog.

"Aral, that's brilliant! If we can bleed off enough of the flare . . ."

Siri's hand lifted to match mine and something dense and black, like liquid tar or condensed night, speared out ahead of us. It branched and twisted in the air, sending out smoky tendrils. Where they met the threading forks of my magelightning they clung and twisted, braiding darkness with light and drawing the two streams of magic closer and closer together.

Within seconds, they met and spiraled into a whirling phantasmagorical spike of black and silver destruction that built and built as the gate poured nima into us and we vented it forward in turn. I felt a deep connection with Siri then, as if the blending of our magic was somehow twining our souls together as well. It started at our joined hands and worked up and through my whole body. Somewhere in there I lost any sense that I controlled the lightning blasting forth from the palm of my free hand. I had become little more than a channel for the magic to pass through and I knew that I couldn't have stopped it if I offered up my heart on a platter in exchange.

From the inside, I couldn't say how long the mad scramble to escape the failing gate continued. Seconds? Minutes? Ten thousand years? Time had no meaning within the compass of the event. It went on forever and a day, and was over in an instant when we stumbled our way out through the jaws of our gate. We made it a half dozen steps before collapsing to our knees with a splash, still holding hands. My other arm remained fixed at full extension for a few heartbeats longer as the power of the gate continued to flow through me and on into the lightning.

It tapered off in bursts, like blood flowing from a mortal wound—a slow pulsing that falls away with each new cycle of ebb and surge from the dying heart as it fails. As the gush of power faded almost to nothing, the silver and black spike burst asunder. I felt a faint crackling in my other hand, then looked down to see a globe of that same mixed energy where Siri's hand met my own, obscuring our flesh. It continued to hold there for one long beat before I felt my ring heat, and smoke rose from it, devouring the globe from within.

What the hell?

No idea. It was Triss, returning from wherever the power of the gate had sent him just in time to answer the question I hadn't realized I was asking. *What happened? How did it get so dark, and why are we kneeling over Parsi's corpse?*

Huh?

Parsi. A generation and a half older than you. Paired with Shade Zissatha who took the form of a huge rat. Are you all right, Aral?

Of themselves, the words made individual sense. But it wasn't until I actually looked in front of me and saw the corpse half-afloat in the puddle where Siri and I had ended our staggering progress that I understood their meaning.

One of the ex-Blades we were following had ended her journey here, her red-tinged grays now stained a deeper crimson with the blood that flowed out of the gaping hole in her lower back. Another cut ran across the top of her shoulders where someone had sliced away her sword rig after she died. Looking beyond her, I spotted another dozen or so corpses, mostly Sylvani or Tolar.

As I watched, one of the latter started to drift slowly from left to right when the water flowing down the middle of the cross street deepened enough to float the body. I had no doubt that more would follow, as the storm showed no signs of abating. Beside me, Siri coughed and pulled her hand free of mine.

"You alive?" she asked, her voice husky.

"I think so."

"Good." She took a deep breath and braced her palms against the street, clearly preparing to get up.

I didn't yet have the ambition to join her, but knew I would have to move soon. As I gathered myself to take that first step, my eyes flicked across the bodies, sorting out the scene. There had been another battle here, smaller, but still with at least three sides. I saw at least one filathalor badge and another that displayed a disembodied eyeball trailing a raw optic nerve. The symbol of a third buried god, perhaps.

Aral, I can taste a shadow trail here. Faran following Kelos following . . . Iander and Ssalassiss maybe. Were you following them?

Yes. I tried to think back to what I had seen of Iander's skill. He was two generations older than I and quite good, but never good enough to break through to the very top of the Blade hierarchy. Ssalassiss I remembered less well—elephant formed, perhaps . . . I pushed it aside as not worth worrying about. *Whoever it is, they probably have the key.*

Damn. I hate to say this because I can feel how tired you are, but we have to go after him right now . . . if it's not too late already.

What? Too late? I asked. *Why?*

The trail leads into the street.

I don't . . . Oh, fuck.

Running water is one of the few things that can break a shadow trail nearly as fast as fire or sunlight. I forced myself upright, then had to lean forward and brace my hands on my knees to keep from blacking out as the blood rushed out of my head.

"Aral, what is it?" Siri touched my shoulder. "Are you all right?"

I was about to answer when a half dozen Sylvani wearing the badge of the disquisition came splashing into view from down the street. They wore cuirasses and half helms, but no other armor, and they were coming straight toward us. Two had obviously magical rods that they now pointed our way, and all had weapons at the ready.

"You there, don't move!" the leader called out.

20

---◆---

Sometimes, all you can do is what you must.

Triss, tell Kyrissa to relay a message to Siri. We don't have time to do this nicely. I'm moving on five.

Done.

I took a deep breath and stood, letting my hands fall to my sides, inches from the hilts of my swords. If I'd had the time, I would have offered the disquisitors the opportunity to find someone else to bother. But I was all out of time. And so were they.

Triss released control as my mental count hit four. I shrouded up, drew my swords, and dove forward all in one continuous flow of motion. I hit the water-slicked surface of the street on my belly and chest, sliding toward the nearest of the disquisitors with my blades crossed in front of me.

When I felt my edges bite into his shins I drew the hilts back and down toward my sides, scissoring the tips together and taking his feet off a few inches above the ankles. The motion slowed my slide but didn't stop it, and the disquisitor tumbled into the street behind me. Borrowed darksight showed me another of the Sylvani lining her rod up on the forward point of my wake. I snapped my arms in tight and rolled sideways, cutting my own cheek as one of my blade tips jarred into the low curbing along the street's edge.

I barely noticed it through the blinding pain I felt as the rod sent a thick spear of brilliant light into the water where I would have been had I continued forward on my original path. The blast didn't touch me, but the brightness burned a vicious trail across my darksight and feathered the edge of my shroud. Through my borrowed Shade senses the intense flash tasted of morning sun shining across fields of ice and new snow. It hurt *cold* and suddenly there were chunks of ice floating in the water around me.

My initial plan had called for moving on to the other, closer rod wielder after cutting the feet out from under their leader. I revised that in light of the near miss. Smart enough to aim at a wake meant smart enough for other tricks. She needed to die fast. I rocked back onto my shoulders and vaulted to my feet, facing toward her. I needn't have bothered. The rodswoman's head left her shoulders before I could take two steps. Siri dropped her shroud then and threw me a reckless salute.

The remaining disquisitors all focused on her as she had intended, with the remaining rodsman dropping to one knee to steady his aim. Before any of them could follow through, smoke and shadow boiled around Siri and she vanished again. The rodsman whipped his head back and forth in confusion as he tried to spot his target. I leaped toward him, extending my right-hand sword in a sliding lunge that ended when my point stabbed into the side of the rod an inch or so below its fluted tip.

I didn't know what sort of spell structure had been used in the weapon's creation, so it was a calculated risk—one that paid mixed dividends. The thing came apart with a really spectacular bang, killing its wielder. But the blast grabbed me by the point of my sword and tossed me away, a motion I converted into a series of spinning jump kicks to stay on my feet in the sloppy street. I managed to hang on to my right-hand blade through the whole thing, though my hand and arm felt like a giant had slapped me.

I heard a scream and turned my head far enough to see a swordswoman lose her weapon and the hand holding it out of the corner of one eye. The cry turned into a breathy gurgle an instant later as Siri's second sword skewered her throat.

When the remaining disquisitor broke and ran, I would have let her go. Siri was less forgiving. A rope of bubbling night hit the back of the disquisitor's neck in the gap between helm and back plate and she suddenly collapsed in on herself.

Elapsed time? Less than two minutes.

I was just reaching back to sheathe my swords when the Mouse Gate exploded.

Heat and light hit me like a sledgehammer, throwing me backward through the air. Somehow, I managed to get my swords out of the way before I landed on my back in the street, but I lost them both in the process. If there hadn't been a foot and a half of water to cushion my fall, I'd probably have died when my head smacked into the roughened diamond surface. As it was, the world went bright red for several long seconds and I sucked what felt like a pint of rainwater into my lungs when my body went limp and floppy.

For a moment, I thought I might drown, but then I got enough feeling back to roll over and force my head back above the surface. I came up coughing and gagging, and nearly went back under when one hand slipped as I vomited up most of the water I'd just swallowed. For perhaps a dozen heartbeats I stayed there on hands and knees wishing I could just give up on the whole damned thing and go home to Tien.

You and me both, Triss sent, surprising me.

Shouldn't you still be under?

You lost control rather spectacularly when you hit your head. It was hard to sleep through. Oh, and I've got your swords pinned against the current.

It was only then that I realized my shroud was gone and Triss had extended himself forward through the water—that said a great deal about just how hard I'd hit my head. *Thanks! Are they that way?* I pointed along the line of shadow with my chin.

Yes, maybe eight feet. And, hurry. Something took a real bite out of me while I was out, and the effort's costing more than it should.

Disquisition. I crawled slowly forward. *Some kind of enchanted rod. Lots of light, but viciously cold. Might be designed to trap rather than kill. Not sure. Ah, there.*

Using my link to Triss as a guide, I had found one of my

hilts. I put the sword back in its sheath before looking for the other. My hands were shaky and I needed both of them to get it in place safely. I couldn't help but think how very much better a hot pot of brewed efik would make me feel just then, or even a couple of beans. I could almost feel them crunching between my teeth, and I don't believe that I could have resisted the impulse if I'd had any to hand.

As I secured my second blade, I heard a splash over the hammering of the rain and glanced up. Siri was slogging her way toward me, looking as drowned rat as I felt. I forced myself not to ask if she had any efik. It was harder than it had any right to be.

"I found the trail," she said. "It goes that way." She waved an arm vaguely uphill, then leaned down to offer me her hand. "Come on."

"What about all the water?" I asked as she dragged me onto my feet. "Hasn't it broken the trail?" Leaning against each other, we started to force our way upslope against the current.

"'S not deep enough. The reason you can't trace a shadow trail across deep water is that the scent is dispersed by the movement. As long as whoever we're after is walking along the bottom instead of swimming, we can follow them."

"Oh. I guess I hadn't realized." All the times I'd tried to follow a shadow trail into water had involved a river. "That's good."

We both shrouded up, though I let Triss run the show this time. I wanted the advantage of his insights as well as his elemental abilities. We spent the next three hours following a shadow trail through the backstreets and alleys of Sylvas as Iander slipped his way ever deeper into the heart of the giant city. If there had been any doubt we were on the right track, the occasional scatter of corpses would have disabused us of the notion. Mostly they came in twos and threes, though we also hit a number of singletons, and two more significant battle sites with over a dozen dead.

The vast majority of the bodies that had any kind of identifying marks wore either the snarling filathalor or the smoking ember—no surprise given the extra time the Changer and the Smoldering Flame had to prepare after Kelos revealed the possible existence of the key to Siri and, through her, to Ash. But, I also saw the badge of the eyeball again twice, three officers of the disquisition, a lightning bolt, a fanged and grinning mouth, and something abstract that reminded me of nothing so much as a half-eaten egg roll. There might well have been others, but we were in too much of a hurry to give the bodies more than the most cursory of examinations.

In addition to the variety of allegiances displayed by the various corpses, the methods of their deaths showed more than the average level of creativity. The fallen had succumbed to spell and sword, spear, bites both massive and minor, and at least two had taken Asavi darts. That last had me eyeing the skies warily and wishing the rain didn't make it all but impossible to keep an eye out for tiny flyers.

"At least we're gaining on them," I said as I toed the latest victim onto her back. Blood from a torn-out throat almost obscured the filathalor badge at her collar.

"Not fast enough," replied Siri. "It's clear the buried gods have some way of tracking the key now that it's out in the open. And, we're stuck trailing along at the end of the parade."

"Look at the upside," said Triss. "If they *couldn't* track the key, Iander would be long gone by now. It's only the fact that all the fighting is slowing him down that's letting us catch up to him at all. Even with a fresh scent, we'd be moving slower than he is if we didn't have the cultists running interference."

"True," replied Siri. "But I *hate* playing catch-up. It leaves us way too vulnerable to the unexpected move."

It was a worry that proved all too prescient a half hour later when we followed the trail to the mouth of an alley that opened into a broad plaza. A spike of malachite vanished into the rain-drenched skies at its center—the tallest tower I'd yet seen in a city filled with high buildings.

The area was lit with dozens of bright magelights on portable stands. They illuminated the site of a significant battle that had claimed the lives of at least a double score of velyn—mostly Sylvani. Soldiers were everywhere digging through the aftermath, as were the city watch and dozens of officers of the disquisition. The gates of the tower lay in twisted ruin, and the fighting had clearly been thickest at its base.

"Fuck!" Siri caught my wrist and pulled me back into the

depths of the alley before I'd had a chance to fully register the scene. "We're too late, by far. I should have realized the trail was leading us here and tried to cut them off. We'll never catch them now. Fuck, fuck, fuck!"

I grabbed her shoulders. "Siri, stop swearing and tell me what we're seeing." I'd never been to the Sylvani capital before. "We can get through the soldiers if we have to." I wasn't sure how, but we could find a way.

"Doesn't matter. If Iander's still got the key, he's out of the city by now and there's no way to follow his trail."

"Back up."

"That's the Tower of the Voice, Aral—the Inspirium Vo!" Siri snapped as if that explained everything.

"And?"

"What? Oh, right. You've hardly spent any time in the empire. Come on, the disquisition's all over back there and we need to move away from any god-sniffers they might have. We can walk and talk."

I let one of my hands fall away, but left the other on her shoulder as she turned and started leading me back the way we'd come. "Tell me about the tower."

"Sometimes, the empress needs to convey a physical message which, for ritual reasons, can't be sent via a teleport gate. Don't ask me about the whys. I've had it explained to me a half dozen times and it still doesn't make any sense. Suffice to say that the Sylvani have fundamentally different priorities than we do, and let it go. In those cases she will send the sealed scroll to the tower."

"All right, I'm with you so far."

"The Inspirium Vo is over a mile high, and they keep a stock of wind-carpets at the top."

"And, there you've lost me."

"Enchanted rugs, fifteen feet wide and twenty-five long. They're woven with a pattern that attracts the more powerful sort of wind elemental—breeds that can only be found in the upper air. Launch a wind-carpet off the edge of the tower and the elementals will catch it and keep it aloft indefinitely because of the power of the pattern. It's nowhere near as fast as a gryphon or a roc, but you can carry more, and any idiot can fly one with minimal training."

"How do you land it?"

"Once you've got an elemental engaged, they'll usually stay with the carpet long enough to see it safely to ground. But it's a one-way trip. None of the greater winds will spend more than a few seconds that close to the earth, and you'll never get it back into the air without them. The rugs usually make their way back to the tower rolled up in the back of a cart."

"So, what you're telling me is that Iander is *flying* north to the wall even as we speak."

"Assuming he's still alive, yes."

"What about Faran and Kelos?"

"Your guess is as good as mine. If they made it up the tower before that mess back there filled up the plaza they might have gone after him, either alone or together. But even if we could get through, there's no point. We have no way to track the key through the air. Fuck!" Siri turned and slid down the wall of the alley we'd been walking along, slipping my grip in the process and landing with a faint splash. "I don't know *what* we do now."

I wanted to join her, but I knew that if I sat down I wouldn't be getting up again anytime soon. "Well, if we can't follow them, maybe we can get ahead of them."

"I don't see how." Siri sounded utterly defeated. "Steered properly that carpet could take Iander all the way to Heaven's Reach without ever coming within a mile of the ground."

"That's only if nothing stops him. How vulnerable are these carpets?"

"To attack? Very. It's one of the reasons they've never gone into wider use. There must be a hundred ways to knock one out of the air."

"Then he's never going to make it to the border on that thing. There are too many players who don't want that to happen, among them some very angry Asavi."

"Good point." Siri's voice took on fresh hope. "So, say the carpet is destroyed. Then what?"

"If Iander lives through whatever takes out the rug, he can convert his fall into a sail-jump with Ssalassiss and glide to the ground." That was a good thing to remember. If Faran had been crazy enough to follow along on one of the rugs and it went down she'd have a good chance of landing in one piece. "The fall probably won't kill him, but he's going to have serious problems when he lands. That key is going to keep drawing in the cultists, so there's bound to be someone waiting for him."

"Probably several someones," agreed Siri. "But the badges tell the story there. Any other buried gods will be playing catch-up to Smoldering Flame and the Changer."

I nodded inside my shroud. "Sure, because Kelos tipped them both off when he brought you into this and you shared the information with Ash. It's given them extra time to prepare. That's good actually."

"And, now *you've* lost *me*."

"It narrows the field. Iander is quite skilled, but he was never among the best of the Blades. As long as he's holding on to that key he's got a giant target painted on his back. If he can't fly all the way out of the empire or find some serious help, I don't see him making it out of this mess alive. Nor even as far as the border. He's simply got too many people hunting him. Once he goes down, the key will almost certainly fall to one or another of the sets of cultists."

"Unless Faran or Kelos get hold of it," said Siri.

"If Faran gets it, that's as good as you or I."

"And what about Kelos?" Siri asked. "He *says* he wants it so he can keep it out of the Son of Heaven's hands. And implies that he might use it to restore Namara if he can."

"But you don't trust him any more than I do. I have no idea what he wants, but the odds that he ends up with the key are pretty low. Not nearly as low as I would like, but there's nothing we can do about that. We've already lost our chance at the clean kill. Now we have to play the odds and hope. That means betting on the cultists. Since Smoldering Flame and the Changer have the bulk of the soldiers on the field, the key's likely to end up with one of them in the long run, even if Hairy Eyeball or that Lightning Bolt god get it for a while first. Given that, what are they going to do with the thing?"

"If it really is a tool for divine resurrection, they'll have to bring it back to the tomb of whichever god they serve," answered Siri. "The bindings that hold the buried ones in the earth are far too strong to be broken from any distance."

"Which means the key is either going to end up at Castelle Filathalor or wherever it is the Smoldering Flame is buried."

"The Brimstone Vale." Siri's voice sounded cold and dead when she said the name. "I know the place."

"Then that's got to be our choice. Ash and Kayla hold Castelle Filathalor, and they don't seem the sort to go down without a hell of a fight. We'll have to let them deal with the Changer, at least initially—if we could send them a message that would help. Where is this Brimstone Vale? Can you get us there? Before the key?"

"I could make the trip on my own easily enough. Maybe I can do that and you can go to . . ." She broke off into a fit of coughing. "Dammit, no. Get out of my head, you bastard. Aral, you *have* to stay with me no matter what I tell you after this moment." She went into another fit of coughing. "The closer I am to the tomb, the more influence the god will have over me, and I can't guarantee I'll be able to fight it. You may have to kill me."

I felt a chill in my guts. "Not an option. But we *do* stay together from here on out, no matter what."

"Aral." All she said was my name. No argument. No pleading. It was all she had to.

"Not unless there's no other choice," I whispered.

"Thank you."

Oh, Aral. I am so sorry.

I didn't answer Triss. I couldn't.

Instead, I squatted down and took Siri by her ring hand—and, it was only as I did so that I realized I could *feel* exactly where it was. "Come on. We need to get moving. *Can* you get us both there?"

Siri let me pull her to her feet, but she didn't answer me immediately. Then, "I think so. We'll need a fire, a big one by preference. This is going to take a lot of smoke. Smoke . . . and sex."

"Excuse me?"

Siri laughed. "Deep magic. We have to be one symbolically, and sex is the fastest way to make that happen, especially given these." She touched the ring of smoke that banded my wedding finger. "Let's go light a fire."

It wasn't the answer I'd expected, but . . . I grinned. "If we must, we must." As ritual magic went, that sounded like a hell of a lot more fun than the way such things usually played out.

* * *

There is something utterly disconcerting about starting a house on fire on your way *into* the building. Especially when your next step is to head upstairs to find a bedroom for a quick roll in the blankets.

We'd had to travel more than a mile out from the city center to find a small place with a structure that both would support a real fire and had any distance from its neighbors. I hated that we had to pick a place in a human slum where the buildings were poorly built and made out of wood. It was exactly the sort of neighborhood where a fire could do the worst damage, but the great gemstone palaces of the Sylvani inner city were all but fireproof, and once again time was our enemy.

The need to retain our swords and other gear limited our options, but at least we didn't have to worry about the smoke and fumes—Siri's divine infection protected us from both. Despite mutual exhaustion, things proceeded much as you would expect them to right up until the . . . critical moment, when we dissolved together into . . . smoke.

21

———◆———

Purity of being is a state not suited to the human condition.

Time means nothing to smoke, so I cannot say how long I spent merged with Siri in a form I was never meant to assume, or in traveling through the elemental place between worlds in that shape. I can only say that I would prefer to die rather than return to the formless perfection of such an existence.

Smoke has no soul, no will, no feelings. In taking its shape you divorce yourself from the most fundamental aspects of being. I don't know where they went when I didn't have them. I only know that having them restored to me served to emphasize the horror of the loss.

As we re-formed out of whirling nothingness in the Brimstone Vale, I fell away from Siri, collapsing into a ball on the ground. The return of sensation and self brought with it a comfort and a terror that left no room for anything else. A six-year-old child with a sharp stick could have killed me in the first long minutes that followed my reentry into the world of individual existence. I was simply incapable of doing more than lying on my side and breathing.

But the awareness of self inevitably brought with it the

awareness of time passing and, ultimately, a renewal of urgency as that time slipped away into the all-devouring void of the past. With urgency came action. First on the list, pulling my pants back up and retying them around my waist. As my fingers fumbled to remember what it meant to exist, I felt Triss begin to stir as well.

That was . . . not an experience I would care to repeat. The smoking void is even more unlike the everdark than the everdark is unlike this world. I will not return there willingly.

You're not alone in that, Triss. I . . . ugh. No. Never again. Where is Siri?

Fuck. I looked around and saw nothing but a rocky wasteland devoid of any life. Here and there water boiled in small pools stained yellow with sulfur. But most of my view was obscured by columns of smoke that rose out of the countless vents pockmarking the floor of the narrow valley. *I don't see her anywhere.*

Without thinking, I flipped myself up and onto to my feet. ". . . huh."

What is it?

An unexpected gift from the Smoldering Flame and our time in the neverwhere between the worlds. I ran through a quick series of exercises designed to test the limits of a body's injuries. *I seem to have mostly recovered from the wear and tear of the last few days. The only thing that still hurts is the cut on my cheek.*

It's a deep one. How did you get it?

Caught the back of one of my swords as I was getting out of the way of that rod blast at the Mouse Gate. I started to follow Siri—only realizing in the moment that I did so that I still knew exactly where her ring was.

Interesting. Assuming that you're right about the source of your healing, it would suggest that the buried god's power is unable to touch a wound inflicted by the tools of Namara. I wonder if there are any other effects.

Nothing that I'm currently noticing, but maybe time will reveal more changes.

The Brimstone Vale was a place rich with smokes and steams and rife with half-hidden pits full of scalding water or

boiling mud. It would have been the easiest thing in the world
to get lost if I hadn't had a personal lodestone in the shape of
a wedding ring. As I picked my way amongst the many hazards,
I found myself taking sudden unplanned sidesteps and unexpected turns that took me forward through the maze without
ever leading me down one of the many dead ends I saw around
me. My ring seemed to be guiding me to Siri by the best possible route.

Within a matter of minutes I arrived at the heart of the Vale.
There, a wide-mouthed marble chimney rose up from a low
dome of the same swirling gray stone. A heavy iron door
opened out of the nearer side, giving the whole the appearance
of some great beehive oven meant to cook for armies. A fallen
and soot-darkened grave tree lay off to one side. Siri knelt in
front of the door, her hands on her sword hilts and her whole
body shaking as if with some great effort. Kyrissa hung in the
air behind her, slowly sculling smoke-feathered wings.

"Siri?" I kept my voice low and gentle, not wanting to star-
tle her.

"I'm trying to fight it, Aral, but he's so very close to free."
She didn't move when she spoke, but Kyrissa turned to me and
nodded. "I can feel the dagger of the goddess burning in his
chest as though it were my own. It's little more than a ribbon
of slag held together by hope at this point. . . . Help me!"

"How?"

"I don't know. I don't know. I don't . . . It comes!" Siri drew
her swords and leaped to her feet in one smooth motion, her
voice shifting into a deeper register as Kyrissa coiled around
her protectively. "The key, it comes! Even now, it approaches
the vale."

She turned and looked at me, and where her eyes should
have been there were only pits of smoke. "There is a running
battle—one with many sides. Followers of the Changer, Cor-
pus, Ugrit Earthshaker, Asavi hivelords, the deniers of the
divine . . . and all with Namara's bitter shadows nipping at their
heels. My disciples cannot hold against them for long. They
have lost too many getting this far and they will fail. You must
go and fetch me the key."

"Siri?" Reluctantly, I drew my own weapons.

She touched the swords of our goddess to the sides of her

throat, pressing the flats into her flesh until it bulged around the steel and blood began to flow along the edges. Kyrissa hissed angrily and moved her chin to rest atop Siri's head. Slowly—ever so slowly—the smoke in Siri's eyes receded back into her irises, leaving the whites clear, if bloodshot.

"I'm here, Aral." She lowered her swords, and the smoke-feathered serpent slipped back into her shadow. "Barely."

"For how long?"

She shrugged and smiled ruefully. "I wouldn't trust me at your back if I were you. Might also be time to start thinking about a divorce."

That's not good, sent Triss.

Not one little bit.

"I'd rather not." I held up my hand with its smoky ring. "I rather like the way this looks."

Siri's smile slipped into something much more wistful. "It is a pretty bauble, but one that may soon outlive its usefulness. Triss?"

The shadow of a dragon formed at my side. "Yes."

Siri straightened her back, and her words came out slow and clear. "I speak now as head of our order. If you feel yourself start to grow feathers of smoke, take Aral's finger off for me. If I try to countermand this order later, ignore me."

Triss bowed formally. "I will see it done, First Blade."

"Thank you. Aral, I am myself, but I don't know how long that will last. A half dozen disciples of the Smoldering Flame have just entered the vale. They are pursued by at least a score of velyn of varying allegiances, as well as at least one shrouded Blade."

"Kelos?" I asked, letting the interchange between Triss and Siri slide—I knew both well enough to recognize an argument already lost.

"Or Faran, but more likely both, given the way the fight has gone thus far. At least that's how I judge it seeing what I have through the god's eyes."

"Speaking of which . . ." I nodded toward the great oven.

"For the moment we have the same goals, so he has released me. How long that will hold I can't say."

"I'm glad that he has," I said. "But, you'll forgive me if I don't take it entirely at face value. *Why* did he let you go?"

"Mostly to prevent me from killing myself. There's still enough of the dagger left in his heart for me to manage my own end . . . for a little while longer at least. He very much wants me alive if he can keep me that way. For his own purposes, of course."

I felt a sudden weight of presence. *A dead servant is no servant at all.* The god's voice spoke directly into my mind—and, presumably, Siri's as well. *You are a powerful tool, Siri of the Blades. I would not waste you if I am not forced to it, nor blunt such a carefully honed edge. I want you well and in my service. You, too, Aral Kingslayer.*

"I will not be your slave," replied Siri. "I will die first."

Do not be so quick to reject what I can offer you, children. You are of a kind who works better of your own will than as a puppet. I do not want you as slaves, though I will serve you thus if I must. No, I want you willing. Eager even. Both of you, and I can offer that which will make the deal a sweet one.

"Somehow, I doubt your sincerity," I replied.

Then you are a fool. Heaven's Emperor betrayed and murdered your Namara. Heaven's gods are your enemies as surely as they are mine. Is that not an excellent basis on which to form an alliance? The destruction of those who have committed the gravest of wrongs against us all—those who even now seek to slay you as they would slay me. Heaven destroyed Namara for the same reason that it destroyed my kind. Because we were a threat that would not be controlled.

Fetch the key and raise me from my tomb and I will become the new God of Justice. A fresh order of Blades will rise to strike back against the tyrannies of the mighty and you two will lead them. The corruption of the system that you have spent your whole life fighting is rooted in the corruption of Heaven. You have seen the powers I have given Siri—smoke and shadow united. You will become unstoppable assassins in the service of the right. The Son of Heaven will fall first, but he will not be the last. Heaven itself will learn that Justice is inescapable.

I shook my head. "As much as I might like the fantasy of visiting justice on those who slew Justice, it all seems a bit grandiose, don't you think? To believe that the Emperor of

Heaven could have anything to fear from a handful of human assassins."

The god laughed in my mind, a cold and mocking sound. *Grandiose? Do you not understand, even now, with all that has happened? He already fears you.*

"That's madness!" I spat.

Is it really? Your goddess died for the threat she posed to Heaven. A threat that did not die with her.

"What are you talking about?" I didn't know why, but I was certain the god believed what he was telling me. That was almost more terrifying than the idea that he was insane.

The legacy of Namara is in your very hands and still you cannot see. Your goddess died almost without a fight because she had long since given up the bulk of her power to her disciples. She sank her soul and her strength into the swords of her chosen champions. In each hand you hold a splinter of the goddess you served, a physical embodiment of Justice's power to execute. Deliver it with justice in your heart, and it will slay even a god. I know. One such took my life.

"But only for a time," said Siri. "Even now you are a hair's breadth from rising again."

But that is my curse, and the curse of all my kind, bequeathed us by the first Emperor of Heaven with his final breath—to lie forever in the grave undying. The current rulers of Heaven are neither bound nor guarded by such a fate. They can die, if not easily, and the swords you carry are one means to that end. Never doubt that Heaven already fears you.

But we have spent too long in converse. The key enters my vale and but four of my disciples remain to guard it. Go. It must not fall into the hands of the Changer, or worse, the disquisition. Slay all who would keep the key from you. When you are done, come back to me and we shall see whether we cannot find our way to a bargain.

Abruptly, the sense of a mighty presence vanished, and I staggered at the feeling of a great weight suddenly lifted. Warily I held my blades up and looked across them at Siri. "Can all that be true?"

"I don't know." She turned her own swords this way and that as if trying to see deep inside the light-absorbing blackness of the divine steel. "I really don't. But the god *has* removed himself from my mind as completely as it is possible for him to do. I feel more myself than I have at any time since Namara's death."

"So, what do we do about it?" I asked.

You're not seriously entertaining his offer, are you? Triss demanded. *To let* that *become Justice?*

I shook my head. *No, of course not. The Smoldering Flame says* justice *when he means* vengeance. *I* want *vengeance, too, but I will never make it my master.*

Siri moved then, sheathing her swords with the same practiced grace I had seen her exhibit ten thousand times before. I raised an eyebrow.

"It's a long run from here to the far end of the vale," she said. "Doubly so carrying naked steel."

"So, we *are* going to get the key, then?" I looked deep into her eyes. The smoke was there in the depth of her irises but thin and barely moving.

A threat still, but a distant one, I think, observed Triss.

I agree. I flipped my swords around and put them away.

Siri nodded as I did so, and if she heard the buzz of our mindspeech, she showed no sign of it. "For the moment, our interests and the god's run in parallel. We need to recover that key, if only to keep it away from the other buried gods."

"What do we do with it once we've got it?"

"I don't know. Time enough to figure it out later."

"Perhaps it would suit best to give it to the disquisition," I said. "Of all the players in this they're the only ones I can think of who want to see the rising of their buried gods less than we do."

"I don't think that will work," said Siri, but her hand jerked in what might have been squeeze code for *yes*. "But for now, time is short and we need to run. Follow me."

Shadow bloomed around her and she vanished, but with the bond of our rings to guide me I had no trouble following in her wake.

The last pair of the Smoldering Flame's cultists stood back-to-back within a crudely executed ward a hundred yards into the vale. They had forsaken all semblance of an offense in favor of simply trying to maintain the ward. Spells representing every one of the greater and lesser elements licked out at them from their many enemies, now from one side, now from another. As the blasts hit the dome of protection that rose from the diagram, they outlined its boundaries and occasionally bent them inward.

They can't possibly hope to hold for long, I sent. *What were they thinking?*

That relief would come from their god, I imagine . . . and so we have.

I didn't like to think of us in that way, but I couldn't logically argue with Triss. The Smoldering Flame probably had sent them a message to fort up and await *our* arrival. It made my bones itch to serve his interests that way, but I vowed in my heart that the alliance would last only as long it served our interests.

I hope we can make that stick, Triss sent in the seconds before he released all control and sank into dormancy.

Me, too, I whispered into his dreams. *Me, too.*

Siri broke left as we approached the loose circle of enemies surrounding the Smoldering Flame's cultists, so I went right. A trio of cultists of mixed following had taken up position behind a low ridge, their differences with one another apparently put aside while the key was held by another faction. All three laid their length on the ground, taking advantage of the cover provided by the rise, despite the fact that the Smoldering Flame's disciples weren't returning their attacks.

They never saw me coming. Five running steps, a high leap, and they died. Two pinned to the earth by my swords. The third, lying between the others, when my full weight landed heels first on the place where his spine met his skull, hammering the lip of his own gorget into the weak point there with the crack of shattering bone.

I moved on without looking back, working my way farther to the right as I felt Siri moving left. The broken ground made excellent cover, especially as the smoke and steam pouring up from the many vents grew slowly thicker and wilder, providing us with ever better concealment.

That was no coincidence. I could feel the Smoldering Flame

exerting his will on the landscape of his domain to aid us. Nor was that the only way he influenced things. Subtler and more worrying by far, I found that I knew the vale as well as I knew my own neighborhood in Tien. Worse, I hadn't noticed it happening until I was already taking advantage of the results. The god might be trapped in his tomb and running out of willing allies, but he was far from helpless here on his home ground.

My next kill was more aware than the first set had been, spinning to face toward me as I slipped up behind her, though I didn't know how she sussed out my approach. But the blind spot defeated her staring eyes and she died when the point of my sword drove up under the chin piece of her helm, stabbing through the roof of her mouth and into her brain. Still, she was very good, and even in dying, her parrying dagger skidded painfully across my ribs in a thrust that missed going deep mostly by chance.

I moved on again, this time with blood slowly saturating the rough bandage I slapped over the wound in my side—oh, to have my trick bag back with its pastes and plasters. Somewhere to my left the ward fell, and with it the two remaining cultists of the Smoldering Flame.

The woman who would have been next on my list died before I could reach her. When the ward fell, she vaulted over the boulder she'd been hiding behind and sprinted toward the fallen cultists and the key, only to have the ground split in front of her feet and throw her into a scalding mud pot. I blocked out her screams and moved on.

My fifth target wore the badge of the disquisition and had his back to a rocky spire. He didn't move when the wards broke, just hunkered down against the tall spur of rock and kept his paired battle wands out in front of him—a patient man. That was going to be a problem. Or, at least, I thought it was.

But even as I tried to formulate my best approach, I felt a sudden tug on my ring and the smoke curling out of the ground on his other side took on Siri's form. Her sword licked out like the tongue of a snake, sinking deep into the bend of his elbow where the armor was thinnest, making him drop his right-hand wand. He spun toward her, firing off a shock of pink spell-light with his remaining weapon. By then, the smoke was just smoke again, and Siri had returned to the far side of the field.

Before the disquisitor could turn back around I was there,

delivering a pair of heavy, chopping blows from behind. My first sword shattered the thick crystal helm that protected his head, and my second split his skull to his teeth.

I quickly moved on. With Siri's new abilities and the god using the very environment to help us, it wasn't a fight so much as butchery. I felt my stomach turning slow backflips as Sylvani who never had a chance died beneath my swords one after another.

And then, almost before I knew it, the slaughter was over. When I moved toward the next place I would have expected one of our enemies to hole up, I found only a corpse— prematurely cold and stiff as the venom of a basilisk slowly turned her to stone. Kelos and Malthiss had been there before me. Which meant it was time to turn toward the center of the field.

When I looked that way, I found that I could only see one of the fallen cultists, and that, a partial view. It took me a beat to recognize the weird blurring for what it was—the blind spot and a shrouded Blade. And not Siri, whose presence I could feel farther away.

"Kelos!" I yelled as I sprinted toward the key. "Siri, hurry! Kelos is grabbing the key!"

But then Faran dropped her shroud. "It's me!" She raised a hand with something dull and brass sticking through her fingers. "They're all dead. I've got it."

I was ten feet away when the air behind her blurred. Something touched the back of Faran's neck with the faintest glimmer of spell-light. Her knees sagged and she slumped toward me. I lunged forward and caught her by the shoulders. For one brief instant the key seemed to hang in the air above her open hand, then it blurred away into darkness.

Kelos! "If you've harmed her, I'll kill you." The words came out cold and hard and alien. More like a deadly anger speaking through me, than me speaking them myself.

"I would sooner destroy one of my own swords than hurt the girl." Kelos spoke out of darkness. "She is the future of justice."

By then I could see that Faran was still breathing. Some of the cold fire in my chest faded as I eased her to the ground. Some.

Another voice spoke out of darkness, this time behind Kelos. "You will put the key gently on the ground, or I will kill you where you stand."

"Will you really, Siri? When I am your only chance at holding on to your soul?"

"What do you mean?" Siri's answer came back slow and stilted.

"The key, of course. If it stays here even an hour longer, your inner fire will awaken with the god as he finishes burning away the dagger in his heart. At that point, for all intents and purposes you will cease to exist. You have to know that. Here, a small gesture of faith." He dropped his shroud, and I let out a hiss at how much closer to me he'd slipped without my having any inkling—he stood now directly above Faran and me, his arms crossed. "Let me go, and I can get this bauble out of here before the Smoldering Flame bursts into fresh fire."

Siri's shroud fell, too. She was standing a yard behind Kelos, one sword back in a high guard, the other forward, its point lying a few inches below Kelos's left shoulder blade. "I'm afraid . . ." she said, and her voice suddenly shifted lower and deeper as the god took control of her, "that you're too late."

She lunged, and her sword punched straight through Kelos, its point emerging just below the ribs on the left side where it slid to a stop less than an inch from my right eye. Before I could move away from the threat of Siri's sword in front of me, a deep crunch sounded from behind, and I heard the voice of a god there.

"I am already awake."

22

———◆———

Without a word, Kelos slid forward off of Siri's blade.
Without a word, I caught him and laid him beside
Faran.

Without a word, I rose to face my wife, drawing my swords
as I did so.

Her eyes were full of smoke, her face blank. The only indication of any inner turmoil was the faintest of tremors in hands
that I had never seen shake.

The god spoke from behind me again, **"Face me, Kingslayer. We have a deal still to make."**

My shroud fell without my wishing it and I could sense Triss
trapped somewhere deep within my shadow unable to act or
awaken. I could do nothing for him and I felt a great pressure
to turn around as the word and the will of the god beat down
upon me. I knew that I couldn't hold out long against such a
power, that in a moment I would have to turn away from Siri
to face the god whether I wanted to or not. My only chance lay
in working that to my advantage.

I took a deep breath and let it out, releasing my thoughts
and emotions with the air in my lungs. I couldn't afford to tip

my hand in any way. I would get only one chance at this.
Maybe. Even if I succeeded, I might well die. Either directly
at the hand of the god, or by proxy with one of Siri's swords in
my back.

"I told you to face me."

I felt the pressure of his command growing stronger, unbear-
able almost. My left foot began to pivot slowly against my will.
Now!

I converted my slow turn into a sharp spin, whipping my
swords into position for a thrust straight at the god's burning
heart as I did so. But then the ring of smoke on my finger
pulsed and I slowed, grinding to a near halt in mid-strike. My
sword continued moving toward the god's chest, but almost too
slowly for me to perceive it. At the current rate, I might move
a few inches in the next hour.

The Smoldering Flame was taller than Ash—eight feet
maybe—and even more perfect of feature. But the Sylvani lord
had appeared as one filled with the dimming light of the
westering sun, pale but still noble. The power within the god
was dark and sullen, like the red glow of coals ready for the
torturer's irons. His was a fire of the earth, reflecting his place
among the fathers of the fathers of the Durkoth.

A narrow diadem of red-hot iron wrapped his brow, burning
the skin beneath it crisp and black. Above, his head simply
ended as thick smoke poured from the open top of his skull. It
trailed down his back in a great cloak that rolled out behind
him to form a yard's long train.

A sleeveless shirt of iron rings glowed dully on his chest
and back, and the skin beneath was as black and burnt as his
brow. Likewise the skin of his hips and thighs where a short
skirt of the same iron mail burned into his flesh. When he
moved, raw red cracks opened in his skin, but if it hurt him he
showed no sign. He shook his head gently now and crossed his
arms like a disappointed father.

**"Oh, child, did you really think that you could fool me?
That I would not see the ploy in your mind and stop it before
it could start? Truly? Speak."**

I felt the power that held my voice in near stasis with the
rest of me ease. I didn't particularly want to answer the god
with anything but curses, but if the only tool allowed me was

words, then I'd best use them. "I had hopes in that direction, yes."

At the same time I sent, *Triss?* But he remained deep in his dreams of darkness, and the part of my will that might have roused him felt as cold and slow as my body.

"When you married the Siri, you married me in the same instant. I can see your heart more clearly than you can. I know how much you want to kill me, and still I would bargain with you. With *both* of you. Siri, come forward."

Siri slid up beside me, her swords still frozen in thrust and guard, her hands shaking more visibly now as she fought against the god's will. The Smoldering Flame stepped closer. That put his chest mere inches from my sword's tip, but it might as well have been a league away for all the speed of my movements.

"I could take the key from you now and bind you to my will so deeply that you would barely even feel the chains. But I said that I wanted you willing, and I meant it. Worship me and I will give you the justice you long for. I will *be* Justice, and there will be a cleansing the likes of which this world has never known."

"I will not serve Vengeance and call it just," I said.

He shook his head. **"This is your last chance. Siri, you have known my touch for longer. Can you not convince your husband to our cause? It is time now to put aside your swords and come to me. They can but prevent me for the briefest of times. You must know that you can't resist me forever."**

"No, I can't. But then, I don't have to." With a sudden vicious twist, Siri brought her guarding sword down on her own forearm and said, "I divorce you, Aral."

It shouldn't have been enough, but it was. Flesh parted like water before the steel of the goddess, and Siri's thrusting hand fell away. The hand that wore a ring of smoke, fading now as it lost its connection to her soul.

Before I could even realize what that meant, my own ring puffed away into nothingness, and the binding will of the god went with it. My body was my own again. My thrust, halted for so long, punched forward now, shearing through burning iron rings to find a home in divine flesh.

I felt the tip of my blade slide into the heart of a god. Felt as it continued onward to burst out through the charred skin of his back. As the mail there slowed but didn't stop the impetus of my thrust. The guard of my sword slamming into his chest to finally stop my thrust. Searing pain as iron rings, heated to a red glow, branded my thumb and the knuckle of my first finger, forcing me to let go my hilt.

But none of that came close to the horrible sense of violation I felt when the god's presence invaded my soul. As the Smoldering Flame died for the third time, I felt the essence of him come slithering up along the line of my blade to worm its way into my heart.

The god fell, landing hard on his back and driving my sword deep into the soil of the vale. In the same instant, Triss screamed in his dreams and my shadow shifted, becoming once again the familiar dragon shape. But something else had shifted as well, and wings that once were wholly dark now sported a line of faint smoke along their trailing edges. It wasn't as dramatic as the feathers Kyrissa wore. Not yet, at least. But it would come. I could feel it in my bones, and there was only one way to stop it.

I reached for my sword. . . .

Siri caught my wrist with her one remaining hand and her grip was cold iron. "Aral! You can't. Not that way. If you withdraw the sword he will rise again."

Smoky worms crawled through my soul, polluting me in a way I could never have imagined. I turned to look at Siri hopelessly. "But, he's . . . I can't—"

"I know, Aral. I know. I know. No one better. You won't have to. You need only abide it a few moments longer."

I stopped trying to shake off Siri's hand. I had said that I would walk into a fire for her. How could I refuse her the smoke? For the first time since the Smoldering Flame had fallen I actually looked at Siri.

Her left arm ended midway between hand and elbow, the stump covered by a thick layer of pure shadow where Kyrissa had made of herself both tourniquet and bandage. Her skin above the shadow was only a few shades lighter, but it was sheened with sweat, and I could only imagine the pain she was in. I lifted my eyes to meet Siri's—they were clear of any hint of smoke—and I nodded slowly and deliberately.

She smiled back at me. "Thank you." The smoke was gone from her hair as well.

"What do you need me to do?" I asked.

"Hand me my sword—the one I'm still holding on to. I'm a little shaky at the moment, or I'd get it myself."

I bent down and pried the fingers of her severed hand free of the hilt. I was about to give it to her when I realized what she intended.

"Siri, you can't." I touched the smoke wisping along the edge of Triss's nearer wing—he was trembling, but he didn't say anything either aloud or mind-to-mind. "It's too monstrous. You're only just free of him now."

"There is only one way to bind him for the long run, Aral. It's your blade or mine, and, frankly, I'm not going to have much need of a second sword given this." She touched her arm a few inches above the place that it ended.

I shook my head. "It's not fair."

"No, it's not. Give me my sword."

But still I hesitated.

"Don't make me make it an order."

I reversed the sword and extended it to her, hilt first. "You don't have to do this. I *will* bear this burden for you if you ask it of me." It cost me dearly to make the offer, but I had to do it.

"I know that you would. That's part of why I can't ask." She took the sword from me and drove it deep into the heart of a dead god. Smoke bloomed in her hair as she turned to face me again. "Your turn."

As my sword slid free of the god's chest, I felt the worms of his presence withdraw from my soul. It was like being born anew, fresh and clean and impossibly young again. Triss collapsed back into my shadow with a sigh, and I felt his awareness fade into the deep dormant state that he sometimes fell into when he needed time to recover from some trauma.

I sheathed my blades and turned back to Siri. "It's inadequate to the moment, but thank you. I . . ."

She reached out and touched her finger to my lips. "I know." She pushed her shoulders back in the manner of one settling a heavy pack into place. "We'll talk of it later. For now, there's still much to do, starting with the key."

We both turned then, and . . . "Son of a fucking sow!" I yelled.

Siri snarled, "I should have killed him!"

Kelos was gone, and, with him, the key.

"I would have, too," she said. "But I could feel that was what the god wanted of me. And so I aimed so very carefully. More fool me." She shook her head. "Do you know how hard it is to thread the line beneath heart and lungs but over the lesser organs?"

"I've never tried it, but I can imagine. Dammit! We have to go after him."

Siri shook her head again. "*You* have to go after him. The shape I'm in I'd only slow you down. That, and someone has to take care of Faran and getting the Smoldering Flame back into his tomb. But, we've no time. Go!"

I went, pulling my shroud around me as I sniffed out Kelos's shadow trail.

How can he keep going like this, hour after hour? I sent.

He is Kelos.

For two days I had run along his backtrail never daring to slow or to sleep, lest he use the opportunity to break his scent or simply double back and remove me from the scene. He'd taken a god-damned sword through the torso, and he was still running fast enough to keep me from ever gaining more than a few seconds at a time on him. Some of that was my own injury. The dagger that slit my ribs hadn't gone deep, but it was another of the cursed weapons of the cultists, and it bled slowly but relentlessly, robbing me of strength a drop at a time.

On the upside, we hadn't yet had to contend with any cultists or other competitors for the key. Whether that was because of our encounter at the tomb of the Smoldering Flame, or because of something Siri was doing to draw attention, or if Kelos had some way to mask the presence of the key, I couldn't say. All I could do was continue to lope along in my old mentor's wake.

Aral?

Yes?

Unshroud your eyes and tell me what you see.

I did. *Oh hell.*

That is *the wall ahead, then? I wasn't sure. It's too bright for me even here under the trees.*

It is. I wish I had some idea where old smoke and mirror's tomb was so that I could tell you what part of the wall we're seeing. But we could be anywhere between Tavan and the sea. Wherever we are, it's a heavily populated section.

I pushed harder, forcing legs that felt like sacks of rice to move faster. I was not going to let Kelos take the key beyond the bounds of the empire if I could avoid it. As we got closer to the wall, the shadow trail started to angle to the left, aiming toward a place where the buildings thinned out. It grew fresher as well, which made me hope that the old bastard's strength was finally waning.

Then, a few hundred yards short of the wall, I saw him. Or rather, I didn't see a bush. One moment it was there. The next gone. Then back again. I was close, so very close. But not close enough. I *would* catch him but not before he got to the wall.

I think we've got him, I sent. *If he can't pick his pace up again, I'll catch him within a mile of the other side.*

Unless he's got a last trick up his sleeve, Triss sent glumly. *Something about the wall, maybe?*

Who knows? But there's nothing we can do about it.

I ran on, scanning ahead for signs of his blind spot. It ate another bush. Then a stand of taller grasses. Finally, when I was less than a hundred yards shy of the wall, it bit a piece out of the structure itself.

The blur moved up . . . touched the top . . . and a mighty chime sounded, like the gods themselves striking a silver bell the size of the palace at Tien. The sky went gray and dark, though no cloud marred its vault.

Kelos's shroud fell, exposing him in an awkward crouch atop the wall—poised on one hand and the balls of his feet. His other arm was stretched back behind him at an odd angle, and I realized that his hand was still on this side of the wall, almost as though it had caught in some invisible trap in the air when he tried to cross.

A webwork of lightning ripped across the sky, filling it from edge to edge with a net of bolts that burned on and on, unfading. Triss shrieked at the sudden brightness and hid himself within my shadow. A single thread of lightning rolled down from the sky to touch the wall between Kelos's feet and hold there.

He bellowed like an old bull gored by a younger rival and his trailing hand opened convulsively. A narrow strip of brass flipped and spun upward from his palm. For one brief moment, it seemed to float in the air. Then the lightning thread moved, jumping from the wall to the key. The brass shone suddenly bright as it shot upward along the line of lightning.

The chime sounded again, lower and more brassy this time, and the lightning web shattered and went dark. The afterimage hung in front of my eyes for three long heartbeats. Then it, too, faded . . . sort of. The knots where lightning had met lightning hung on, and even started to grow larger as though they were falling from the sky.

I don't . . .

What? sent Triss.

And then I knew, and I started to laugh. It served the old bastard right.

What is it?

Before I could answer, a distant tinkle marked the sound of the first bit of falling brass hitting a roof in the city of Wall. All over the empire it was raining keys.

The wall, I sent. *I should have realized what that meant when it sniffed around my swords, but I didn't understand then that that was what was happening. It's a ward against god-magic, specifically, the god-magic of the buried ones, and the key is very powerful god-magic indeed.*

You mean that it's here to stop the movement of the key specifically?

Not just the key, no, but the key is the most powerful manifestation of the buried gods, short of one of them showing up in person. Of course it can't cross the wall.

I wonder what it would do to Ash's sword? asked Triss.

Nothing good.

When I caught up to Kelos, he was laughing, too.

* * *

"**I'm** still not entirely sure that I understand what happened," Faran said from her place beside the fire.

"The key can't pass the ward of the wall," I replied.

"Yeah, I got that part, but what happened to it? And, more importantly, why let him live?" She nodded toward Kelos, who was brooding on the far side of the hearth.

I shrugged. The four of us were sitting at the very end of one of the long narrow taverns on the human side of the city of Wall. The locals had scattered away from us like minnows who fear the shark.

I still wasn't sure how Kelos had talked me out of killing him at the wall. Or, later, and even more surprisingly, talked Siri out of it. Part of that was convincing us that he still had too many secrets that we needed to know. Especially if we were going to do something about the Son of Heaven, an open question at the moment, though I was beginning to think I couldn't leave it that way for much longer. But that wasn't all of it, nor even most of it.

No, if I was going to be truly honest with myself, he had done it by being the father that neither of us had ever had. For both of us he stood on the threshold between love and hate. I don't know about Siri, but while I might be able to kill Kelos in a fit of anger, or to prevent him doing some greater harm, I don't think I could ever take his life simply for what he had done, however horrible.

It was ironic, really. If I were still the man he had tried to make me at the temple, he would already be dead. The young Aral, the black-and-white Aral, the Aral who had killed Ashvik? He would have killed Kelos without hesitation. It would have been the just decision. Now . . . well, the Aral of now hadn't the certainty for it. As for Siri? I couldn't speak for her reasons, but she didn't seem any more capable of putting Kelos to death than I was. Perhaps the god in her head had burned away what certainty she had left.

As for Faran? She seemed to have gone along with the whole thing out of respect for Siri and me. That, or because the headaches continued and she didn't want to start that argument with me quite yet—which was as likely an explanation as any. The look in her eyes when she glanced his way now was cold enough for that, and I suspected she was trying to figure out how exactly to take him when the time came.

In a move that seemed almost a deliberate confirmation of my suspicions there, her right hand fell to caress the hilts of the pair of Namara-forged swords leaning against the arm of her chair—Parsi's. It was Faran who had taken them from the older Blade's corpse, and I couldn't fault her for it. I only regretted that Iander's had fallen into the hands of the disquisition after his wind-carpet went down.

"Well?" She squeezed the nearer of the hilts as she prompted me again. It was a profoundly possessive gesture, and who could blame her? She had waited years for those swords. "What about all those keys? What was that about?"

"I really don't know," I said. "That wall is magic on a scale that's hard to conceive. Siri's the expert there. . . ."

Siri shook her head. "It's beyond me, though I *can* speculate. Aral and Kelos each picked up two or three keys and looked them over closely." She turned to me. "You said there was nothing special about them."

"Except for the bit where they faded away a couple of hours later," I replied.

Siri ran her fingers along the line of one faintly smoking braid. "The really big magics have a sort of life of their own. They have to in order to do their jobs, especially if they're long lasting and the task they're designed for is complex enough. The wall is the biggest and most permanent piece of magic I've ever heard of, and if there's a task more complex than guarding against the constant attack of the buried gods, I have a hard time imagining it."

"All right," said Faran. "I'm with you so far."

"The wall may not live and breathe and think in the way that we do, but neither does a Shade. And we would never underestimate them. What I think happened is that all of those keys were *the* key. At least in potential and for a little while. The wall's purpose is to keep the buried gods under control. The awareness of the key and its position had them all waking up and wrenching themselves free of their graves. In order to end that uprising, the wall had to break the attention of the buried ones. It did that by scattering the focus across a million little shards of potential, only one of which would eventually become the true key again once it landed someplace safe. At least, that's how it . . . feels to me."

Triss and the other shades had chosen to remain concealed within our shadows—at least until we left the common room—though they had cheated the light a bit to put them all in contact.

Now he spoke into my mind. *If that feeling comes from where I think it does, better her than us.*

I nodded. *We owe her. Now, more than ever.*

Agreed.

I looked sadly at the stump of her left arm . . . and then had to suppress a sudden shiver.

What is it? asked Triss.

I . . . It's gone now, but for just a second I thought she'd grown a new hand. One of smoke . . .

I stood. "I think I need to get to bed. I'm feeling a bit woozy."

"No surprise there," said Siri. "You damned near bled out through that little cut on your ribs. If I hadn't drawn the curse . . ." She looked down. "You scared me there, old friend."

Me, too, added Triss.

Kelos growled, "You should take better care of yourself, boy."

And that was too much. I must either challenge the man or walk away for a time. I chose to walk away. I needed the sleep anyway.

As I closed the door of my room, Triss shaped himself out of shadows on the wall opposite the fireplace. "I wish I knew where the key went. We went through so much to try to recover it, and now it feels almost like we've lost."

I smiled. "It was never really about the key, Triss. At least, not for its own sake. It was always about Siri and her problems. Going after the key was always a means toward that end."

"I suppose. . . ." He didn't seem entirely convinced.

"No supposing about it. We got into this because Siri needed our help. The Smoldering Flame was slowly devouring her. Without us he would have owned her soul."

"But she's still bound to him."

"By her own choosing this time, and in a very different degree. The cost was high, but I think that we did what we set out to do, and that Siri would agree."

"She would indeed," said a voice from behind me.

I drew my swords and spun before my wits caught up with my reflexes and I recognized Siri's laugh.

"Gently, Aral," she said even as I relaxed. "It's only me." She was standing in the mouth of my empty hearth, and she smiled now, her teeth flashing white in the dark. She patted the mantelpiece. "I let myself in. I hope you don't mind."

"Not at all," I replied.

"He's right, Triss. When I needed you the most, you were there for me. I owe you my soul, and that's a debt I can never properly repay."

"There is no debt, Siri, not from my side of the ledger. If there's anything I can do for you ever, all you have to do is ask. Speaking of which, I presume you came here for a reason beyond reassuring Triss. What do you want?"

"You." She chuckled, low and wicked, sliding forward into a pool of light from the window as she slipped out of her shirt. "The mission is over, for now, and I thought it might be fun to shack up with my ex."

"I think I could be convinced." I sheathed my swords and stepped forward into her arms.

And so, it ended as it had begun, with the woman and the smoke without fire.

. . . Well, maybe a little fire.

Terms and Characters

———◆———

Alinthide Poisonhand—A master Blade, the third to die making an attempt on Ashvik VI.

Alley-Knocker—An illegal bar or cafe.

Anaryan, Earl of—A Zhani noble.

Anyang—Zhani city on the southern coast. Home of the winter palace.

Aral Kingslayer—Ex-Blade turned jack of the shadow trades.

Ashelia—A smuggler.

Ashvik VI, or Ashvik Dan Pridu—Late King of Zhan, executed by Aral. Also known as the Butcher of Kadesh.

Athera Trinity—The three-faced goddess of fate.

Balor Lifending—God of the dead and the next Emperor of Heaven.

Black Jack—A professional killer or assassin.

Blade—Temple assassin of the goddess Namara.

Blinds—Charms of confusion and befuddlement, mostly used by thieves in the Magelands.

Bontrang—A miniature gryphon.

Calren the Taleteller—God of beginnings and first Emperor of Heaven.

Caras Dust—Powerful magically bred stimulant.

Caras Seed-Grinder—Producer of caras dust.

Caras Snuffler—A caras addict.

Channary Canal—Canal running from the base of the Channary Hill to the Zien River in Tien.

Channary Hill—One of the four great hills of Tien.

Chenjou Peninsula—The peninsula to the north of Tien.

Chief Marshal—Head of the Zhani military.

Chimney Forest—The city above, rooftops, etc.

Chimney Road—A path across the rooftops of a city. "Running the chimney road."

Coals—Particularly hot stolen goods.

Code Martial—Ancient system of Zhani law.

Cornerbright—Magical device for seeing around corners.

Crownies—A derogatory term for the Crown Guard in Zhan, used by the watch.

Crown Law—Zhan's modern legal system.

Dalridia—Kingdom in the southern Hurnic Mountains.

Devin (Nightblade) Urslan—A former Blade.

Dian—A black jack in training in Tien.

Downunders—A bad neighborhood in Tien.

Dracodon—A large magical beast, renowned for the ivory in its tusks.

Dragon Crown—The royal crown of Zhan, often replicated in insignia of Zhani Crown agents.

Drum-Ringer—A bell enchanted to prevent eavesdropping.

Durkoth—Others that live under the Hurnic Mountains.

Dustmen—Dealers in caras dust.

Eavesman—A spy or eavesdropper.

Elite, the—Zhani mages. They fulfill the roles of secret police and spy corps among other functions.

Emberman—A professional arsonist.

Emerald Throne—The throne of the Sylvani Empire.

Erk Endfast—Owner of the Spinnerfish, ex–black jack, ex–shadow captain.

Everdark, the—The home dimension of the Shades.

Eyespy—A type of eavesdropping spell.

Face, Facing—Identity. "I'd faced myself as an Aveni bravo."

Fallback—A safe house.

Familiar Gift—The ability to soul-bond with another being, providing the focus half of the power/focus dichotomy necessary to become a mage.

Faran—A onetime apprentice Blade.

Fire and Sun!—A Shade curse.

Ghost, Ghosting—To kill.

Govana—Goddess of the herds.

Gram—The name of the world.

Greatspell—A major permanent work of magic, usually tied to a physical item.

Gryphon's Head—A tavern in Tien, the capital city of Zhan. Informal office for Aral.

Guttersiders—Slang for the professional beggars and their allies.

Hand of Heaven—The Son of Heaven's office of the inquisition.

Harad—Head librarian at the Ismere Library.

Hearsay—A type of eavesdropping spell.

Heyin—Lieutenant of the exiled Baroness Marchon.

Highside—Neighborhood on the bay side of Tien.

Howler—Slang name for the Elite.

Inverted Crown—A Zhani brand applied to the cheeks or fore-heads of traitors.

Ismere Club—A private club for merchants.

Ismere Library—A private lending library in Tien, founded by a wealthy merchant from Kadesh.

Issa Fivegoats—A sellcinders or fence.

Jack—A slang term for an unofficial or extragovernmental problem solver; see also, shadow jack, black jack, sunside jack.

Jax Seldansbane—A former Blade and onetime fiancée of Aral's.

Jenua, Duchy of—A duchy in Zhan.

Jerik—The bartender/owner of the Gryphon's Head tavern.

Jindu—Tienese martial art heavily weighted toward punches and kicks.

Jinn's—A small cafe near the Ismere Library.

Kadeshar—Chief city of Kadesh.

Kaelin Fei, Captain—Watch officer in charge of Tien's Silent Branch. Also known as the Mufflers.

Kaman—A former Blade, crucified by the Elite, then killed by Aral at his own request.

Kanathean Hill—One of the four great hills of Tien.

Kao-Li—Fortress retreat of the Zhani royal family, upriver from Tien.

Kayarin Melkar—A master Blade who joined the Son of Heaven after the fall of the temple.

Kelos Deathwalker—A master Blade who taught Aral.

Keytrue—A charm to prevent lock picking.

Khanates, the Four—A group of interrelated kingdoms just north of Varya. Also known as the Kvanas.

Kijang, Duchy of—A duchy in Zhan.

Kila—The spirit dagger of the Blade, symbolizing his bond to Namara.

Kip-Claim—Pawnshop.

Kodamia—City-state to the west of Tien, controlling the only good pass through the Hurnic Mountains.

Kuan-Lun—A water elemental, one of the great dragons.

Kvanas, the Four—Group of interrelated kingdoms just north of Varya. Sometimes referred to as the Khanates.

Kyle's—An expensive Aveni whiskey.

Last Walk—The road leading from the Smokeyard to the traitor's gate in Tien.

Leyan—A onetime journeyman Blade.

Little Varya—An immigrant neighborhood in Tien.

Loris—A former Blade.

Magearch—Title for the mage governor of the cities in the Magelands.

Mageblind—Mage term for those without magesight.

Mage Gift—The ability to perform magic, providing the power half of the power/focus dichotomy necessary to become a mage.

Magelands—A loose confederation of city-states governed by the faculty of the mage colleges that center them.

Magelights—Relatively expensive permanent light globes made with magic.

Magesight—The ability to see magic, part of the mage gift.

Mage Wastes—Huge area of magically created wasteland on the western edge of the civilized lands.

Malthiss—A Shade, familiar of Kelos Deathwalker.

Manny Three Fingers—The cook at the Spinnerfish.

Marchon—A barony in the kingdom of Zhan. The house emblem is a seated jade fox on a gold background.

Maylien Dan Marchon Tal Pridu—A former client of Aral's.

Mufflers—Captain Fei's organization, so known because they keep things quiet. Officially known as Silent Branch.

Nail-Puller—Tienese street slang for a freelance torturer.

Namara—The now-deceased goddess of justice and the down-trodden, patroness of the Blades. Her symbol is an unblinking eye.

Nest-Not—A ward to prevent vermin infestations.

Niala—A Varyan liquor flavored with efik.

Nightcutter—Assassin.

Nightghast—One of the restless dead, known to eat humans.

Night Market—The black market.

Nima—Mana, the stuff of magic.

Nipperkins—Magical vermin.

Noble Dragons—Elemental beings that usually take the form of giant lizardlike creatures.

Nuriko Shadowfox—A legendary renegade Blade killed by Kelos Deathwalker. Also known as the Kitsune.

Oil-Smear—A charm to ward against eyespys.

Old Mews—An upscale neighborhood in Tien that burned to the ground.

Orisa—God of sailors.

Oris Plant—A common weed that can be used to produce a cheap gray dye or an expensive black one.

Others—The various nonhuman races.

Palace Hill—One of the four great hills of Tien.

Petty Dragons—Giant acid-spitting lizards, not to be confused with noble dragons.

Poison—Gutter slang meaning toxic or too hot to deal with.

Precasts—Active spells kept precast and at the ready.

Pridu Dynasty—Hereditary rulers of Zhan from around 2700 to the present day.

Prixia Dan Xaia—Clan chief of Xankou.

Qamasiin—A spirit of air.

Quink—Slang word meaning, roughly, freak.

Rabbit Run—An emergency escape route.

Rehira—A high-end black jack in Tien, one of the few who's not a mage.

Render's Way—A street in Tien.

Reshi—A clanate in northern Zhan.

Resshath—Shade term of respect meaning, roughly, teacher or sensei.

Restless Dead—Catchall term for the undead.

Riel—Currency of Zhan, issued in both silver and gold.

Right of Challenge—Part of Zhan's old Code Martial.

Risen, the—A type of restless dead, similar to a zombie.

Royal Monetist—Chief financial official of Zhan.

Sailmaker's Street—A street in Tien.

Sanjin Island—Large island in the river below the palace in Tien.

Scheroc—A qamasiin, or air spirit.

Sellcinders—A fence or dealer in hot merchandise.

Serass—A Shade, familiar of Alinthide.

Shade—Familiar of the Blades, a living shadow.

Shadow Captain—A mob boss.

Shadow Jack—A jack who earns his living as a problem solver in the shadow trades.

Shadowside—The underworld or demimonde.

Shadow-Slipping—The collective name for the various stealth techniques of Namara's Blades.

Shadow Trades—The various flavors of illegal activity.

Shadow World—The demimonde or underworld.

Shaisin—Small town in Zhan, baronial seat of Marchon.

Shanglun—A river dragon.

Shan Starshoulders—The god who holds up the sky, current Emperor of Heaven, lord of stability.

Shatternot—A charm to keep windows from breaking.

Shinsan—A water elemental, one of the great dragons.

Shrouding—When a Shade encloses his Blade in shadow.

Silent Branch—The official name of the Mufflers.

Siri Mythkiller—A former Blade.

Skaate's—A premium Aveni whiskey.

Skip—A con game or other illegal job, also a "play."

Sleepwalker—An efik addict.

Slink—Magical vermin.

Slip—A person who tries to get out of paying back a money-lender. Also known as a debt slip.

Smokeyard—The prison in Zhan where traitors are held on their way to execution.

Smuggler's Rest—The unofficial name of the docks near the Spinnerfish.

Snicket—Alley.

Snug—A resting place or residence.

Son or Daughter of Heaven—The title of the chief priest or priestess who leads the combined religions of the eleven kingdoms.

Sovann Hill—One of the four great hills of Tien.

Spinnerfish, the—A shadowside tavern by the docks.

Sshayar—A Shade, familiar of Jax.

Ssithra—A Shade, familiar of Faran.

Starshine—Elemental being of light.

Stingers—Slang term for Tienese city watch.

Stone Dog—A living statue, roughly the size of a small horse. The familiar of the Elite.

Straight-Back Jack—A shadow jack who gets the job done and keeps his promises.

Stumbles, the—Neighborhood of Tien that houses the Gryphon's Head tavern.

Sumey Dan Marchon Tal Pridu—Baroness Marchon and sister of Maylien.

Sunside—The shadowside term for more legitimate operations.

Sunside Jack—A jack who works aboveboard, similar to a modern detective.

Sylvani Empire—Sometimes called the Sylvain, a huge empire covering much of the southern half of the continent. Ruled by a nonhuman race, it is ancient, and hostile to the human lands of the north.

Tailor's Wynd—An upscale neighborhood in Tien.

Tangara—God of glyphs and runes and other magical writing.

Tangle—Charms of confusion and befuddlement, mostly used by thieves in the Magelands.

Tavan—One of the five great university cities of the Magelands.

Tavan North—The Magelanders' quarter of Tien.

Thalis Nut—A nut that produces a poisonous oil.

Thalis Oil—A toxic oil used by the Blades both as a poison and for the oiling of hinges and other hardware.

Thauvik IV, or Thauvik Tal Pridu, the Bastard King—King of Zhan and bastard half brother of the late Ashvik.

Thieveslamp/Thieveslight—A dim red magelight in a tiny bull's-eye lantern.

Thiussus—A Shade, familiar of Nuriko Shadowfox.

Tien—A coastal city, the thousand-year-old capital of Zhan.

Tien, Duchess of—Jiahui Dan Tien, cousin of the king.

Timesman—The keeper of the hours at the temple of Shan, Emperor of Heaven.

Travelers—A seminomadic order of mages dedicated to making the roads safe for all.

Triss—Aral's familiar. A Shade that inhabits Aral's shadow.

Tuckaside—A place to stash goods, usually stolen.

Tucker—Tucker bottle, a quarter-sized liquor bottle, suitable for two or for one heavy drinker.

Underhills—An upscale neighborhood in Tien.

Vangzien—Zhani city at the confluence where the Vang River flows into the Zien River in the foothills of the Hurnic Mountains. Home of the summer palace.

Vesh'An—Shapechanging Others. Originally a part of the same breed that split into the Sylvani and Durkoth, the Vesh'An have adopted a nomadic life in the sea.

Warboard—Chesslike game.

Wardblack—A custom-built magical rug that blocks the function of a specific ward.

Westbridge—A bridge over the Zien, upriver from the palace and the neighborhood around it.

Worrymoth—An herb believed to drive away moths.

Wound-Tailor—Shadowside slang for a healer for hire.

Xankou—A clanate on the Chenjou Peninsula, near Kadesh.

Xaran Tal Xaia—Bastard half brother of Prixia Dan Xaia.

Zass—A Shade, familiar of Devin.

Zhan—One of the eleven human kingdoms of the East. Home to the city of Tien.

Zishin—A sergeant of the watch answering to Captain Fei.

Currency

Bronze Sixth Kip (sixer)
Bronze Kip
Bronze Shen
Silver Half Riel
Silver Riel
Gold Half Riel
Gold Riel
Gold Oriel

Value in Bronze Kips

~0.15 = Bronze Sixth Kip
1 = Bronze Kip
10 = Bronze Shen
60 = Silver Half Riel
120 = Silver Riel

Value in Silver Riels

0.5 = Silver Half Riel
1 = Silver Riel
5 = Gold Half Riel
10 = Gold Riel
50 = Gold Oriel

Calendar

———

(370 days in 11 months of 32 days each, plus two extra 9-day holiday weeks: Summer-Round in the middle of Midsummer, and Winter-Round between Darktide and Coldfast)

1 *Coldfast*
2 *Meltentide*
3 *Greening*
4 *Seedsdown*
5 *Opening*
6 *Midsummer*
7 *Sunshammer*
8 *Firstgrain*
9 *Harvestide*
10 *Talewynd*
11 *Darktide*

Days of the Week

———◦•◦———

1 *Calrensday*—In the beginning.
2 *Atherasday*—Hearth and home.
3 *Durkothsday*—Holdover from the prehuman tale of days.
4 *Shansday*—The middle time.
5 *Namarsday*—Traditional day for nobles to sit in judgment.
6 *Sylvasday*—Holdover from the prehuman tale of days.
7 *Balorsday*—Day of the dead.
8 *Madensday*—The day of madness when no work is done.

Read on for an exciting excerpt from
the next book in the Fallen Blade series

DARKENED BLADE

by Kelly McCullough
Coming May 2015 from Ace Books!

The dead should stay dead.

For six years after the fall of the temple, I believed that Kelos had died defending our goddess and our people. Then I discovered what really happened and that he was still alive. I wish that he'd stayed dead.

I had climbed to the top of our little tower, an octagonal deck surrounded by a low wooden wall. The sun had long since set, but the moon was bright for eyes trained to the darkness, and I could see well enough. The wall stretched away east and west, its shape picked out by the magelights and oil lanterns glowing along its length, like some phosphorescent eel from the deep ocean.

"I liked him better when he was a corpse," I said.

"It's never too late. . . ." Faran's voice spoke from behind me.

I turned, looking for the deeper bit of shadow I must have missed when I first came out on the rooftop. I found it in an angle of the wall not far from the stairhead, or at least thought that I did—a shrouded Blade is all but invisible, especially at night. I crossed my arms and waited silently. A moment later the shadow thinned and resumed Ssithra's phoenix shape, revealing Faran, who sat cross-legged with her back against the boards.

She lifted her chin. "It's really not too late, you know. I could go back downstairs and kill him right now. Or . . . you could."

"That wouldn't solve the problem."

"It would put an end to it."

"No, it would only put an end to Kelos. It wouldn't undo the fall of the temple or the death of Namara or any of the other horrors he helped perpetrate."

And it wouldn't salvage your memories of the man he was before he did those things, Triss said quietly into my mind. *That man is already dead, and with him a part of you.*

That, too.

Faran rose to face me, and her eyes were on a level with mine. "Then what is the lesson?"

"Huh?" I asked.

"You took me on as your apprentice, right?"

I nodded.

"So, teach me. How can you stand to let him live after all that he's done? How can that be right? Namara's Blades exist to bring justice to those who would not otherwise receive it, those who are protected by power from the results of their actions. Doesn't Kelos fit the bill?"

"Namara's Blades are gone."

"That's a dodge, Aral, and a pretty bad one at that. You're still here and the ghost of the goddess told you herself that you should seek justice, that you should continue down the path she set you on."

"I don't know." I turned my back on Faran and looked out into the darkness again. "I don't want to kill him."

"Not two minutes ago you said that you liked him better as a corpse."

I nodded. "I did that. But the corpse I liked him as was a martyr to our goddess, not a traitor to her. That ship sank. Now he wants me to kill him, or if I won't do it, Siri or you. He believes that he deserves to die for his treachery."

Faran put a hand on my shoulder and turned me to face her. "He's not wrong."

"No, he's not. But what will it accomplish? He wants to die

for his crimes, but he doesn't repent them. He would do the same thing tomorrow in the same circumstances. He believed then and still does that by giving people hope for justice, Namara was relieving pressure that otherwise would have destroyed a corrupt system of governance. Is he wrong about that?"

"I don't know." Faran sighed. "In the lost years I made my way in the world by spying and commissioned theft. I saw a lot of corruption in the ruling classes, and I didn't do anything about it because: hey, my goddess is dead and it's not my fucking job. Then I found you, and you showed me that there may be something to this whole justice business even without Namara to show us the way. But I don't see it as clearly as you do. *Is* the system so corrupt that the only thing to do is burn it down and start over? Or is it more important that we keep righting the individual wrongs?"

"That's really the question, isn't it?" asked Triss. "The big one that we're all fighting about without actually talking about it. Do we kill Kelos because of what he did to Namara, or do we back his play and move against the Son of Heaven?"

"And even that oversimplifies things," I growled. "Killing the Son is surely justice of the kind we were raised to deliver. He is practically the personification of injustice rendered untouchable by power. If ever there was a man who deserved to die on the sword of a Blade, it's the Son. Killing him would certainly serve the old ideal."

"But then there's the risen problem," said Faran.

I nodded and began to pace. The Son was more than just a priest; he was a rapportomancer—a very specialized sort of magic user as well, one with the familiar gift but no talent for actual spells, and his familiar . . . That was the rub. His familiar was a sort of death elemental, a strand of the curse of the restless dead.

In the shape of the risen, the Son's familiar wore the bodies of thousands of nobles and priests all through the eleven kingdoms, maybe even tens of thousands. They were hidden risen, monsters who used the blood of the living to disguise their undead condition. Killing them individually was as just as killing the Son himself. But all at once . . . that was another thing entirely. What happens to a civilization when you remove the structures that rule it?

Kelos believed that a new, more just system would arise from the ashes of the old, that the inevitable civil wars and banditry and bloodshed would all ultimately prove to be worth it. Nuriko Shadowfox, his sometime lover, sometime foe who had started him down the path he now walked, had been even more radical in her plans. She didn't believe in government at all, thought that somehow eliminating it would lead to a new and better world. Her plan had been to destroy the system and then to spend the rest of her life preventing a new one from growing in its place.

I didn't know what I believed, but I knew damned well that killing the Son would result in a bloodbath of epic proportion. For every one of the risen that died with the Son, tens or even hundreds of innocents would fall in the chaos left behind. If the weight of my dead was already crushing me when they numbered in the hundreds . . .

"I don't know what to do, Faran. It was so much easier when the goddess told me where to go and who to kill. The responsibility was hers. I *hate* being the one who has to make the decisions."

"Would you go back to living that way . . . ? If you could?" Faran's tone was gentle, her expression sympathetic, but the question was as sharp as any knife and cut straight through to the pain that knotted my gut.

I desperately wanted to say yes. But . . . "No. I have seen too much of life's grays to ever go back to that kind of certainty. Even knowing, as I now do, that Namara herself was uncertain . . . No. I lie to myself when I say the responsibility was hers. My actions were and always have been my own, and somewhere down deep I've always known that. If the responsibility for what I do belongs to me, so do the choices. I couldn't go back to being a tool in another's hand if my soul depended on it."

"Then stop letting Kelos manipulate you."

Her mind is as sharp as her blades, sent Triss. *She's grown so much since we first found her.*

I laughed a grim little laugh. "That would be much easier to do if I knew what he was trying to bend me into doing, and whether or not what he wants of me is the wrong thing to do. Because the flip side of the risen problem is that allowing the

Son to live is a decision with heavy consequences of its own. How much of the evil done by and for him am I responsible for if I refuse to end his life?"

That was the question that made me feel as though I were carrying shards of broken glass around in my chest.

Triss rose up and wrapped his wings around my shoulders. "Sometimes you come to a place where there are no right decisions and all paths lead to fell ends."

"And then?" I whispered.

"You still must choose your way," said Triss.

"But I don't know how. . . ."

Faran stepped closer then, taking my hands in her own. "You do, you know."

"If so, I can't see it."

"That's because you're looking at it the wrong way. The question is not, what should you do? It's: who do you want to be?"

"I don't understand."

"You cannot control everything that will result from your actions; you can only control the actions themselves. If you died tomorrow, how would you want to be remembered?" She put one palm on my chest where the goddess had touched me. "Who are you, in here?"

I thought back to the decisions I had made over the last few years as I'd crawled my way back out of the bottle and the gutter, what I had done that had made me proud, where I had failed. . . . I might hate the answer that led me to, but I couldn't deny it any longer.

I took a deep breath. "I must kill the Son of Heaven, or attempt it, at least."

Faran nodded, but she also asked, "Why?"

"I am a killer, a slayer of monsters. It's what I was born to do. It's what I trained to do. It's who I am. Who knows, that may even make me into something of a monster myself. But if so, I am a monster whose job is taking greater monsters out of the world. I may not be able to stop new ones from rising up where I have slain the old, but I can't let that stop me from doing the job I was made for, and the Son is a very great monster indeed."

It was a scary decision, but it was the right one; I could feel it in my heart where it beat under Faran's hand. I covered it with my own. "How did you get to be so wise, my young apprentice?"

"I have a good teacher, old man." She pulled her hand free of mine and very gently leaned forward to kiss me on the cheek. "Who is also a good man, and no monster." She turned and walked back to the head of the stairs.

"Thank you," I said as she started to descend.

She nodded but didn't answer me back.

"What about Kelos?" asked Triss.

"I don't know. But it matters less now."

"How so?"

"If I must kill the Son of Heaven, he can help me—none better. But even with all the help in the world, this will be a very difficult play. The chances that either of us will survive the attempt are not great, much less both of us."

Triss snorted. "What you mean is that you're hoping to push off the decision long enough for it to become somebody else's problem."

"Or no problem at all, yes. Is that so wrong?"

"No. If we're going to go against the Son of Heaven, we will need all the help we can get, and, sometimes, the enemy of my enemy is enough to get you through to the end."

I had made my decision, and I believed it was the right one, but somewhere, down deep in the back of my mind, a voice kept saying: *But what if you're wrong?*

I appreciate irony as much as the next man. I just wish it didn't have to be quite so biting when you were on the receiving end.

"Absolutely not." I slammed my palm down on the tabletop. "I will not have anything to do with that woman." Faran had already stormed out, while Siri sat quietly behind me, radiating a sort of cold rage.

Kelos looked stubborn. "Don't go all squishy on me now, Aral. We need allies and I can't think of a better one. At least talk to her. We share a common enemy."

"Yes, and she's part of it."

Kelos crossed his arms and waited. Siri leaned forward and

put her hand on my shoulder. It reminded me of the one she'd lost—a price willingly paid for ending a greater evil.

I sighed. "All right, I'll talk to her, but I won't promise not to kill her when we're done."

Kelos grinned. "That works for me. If you come to an agreement, we advance things in one way. If you kill her, we do it another. Chaos to our enemies and all that. I'll tell her you're on your way down."

He went to the stairs and headed down to the pub below.

"Siri, am I doing the right thing here? I mean, this is the fucking Signet of Heaven we're talking about."

She shrugged. "Probably, but I wouldn't let Jax in on this part of the deal when we bring her into the matter."

I shuddered at the very thought. The Signet was the head of Heaven's Hand, the Son's own personal sorcerous storm troopers, and the people who had tortured Jax more than half to death when she was taken prisoner in the fall of the temple. Actually, there were any number of things I didn't want to mention to Jax. Like the way Siri had lost her hand, for one. Jax was my ex-fiancée, and I didn't fancy explaining the weird magical mess that was my brief and unexpected marriage to Siri, or the bloody but amicable divorce that had ended it. . . .

Triss had followed Kelos to the head of the stairs. Now he looked back at me, his posture questioning.

"All right, I'm coming." As I reached the head of the stairs, he let his dragon shape go and faded back into my shadow.

The taproom below was all but empty, a very unusual circumstance here in the early hours of the night. The only members of the local crowd who remained belonged to the staff of the inn, and *they* didn't look any too happy about being there. I couldn't fault them for wanting to leave given the newcomers— a half dozen members of Heaven's Hand. Priests and sorcerers of the most deadly and fanatical sort. I wanted to leave, too.

They had shed their uniforms for loose dark pants and shirts cut in the style of the steppe riders of the Kvanas. They weren't fooling anyone. Everything about them spoke to their true origins, from the hard, cold expressions on their faces to their military bearing and the many weapons that hung in use-worn sheaths at hips and shoulders or tucked into boot tops. Long ponytails bound with the ritual knots of their order identified them more exactly for any who knew what to look for. And then there were the Storms.

Each of the six companioned a cloud-winged familiar. The Storms were elemental creatures of air that assumed a myriad of forms, everything from the lucent shapes of huge gemstones to wheels of golden flame and abstract swirls of color. Their only commonality one to another was that they flew on wings of cloud.

The obvious leader of the troop was accompanied by a tight bundle of colors and tentaclelike streamers that reminded me of nothing so much as an octopus trying to conceal itself on a bright coral reef. She had taken a seat at a small table not far from the base of the stairs, where she sat as ramrod straight as if she were occupying a bench in the front row of the master temple at Heaven's Reach. Her followers had ranged themselves around the room in a loose cordon that allowed them to see every entrance and exit and to cover each other as needed in case of assault. I had to give them points for execution at the same time I deplored their very existence.

Kelos, being Kelos, had taken a stool at the bar with his back to almost everyone, like he was daring someone to stick a knife in it. Tempting as that idea sounded from time to time, I ignored him in favor of approaching the woman at the table. A second glance refined my first impression. For one, she was absolutely ancient, her hair bone white rather than the blond I had first thought, and the lines in her face many and deep.

If she were not a sorcerer I might have guessed her age at eighty, but her life was tied to her familiar's, and the Storms, like the Shades, may live for hundreds of years. For her to have aged so much, she must be at least three hundred, and maybe as old as six hundred.

"I am five hundred and thirty-eight," she said, her voice crisp and more than half-amused. "Also, I don't read minds, just faces, and I've had lots of practice. My name is Toragana, and this is my second time wearing the ring." She waved her right hand, where the Signet's insignia of office circled her thumb. "After a hundred and ninety years of retirement in a peaceful hermitage, I have been drafted back into the job, and I am not at all pleased about it. Now, sit. We have much to talk about and our time is short. The Son would kill us all if he knew I was here talking to you. Besides, I'm ancient and angry. Apoplexy could carry me off at any moment."

I suppressed a grin and sat. Despite all the weight of history and blood that lay between our two orders, I found myself instinctively liking this woman. "Angry?" I prompted.

"Extraordinarily so. Mostly at Corik Nofather. First for failing to succumb decently to the risen curse fifty years ago, thereby sparing me the trouble of doing something about his continued reign as the Son of Heaven. Second, for doing such a horrible job on the throne, *necessitating* my doing something about it. Third, for being an inhuman monster, which makes doing something about it a task that requires me to seek help in that task. And, before you put on the curious tone and say, 'Mostly?' I'm also mad at myself for hiding away in my hermitage and missing out on the chance to simply kill the little bastard off before he got too powerful for one old woman to handle."

I like her, Triss sent rather bemusedly.

So do I. This time I couldn't stop a grin. "So, you know what he is, then—" She cut me off with a chop of her hand.

"Yes, and all of his history, though I haven't been able to do anything with the information, since he's converted the bulk of the curia into undead slaves." She sighed. "I admit it's an improvement in some cases, but still, it complicates things. The only ones I've been able to bring in on this are certain members of my own order and that idiot Devin Nightblade."

I started at the name of my onetime best friend, now head of the rogue Blades, who had gone over to the Son of Heaven after the fall of the temple. He had been Kelos's chief pawn in the matter, and he hated me with a rare vigor.

She nodded at my reaction. "A piece of work, that one. Venal, dumb in a clever sort of way, and more than half a coward. He speaks very highly of you, which would have been enough for me to look elsewhere for help if it weren't for the fact that it's obvious he despises you and that it pains him to feel the way he does about your abilities."

"So, he sent you here?"

"No, I sent me here. Devin—gods help us—heads one of the five branches of Heaven's forces on earth. I head another. Together we *ought* to be able to push the Son off his throne without any help. But in addition to Devin's cowardice, his fallen Blades are bound by terrible oaths that prevent them from acting directly against the Son, and my own order is a hollow shell of what it once was. For which, curse Corik's name for five thousand generations." She spat on the floor.

"As much as I agree with you about the Son of Heaven, I'm finding it hard to feel a lot of sympathy for you after what your order did to mine."

Her mouth tightened at that, but she nodded. "I can understand your position on that conflict. What would you say if I told you that I mostly shared it?"

"I . . . What?" That was not what I had expected.

"That attack killed over half of the active members of my order, and it utterly destroyed our command structure. Nor was that result unintentional. The Son cannot convert mages without revealing himself, and that means that his control over the Hand has always been the weakest element of his command of the forces of the church. Since he took office, he has been systematically throwing our most powerful and independent members into the riskiest of situations, and the pace has accelerated dramatically of late.

"Seven Signets have died in the last ten years. Two at the fall of your temple. One in an ill-planned mission to Aven. Another, you killed two years ago at the abbey outside Tavan. One vanished shortly afterward; no one knows where. One fell in the battle understairs during the conflict over the Key of Sylvaras. His replacement was executed for treason three weeks later. Discounting half-trained novices and dotards like myself, the order has a fifth as many members as it did when your temple fell."

She slammed a fist down on the table. "The Son has killed more of us than your Blades have. After the death of the last Signet, there were only three active officers who have held significant command roles in the organization, and not one of them felt up to the task of assuming the office—which is why they came to me. Privately, and *before* I took the ring, the three of them told me that they thought it would be a death sentence for any of them to do so. All of them were willing to offer up their lives if they thought it would save the order, but not one of them believed they could make a difference."

"And you think you can?" I asked.

"I honestly don't know. But I had to try. That's why I'm here. The Son has made *this* into little more than a shiny bauble." She took off the ring and tossed it to me.

Reflexively, I caught it out of the air. When I opened my hand to look at it, I realized for the first time what was missing. "What happened to the magic . . . ?"

I held it up to my eye and looked through the circle at Toragana. I had held the ring of a Signet before. Two of them, actually, and each had glowed brightly in magesight, infused as they were with many spells. Among other enchantments, they were, or had been, keys that opened every one of the many wards that guarded the great temple at Heaven's Reach.

"Two years ago *someone* slipped into the Son's bedroom." Toragana gave me a pointed look.

"Really?" I asked, my face as blank as I could make it.

"Really. Though the story has not been widely shared beyond the upper echelons of the temple, the intruder stabbed two swords of your goddess into the headboard of the Son's bed bare fractions of an inch above his face. When the Son woke, he ran into them, putting twin slices into the flesh over his cheekbones. Those wounds have never healed."

"That's fascinating," I said.

"Oh, do stop. Kelos was the one outlawed for the thing— losing his place as head of Heaven's Shadow to Devin—which is part of why I sought him out. But he's already told me who actually marked the Son's face, and how, and why. That's also when he told me that you're the one I have to deal with if I want your people to help us with the Son."

"Me, not Siri?" She nodded and, wondering what Kelos was up to, I glanced over her shoulder to where he continued to pointedly ignore us all. "Interesting."

"Look, I don't care about your internal politics. What I care about is rescuing my order and my religion from the half-risen monster who currently heads it."

"How did you discover the Son's true nature?"

"After you left the Son with those slices on his cheeks, he went a little mad—paranoid and vindictive. He executed every guard who had been within a hundred yards of his rooms that night. Then he cut off all access to the innermost temple for the Hand, the Shadow, and those members of the Templars who are also mages. He restricted entry to a very few at first, his risen slaves within the priestly hierarchy and the military orders. But that also restricted his ability to get things done, so he started converting more and more risen. Concealing their true nature takes enormous amounts of blood. Too much to hide. Combine that with things that I scared out of Devin, and I knew what the truth had to be."

"That's when you decided to come to me."

"Well, Kelos initially, but yes. Will you help me make war upon Heaven's Son?"

I took a deep breath as I tried to decide how to answer her. That's when a large boulder smashed right through the Fallowsside wall of the Roc and Diamond at shoulder height. It passed directly over the table where Toragana and I faced each other before punching out the wall on the other side. A few inches left or right and it would have killed one or the other of us.

Triss wrapped me in a shroud of darkness as I rolled backward out of my chair. In a handoff we had practiced thousands of times, he released control over his senses and substance to me as I bounced to my feet. My view of the world changed as my own vision became irrelevant and I shifted to seeing through Triss's borrowed darksight. Color went away as textures and how they reflected or absorbed light became central to my awareness, and shadows took on a depth of meaning beyond anything I can ever hope to describe. . . .

As I drew my swords, a tattered horde of risen came pouring up the main stairway from the lower level.

The Son of Heaven had moved first.

No one can escape his past.

FROM

KELLY McCULLOUGH

CROSSED BLADES

a FALLEN BLADE NOVEL

For six years, former temple assassin Aral Kingslayer has been living as a jack of the shadow trades, picking up odd jobs on the wrong side of the law. But the past is never dead, and Aral's has finally caught up to him in the beautiful, dangerous form of Jax Seldansbane—a fellow Blade and Aral's onetime fiancée.

Jax claims that the forces that destroyed everything Aral once held dear are on the move again, and she needs his help to stop them. But Aral has a different life now, with a fresh identity and new responsibilities. And while he isn't keen on letting the past back in, the former assassin soon finds himself involved in a war that will leave him with no way out and no idea who to trust...

"McCullough evokes a rich and textured setting of back alleys, rooftop hideouts, dank dungeons, and urban magical grime. Call it fantanoir." —SF Reviews.net

kellymccullough.com
facebook.com/Kelly.McCullough
facebook.com/ProjectParanormalBooks
penguin.com

M1257T0213

FROM AUTHOR
KELLY McCULLOUGH

the faLLeN BLaDe seRies

BROKEN BLADE

BARED BLADE

CROSSED BLADES

BLADE REFORGED

---

pRaise foR the faLLeN BLaDe NoveLs

"Stories by Kelly McCullough are one of a kind."
—*Huntress Book Reviews*

"A fascinating world."
—*Fresh Fiction*

kellymccullough.com
facebook.com/Kelly.McCullough
facebook.com/ProjectParanormalBooks
penguin.com

M1258AS0213

Penguin Group (USA) Online

What will you be reading tomorrow?

Patricia Cornwell, Nora Roberts, Catherine Coulter,
Ken Follett, John Sandford, Clive Cussler,
Tom Clancy, Laurell K. Hamilton, Charlaine Harris,
J. R. Ward, W.E.B. Griffin, William Gibson,
Robin Cook, Brian Jacques, Stephen King,
Dean Koontz, Eric Jerome Dickey, Terry McMillan,
Sue Monk Kidd, Amy Tan, Jayne Ann Krentz,
Daniel Silva, Kate Jacobs...

You'll find them all at
penguin.com

*Read excerpts and newsletters,
find tour schedules and reading group guides,
and enter contests.*

Subscribe to Penguin Group (USA) newsletters
and get an exclusive inside look
at exciting new titles and the authors you love
long before everyone else does.

PENGUIN GROUP (USA)
penguin.com